Cold Heart

冷酷

REIKOKU

Cold Heart
Yamabuki vs. the Shinobi Priest

Sword of the Taka Samurai
Book Three

Katherine M. Lawrence

Toot Sweet Ink
tootsweet.ink

Boulder

Cold Heart: Yamabuki vs. the Shinobi Priest (Sword of the Taka Samurai Book Three)
Copyright © 2018 Katherine M. Lawrence
All rights reserved.

Series editor: Laura Lis Scott

Cover, interior design, and maps by Laura Scott
Copyright ©2018 Toot Sweet Inc. and Laura Scott
All rights reserved.

A Toot Sweet Ink Book
Published by Toot Sweet Inc.
6525 Gunpark Drive Suite 370
Boulder, CO 80301

Visit us at tootsweet.ink

Toot Sweet Ink is a trademark of Toot Sweet Inc.

Library of Congress Control Number: 2017963515

First Edition
ISBN: 978-0-9912667-7-7 (trade paper)
ISBN: 978-0-9912667-9-1 (ePub)
R. 1.0.2

Dedication

To my mother, Lilith,
the real-life Lady Taka.

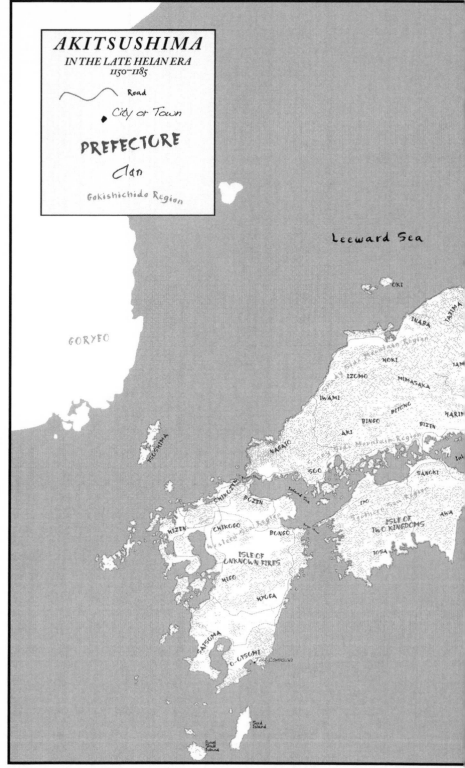

AKITSUSHIMA
IN THE LATE HEIAN ERA
1150-1185

Road
City or Town
PREFECTURE
Clan
Gokishichido Region

Leeward Sea

GORYEO

OKI
INABA
TAJIMA
HOKI
IZUMO
MIMASAKA
IWAMI
BITCHU
HARIMA
BINGO
BIZEN
AKI
NAGATO
SUO
SANUKI
IYO
Inland Sea
Tsukiura Seas Region
CHIKUZEN
BUZEN
ISLE OF
TWO KINGDOMS
AWA
HIZEN
CHIKUGO
BUNGO
TOSA
Western Seas Region
ISLE OF
UNKNOWN FIRES
HIGO
HYUGA
SATSUMA
O-OSUMI
Two Compass

Bird Island

Small
Island

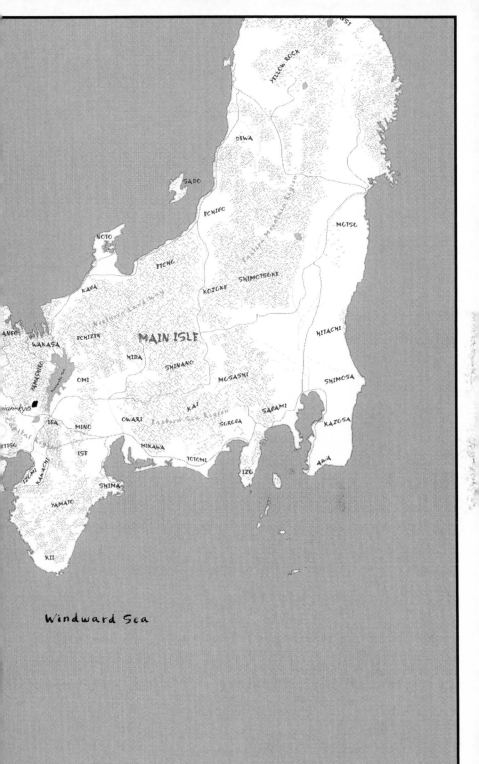

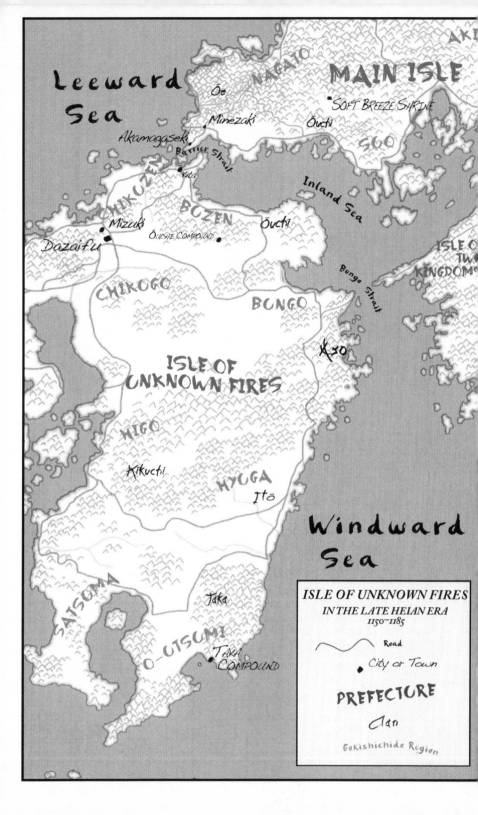

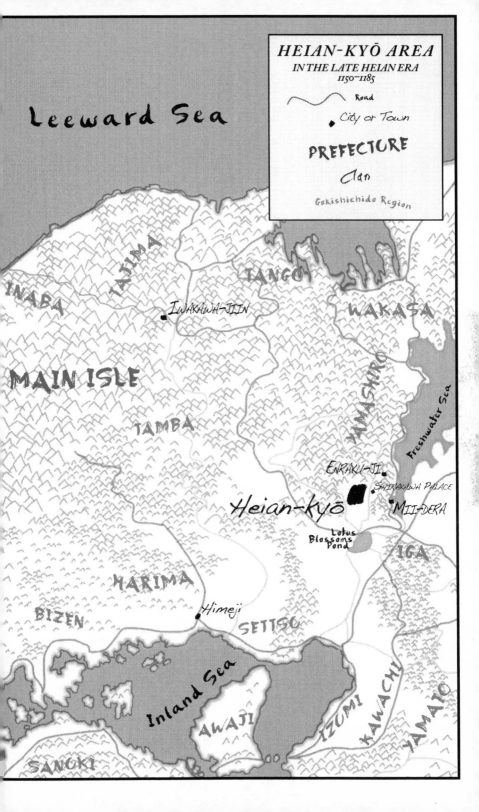

TABLE OF CONTENTS

MAPS . . . . *vi*

COLD HEART 1

EXTRA: EXCERPT FROM *COLD TRAIL* . . 273

AUTHOR'S NOTE 278

CHARACTERS 279

GLOSSARY 281

JAPANESE YEARS, SEASONS, AND TIME . . 290

ACKNOWLEDGMENTS 294

EDITORIAL NOTE 295

ABOUT THE AUTHOR 296

BOOKS BY
    KATHERINE M. LAWRENCE 297

ABOUT TOOT SWEET INK 298

Long before it was called Japan,
the island empire was known
to the world as Akitsushima,
the Autumn Creek Land,
and among its samurai,
one of its mightiest warriors was
a woman named Yamabuki.

Cold Heart
Yamabuki vs. the Shinobi Priest

Sword of the Taka Samurai
Book Three

Spring 1172:
Known as Year of the Water Dragon,
Second Year of Shōan,
eight years prior to the Genpei War
and the ensuing struggle
for the mastery of Japan
that tore the realm apart
and ushered in the era of the warlords.

ONE
THE HOUR OF THE OX

W HEN YOUNG YAMABUKI was still innocent, the holy men warned her about the Hour of the Ox, the longest and darkest hour of the night. They said that at the beginning of the Fourth Watch, when eight bells tolled, ten thousand fissures yawned wide, releasing unclean things from the underworld. Under darkness, the contagion floated free, finding cracks in doors and vents in roofs; and having gained entry, these phantasms descended on fitfully sleeping souls, their sinewy tendrils probing the smallest clefts in closed eyes and creating only the slightest of ripples as they slithered under the lids and penetrated the sleepers' dreams.

Moved by these tales, the young princess asked, "Can spirits rising from the *jigoku* ever be good?"

Every priest and every monk declared that no thing from the dark realm was benign—not even slightly for they were no longer capable of human feelings. Once drained, the heart shriveled inward with emptiness.

"But couldn't the hearts of lost spirits be refilled?"

The holy men explained, "If such a thing still had a heart, which was doubtful, it would be *reikoku*—a cold heart. Unbeating and incapable of ever being warmed."

"Ever?"

"Never."

And yet, for whatever obdurate reason, Yamabuki did not believe them. What did celibate men know of hearts anyway? Perhaps all that the lost spirits needed for deliverance was but a single spark of kindness. Love?

Two
DEATH POEM

Nine Bell Strikes, Hour of the Mouse
One day past Full Moon of Unohana Month
Sixth Day of Rikka
Second Year of Shōan, Year of the Water Dragon
10 May 1172
Minezaki, Nagato Prefecture, Main Isle

U NDER LAMPLIGHT, YAMABUKI LIFTED the tip of the writing brush.
She gazed at its bristles fat with glistening black ink, then looked
down to the still-wet calligraphy on the rough cut rice paper within the
writing box. As the ink dried, she looked for any flaws in her brush strokes
of the exalted language of Qin.

And as was her custom, she repeated the *kanji* in her native tongue,
enunciating each line in her studied high court accent.

> *One person.*
> *One sword.*
> *Bringing death the first time.*

Be parsimonious. That was what Lord Nakagawa advised when he suggested she record her journey in a pillow book. Was there any more to say?
Maybe just three lines was a bit *too* succinct. Only after she mouthed the
words a second time did she realize, *I've written a poem.* A poem about
killing. "Only this morning," she whispered to the paper, as if it were capable of listening.

What a discordant day. It had dawned so clear and bright and full of
hope, but by the Hour of the Horse, as the rain poured down from darkened skies, three men lay dead at her feet. She pushed away the image
of the bodies sprawled in the mud, replacing it instead with more hope-
ful recollections.

She thought back to the previous evening, when she had summoned Ryuma, asking him to bring saké to her chamber at the Inn of Young Bamboo. She bade him enter and by dim brazier light invited him to share her wine and her body. In hindsight, enticing him was perverse in almost every sense of the word. Imagine: inviting a commoner, who at best might be called Master of Horses, and at a mere inn at that, to make love to her, a warlord's daughter. And yet their stations mattered little in that moment of unfinished business. Throughout the evening they had hardly exchanged words, but once he entered her bed chamber, she allowed her gaze to linger. No longer the gruff bodyguard, he broke into a boyish grin. By brazier light she fixed her eyes on him.

After sharing their first bowl of saké, he took a long breath, looking deeply into her eyes, and she, after a measured moment, turned her head away, ever so slightly. Letting her glance linger she sighed, slowly lying back in the bedding. He dropped to his knees, loosened his waist sash, and pulled off his tunic. Her toes curled.

It wasn't that she hadn't seen naked men before. She had seen lots of them. Her father's rough soldiers, not always the most modest of men, went about nearly naked when laboring during the humid rainy season. She had taken only a passing interest, noting the similarities among their muscular bodies, pondering the differences between her body and theirs, and then mostly given it no further thought—at least not until she grew older.

She had also seen Ryuma naked as well, six years ago, not long after he had undergone his *genpuku* coming-of-age ceremony at twelve summers. At the time, Yamabuki had one more year before she observed her own female maturity ceremony, *mogi—adult clothes*. And yet when they stole away, it was their intent to remove every bit of their clothes in order to quench their mutual curiosity in each other's "adult" bodies. Back then it had not been easy for the two youths to find privacy at the inn where her father's retinue, numbering some seventy assorted body guards, Taka royalty, and their handmaids, and hand-men, and other highborn, bedded down for the night.

The two youths stole off to a secluded corner of the stables where, without uttering any words, showed themselves to each other. Innocently. Purely. The youthful Ryuma proved nothing like her father's soldiers. He was beautiful, his body lithe like hers, only taller and stronger. Unsure of themselves, yet without shame, they had exchanged nothing more than prolonged stares.

Last night, still without shame, they did not stop with just furtive glances. Excited, she had slipped into his embrace. The memory was still vivid, his scent still fresh.

Yamabuki set down her writing brush. *I'm not going to recount the details of that!* Upon conclusion of her travels, custom dictated that a pillow book was to be read aloud to those at the Taka Court. Reflections on Ryuma and his special place in her heart would not be shared with them.

She took a deep breath as a second thought crossed her mind. In the throes of their passion and gasping, she had pushed aside the reality that his seed might take root. Every time a woman made love with a man, afterward there was always *that* to think about. Yamabuki's rhythm with the moon—the "tide," as the common women of Ō-Utsumi in their indecipherable provincial dialect called it—usually arrived around the time of the Dark Moon. *Fitting.* Didn't the diviners always remind her that she was born on Dark Moon's night in Gods Month in the First Year of Kiūju? The court magicians, upon learning of her tidal rhythm, had sent a self-appointed delegation of *onmyōji* to pronounce that the most likely time for Yamabuki to conceive a child was at the Full Moon. *My low tide.* She laughed to herself, thinking of all the sly slangs associated with that.

Actually the diviners had said "auspicious" and not "likely," but she had grasped their meaning. Was last night *auspicious?*

"Bah!" *Why am I even thinking this way?* What did the onmyōji know about the time women conceived? Or of birth! They were never around when that happened. Instead the *sanba*—the woman who knew the ways of birth—did what was needed to bring the child into this floating world of sorrow.

For that matter, what did diviners know about anything? They had said that *this* morning, the sixth day of the Rikka cycle, marked the auspicious beginning of summer.

Auspicious. Auspicious. Everything was *auspicious* to them, or just the opposite. Good omens. Bad omens. The good portent of a barking dog at sunrise. The bad luck sure to befall anyone who changed clothes before the evening meal. Travel on this day, but not on that. Traveling northeast was safe under a waxing moon, but dangerous under a waning one, and very badly aspected under the Dark Moon.

But there was nothing auspicious about today. The three killers had awakened on the same auspicious morning and had the same auspicious crossing of the Barrier Strait on the same single-masted *kobune* as she, but it had not ended auspiciously for them. She had cut down all three. When it was over, at least the rain and ice that poured from roiling clouds had veiled her angry tears. She wiped them from her eyes and then the blood from her blade, leaving the bodies where they fell. What else could she have done? She was not going to simply stand in the freezing cold waiting for local authorities over whom she had no control to arrive and pester her with impertinent questions about who she was and why these assassins had chosen her in particular.

She had turned her back on the bodies and rode in the direction of the Pass of the Setting Sun, and by day's end she had settled in armorer Kōno's guesthouse, on the wrong side of the mountains in ever-worsening conditions, still ten, maybe even fifteen days away from her destination, the Imperial City.

Yamabuki picked up the writing brush. After all, she had to write something. She balanced the brush between the thumb and first two fingers of her left hand—fingers calloused from years of practice with her bow, the same fingers that notched and leveled an arrow while drawing back the bowstring. Lord Nakagawa had called her attention to the similarities in the art of archery and calligraphy: In each and in both, mastery arose out of a balance of intent and abandon. In holding an arrow, or in holding a writing brush, she had to keep a firm but not too tight a grip. All else flowed from her ability to maintain that balance. Firm, but supple. Qualities she aspired to within herself.

I'm getting philosophical. She laughed. She always got philosophical when she drank saké.

She set down the brush and took up a small steel mirror. She recalled the old saying, *"A man's soul rests in his sword. A woman's, in the mirror."*

She scoffed. *Where do I figure in this?* She gazed into the fine-polished surface, her eyes focusing on the gash along her left cheek, the only obvious wound from the afternoon's fracas—and from a rock at that—a last desperate ploy of the assassin whose life she ended with a simple blade thrust. Would her face heal without a scar, like armorer Kōno had predicted? She put the mirror down on its face and picked up her writing brush again, working the bristles against the ink stone.

I need a poetic beginning. She decided to model it on the Pillow Book of Lady Sōshi. Snow in the mountains on the first day of summer? Lady Sōshi would likely have found that fascinating. *Maybe begin with tonight's first snowflakes.* When had the first snowflakes arrived? Long after the five rowdy Ōe clan sakimori had stumbled into Unagi's rundown Saké House. They were already drunk, but then again, so was she. Nevertheless she spared them. After all, they had not participated in Blue Rice's murder, and there had already been too much killing for one day. But that did not mean she was too timid to mete out punishment for their inaction when Misaki killed her friend.

Suddenly she felt the brush come alive. She smiled and with a flourish wrote:

Mountain Snow.
Summer Night.
The battlefield, atop spilled saké.

She rewet the brush. *Why am I so upset about someone I hardly knew? I only met Blue Rice this morning.* And yet during the hour-long trip across the Barrier Strait, she had grown to like him. *Strange*, the young princess mused to herself. Was there also not an old saying: "*A friend for life is first recognized in but a slice of time*"? Alas for Blue Rice, the lifetime friendship lasted scarcely two hours.

Yamabuki tried to make sense of a senseless murder, but no matter how much saké she sipped, it made no sense. Blue Rice was killed over nothing—what amounted to a skill-testing murder by someone who wanted to show off his bowmanship. Had she been back in Great Bay Prefecture, where her father ruled, she would have seen to it that Misaki was punished—and severely. However, warlord's daughter or not, her wishes and her authority were of no consequence here. She was not in her home province, not even on her home isle.

On the other hand, none of the guards had connected her with the helmeted samurai in dark green battle armor they had challenged at the boat landing. All they saw was a lone woman in an orange kimono, porcelain-white *oshiroi* makeup, and waist-length black tresses whom they took for a *yahochi*, a woman of rendezvous. Were they so drunk that they failed to notice her sheathed short sword? Apparently. When one of their number tried to snatch her bottle of saké, she broke his wrist with a single strike of her scabbard—and when two cohorts came to his aid, she bashed one in the ribs and knocked the other unconscious with a cracking wallop against his jaw.

The Gentian samurai who leaned back in the corner, away from the fracas, had laughed at the scuffle as if it were endlessly entertaining. At least the saké he offered her afterward in his private quarters at the House of Red Banners proved equal to his claims about its taste and potency.

She'd had every reason to get drunk, and every reason to stay the night with the man who identified himself as Minamoto Yoshinaka. She had seen his armor under repair, in Kōno's shop; likely he was all he claimed to be. When she told him about battling the two *ninja* and the fencing master, he spoke of his own first duel, describing feelings similar to those she felt. He understood her—a rarity throughout her young life. It might have been nice to lose herself in his powerful arms. To be embraced in that way was indeed to her taste; two warriors, even if one was a woman, might have much to admire in each other. The same arms that could effortlessly wield a weapon could also transmit feelings of love, and if not love, at least lust, and of course even more drink.

But two different men on two different nights?

She sighed. Maybe no more needed to be written. Besides, the saké had made her sleepy. She cleaned her brush and set it aside, replaced the top of the small wooden box that held the pillow book, turned down the brazier, and, for the eleventh night, slept in a strange room, this night alone. She found warmth in her bedding.

Maybe Yoshinaka and she had unfinished business. After all, no one would be going anywhere if this snow continued. She pictured his powerful arms, imagining his shoulders and his legs. She let her hand slip down to where her own legs came together, her fingers beginning to caress the soft developing wetness. Yes . . . maybe some unfinished business.

THREE

THE LAKE OF DREAMS

S HE HEARD A SMALL TAPPING at the door to her chamber. Would Yoshinaka have been so crass as to have followed her? Warrior or not, this would not go well for him. She smoothly slid her left hand to Tiger Cub's hilt and gripped its leather and silk windings. With her thumb, she pushed, loosening the blade very slightly from its scabbard.

Next came a tiny giggle. It was that of a small girl.

"Kouma?" Yamabuki whispered.

Another giggle. Was the girl was already inside? If so, she had slipped in ever so softly.

Yamabuki said, "You're up late. Does your father know you are walking about in the night?

"No," a voice answered tentatively.

"When I was your age if I had been caught wandering around near the Hour of the Ox, my father would have been quite cross with me."

"You are afraid," Kouma said in a small voice.

"Oh?" Yamabuki replied in a voice equally soft.

"You're afraid people will hurt you. And you have to hurt them instead."

Yamabuki wondered if that was true.

Kouma giggled and said, "Those were bad men and you scolded them good."

"At the saké house?"

The girl giggled again.

My what a small town. Word travels fast. Even children know things within an hour of them happening.

The little girl's voice came closer. "This is a good place. My father likes you. You will sleep. No bad dreams."

No bad dreams. Yamabuki laughed softly to herself. The girl moved through the shadows. Yamabuki thought she heard the door slide aside as Kouma softly left the chamber. Yamabuki was alone and too tired to open the door to see where Kouma went. Instead, she wandered ever deeper into a dream state. She saw the fencing master, Shima, though not as she saw him in death. He wore the same indigo and orange armor, carried his *nodachi*, and displayed the *hanabishi* clan symbol. He seemed pleased to see her.

"Death walks the road," he said in the dream. "Saburo will be here soon."

"Let him come," she heard herself say. She would rest for now. She was deliciously drunk. Happily she fell further into a very deep, profound, and peaceful sleep.

Four

Shakuhachi

A DEEP-THROATED BELL'S REVERBERATION broke over Yamabuki's dream like a crashing wave. *The Taka compound is under attack!* She reached into the darkness finding the long sword, and sat up, gripping Tiger Claw's hilt. "Tomoko! Hana-ye! Bring my armor!" Yamabuki had to report to the marshaling yard, ready to stand at her father's side.

The bell echoed a second time. *Where are my handmaids?* When the bell reverberated a third time, she realized, *I'm not at the Taka compound. I'm in armorer Kōno's guesthouse.* This was not a tocsin, but a temple bell, a large one at that, announcing the hours of the night. She softly laughed at herself. Relieved. She set Tiger Claw back down and listened to the reverberations dying away, counting how long until the next peal. Seven long breaths. No ordinary bell this, not even by Taka standards. An *ōgane*, the largest and most deep-voiced. It was said ōgane resonated to the nethermost places striking terror into the doubtful hearts of the vile things that lurked there.

Between the waning strikes, a whistling breeze arose. Granulated snow pattered the walls. Hissing. Trees just outside the entry door creaked. Buffeting gusts—thunder without lightning—blew through the night. The dull red *irori* fire pit's coals pushed back against the gloom, but did not cheer.

The ōgane continued tolling. *Five . . . six . . . seven . . . eight . . .* and then nothingness.

Eight strikes. Hour of the Ox.

She detected scratching. *Mice?* Her hand slid to the three scrolls, her fingers gliding over their rough silk husks. Intact.

A child's playful laughter rose above the wind. Kouma? Was the armorer's young daughter wandering in the storm? The giggling continued. Shadows dashed across the wall. *Inside? No—outside.* Someone tapped the window shutters and tittered. Yamabuki left her bed to peer through the slats. The night skies had completely cleared. A moon ringed by a muted rainbow haze illuminated the virgin snow. A steady breeze lifted flakes off the pines, carrying the snow horizontally, but not so thick that she was unable to see two figures, one tall, one tiny, trudging toward the night-soil pit. Kouma and her mother?

Night-soil pits were deep and dangerous. There were oft-repeated cautionary stories, delivered with dark laughter about those who fell into the pit and ended up drowning or suffocating in *kuso*. The indignity of such a death!

Yamabuki returned to the bedding and pulled the blankets tight. Had she been back at the Taka compound, so close to the ocean with its rains, fogs, and mists, her handmaids would have tended the fire to beat back the inevitable dampness. In the *nurigome* bedchamber of her personal, palatial *shinden-zukuri* estate in the Taka compound, on more than a few nights, Yamabuki had invited Tomoko and Hana-ye to stay with her after the fire caught. Beneath the curtained sleeping canopy, the three girls huddled for warmth—sometimes for something more.

But alone in Kōno's guesthouse, she had to make do with dying coals. She traced the threads of smoke as they snaked up into the dark rafters, barely making out the roof vent. She closed her eyes. The wind continued whistling, rising and falling, soothing—almost melodic. She let her mind follow. Indeed it *was* a melody. A flute. A *shakuhachi*. Yamabuki shifted. Who would stand out in the storm playing a flute? She doubted it was the armorer's wife, and surely it was not little Kouma. Who then? A master musician.

The notes formed in her head, and then she recognized the melody: "The Song of the Swan," a song from her childhood, a song that Giichi had played the afternoon she had arrived in the city by the River of Wild Ducks. The day he died.

FIVE

WHO COULD EVER FORGET YOU?

THE FLUTE'S NOTES CARRIED her through her dream to the glossy smooth floor of the Palace of Black Plums, where on hands and knees, as she had been instructed, Yamabuki bowed so low that her forehead touched. In the lacquered mahogany planks, the slightly distorted image of the ageless Dowager in bright colorful robes, sitting stiffly on the dais, gazed darkly at the girl. The young princess, almost five springs of age, knew to remain still, saying nothing, until the signal—a small nod from her mother, Lady Taka, whose face also floated within the floor's reflection.

The subtleties of the Ceremony of Presentation had been painstakingly conveyed to Yamabuki during their journey from Great Bay Prefecture to the Imperial City. Too young to merit her own personal *goshoguruma*, Yamabuki rode in her mother's curtained coach, the largest and most opulent of the six ox-drawn carts, with embroidered silk tapestries lining the walls and soft pillows to cushion the ride; and it was there that Lady Taka had stressed that the girl, the eldest surviving child of the daimyō, was to be polite to the Dowager—exceedingly polite, as polite as if she were being presented to the Emperor Himself.

At the mere mention of the Son of Heaven, Yamabuki had filled with excitement. "Is it because she's one of the Mikado's wives?"

"*Īe,*" Lady Taka answered—in the polite form, already setting the prescribed tone. "The Dowager is not married to anyone anymore. She is your father's mother. The wife of your dead grandfather, Taka Jirimu. She watched over you after you were born. Remember her?"

Yamabuki brightened. "Snowy hair?"

Lady Taka nodded, obviously pleased. "Remember anything more?"

"Big."

Lady Taka's eyes twinkled. "Big to someone so small. You were but three springs when we returned home to Ō-Utsumi Prefecture. I am surprised you remember her at all."

"Will she remember me?"

Her mother suppressed a small laugh. "Who could *ever* forget you?"

On horseback, her warlord father led more than forty of his personal bodyguards as escort to the six lavishly decorated two-wheeled royal carts as they rolled ever northward, their wooden spokes turning, their axles squeaking and moaning, the oxen snorting. Traveling only by daylight, the Taka caravan paused every night at one of the acceptable *ryokan* along the road, where they could eat and sleep in comfort.

It was on the twenty-sixth day of the journey that the caravan approached the Imperial City and was met by a concert of faraway temple bells that tolled out the second quarter of the Hour of the Monkey. A dark horse came apace of the cart. A moment later, the melody from a shakuhachi succeeded the bells, rising above the rumble of wheels and clop of hooves.

Lady Taka pulled the cart's blue gossamer silk window curtain aside to afford Yamabuki a better view.

In full battle gear, save for his iron facial mask, Giichi rode alongside, his head shielded by his heavy *kabuto*. Yamabuki squealed. Giichi turned toward her, and Yamabuki now saw his unshielded face—black silky beard, his eyes dancing just as mischievously as hers.

"This is for you, little Princess," he said and put his lips to the tip of the flute. And as the song emerged from his shakuhachi, he nudged his horse in the flanks and rode ahead, never missing a note.

Yamabuki poked her head out of the stuffy cart.

The kicked-up dust twirled in the breeze of the autumn afternoon. Behind, two other carts carried Lady Taka's *nyōbō*, her attendants, followed by the Taka rearguard on horseback. It was a familiar view, so the young princess paid none of them any mind.

It was far more exciting to watch Giichi ride forward past the three other Taka goshoguruma as the cortège headed toward a city that stretched everywhere she could see. In fact, the entire valley was filled with countless structures adorned with bright roofs of different colors gleaming in the sun. Now and then, she could see down wide streets that seemed to go on forever.

"There are so many buildings!"

"Hai," Lady Taka said.

"It's so big."

"You were born in this city, at the Palace of Spring Snow, among the Itō clan."

Yamabuki pulled back inside and excitedly asked, "How many people live here?"

Lady Taka gave a quick nod. "Remember when Lord Nakagawa had you write all the numbers between one and a thousand?"

Yamabuki shook her head solemnly and sighed. "That took a long time."

"Now imagine that each number was one person."

"That's many people," she said with awe.

"Now imagine doing the exercise four hundred times in a row. That's how many people live in the city."

Yamabuki, amazed, briefly poked her head out the window again. "How do they know? Does everyone line up to be counted?"

"The Emperor has people who take care of such accountings for Him. He needs to know how many people there are, and in which places. This is how He decides how much we send in the *koku* tax."

"Koku tax?"

"The wagons that carry the rice boxes at the end of the year. You remember them, no?"

Yamabuki nodded, picturing the long train of carts under guard led by Counselor Mizumaki. In the late autumn, the procession headed to Heian-kyō loaded to capacity with tightly-packed bales of Ō-Utsumi's rice harvest. And the following spring, the carts returned empty.

"The more people, the more koku needs to be sent, so the Emperor keeps a close count on how many subjects He has."

The clomps of hooves on wood accompanied a rumbling that shook the entire cart. Yamabuki grasped her mother's hand to steady herself and asked, "How many subjects are in Great Bay?"

"It would be fifty times the number that you wrote out for Nakagawa."

"Not as many as in Heian-kyō?"

"No. Not nearly as many."

"In the whole prefecture? Not as many?"

"No. Not as many."

The cart paused, silencing the rumbling, but snorts and restless thumps of horse hooves on wood continued.

This was all very strange to the young girl, who asked, "Why are we stopping, mother?"

"We are at the Welcome Gate checkpoint."

"What are they checking?"

"Everyone who enters the city must identify themselves to the gokenin guards and state their business."

"Even a daimyō?"

Lady Taka nodded. "Everyone."

Yamabuki leaned out the window again and saw the entire retinue stopped on a long bridge across a wide river. The guards, looking fierce in full armor like her father's warriors wore—but gold-and-black instead of Taka green—and carrying long spears with blades that glinted in the sun, walked down the line of carts and among her father's mounted escort.

Yamabuki scowled. "They aren't Taka, but they walk right up."

Her mother said, "Back when the Emperor lived on the Isle of Unknown Fires, the Taka clan protected Him, and when the Emperor moved the Imperial City back to Main Isle, he took several of our banner men with him because they were such fierce fighters. We share an ancient lineage with these very guards."

Before Yamabuki could ask any more, the cart lurched back into motion and riders began to move again, on through the gate and into the bustling city with wide avenues and large buildings. And indeed it was as her mother said. There were more people here than Yamabuki had ever seen in one place. They were of all types and wore every manner of clothing—some lavish, others almost naked. Merchants, soldiers, monks, farmers, entertainers, women in holy robes, artisans, and some of the most beautiful women imaginable beneath giant parasols and flanked by attendants.

Yamabuki watched the spectacle as riders at the front of the Taka entourage warned everyone to withdraw, for a warlord and his bodyguard were approaching. The people scurried to get out of the way, giving perfunctory bows to the procession as it advanced down the twenty-horse-wide thoroughfare. The babble of voices drowned out the rumble of the cart wheels and horses' hooves. Other royal carts with other banners moved in different directions through the ocean of people.

All of a sudden, a rider came apace the Taka cart—her father, the daimyō himself. His bodyguards fanned out. Ahead, in the distance, Yamabuki caught a glimpse of magnificent roofs. It had to be the Emperor's palace. She squeaked with delight. Her father flashed a look at her, eye to eye, and she fell silent.

"Soon," he said flatly to her mother. "Be ready."

He spurred his horse.

Yamabuki's face fell, and she sat down on her pillows. "Why did father not smile?"

Lady Taka pulled the cart's window curtains down. "Your father is missing us already." Yamabuki saw fleeting sadness in her mother's eyes.

"How long will we stay here?"

Lady Taka sighed. "It will be a year, Kouma."

"How long is that?"

"Remember when you went with uncle Tachibana to see the wreck of the ship that brought the horses that fell from the skies?"

Yamabuki nodded.

"That was a year ago."

"That is a long time."

"It is."

"But father will be with us?"

"No, Kouma, he won't. By the next moon, he will return to Ō-Utsumi. Great Bay Prefecture needs its daimyō."

Yamabuki frowned. "We will stay here?"

"We will, and then we will return home again, and until that time we will live at the Palace of Black Plums."

Yamabuki put her head out of the window again, catching her father as he moved to the head of the procession. Finally fully understanding the purpose of the journey, she felt a pang, missing him already.

As she sat down, her face must have expressed the same, for her mother suddenly became cheerful and touched her daughter's hand. "We will see all the wonders of the Imperial City. Maybe even glimpse the Mikado Himself." Lady Taka squeezed Yamabuki's hand. "The time will go fast."

"Why do we have to visit for so long?" Yamabuki looked puzzled.

"It's because the Emperor likes having the family members of every daimyō close to Him so He can protect them if there is ever any trouble."

"But isn't father better at protecting us back in Ō-Utsumi?"

Lady Taka smiled sagaciously. "You are very perceptive for someone so young."

Yamabuki was not sure what was so perceptive about this, for it made no sense to her that the Emperor would need to have them in the Imperial City.

It was then that Etsu, on horseback, came alongside the wagon, bringing his mount to a walk. "*Denka!*" he called loudly.

Yamabuki's mother looked out without lifting the silk curtain, for decorum demanded that once she was within the city, she not reveal her face to a bodyguard, even though at the Taka compound she trained, rode, and practiced weapons with all of them. Today protocols were to be meticulously followed.

"The Palace of Black Plums!" Etsu pointed up the Suzaku boulevard, and with that he kicked his bay in the ribs and took off at a trot.

Indeed the wagons had finally rolled up to the Taka legation. The mounted bodyguard, in a crescent formation, waited as the lumbering six carts rolled to a complete stop.

Giichi, two riders over from the daimyō, smiled and nodded toward her. He put the shakuhachi to his lips and once again blew out the notes of the "Song of the Swan."

And Yamabuki drifted between sleep and consciousness, between childhood and adulthood. Between knowing where she was—and yet lost. Was she at the Palace of Black Plums? Or was she in Kōno's guesthouse?

The notes of the flute merged with gusts of wind even as Giichi stood close by, grinning at her, lifting the flute but not playing as he pointed it at the door, which then slid open on its own.

He beckoned her to follow.

Six

Dead Men Can't Be Interrogated

AND AS THE LILTING MELODY echoed across the gardens, Yamabuki found herself inside the open, high-ceilinged *shinden* of the Palace of Black Plums, where everyone in her family sat with the daimyō, each in order of rank: first, the Dowager; next, Yamabuki's mother, Lady Taka; then Yamabuki's uncle, the daimyō's brother, Prince Tachibana, with his highest ranking wife, Yuma, and their eldest child, Atsumichi, who was even younger than Yamabuki and accordingly wore the expected feminine gossamer veils of a royal son many years away from majority. The solid black-lacquered wooden *shōji* were slid aside, and in the broad *hisashi* corridor others of the Taka retinue knelt at various distances further from the daimyō, as protocol required.

A tray of the delicacy *fugu* was brought forth and, as was the custom, offered to the daimyō first.

Laughingly, Giichi said, "Oh, *Tennō*! Fugu must be correctly cleaned. I can't let you eat a fish without making sure no poison lingers. So"—and he reached for a random piece of the fish—"please forgive me and let me taste it before you."

The flute melody continued as he lifted the morsel into his own mouth. He smiled as he chewed.

And then his eyes grew round. He gagged, fighting to draw breath. He reached for his throat. He tried to make words, but they came out garbled. Here and there, laughter erupted. But then Giichi fell forward, crashing onto the food trays.

Yamabuki, now seeing herself as a very young child sitting among the retinue, screamed in terror.

As Giichi fought for every breath, her father leapt to him, rolling him over, meeting his retainer's eyes, which grew evermore panicked. For the first and perhaps only time ever, Yamabuki saw her father look helpless.

"His stomach! Cut his stomach," Etsu shouted, pulling his dagger.

Lady Taka rose up. "No! That will kill him for sure."

Some people put fingers down their own throats to induce vomiting, even though they had not eaten any of the fish. Others shouted, calling for action, but what action should they take? Atsumichi sat sobbing into his sleeve.

"Calm yourselves!" the daimyō barked.

Prince Tachibana grabbed his sword and rose up in one motion.

Yamabuki again moved like a disembodied spirit, floating after Tachibana. In a few strides, her uncle was out of the shinden, storming down a covered walkway across the estate grounds and into the kitchen, where fifteen people, all members of the chief food preparer's family, stood stunned.

"Who?" Tachibana demanded.

"You—" stammered the chief of food, who held a boning knife at his side.

The prince's sword flashed, and blood flew in every direction. The old man fell dead. Sword still at the ready, Tachibana looked for his next target: the old man's son, who had stopped in the midst of cleaning more fugu.

"*Nooo!*" the dead man's wife screamed. Crying in anguish, she threw herself around the youth, shielding his body with her own.

"Stand aside," Tachibana thundered, lifting his blade high, "or I *swear* I'll take both of you with one cut!"

The woman remained frozen.

Lady Taka burst into the room. "Hold!" She placed herself between Prince Tachibana and the would-be victims. "Put your weapon aside! Dead men can't be interrogated."

Tachibana snarled, but Lady Taka stood her ground and glared back.

The scene faded. Giichi and all those in the Palace of Black Plums vanished, as did the melody. Yamabuki opened her eyes.

She lay near the irori in the guesthouse. The room was as dim as ever. *I was dreaming.* A coal in the irori popped and flared, and the bright yellowish flame flooded even the darkest corners of the room. The outer door slid open. A figure stood framed in the entry.

Yamabuki gulped. "Blue Rice?"

SEVEN
I BUILT THE MEMORIAL
IN YOUR HONOR

I T'S BITTER COLD, YAMABUKI-SAN," Blue Rice said, and forcefully he slid the outer door of the guesthouse shut. "There! That will keep the heat in." He clomped his *fukagetsu* against the planked floor. With each stomp, snow clumps flew until he had shucked his straw boots clean. He left them in the entryway and glided toward the irori, bending forward, warming the palms of his hands near the fire. Even by the glow of dimming coals, his breath steamed.

Clad in only her thin red silk *shitagi*, Yamabuki stood up. It did not occur to her that decorum had been breached—let alone that she chatted with a dead man. He acted as if he were her equal. He should have addressed her as Taka-*gimi*, not Yamabuki-*san*, as though they were familiar.

When had he learned her personal name? She had never revealed it to him—nor he his name to her. Only because of the blue circular rice-ear *mon* decorating his simple tunic had she taken to calling him Blue Rice. Yet none of this strangeness gave her the slightest pause either. Indeed she was eager to speak with him.

"I'll wager the wine at Unagi's drinking house tastes dreadful," Blue Rice said. "You should have taken me up on my offer of saké when you had the chance."

He grinned and held out to her an unstoppered flask—a white porcelain bottle with the same mon as on his tunic.

Something told her she should not accept it. She vaguely recalled what the holy men warned: If the living ate or drank anything offered by the dead, the flesh of the recipient would immediately start to decay and rot.

"Thank you, no," she said. "As I told you when we boarded the shout boat, the innkeeper filled my canteen with his best saké."

"You have any left?"

"No."

"Then you *did* take my advice: drink enough saké and you won't get seasick."

"I drank only a bit."

"What? Not good?"

"Delicious."

Blue Rice threw her a curious look.

Yamabuki grew pensive. "I poured much of it over your cenotaph."

"You wasted it?"

"No. I built the memorial in your honor."

Only now did she grasp the fact that two arrows protruded from Blue Rice—one in his side, the other in his chest. Both wounds seeped blood. *Why did I not notice that before?* She asked, "Did the arrows hurt?"

He contemplated the feathered shaft protruding from his side. "I think it did." He paused. "Yes. When it went in, it was very painful."

"Misaki's second shot went straight into your heart."

"I remember only one arrow."

"Maybe that's good. If I were to die, that would be the best way to go. Not feeling. Not knowing." She sighed. "I killed a man today. The fencing master. His name was Shima. He was aboard the kobune. Remember?"

"Big man. Double-long sword. Ōuchi clan?"

"Hai." She glanced at the door, almost expecting Shima to walk in. But the door did not move. "We dueled. He didn't die straightaway. He teetered for several moments after I drove my sword into his side. Stood gasping. Whispered some final words." She shook her head, reliving the moment. "Had my blade thrust been truer, he would not have made any sound."

Blue Rice looked at her intently. "I need to ask you something."

"Is that why you have come to me?"

"I was to rendezvous with my sister. We were to meet in Minezaki, where the North Road crosses the East-West Highway. Will you tell her I won't be meeting her?"

"How can I bear bad news to someone I've never met?"

For the first time, Blue Rice seemed distressed. "Who else can tell her? You were there. You have to tell her what happened."

"I don't even know what she looks like."

"She will be coming from the Mountain Country. From the East. She'll be wearing an *Ine* rice crest identical to mine."

Yamabuki took a deep breath. "Can you describe her?"

He smiled whimsically. "She calls me Risu." Squirrel. "She found me climbing a tree—"

The ōgane boomed, startling him.

"Fifth watch. Hour of the Tiger," Yamabuki said.

Distracted, Blue Rice moved away. "I must leave."

The wind picked up, rattling the guesthouse. Blue Rice grew transparent before her eyes.

"Wait!" she called.

He slung the outer door wide and ran into the snowy night. It closed by itself with a bang. Yamabuki thought to run after him. *What is his sister's name?* Yes. She would have to run after him and ask.

Only then did she realize that she lay on the floor. Unable to move. How terrible it was to be unable to move! Was this what it was like to be dead? Maybe she had frozen to death and just did not know it. *Maybe you don't know when you die; you simply go on afterward in a dream.*

She tried to scream but no sound came.

EIGHT

FILL THE FISSURE TO THE JIGOKU

Five Bell Strikes, Hour of the Dragon
Two days past Full Moon of Unohana Month
11 May 1172

Y AMABUKI'S HEAD THROBBED. Even within the warm bedding, she sensed the day dawned bitter. The coals in the irori had turned mostly to whitish ash. Gusting mountain winds blew ice through the ceiling's smoke vent. Snowflakes the size of sand grains disappeared in the fire pit's rising heat. The lingering vapor shimmered. If she were home at the Taka compound, by now someone from the household staff would have been attending to the fire. *I have to get up. The fire is not going to tend itself.* She propped herself up, checking the scrolls. Intact and dry.

Pieces of memory, or rather dream fragments, came to her. Her personal sword lay within reach, not her long sword—that had been only part of a dream. Of course it would not be there. Armorer Kōno was to polish Tiger Claw.

She gathered herself, tossing off the quilts. The chill took her breath. Toes freezing, clad only in her white shitagi, she went to a stack of small logs—any one of them no larger than her forearm. *How many should I use?* She decided immediately, not wanting to stand around deliberating while she froze. *Five should be enough.* That was the number the samurai back home used when they made fires at camp. She tossed the logs on top of the coals and ash. The pinewood smoldered.

There was no sand-filled night-soil box in the room. *I will have to use the pit outside.* She did not look forward to that. Still shivering, she peered through the window slats. Sunlight shimmered on the snow-covered ground under cloudless blue skies.

She coughed. The fire struggled, producing more smoke than heat—a lot of smoke, which hung low, thickening in the air rather than escaping through the roof vent.

Now gasping, eyes stinging, blinking through tears, she quickly donned the orange kimono and slipped the three wax-sealed dispatches into its ample sleeve pockets, pushed Tiger Cub through the sash, and pulled on her fur boots.

She slid the outer door open and rushed outside.

Cold assaulted her face, but at least it was clear and fresh. Lifting her arm to shield her eyes, she squinted up the glaringly bright mountainside toward the Pass of the Setting Sun. Snow blanketed everything. Ice sparkled at the summit.

Lower down, Yamabuki noticed smoke—or rather vapor. A rivulet of steaming spring water emerged from the cliff base near the third structure, where the armorer's wife and Kouma lived. Such springs could range from tepid to scalding hot, and often smelled of rot. This one did not.

Everything slowly took on a red cast. *I'm going snow blind.* She looked down, searching for any footfalls to make the walk to the night-soil pit easier. The only imprints were her own—from last night, headed in from town—and now largely buried by new snow. Had she only dreamt Kouma's visit, or were Kouma's tiny feet so light that they made ne'er a dent? What of her mother? Dreamt as well?

Momentarily putting off the ordeal of the night-soil pit, she decided to look in on her mount in the stables. Picking up her steps, she waded past the complex of five armory buildings on the snowy plateau. In a few strides, she passed into the shadows of the cliffs. No longer bedazzled, her snow blindness faded.

The stable abutted the sheer rock face of the notch. The plank walls were partially open to the elements, allowing feed to be easily tossed into eating troughs. Someone had thrown a thick horse blanket over her jet-black colt, who stood quietly and quite serenely inside. Similarly draped was one other fine mount. She wondered if it belonged to Yoshinaka. It certainly looked splendid enough for a young warlord.

The shed, warm and musty, seemed to agree with Mochizuki. His skittishness of yesterday at the windswept seashore seemed to have evaporated. He looked up from the rice straw, and his big, brown, moon-round eyes met hers. Then he went back to his champing. She whispered as she came right beside him, "I'll get you out of here soon, Mochizuki. I know this is not a place for someone who loves to run as much as you do." He paid her no further attention, even as she stroked him. "Hmm. Maybe you know something I don't."

She looked back across the snowy grounds. As soon as her armor was repaired and sword was polished, she needed to resume her journey. But an attempt to cross the pass late in the day with the new-fallen snow did not seem like a good idea.

Yet it was unwise to remain in Minezaki. Others were on her trail. Yoshinaka seemed convinced. And Shima had actually identified Gankyū, the master assassin. And the false monks? She didn't want to accept it, but wanting it not to be true would accomplish nothing: Someone had sent assassins after her—someone who knew where she was going, someone who knew about the scrolls she carried. Someone: a traitor within the Taka.

She drew in a deep breath. There was nothing she could do about that now, except survive—and she'd proven to herself she was capable of defending herself. Once she reached the Imperial City, her clan could send messengers to warn her parents in Ō-Utsumi.

Having put off the inevitable as long as she could, she left Mochizuki to his munching and headed out to the night-soil pit.

As she approached the open trench with its crude wooden handrails, she looped her long hair, still tied in ribbons, around her neck. Hiking up her kimono and using the wooden handrails to brace herself, she straddled the pit. Cold wind blew through the fissure. Yamabuki shivered more than ever, though she was thankful that the pit's ripeness was all but gone. To think, she had left the comfort of the Taka compound for *this*—the real world of a warrior.

The snow glared, and again the reddish cast of snow blindness returned. *Just like the fire last night.* Things from the underworld had come through the cleft in the earth. *Perhaps I shall now fill the fissure to the jigoku.*

Yamabuki, teeth chattering, laughed.

But then she noticed thick bluish-white smoke belching from the guesthouse.

NINE
IT APPEARS I'M BEING COURTED

Y AMABUKI GASPED AND BROKE into a run, fighting her way through
the drifting snow. No flames were in evidence, but as a child she
had learned firsthand the unpredictability of fires. In an instant, an entire building could erupt.

The entry door stood wide. Someone was inside.

Mari.

The girl must have sensed Yamabuki's presence, for she looked toward
the entry and smiled kindly, pulling the last of four logs from the irori,
leaving only one. Already the smoke was clearing. Yamabuki sighed in
relief and entered.

"Just to be sure," said Mari as she gave a quick, small bow to Yamabuki
before slipping past her and tossing the smouldering wood out the doorway into a snow bank.

"I'm afraid I caused this," said Yamabuki.

"Not at all." Mari returned and now bowed again with a polite smile.
"In the mountains it's harder to get smoke to rise. And the firewood's always damp."

*Mari spares me embarrassment and she now acts like it was in no way
my fault.*

Still standing in the genkan, Yamabuki took off her fur boots, putting
them next to Mari's straw pair, and stepped inside.

Mari picked up a small iron kettle. "I've brought some hot food. Hot
food fights the cold." Yamabuki braced herself for more *kibi.* "*Nabe!*" Mari
beamed as she lifted the lid off the pot. Nabe, of course, was the word for
kettle, but inside was what counted—hot broth and vegetables.

Yamabuki brightened. "I shall now eat like a sumo player!"

Yo-ichi appeared in the doorway carrying a tray of covered wooden bowls. He kicked off his straw snow sandals, but came no further than the genkan and bowed. Mari took the tray, presenting steaming unhusked rice to the warrior.

"I see." Yamabuki grinned. "I get the rice grains and you give my mount the rice straw."

Yo-ichi shifted uneasily and grew slightly red faced.

Mari giggled, eyes twinkling. "Samurai-*sama* is just making light."

Yamabuki laughed good-naturedly. But Yo-ichi hovered near the door, grinning uneasily. He was probably not used to women's patter.

Mari bowed yet again. "Last night we weren't ready for guests. Millet was all we had. Not a worthy meal for a samurai. I hope you'll like this better."

"I wasn't hungry last night," Yamabuki lied. "But I'm hungry now."

Yo-ichi left, promising to return shortly.

Mari placed onto the food tray a dark-blue flask bearing a white felwort mon. "The Gentian samurai left it for you early this morning."

"What is this?" Yamabuki asked.

"He said it's saké. And I was to also give you this." She held out a beautifully folded paper.

Yamabuki hummed skeptically and unfolded the note. It still smelled of fresh ink.

> *To the warrior of saké and ice*
> *May this flask soften the road's hardships*
> *Come to the House of Red Banners*
> *So we can again drink together*
> *To forget our homes.*

It was written entirely in the calligraphy of Qin. A schooled hand. *So much for his claim of bare literacy.* She snorted in exasperation. *It appears I'm being courted.*

A worried look crossed Mari's face. "Is it a challenge?"

"Not to a duel, if that's what you think," said Yamabuki. "Just a poem."

Mari sighed, relieved.

Yamabuki reconsidered. "Well, maybe a challenge, but of a different sort. You know—" She smiled slyly and shrugged.

Mari gave her a questioning look.

"The kind between a man and woman."

Now Mari blushed.

Yo-ichi returned, bearing a bundle.

"Your clothes." Mari took the bundle from him. "I apologize if I failed to clean them enough." She brought forth Yamabuki's folded kimono and hakama.

The clothes had been pressed. Yamabuki lifted the split riding skirt, which had received the worst spattering of blood; the distinctive rough silk with the green tortoise-shell pattern now betrayed not the slightest hint of it. Not even the scent. It was as if Mari had switched out the hakama for a new one, but that was impossible. The pattern was unique. Getting the blood out silk must have been something an armorer's daughter had learned as part of the family livelihood.

"Will you please help me into my own clothing?" Yamabuki asked.

At this, Yo-ichi left.

Mari stepped over to slide the outer door shut.

Yamabuki took the opportunity to quickly remove the scrolls from her sleeves and set them, along with her short sword, against the wall in the shadows. Hopefully the girl would not notice them.

As Mari returned, Yamabuki nodded. "Your brother has good manners."

Mari bowed and eased the borrowed orange kimono off Yamabuki's shoulders. "I hope the Kōno family kimono kept you warm," Mari said.

"Very. It was warm and fit perfectly. And last evening, wearing it, I was able to move about not as a warrior, but as a person who might live in Minezaki. I wore makeup, so I don't think anyone recognized me, either."

"Makeup?" Mari tried to suppress a small gasp.

Yamabuki pointed to her own left cheek. "Perhaps I am vain, but the gash on my face had to be covered, which meant I had to cover the rest of my face as well, no?"

"And no one bothered you?"

"Bothered me?"

Mari's expression grew strained. "In this town, if anyone—man or woman—wears makeup, it means the person is available for a rendezvous." Yamabuki must have blanched, for Mari hastily added, "But I know that since you carry a sword, no one would make such a mistake."

Yamabuki cleared her throat. "No. Nothing like that."

Mari took the orange kimono from Yamabuki, set it aside, and began to help her into her own garments.

As the young girl fussed, Yamabuki said, "You've cleaned my clothes so beautifully. I doubt our clan tailors could have done as well."

Mari brightened. "Hai!"

When she had finished and Yamabuki was fully dressed, Mari collected the Kōno clan kimono and bowed. "I hope you find your meal satisfactory." She stepped into the genkan and bowed again before opening the door.

Yamabuki called out, "What about your boots?"

"My boots?"

"The straw boots by the door. Next to mine."

"Too big for me," Mari answered, genuinely surprised.

"Yo-ichi's?"

"He's smaller than me."

"Whose then?"

A look of puzzlement flashed across Mari's face, but it was replaced by a smile. "They do not belong to any of us. These are mine," she said, sliding her feet into a small pair of winter sandals. She quickly left.

Alone, Yamabuki retrieved the three scrolls and slipped them into the safety of her kimono's ample sleeve pockets. Yes. It felt good to be back in her Taka clan colors and crests. She sat before the food tray. At last, a chance to enjoy a warm meal. She took the first mouthful, and it was like Mari had said. The food warmed her. She savored every bite, feeling her strength returning.

What would her two handmaids think if they knew about the past eleven days? She had met so many new people, especially people as young as she, many even younger—and none, apart from Yoshinaka, was *kuge* class. Growing up, the few young people she'd known were the sons and daughters of her uncles and aunts and of her father's senior council, all kuge, though none were like her. And she knew it. So did they.

For them, everything was about rank, appearances, currying favor and ingratiating oneself. The other highborn females showed little interest in training horses or mastering weapons, though some had at least a nodding acquaintance with *naginata*. Most, however, spent the entirety of their waking hours composing poetry and music and singing—much of it mediocre and all of it derivative—or thinking about how to look more fetching. And this carried over to the young males as well. Not long after their genpuku, they quickly learned that professing a love of poetry and music provided a convenient cloak for their lusts. They composed poems and songs, even more mediocre and derivative, dedicated to attractive girls of lower court rank.

None of these men, however, had dared entreat Taka-gimi. Courting a warlord's daughter was impermissible—not that Yamabuki was interested. She told Tomoko that she did not care for, nor did she have even the slightest use for, these young men, who were still mere boys, genpuku or not. No wonder she'd found a stable boy grown to manhood more fetching than any of them. Ryuma had been the first to cross a line that no youth at the Taka compound would have dared approach.

She had always thought that her life was governed by so many rules: what she could and could not do; where she could and could not go; what she could and could not say; how deeply she had to bow to whom, depending upon rank. And yet now she found that the *nanigashi*, what the kuge called commoners, were just as restricted, only in different ways, including what boys could and could not do, and what was expected of girls and what they were not permitted. They were just as trapped as anyone at court. And it seemed the rules were just as complex—perhaps even more so when they encountered samurai, who were known to react unpredictably, even violently, if they felt imposed upon.

She recalled at the Barrier Strait when the young oyster girl offering to sell part of her catch to Yamabuki had hidden any fear. At the Wakatake Inn, Ishi-tsuki and Chi-ye, neither of them any older than Mari, had instructed Yamabuki in the steps of the fiery dances of the *toi*. At the site of yesterday's duel, the knees of the farm girl carrying cloth to market had buckled upon seeing Yamabuki wipe blood from her blade, but the girl then braced up and maintained her composure. When Yamabuki had arrived in Minezaki, its townspeople were taciturn but for Kani, a youth who summoned the courage to answer her instead of turning mute. It was he who told her about the armory— where at sunset Yamabuki encountered the adorable child beating an already dead rat with a stick—a little girl with whom she shared the same childhood sobriquet: Kouma.

And then there was Mari, who had treated the guesthouse as though it was Yamabuki's royal chamber. In many ways, she substituted as Yamabuki's handmaid; and likewise Yamabuki was allowing herself a familiarity with this girl that she might otherwise not have displayed.

It occurred to Yamabuki that something was changed about herself, and not just from the killing. In each of the prior trips to Heian-kyō, others had always decided the route; others had always negotiated with merchants and ferrymen along the way; others had always dealt with threats natural and human. Though she had grown up with the autonomy afforded a girl of high birth, only now did she begin to fathom that what she had thought of as her freewill and independence was nothing of the kind. Others had decided practically everything, and she in contradistinction had decided very little—if in fact anything. But now, away from the rules and customs of life back home, she had freedom to do as she pleased, to talk to whom she pleased in ways she pleased, and to go where she wished.

She decided she liked that. Maybe she was more like the Dowager than she cared to admit. Maybe her grandmother's blood ran strongly in her veins, and no one was going to tell Yamabuki what she could do and could not do.

Was that what her mother feared? That Yamabuki would be too independent? And never marry?

Her thoughts drifted back to Yoshinaka. She felt a smoldering attraction. He was handsome like Ryuma, yet he was also so like herself, raised much like she had been raised. Yoshinaka had been forced to do what she had been forced to do—kill. And yet he retained a poet's soul.

She pondered his poem of invitation to share saké. What else could she do in this boring little crossroads town until the pass cleared?

"Samurai-sama!" a young voice shouted. "Samurai-sama," he repeated, now louder and more urgent.

"Yo-ichi?" She put down her food and *hashi* and slid the outer door aside.

The young boy, eyes panicked, panted for breath. "My father begs your help."

"Help?"

"Survivors!"

TEN
STRIP HIM!

THE DOUBLE DOORS at the back of the armory stood wide, likewise the front, allowing Yamabuki a clear view right through and on up the Ledge Road, where Yo-ichi thrashed through waist-high drifts, snow flying with every stride as he chased after his father and brothers.

Inside, Mari knelt over a man who lay in a heap next to the forge. He was either unconscious or dead. She tugged at his outer clothing—a straw winter cape and hat which she pulled loose. Beneath he was clad in Ōe clan armor.

"You know him?" Yamabuki asked.

"No."

Yamabuki bent down. It did not look good. A mass of ice balls the size of cherries clung to the man's beard. His mane of hair, crystalline and matted, held fast to his cheeks, his eyebrows and mustache caked in frost. His eyes fluttered and his lips moved, though only imperceptibly. He moaned.

"He's coming around again." Mari raised a cup to the man's lips and whispered to him, "Slowly now."

"Hot water?" Yamabuki leaned to get a closer look.

"Warm. Not too hot or it can burn him—just as bad as the frostbite." She looked up, eyes sad. "He's drifting in and out."

"Did he say anything?"

"Only a little. The snow came suddenly. The horses died. The night fell." Mari shook her head. "That's all I got from him. That and that some unseen thing attacked him."

Shouts echoed off the rock walls of the notch.

Mari looked up. "It's father."

Outside, Eiji and Fuyuki trudged toward the armory, bracing up another survivor between them, a man in full armor. They were most of the way back when the man slipped from the boys' grasp. Try as they might, they could not get him back to his feet. Kōno marched up, waving his sons aside, stooped over, and hefted the man over his shoulders.

He's strong as a horse.

Kōno called out, "Mari! Heat water! Heat lots!"

"Samurai-sama," Mari interrupted. "I know I should not ask, but could you please give him some more warm water?"

"Oh." Yamabuki turned. "Of course." Yamabuki moved closer, and mirroring Mari, she lifted his head so it rested against her knee.

"Give him only a little at a time." Mari formally bowed and then fetched a nabe iron kettle and rushed out the back to the hot spring.

The ice in his hair and face began to thaw where it touched Yamabuki's hem. *How cold his skin is.* She put her hand against his cheek and the ice there took to melt. He opened his eyes and through frosted brows and lashes looked at her kindly. The beard around his mouth was no longer totally ice encrusted. She could see his once-blue lips turning pink. He mumbled, "*Dōmo.*" *Thanks.*

Mari returned, the kettle brimming with water.

How can a willowy girl be so strong?

Mari placed the kettle on the forge to heat.

Kōno Taro, breathing heavily, entered the armory with the second victim slung over his shoulders. Gingerly protecting the man's head, Taro lowered him onto the floor in the center of the workshop. The armor clanked against the planking. Coming to rest, the man lay still as a doll.

Taro stood, catching his breath. Mouth drawn and jaw clenched, he looked at Yamabuki and slowly shook his head.

Eiji and Fuyuki entered, stomping the snow off their winter sandals.

A look of renewed determination crossed Taro's face. "Strip him!"

As if receiving orders from a *tai-shōgun*, they moved as one. Eiji, Fuyuki and Yo-ichi pulled off their own cloaks, tossing them aside, and began pulling away the supine man's outer garments. Underneath, he too wore Ōe clan armor.

"High ranking," Taro huffed.

"He's a *kashira*, judging by the ornate *yoroi*," said Yamabuki.

The Kōno siblings rapidly but respectfully unknotted the binding cords they could reach, then gently rolled the commander onto his side to get at the other disparate fastening points. He did not resist in the slightest as they removed the individual pieces of armor.

The forge fires burned high and hot. Even with the front and back doors thrown wide open, snow that had been tracked in had turned to melted puddles pooled on the fine pine floor.

The kashira's face remained covered by a scarf. Only his half-vacant eyes showed. Mari stooped down and tenderly removed the shawl, revealing his black shaggy beard and long mane, all crusted with hunks of snow. The two elder brothers pulled off the rest of his clothing, right down to the shitagi. And then even it came off. Naked and pallid, the warrior lay on his back, too cold and too near death to shiver.

"Water!" cried Taro.

Yo-ichi and Mari rushed over to the forge and returned hefting steaming nabe. With his fingertips, the armorer touched the liquid in one cauldron. "Hum," he murmured approvingly, pulled back his sleeve, and shoved his arm in up to the elbow. "Perfect!" He nodded emphatically. "Eiji, Fuyuki. Drench him." He gestured at the kashira. "And don't forget the hands and feet!"

The two brothers cautiously poured—a gentle flow, but enough to cover all of him.

Mari and Yo-ichi brought more kettles forth, and the elder brothers poured a second round of water over the naked man. But the kashira lay as still as ever.

"Hotter water!" Taro called out. "Hotter water!"

Mari stoked the fire. Yo-ichi delivered a heavily steaming cauldron, one the armorer could barely keep his hand in. "Good!" Taro started pouring.

The kashira did not blink, move, or mutter.

Tossing the empty cauldron aside and dropping on all fours, Taro pressed his ear to the man's chest. He laid his fingertips against the man's neck. Darkness crossed Taro's face. "Too late."

Eleven

Strange Things Walk the Road

T HE LIGHT OF THE FORGE FLAMES shone brightly, revealing Taro's grim expression as he gazed at the unconscious man, whose head lay on Yamabuki's knee. In a soft voice, he said, "This one was barefoot when he arrived."

"Barefoot?" Yamabuki shook her head.

"He lost his boots. He said that during the night something pulled them off."

"Something?" Yamabuki made a face.

Taro nodded sagely. "Strange things walk the road to the pass. Disquieted spirits cling onto the living and pull others into the abyss."

She cast a skeptical look. "Disquieted spirits?"

"There were two other soldiers. I doubt they made it. After the thaw, we'll find what the wolves and scavengers haven't picked clean."

Mari came over and draped a blanket across the warrior. She then took over the ministering, resting his head on her knee.

Yamabuki stood and said, "So this man is the only one who will live."

Taro grunted and led her a few steps away. "Maybe not even him."

"He's warm and breathing. Surely—"

"His toes—" Taro pointed at the man's feet, which protruded from the blanket. "Look at them. *Tōshō.*"

Yamabuki didn't understand. From what she saw, color had come back to the feet—save for the toes, which were as colorless as ice. "You'll warm the toes," she said hopefully.

Taro shook his head. "The ice kami has already feasted on the flesh. Once warmed, the toes will turn black. Rot. And then the blood fever will come. After that—" Taro shrugged. "A terrible way to go."

"Can't anything be done?"

"Yes, but he won't let it happen."

Yamabuki cocked her head. "Won't let what happen?"

"We take off the frozen parts before they turn black."

"Take off the frozen parts?" She took a deep breath. "How?" She already suspected the answer.

"We cut them off. But he won't agree. It's all his toes. And two of his fingers."

"So we do nothing?"

"By the time they finally agree, it's always too late."

The man still breathed, though shallowly.

"He has no hope, then," Yamabuki said sadly.

"Who knows? The blood fever kami usually doesn't spare anyone."

"You can reason with him."

Taro walked over to a box. "He won't want to reason with *this*." He lifted a saw with tiny razor-fine teeth like inside a shark's mouth, its handle dark with bloodstains. "This will cut through flesh and bone quickly."

"How long does it take to cut toes off?"

"About the length of a shriek."

"All of them?"

"Each." Taro straightened and looked Yamabuki in the eye. "I won't give up, but the challenge is to get his permission."

Keeping the saw behind him, out of man's line of sight, Taro approached the injured survivor, bent down, and spoke soothingly.

"Can you hear me, samurai-sama?"

Awake after all, the Ōe warrior weakly nodded.

Taro gently pulled the blanket back from the man's feet. "Your toes. You see them?"

The man opened his eyes and lifted his head to look. Then he sank back and nodded again.

Taro sighed. "Not so good. The Yuki-onna must have brought the storm in hopes of embracing someone. She hoped to turn you into ice. You're lucky. All she got were your boots." He gave a sad chuckle.

The warrior managed a crooked smile.

"But then the *kami* of snow came"—Taro pointed to the toes—"and touched them, and two of your fingers. They're all white, just like the

Gods. But mortal people can't have God parts. God parts kill us. Thus your kami toes must be taken off."

Nearly ice-white already, the man grew even more pale. He shook his head. "No," he whispered. "The kashira won't permit it."

"The kashira." Taro's face was grim. "He didn't make it, but I'm sure he'd tell you to heed my advice."

The warrior rolled his head to the side and looked at the kashira's naked corpse lying in the morning sunlight. His mouth twisted, and he turned his gaze toward his toes, his face set.

"It is up to you, but if we don't do this, you'll die," Taro said sadly.

"A warrior is not afraid to die," said the samurai with veiled pride.

"This is true. But we are talking about *life* here and a battle which you could survive."

"A warrior with no fingers? Death is better."

Taro glanced at Yamabuki as if to say his prediction had been correct.

Yamabuki screwed her face and broke in. "You are right handed? Draw the bow string with your right, no?"

The warrior looked up at her. With darkening eyes, he nodded.

"We've all met warriors who have lost fingers either in skirmishes or forfeit for making mistakes. Someone who has lost an ear or an eye or even a nose and have gone on to become illustrious, no?"

Slowly he nodded.

"For you, it's only two small fingers," she said with assurance. "Afterward you'll still pull with the thumb and first two fingers, same as always. Same as everyone."

He frowned, and there was a long silence. He breathed hard and looked to Taro. "How will you . . . take off the God parts?"

Taro revealed the jagged blade. "With this."

"A saw!" the warrior snarled.

"I am fast."

The samurai's eyes betrayed everything—anger, fear, panic, resignation, each turning over in his head.

"No!" He tried to sit fully up.

Mari laid a restraining hand on his chest. "It's the only way," she whispered.

"No! I'll do it myself. With my own blade." Again he tried to sit upright.

Taro touched the man's shoulder. "You shouldn't move."

The guard lapsed back. Weak but resolute, he said, "Hand me my blade."

Taro pointed to the tachi. "It's next to you."

The warrior rolled onto his elbows. With his left hand, he seized the scabbard. With his right, he grasped the hilt to pull—but his fingers could not close, and he moaned in pain, gasping "I can't!" before lying back exhausted.

"I'll do it then," Taro said with gravity.

"No, you won't." Still panting, he gritted his teeth. "But *she* can!" He shot a hard look at Yamabuki.

Stunned, she resisted the impulse to look away, for his eyes expressed a strange mixture—anger and pleading.

"You are proficient?" His words to her were not meant as a question.

She took in a breath, picturing what he was asking, imagining herself delivering a stroke to slice off the man's toes.

Almost growling, the samurai challenged, "Even an *average* warrior can do what must be done in an instant. Are you at least that good?" But it was all the fight he had within him. He closed his eyes tight.

Taro looked to Yamabuki. "With your sword, you could make it go quickly for him. Clean cuts. After, there's the hot pike and my needle. But if he survives that, he has a chance. A fair chance." He looked expectantly at her.

"I don't like this one bit." She realized that she sounded exactly like her mother. "It's savage."

"It's merciful. We need to be quick, while he still has the resolve and we haven't run out of time."

No one had ever suggested that this was any part of her duty. It had been one thing to kill an opponent with a thrust. But to methodically hack away pieces of a man? How was this part of the warrior's code? No one at the Taka compound ever spoke of such an eventuality.

And yet, was this not what *musha shugyō* was about—encountering things she would never experience as a princess in a palace? Yesterday three men had fallen before her sword. What was this compared to that?

Something inside her hardened. Perhaps forever. She slowly nodded. "I agree."

Twelve

Her Forearms Now Bare

ALL EYES WERE ON TARO as he painstakingly tied down the good fingers of the man's right hand.

Yamabuki took this moment to surreptitiously remove the scrolls from her sleeve and casually slip them into an open box of half-finished *kozane*, covering them with the stitched platelets.

Taro now tethered the soles of the man's feet in place against a log.

The samurai murmured to her, "You may use my blade."

"No. I know my own the best."

He closed his eyes and lay back, toes clearly exposed, healthy fingers of his right hand tied back.

Yamabuki pulled a *tasuki* from her sleeve and held one end of the strand with her teeth, freeing both hands. With well-practiced motions, she wrapped the free end of the cord under her right arm, pulling the right sleeve back, then passed it behind her neck and pulled the left sleeve back. Forearms bare, she tied the two cord ends into a bowknot near her right shoulder. Any worthy warrior could finish this action in under five heartbeats.

Face grim, Yamabuki gave Taro a hard look.

"You are ready?" Taro asked.

Yamabuki unsheathed Tiger Cub and nodded.

"We need to purify the blade," said Taro. "Warm water will have to do."

"Is there something better?" she asked quietly.

"*Omiki*," said Taro.

"Sacred saké?"

Taro nodded. "But we have none."

"Maybe not sacredly blessed, but I have saké," Yamabuki said. "Mari?"

The girl stepped forward. "Hai?"

"Bring the bottle the Gentian samurai left."

Mari nodded and dashed off, returning almost straightaway with Yoshinaka's flask.

Yamabuki presented the naked sword, point down. While incanting prayers, Taro poured the wine over the blade. The rivulets washed the steel and trickled to the floor.

"Maybe it's time for him to take a swig too," Taro said, inclining his head toward the man. Yamabuki nodded. The warrior took the bottle in his left and drank thirstily, quaffing almost all of it. Eyes round, Taro's children looked to see what would happen next. Taro waved them away. "Go. There's nothing to see here."

Mari stepped to the forge and started heating an iron pike.

Yamabuki moved into place, focusing her targets: two feet and a hand; ten toes and two fingers. The morning light, amplified by sheets of snow, filled the armory so brightly she saw the afflicted appendages very clearly. They were white like the whitest rock, but there was also blackness in the nail beds. The stark contrast of the alabaster digits against healthy flesh indicated exactly where she was to strike.

She would do it in three rapid sweeps: One right-to-left cut to take the five toes of the left foot in one strike. Reverse in almost the same motion and take the five right toes. Then pivot very slightly to bring the sword down toward his right hand.

The wine obviously dazed the warrior. Maybe that was good. Less pain. He asked somewhat drunkenly, "May I know the name of the samurai who is going to cut me?"

She looked into his haggard face and answered simply, samurai to samurai, "I am known as Taka Yamabuki. And since I am about to do this, may I ask *your* name?"

"Misaki Tada."

Yamabuki stiffened. She looked past the beard and mattered hair. Indeed. It was none other than Blue Rice's killer. And the dead kashira? The same leader who had not lifted a finger to save Blue Rice and merely shrugged off the murder? And the five guards she had encountered the previous night at the Saké House—part of the same contingent? Was the law of karma unfolding before her?

Did Misaki recognize her? Likely not. She had been in full armor when she arrived in Nagato Prefecture. Misaki had been too busy tormenting Blue Rice to pay her any mind.

Now he lay at her feet, neck as exposed as his toes—in fact more so. One quick cut. One simple strike. She eyed his toes and fingers—more difficult targets. His head, so easy. She looked inside herself. She could do it. He would hold perfectly still, not expecting an executioner's cut. Not a word of protest. It would be quick. He would not even know that he was being punished. He would die without further suffering. Painless. He would not suffer like Blue Rice had suffered.

She recalled Lord Nakagawa's discourse on the dichotomy of the sword. He had once said, "*In one moment, an instrument of destruction. In the next, one of humanity.*" Until this morning, she had only understood this abstractly: like the manifold faces of the numberless Gods, more of a riddle than anything else.

Four slow bells struck the Hour of the Snake. She centered herself and raised her sword into the prepare position. Silence fell over the armory. Everyone held their breath. Even the wind ceased to stir.

THIRTEEN
STILL SOME BLOOD

T IGER CUB WHISPERED as it cleaved the air. Three cuts merged into a single blur. Misaki's two fingers dropped straight to the floor. *Plop. Plop.* She wiped her blade with a piece of paper and slid her sword back into its sheath. Everyone stood frozen. Misaki grimaced, but to his credit it made no sound.

"Did she miss?" Yo-ichi whispered meekly.

Taro went to Misaki's feet. "She didn't miss. Clean cuts of a master swordsman," Taro declared as he lifted away the ten severed toes, throwing them toward the open back door. On all fours, he moved over to inspect the stumps where Misaki's fingers had been—and pulled back, gagging. "More!" He pointed to what remained of the little finger. "You were conscientious samurai-sama. Some's left. Just a tiny bit."

Yamabuki eyed the nub of bone—white flesh that did not even ooze. It was an angular piece that protruded uncomfortably close to the healthy digits. If she let herself be careless and nicked his adjacent drawstring fingers, Misaki would never draw a bow again. If she was passing sentence in her home province for killing Blue Rice, would she now demand he forfeit more?

Yet again Yamabuki grimly centered herself. The blade flew. Misaki hardly flinched. Taro bent down a second time for another sniff. "Perfect!"

He grabbed the iron pike from the forge. The smell of hot metal filled the air.

"Brace yourself," Taro warned. He pressed the pike's dull red tip against the raw toe stumps.

Misaki gasped, pulling against the tethers. Burning flesh added to the odor of metal and rot. Taro quickly pulled the pike away.

"Mari," He commanded. Immediately she packed handfuls of snow over the burnt area. The snow reddened. "Still some blood there." Taro drew a pre-threaded needle from his tunic. He spat on the thread, pushing the snow aside and began to sew, moving from stump to stump, wound to wound, stitching points only where blood still oozed.

Yamabuki marveled. Though his fingers and hands were hardened and thick from wielding a hammer, Taro's sewing proved deft and artful.

The air increasingly carried a pungent reek. Yamabuki stepped toward the back door, vowing to hold her gorge until she got outside. She looked down, for it helped contain the nausea—except that now her eyes came to rest on the white frozen toe remnants glistening in the daylight. In three long strides, she headed toward the guesthouse.

Out in the daylight, she doubled over and lost the content of her stomach. After nothing more came up, she cleared her mouth of the remnants of spit-up rice and bitter broth with a handful of fresh snow.

When she re-entered the armory, the putrid odor had all but vanished. None of the severed toes and fingers were anywhere in sight. Mari threw something into the forge and a sizzling sound arose.

Misaki lay very still, his eyes closed. She had heard from seasoned warriors that sometimes people died from blows not judged to be fatal, seemingly survivable blows, but which once delivered, jolted the victim's spirit loose.

"He dead?"

Taro said, "He's had enough for the moment. Let him be. He'll be awake soon enough."

As for the dead kashira, someone had covered him in another blanket.

She turned and gazed out the doorway at the shimmering snow beyond. So beautiful. But such beauty took the lives of the men on the pass, and even one of the survivors had succumbed later to its touch. In fact, but for her sword, no one would have survived.

Her hand gripped Tiger Cub's hilt, curling around the wrapping until her fingers blanched. Yukiyasu's steel was not unlike the snowy morning. Shimmering. Blinding. Deadly.

She released a breath. Only now, after she had killed men in battle and saved a life in need, did Nakagawa's lesson become clear in her mind: "*The sword becomes part of the person who wields it.*"

It was not the sword that determined whether an act was wanton or compassionate. *She*, not Tiger Claw, had struck down the men yesterday. And *she*, not Tiger Cub, had removed Misaki's rotting flesh. Her actions—and to a large extent the course of events around her—were up to her. Not only did she have a hand in her own fate. Her decisions changed the fate of others.

"What a morning," Taro sighed. "I would have started polishing your *tachi* except—" He pointed toward Misaki.

"You said you'd have it today."

"Hai." Taro brightened. "But I did mend your armor, samurai-sama."

"My armor? Already?" She perked up.

On a trellis-like wooden work rack, Yamabuki's dark green yoroi hung by knotted ropes. She touched the *dō*, running her hand across the spot where Shima's nodachi had ripped apart the kozane. The leather lacing connecting the platelets was not just mended—the entire chest protector bore not the slightest hint of a tear. The silk was perfectly matched. Taro had completely restored the armor—as new as the day she had left the Taka compound on this journey.

Taro beamed at her obvious approval and change of mood.   .

"I would like to be fitted," the Taka princess declared.

"Eiji! Fuyuki!" Taro called. "Make yourselves useful!"

The two young men ran up as Taro offered to hold Tiger Cub. The boys immediately set to work, retrieving the *suneate* from the rack and kneeling to attach them to her shins. They fastened to her body each armor component methodically and efficiently as Taro supervised the work, saying, "I admit, I was up all last night, but the armor's intricate and expert construction was sufficiently fascinating to keep me awake. Once I started working the new *odoshi* through the kozane, I lost all track of time."

The boys' tugged on the leather and jerked the silk ties, though no more firmly than did her handmaids back home.

FOURTEEN

ETSU COULD LIFT A HORSE

Eight Bell Strikes, Hour of the Sheep
Second Day of Unohana Month
Eighth Day of Kokuu
27 April 1172

Taka Compound, Ō-Utsumi Prefecture, Isle of Unknown Fires

WITHIN THE OPULENT BEDCHAMBER of her shinden, with suneate and *kote* already snugly in place on her shins and forearms, and the heavy *kusazuri* armor skirt secured around her waist, Yamabuki reached out like a great bird, ready to be wrapped in her upper-body armor. Her two trusted handmaids slid the heavy green-lacquered dō around her torso and tied the silk side fastenings, taking the same pleasure mothers indulge in when fussing over a beloved child.

"The scent is so fetching," Tomoko said with a giddy laugh, "when the armor's new."

"I think it's the fresh lacquer," said Hana-ye. "I don't know why, but the dark green seems to smell the best. Do you think maybe that's why the Taka chose it for their armor's dominant color?"

"Is that too tight, Yamabuki-sama?" Tomoko asked before continuing. "Actually it's that I like the way the leather smells."

Yamabuki smiled. "That's rather *un*-Buddhist of you."

"Ha!" Hana-ye scoffed. "I don't think *all* warriors are Buddhists."

Yamabuki laughed. "If the Emperor is Buddhist, then those who serve Him must be also."

"Buddhists are supposed to be vegetarians, but that doesn't stop us from eating fish." Hana-ye looked pleased with herself and licked her lips.

As her handmaids fastened the ties at her waist, Yamabuki said in mock officiousness, "There's precious little fish in the Imperial City. It's easy enough not to eat something you can't get. We Taka cannot help it if there is only ocean to the east and to the south. We net what the Sea Deity bestows."

Tomoko and Hana-ye giggled quietly. Yamabuki laughed. The banter kept her mind off the import of this, the next-to-final fitting. She knew they keenly felt this as well, for in special honor of this day and the princess whom they served, they wore their best everyday kimono: Tomoko in the cobalt blue Taka colors, and Hana-ye in the Taka's muted red.

In two days, she would have no one to fuss over her. She might not see her handmaids for another year, maybe two. Yamabuki would leave secretly and travel without bodyguards or royal escort. As for the armor, it bore no special badge of rank—merely the obligate crossed arrow feathers, seals of the Taka clan. And Yamabuki had told only Tomoko that Lady Taka had entrusted Yamabuki with a scroll. The princess was to hand it directly to Lady Taka's brother at the Palace of Spring Snow.

Tomoko, Yamabuki's age, had faithfully served the princess for over five years now; Hana-ye, two years younger, for three. Taka princess or not, Yamabuki felt they were as much sisters to her as any sisters by royal blood could be. And now she would be withdrawing from them, leaving an equally empty place in their hearts as well. And so they laughed and tittered all the more.

Tomoko tugged again on the kote on Yamabuki's left forearm. "Good. Tight though?"

Yamabuki nodded. "Much better than what I had before."

Hana-ye said, "This is the second armor set since last spring."

"If you grow any taller," Tomoko teased, "you'll be the tallest person in all of Great Bay Prefecture."

Yamabuki scowled and both handmaids giggled. Then Yamabuki moved about, stretching and bending to test the fit. She was pleasantly surprised by its flexibility. Despite its absence of markings of rank, this yoroi reflected the finest work of the Taka armorers. Always only the best for Taka-gimi.

"It's so bulky and heavy," Hana-ye chided.

"How *ever* can you walk in it?" Tomoko asked mockingly.

"And if you had to swim for it—" Hana-ye prompted, as she always did.

And Yamabuki, as always, concluded with all of them, in unison, "Armor's not for swimming!" And they all laughed.

Yamabuki heard her two bodyguards stir outside the *nurigome*'s heavy doors. The girls fell silent. Yamabuki gave Hana-ye a conspiratorial look and whispered, "Whoever it is, tell them I am not available."

Before the handmaid could utter a word, a voice boomed, "General Moroto summons Taka-gimi!"

"Etsu?" Tomoko asked with surprise.

Yamabuki frowned. "I have to obey."

Hana-ye wondered aloud, "Why send Etsu instead of one of the hand-men?"

Yamabuki shook her head. "Because my father wants me *now*."

Hana-ye called out, "What should Taka-gimi wear?"

Etsu boomed back, "Full armor."

Tomoko asked loudly, "Where does the Great Lord wish to see Taka-gimi?"

"He waits in the marshaling yard, and asks the princess to come with her swords and be ready for hard riding."

Yamabuki said softly, "I'll need my fur riding skirt." The two handmaids pulled it up around her waist, and while Tomoko fussed with the last of the knots, Hana-ye carried over the fur-wrapped scabbard cover. "This too will protect Mochizuki's flanks," she said brightly, clearly trying to add cheer to the moment. Yamabuki smiled.

The handmaids quickly arranged Yamabuki's hair, wrapped it in a *hachimaki*, and set the kabuto in place. And since she went without a facemask, they were extra careful to securely tie the silk knots under her chin to keep the helmet snugly in place. Yamabuki nodded, and Hana-ye swung the doors outward.

Etsu filled the doorway. He was the biggest man, maybe apart from Jun, she had ever seen. When she was a child, a story circulated about Etsu: to build his strength, every day from childhood on he lifted a foal high over his head, so that as the colt grew in size, Etsu's strength grew apace. At first, Yamabuki had believed this story. But three years after her mogi, when the daimyō had presented her with a foal of her own, she tried to do what Etsu was said to have done, but it became obvious that horses grew to maturity far faster than did people. Mochizuki was nearly fully grown, even as a yearling. She felt quite foolish that she had ever believed the story.

Etsu bowed, tipping his bulk toward her, and his voice rumbled, "Denka!"

As the large man led her across the shinden to the outer doors, Yamabuki dismissed her personal guards who normally escorted her everywhere. Etsu surely would be enough protection for her. Besides, she wanted to talk with him.

The warm late-morning air carried the scent of peach blossoms as they crossed her garden. A steady offshore breeze rustled the palm trees. Five white-naped cranes floated directly over the compound, heading into the north, squawking in formation.

"Maybe that's the last of the cranes we'll see until the Time of Cold Dew," she said. "I wonder where they go in summer."

"North," Etsu said flatly.

"Maybe to the Barbarian Isle."

Etsu said nothing.

Yamabuki grinned, looking at the man who towered even over her. "Up close, those birds are tall as a man."

Etsu shrugged. "Some of them taller."

"Maybe when they land they'll chase the barbarians." Yamabuki laughed at her light jest—imagine, these gawky birds chasing giant, hairy *kehito* barbarians across open fields!—but Etsu merely breathed and opened the gate. At times she wondered what Etsu really thought of her. What lurked behind the stony face and granite exterior? She never questioned his loyalty to her father and thus to her, but Etsu was a man of few words. Like a tiger, he hid whatever he thought deep within, behind eyes that revealed precious little.

As she followed him down the covered plank walkway toward the marshaling yard, her own thoughts shifted to two nights earlier, when she had worn three-layered kimono and courtly makeup while following Rei, her mother's lithe, scarred handmaid to Lady Taka's shinden. That rainy night, after giving Yamabuki a single scroll, her mother had said the daimyō would also entrust her with a dispatch. Was her father summoning her to hand her the scroll? Why would he want to give it to her while she wore full armor? With swords? And what about the hard riding?

Only more questions arose as Yamabuki and Etsu emerged at the threshold of the marshaling yard, where ten mounted samurai of her father's personal retinue—Yamabuki recognized each, and could name all—circled the ring, putting their mounts through their paces in an impressive demonstration of horsemanship.

In a royal manner and in the way of a warrior princess, Yamabuki turned to Etsu. "Why has my father summoned me like this?" She flicked a gesture at her armor.

Etsu grunted. "Unknown riders. Warriors. Two, maybe more. Crossing down from the north."

Yamabuki gasped. Nobody dared encroach on Taka territory, especially given the tortuous approach required to reach the compound. "Whose riders?"

Etsu gave her a sideways glance. "Don't know. They slipped away from our pickets."

"Bad pickets," Yamabuki said with disappointment.

"Skilled intruders."

The marshaling yard was immense, circumscribed by thirty sprawling, walled estates of T'ang and Toi architectural styles—each with well-tended ornamental ponds, flowering trees, and lush shrubs that provided shade and tranquility—plus the clan's private Shintō temple, armory, sword works, fletchery, several grand meeting halls, cart houses, and stables—in effect an enormous open-air garden in the center of the compound, except this garden was routinely employed for the purpose of warrior training and preparation.

Now, surrounded by such opulence, the central yard's simple loose-dirt training area roiled with dust as the mounted warriors dashed between decapitated and speared straw dummies that lay scattered.

But this was no training exercise. As if in preparation for battle, the mounts ran bare-hoofed, without their protective straw coverings. Yamabuki never liked exposing her own colt to such hazard. If Mochizuki shattered a hoof or broke his leg, she would have to put him down. Not six moons before, General Moroto had disparaged her sentiment. Such words coming from a warlord's daughter! "What else are battle horses good for if not to rapidly carry riders over uncertain ground? Does the princess weep for every arrow she lets fly in battle?"

Of course, Mochizuki meant far more to her than any bamboo shaft, regardless of what speeches the royal fletchers made about their craftsmanship. And she also had reason to believe that her father cared for his own mount, Kage, at least as much as she cared for Mochizuki. But she knew he could never admit it. How would it look if a warlord hinted he might put a horse's welfare before the objective of winning a battle?

Two and three abreast, the riders thundered around the yard. But her father was nowhere to be seen.

"I thought my father was waiting," Yamabuki said sharply to Etsu.

The ground pulsed. *More riders.* All attention turned to the middle gate, a side entry that was rarely used. Six guards swung it open.

On horseback, her father, General Moroto, burst into the yard, eight mounted Taka samurai at his side.

But there were no prisoners. No heads.

FIFTEEN

TOO TEMPERAMENTAL

YAMABUKI SOMETIMES WONDERED if she took more after her mother or father. Perhaps both; maybe neither. Whenever she gazed at her mother, she wished she could be like her: captivating, strong, talented, and limber, her physiognomy tapered, her complexion pale, her skin milky smooth jade—the ideal of beauty, the impression all the highborn of the Itō clan, including its men, conveyed to the world, even if it required white powder and rose blush to do so. And years of martial practice had repaid her mother generously in terms of health. Unlike say Tachibana's senior wife, who though several years younger looked brittle and walked stooped, Lady Taka could still hit targets with a bow and arrow while riding at full gallop. Since childhood, Yamabuki had heard the flattering remarks that she shared her mother's subtle features. Yet Yamabuki knew she herself lacked her mother's mask of tranquility that so well hid her own passions.

With her father, it was different. More complicated. As General Moroto, the bold and experienced shōgun, his demeanor was anything but tranquil. Hardy and dark complected, he bore the port of Hachiman, God of War, with a round visage that shone like a brooding sun. A mere glance from him instilled a respect and obedience that verged on foreboding—even from Etsu and Jun. In exaltation, his men could not help but follow him. And Yamabuki could be counted among them.

But within his shinden, her father would shrug off all the wildness as if he were shrugging off a heavy cloak. By flickering light, in quiet repose, he read tomes on ancient matters and wrote in his diary about the fine points of statecraft. And he could always be counted on for *Wéiqí*, the board game that the people of Akitsushima called *Igo*, a game which he often won, a game he said was "to be mastered by every daimyō"—and by that he meant Yamabuki.

This morning, as he galloped past her in the marshaling yard, her father was not the man of thoughtful reflection as he raised his bow and stood in his stirrups. In one smooth motion, he drew the bowstring back and released an arrow.

The sound of the snapping string mixed with the arrow's whistle, immediately followed by a loud crack as the shaft shattered the target. The downrange target judge cried, "Hit!" as the two board halves landed in a pile of previously broken pieces.

Without hesitation, a boy who no doubt was being groomed to be a warrior ran from nowhere and set a fresh board into place.

Yamabuki's father, still in rhythm, already had another arrow in hand. In a single motion he drew and released, breaking the second target. He shattered a third. A fourth. And a fifth before finally turning Kage at the end of the run.

At a canter, he rode up to Yamabuki.

"You hit them all," she said with an admiring nod.

"Easy to shoot things that don't move. How nice it would be if targets never shot back." He grinned darkly. "You ready to ride?" Before she could answer, he called out, "Bring Taka-gimi's horse!"

A young groom led across the yard Mochizuki in full battle array—bow and *ebira* stuffed with arrows hooked to the saddle. Her mount shook his head, eyes half wild. He tried to rear. The boy struggled.

"Hold him!" Yamabuki snapped. She snatched Mochizuki's harness. The boy backed away as Yamabuki made sure Mochizuki was indeed ready for hard riding. She inspected the tack, lifted the stirrups, and tested that the saddle was solidly placed.

"Mount up," Moroto commanded.

Yamabuki gave him a long look. "The *yumi* is not strung!" She handed the reins to the stable boy. "Keep him still!"

With one hand she produced a heavy length of *asa* twine from her pocket, while with the other she grasped the bow, which was as long as she was tall, by its middle. Deftly she fastened the twine to the top, bit the loose end, and braced the yumi's tied end in a notched wooden block that lay on the ground—one of many scattered throughout the archery yard for just this purpose. Bending down on her left knee, she rested the bow against her thigh armor and pressed her weight down onto the middle. The laminated hardwood and bamboo composite yielded and creaked under the force. Taking the hemp twine from her mouth, she slipped its free-end knot over the end without looking. The yumi was strung.

"You move like you were in a mirror," Moroto said, commenting as usual on the fact Yamabuki accomplished this left-handed.

"Either side works, Tennō. What if I was wounded?" she answered firmly but respectfully. "I must inspect the arrows."

"No need. The groom's seen to that."

"He's only a stable boy."

"Let's ride out!" Moroto turned about, barely keeping control as his frenzied mount came up on his hind legs—which in turn excited Mochizuki, who tried to break free.

Yamabuki lunged, seizing Mochizuki's bridle before the boy lost control. The colt fought to pull away, but she would have none of it and grabbed his mane. Still he tried to rear. Overcoming the weight of her armor, she leapt, swinging herself up, and placed her left foot in the stirrup. Mochizuki, legs prancing, carved a circle as Yamabuki settled fully into the saddle and adjusted her hold on the reins, shrugging her shoulders, appreciating again the freedom her new armor afforded.

Laughing, Moroto shouted, "You've left him too temperamental."

Yamabuki shouted back, "Just the way I like him!"

The eight riders who had ridden in with the daimyō came alongside. "Tennō! We must escort you!"

Moroto waved them off. "I have all the escort I need." He glanced at Yamabuki.

"Ha!" she barked affirmatively, just like her father's retinue always did. "Where are we going?"

"The Trap! See if you can keep up with me!"

With that, dirt flying, he raced Kage through the open gate.

In an instant, Yamabuki assessed the situation. The Trap, a trail that ran down from the north into Ō-Utsumi by hugging the sea, was the least obstructed, and thus most obvious route for any would-be invaders.

Yamabuki cried out, "Ha!" and Mochizuki leapt immediately into a gallop, pursuing the daimyō out of the compound.

Ahead, already far across the wide hilly pastureland, Moroto had already covered the distance of the well-trodden trail. He dropped out of view.

Sixteen

Count on His Heart, Not His Head

YAMABUKI REACHED THE HILLOCK that overlooked the expansive labyrinthine tangle of ravines, weathered outcroppings, dead ends, blind drop-offs, loops, and uncertain forested links of sandy loam the Taka called the Maze. She knew it as well as the features of her own face. With her riding silks, kimono train and sleeves flying in the wind, she often took Mochizuki for a dash through the serpentine trails and twists.

Her father was nowhere in sight. Below, the trail broke in four directions, each path leading into thickly wooded old-growth trees. The freshest tracks led to the fourth trail—the series of switchbacks that ultimately coursed down into the Trap. If she gave chase, she likely could not close the gap with her father.

But the third trail, which diverged away from the Trap, ran atop the opposite side of a narrow and deep gully. If she leapt the gully, she could join the fourth trail and avoid the switchbacks altogether, emerging ahead of her father. Her colt was powerful enough to make the jump; she and Mochizuki had done it any number of times—though it had never proven a trivial vault, even for her agile colt. The approach was always tricky, for there was no definite path to the precipice, only loose pebbles overgrown with twisted pines.

Today her mount would have to bear her in full field armor.

No time to ponder.

"Ha!" she called out and Mochizuki charged down into the third trail.

Her armor creaked in the saddle. Stones popped, crunched, and crackled under the pounding hooves. Pine pitch rising in the heat of the day mingled with the scent of her own sweat and that of the horse as they raced through the familiar series of thin tree branches. Rich with spring sap, they did not yield in their usual way. Mochizuki seemed not to mind, and her armor protected her from the sting as she burst through them.

"Come on! Come on!" she encouraged him. "You know this!"

She sensed that the extra weight slowed him. She had to count on his heart and not his head, for if he suddenly balked and stopped short, he would throw her, armor and all, over his head and down into the gully.

She shook her head to get the image out of her mind. *I can't let myself think that way!* She urged her colt onward.

The thin path curved slightly uphill, yet even with the additional weight, Mochizuki gained speed. "Now! Now! Now!" she cried, putting her heels against his sides—

And suddenly the sound of hooves stopped.

Mochizuki was in the air. She clutched the reins.

A moment later he cleared the gap, landing hard but firmly on the other side.

It did not go as well for Yamabuki, for her top-heavy armor pitched her forward, and she came out of saddle and stirrups. The world spun. In less than a heartbeat, she would sail over Mochizuki's head. Though every instinct screamed otherwise, she forced herself to release his reins. They were useless.

Instead she grasped his mane, entwining her fingers among the locks before closing her muscular fists. Yet if she held on too hard, she might cause Mochizuki to stumble, even fall—possibly on top of her. Crushed by her own horse. The alternative was to let go entirely and be flung free—and land who knew where?

Mochizuki's next stride changed everything. The colt sprang up from the crouch, and she slammed back into the wooden saddle. Pain shot through her pelvis. She flayed her legs, trying to set her feet into the stirrups, but Mochizuki's galloping motion lifted her up and forward, and the stirrups the danced back, cracking against her shin guards, evading capture. As her mount settled into his rhythmic cadence, she clamped her knees into his sides and re-tightened her hold on his mane. Mochizuki charged ahead, still at full gallop. The reins fluttered back, snapping at her face.

She grabbed the ends with one hand. In the next moment, one foot and then the other found the stirrups.

"Hoh. Hoh. Hoh," Yamabuki intoned. "Step. Step. Step."

Mochizuki, slowed to a trot. Yamabuki pulled back hard on the reins. The colt, still excited, snorted and stopped, breathing heavily. She stretched her body. At the moment, nothing seemed to be broken or stiff, but of course stiffness would come only later.

Breathing harder than her mount, she patted his neck, whispering, "Good boy. Good boy. Did you scare me, or did I scare you?"

SEVENTEEN

THE TRAP

Yamabuki guided her mount down the incline, leaning backward, shifting her weight as much as she could over Mochizuki's haunches. There were no fresh tracks to be seen. If intruders were about, they had not yet been here. Nor had her father. She pushed Mochizuki to a canter to stay ahead of the daimyō as she had planned. The air grew heavy with the scent of the sea, though the high, grassy dunes obstructed the view of the ocean.

She slowed to a stop at the bottom, where the trail opened into an elongated clearing. The Trap. Any approaching enemy would be forced to converge here, pressed together on low ground, vulnerable to defensive attack from the hills on either side.

This was also where the Taka routinely practiced archery. Along the left side, under tall pines, five chest-high posts stood at various distances from the path—one from ten paces back, another thirty paces back, three others in between. The arrangement was designed to make the shots tricky. Unlike the targets in the marshaling yard that were all the same distance from the rider, these were staggered, like a real enemy, and multiple shots at full gallop required constant adjustment for distance.

Someone had kindly left targets atop each post. She decided to warm up her bow arm just a bit. Take out the five targets and she would be the one laughing with warrior spirit when her father rode up.

She circled around to the entry of the range, noting how the pines rustled, tops swaying; wind gusts would cause the arrows to fly unpredictably.

She delivered a small kick to Mochizuki's ribs, and he broke into a gallop. With one hand, she grabbed her yumi and pulled three arrows with the other. Her heart beating hard, she came up in her stirrups, turned her body, eying the first target, and drew the bowstring fully back. Allowing for her horse's movement, she released the arrow slightly early. And without waiting to see if it hit, she focused on the next target.

An arrow whistled by her.

Her mouth went dry. Another arrow flew, whizzing just behind her. Then a third, landing a good five strides away. They came from the distant tree line. Her heart beat even faster. Her anger rose. How foolish she was with intruders about! Now it was she who was vulnerable in the Trap!

For a brief moment she wished she had her arrow cape, but there was no use in wishing for what she did not have. What she did have were two arrows in hand.

She detected movement within the pines. Her first shot fell short. She retrained the remaining arrow in a slightly higher arc. It sailed beautifully until it ran afoul the branches, crackling through. She sensed the arrow struck something—a tree trunk? An intruder?

That sound mingled with approaching hooves—her father riding rapidly toward her. With all her lungs she shouted, "Go back! It's an ambush!"

Another arrow hissed close by.

She pulled hard on Mochizuki's reins. He reared up. She got him to prance, hoping to draw the fire away from her father.

She grabbed more arrows from her ebira, notching and releasing, notching and releasing, notching and releasing "At me! Shoot at me!" she yelled. "Cowards!"

To her horror, Moroto still thundered toward her.

"No! No!" she cried. "Run! Save yourself."

But her father charged forward until he reined Kage beside her.

The arrow volleys stopped.

And Moroto burst out laughing—a deep and joyful laugh.

Yamabuki, her teeth gritted in anger, swung her bow in the direction of the intruders, waiting for a target. Her father might have lost his senses, but she was ready.

His war fan in his mailed fist pushed her bow down. "Careful, before you kill someone."

"What!"

"You're as hot-tempered as Mochizuki!" He chuckled. "Put the bow down."

When Yamabuki skeptically complied as commanded, Moroto called out to the tree line, "You can come out now!"

Moments later Etsu and Jun emerged from the underbrush and made their way down with grins on their faces.

"What—?" Yamabuki began. "How—?"

"While you were busy with the stable boy and Mochizuki, they rode out ahead. As I said, wooden targets don't shoot back."

"They could have killed me!"

"Not with those arrows." Moroto gestured. "Show her."

They lifted the arrows they carried. Jun pushed his finger against the tip of one. Blunted. A hit would have hurt, but likely not seriously.

"They were very hard to aim," Jun said, obviously suppressing a smile.

"And you did not do bad, either," Etsu said, rubbing his shoulder. "Your aim was good. Luckily your arrows are the same."

Shocked, Yamabuki pulled an arrow from her ebira and touched the point. Flat. And soft. Not forged from the *tamahagane* used for arrowheads and sword blades. "Clay?" she wondered?

"And *namari*, for the weight," Moroto said, sounding pleased with himself. "It was all I could do to keep you from checking the arrows. I had to rear up Kage to distract you."

Yamabuki held her tongue, feeling played the fool.

Moroto said in a lower voice, "Next time, we won't be around, and the arrowheads won't be made of lead." He watched her as she absorbed these words. He was preparing her in a way the target range could not.

She took in a deep breath and nodded.

"Let's talk," he said.

Eighteen

No Use for Prisoners

Jun and Etsu remained behind as Yamabuki followed her father deeper into the gully's enchanting stillness, accompanied only by the hoof falls and snorting breaths of their mounts, the creaks of their saddles, and the jangling of the tack. Too sandy for trees here, only grasses and reeds thrived. The scent of salt spray filled the air.

No longer warlord and princess, but more father and daughter, the two riders emerged at the shoreline. The panorama immediately revealed shimmering waters filling the entire east, from northern to southern horizons, beneath a sky that stretched into the infinite cloudless blue.

"This way," he said, turning Kage southward. The two rode for a long while without conversation, riding until the shoreline veered south-southwest. A series of loam hills rose on their right, holding them against the ever-present sea to the east and southeast. The briny breeze touched their faces.

Her father drew in a deep breath. "Smell that, Kouma?"

Gathering herself, Yamabuki huffed, "Why does Nakagawa call me that?"

"Call you what?"

"Kouma."

He laughed. "Don't blame him. Blame me. Actually blame yourself."

Yamabuki knit her brows. "Myself? How?"

"It was the Second Year of Hōgen. You were just two springs and had never been to Great Bay Prefecture. I had not seen you in a year. Everyone begged to see the young princess and indeed it was time to bring you to your true home. When I left Heian-kyō the spring before, you could walk and talk." Moroto paused. "You could talk a *great* deal." He grinned.

"But by the following spring you could gallop. You galloped, swinging a wooden sword and crying out to everyone that you were a pony. You insisted everyone call you Kouma from then on, and so we did. Your first royal edict."

Yamabuki tried to remember. She had been so innocent, and now here she was, wearing armor, about to depart on musha shugyō. Would her father and Nakagawa call her Kouma upon her return?

The shore turned from wet sand to a series of rocky ribbons that resembled petrified ripples of water that paralleled the beach. "Follow my lead," her father said. "This stretch does not favor horses."

He led her up a steep, narrow path marked by uneven rocks both smooth and jagged. By how he rode, it was clear he took this trail often. At several points, the trail resembled more cliff than slope; Kage leapt up from ledge to ledge, sending tiny rocks skittering down. Yamabuki squeezed Mochizuki's flanks and without hesitation he followed, his legs shoving off powerfully, launching her up to float over the saddle until his hooves gained purchase again.

When the path flattened, the horses, snorting from the exertion, settled back into walking. They rounded a small stand of trees and emerged atop a secluded cliff overlooking the expanse of the eastern ocean—a commanding view of the Windward Sea. A steady wind, stronger than down below, rippled their riding skirts.

Her father gazed out at the water. Yamabuki suspected her father sometimes came here to marvel at the mystery of the ocean, the sky, and vastness into which it all disappeared. She looked too, trying to savor the tranquility, but the sheer immensity of the ocean and sky, all they contained, so much that remained hidden, left her unsettled. Why had her father brought her here? Was he feeling sentimental on the eve of her departure? She waited, trying to exude patience that she did not feel.

At last, Moroto spoke. "My father, Jirimu, ruled for many years. Following my genpuku, I took up residence in the northwestern estate house, just as you. It was my father's idea to call me Shōgun, though at my twelfth summer I had yet to establish myself." He laughed darkly. "I was a head shorter than you are now. I lived with six bodyguards, and while everyone called me Shōgun, it always sounded perfunctory—and why not? What had I ever done?" He nodded, staring off in memory.

"Living in the northwest shinden-zukuri can be lonely. Maybe you know a bit of that yourself."

"I have Tomoko and Hana-ye," she said, realizing as the words came out that her handmaids had been permitted for this very reason—to keep her company. "But you had your brothers."

Moroto let out a long breath. "Tachibana was nine summers. Nobuyori, four. How would it look if the shōgun kept the company of mere children, brothers or not? No, I was lonely and profoundly bored."

He laughed softly.

"So one day, I stole aboard a ship sailing to Pearl Shell Island." He pointed out into the ocean. "It is part of the Taka lands, yet it is out of our view. It's a clear day today, but even this high up I can't make it out."

Indeed, she could see only the empty blue expanse.

Her father continued, "It was not easy to get away, but I was strong and limber and made it past the guards undetected and managed to get on the seagoing *fune* making its monthly journey. The trick was to be aboard and undetected until we had set sail."

"As shōgun, why would you have to hide?"

"I might not have needed to, but I could not be sure word wouldn't get out, and then my guards would have insisted on accompanying me, and the whole point was to have an adventure on my own, no?"

Yamabuki grunted.

"It took two days to sail over those waters. I did bring something to eat. I had heard persimmons help with seasickness. But two rough days and one night on the sea and I knew that I was not meant to be a sailor. I thought the worst part was going to be staying cramped between some of the cargo, but the worst part was holding it in. I had to relieve myself. How would it look if the shōgun soiled the cargo? In the darkness, I did what I saw the others do to relieve themselves. I had to turn my backside to the sea and hope I did not fall in."

She tried not to imagine what he described.

"I almost came out of hiding more than a few times, but what kind of shōgun would I be if I could not stay still? I was heartened when on the late afternoon of the second day, the mountains of the isle appeared ahead. I gathered myself, put my long sword through my sash, and crawled out of my hiding place. At first the sailors were angered, but when they saw the crossed feather emblem on my *haori*, there was no room for doubt who I was, and they bowed low. When we landed, I announced myself to the people, and you would have thought the Emperor Himself had come to visit. They didn't know what to make of my visit, but no one questioned who I was."

He smiled, obviously remembering something. "Normally the boat would have sailed once it was loaded again with cargo, but they waited for me, for my orders. It's actually quite a lovely island, but after a few days I grew tired of it."

"And you came home to face your father?"

He raised his hand. "Usually on a fune, we have a few soldiers aboard because of pirates. If it had been known I was on board, my personal guard would have been along with us. In fact, the captain tried to add guards while we were still at Pearl Shell Island, but I would not hear of it. I did not want to be coddled. We had the usual four Taka fighters to repel pirates, and I said that would be enough. And so we set sail."

He glanced at Yamabuki, eyes twinkling. "But as luck would have it, on the way back we were intercepted by a *mifune*. They weren't after our cargo, which was mostly dried fish and a few turtles. They wanted our boat itself, which was hale enough to safely cross the Leeward Sea. Our fighters were outnumbered two to one when they boarded us. And you know raiders have no use for prisoners, not even a young shōgun."

He darkened and shook his head, remembering.

"They did not wear clan colors, but to this day I suspect they were Ōuchi looking for an easy mark. It was the first time I ever used my sword to draw blood. I was far too young to be afraid."

He paused again. Remembering more.

"When the fighting was over, their mifune got away, but not one of the men who'd boarded us was left standing. For the rest of the trip, everyone called me Shōgun like they meant it. Moroto Shōgun. I swore the crew and soldiers to secrecy. Of course they had to agree. A day after we landed, Jirimu Daimyō called me to his audience chamber and asked me how my 'expedition' had gone. I suspected someone in the crew or among the soldiers had been unable to keep his vow of secrecy about the battle. I said as much to my father." Moroto chuckled. "In fact, he had heard nothing of the kind. All I did was to blunder and blurt out the secret. As it turned out, he *did* know I had left, but that was all he knew. I asked why he had not stopped me. And he answered that I was a general, and it was in my purview to make the journey as I saw fit. He was surprised but not shocked to hear of that battle and was not at all surprised at the outcome. He said I had been a credit to the Taka."

Moroto shifted in his saddle and looked her in the eye. "When you lead warriors into battle, you must be seen as strong, confident, capable, and in command. They who follow you must respect you. Staid protocol does not help in crisis. I do not need men bowing to me when telling me someone is about to cut my throat. I need that warrior to take action and not stand on formality. And so in the field, it is good to be a daimyō, but it is even better to be a leader of samurai—a shōgun."

Yamabuki said, "That's why our warriors refer to you as Moroto Shōgun, not daimyō."

"Warriors do not follow a daimyō merely because of his title, or because he carries a sword or war fan. A daimyō must prove himself in his own right. Warriors—armies—follow daimyō who are generals, who have shown courage and wisdom. They follow you because they trust you."

Yamabuki smiled inwardly, for it was true. The Taka warriors trusted Moroto as much as she did. Trusted him and loved him.

Moroto said, "But that sort of respect comes only by doing what they do and not asking for any special favors or dispensation because you are Taka, or because you are a woman."

Yamabuki scowled. Was he accusing her of relying on her privilege? "I have asked for no such thing!"

"Ha!" He snorted. "Don't think that others wouldn't ask for it on your behalf, even with honorable intentions. But what would that make you? A princess who relies on her escort to protect her."

"But we all have bodyguards. You have three *jun* protecting you."

"That's true, but to earn the loyalty of thirty guards, or even three, you first have to prove that you don't actually need them for protection."

"I understand," she said, and she did understand. Was this not one of the purposes of her musha shugyō?

Her father gazed at her, watching her, and his face hardened into the visage of Taka Daimyō. "Yet I cannot allow you to be sacrificed."

Nineteen

REMEMBER WHO YOU ARE

M OROTO SWUNG HIS LEG over Kage's haunches and jumped to the ground. Yamabuki followed his lead, and they walked, leading the horses by their reins. The ground was soft, and it felt good to move her legs. But her mind was full of questions. *Sacrificed? How would I be sacrificed?*

Her father said, "You know the timing of your mogi was entirely my idea. My own mother, of course, had different ideas. You noticed, the Dowager did not attend your mogi. She knew what it meant, that you had all but been made the heir apparent to lead the Taka. Something she still has not come to terms with. She has her own ideas about who you should be and what you should do. When you celebrated with your mother and me—the three of us drank saké together—it was more than an empty form. You are more than Taka-gimi. You one day will be warlord of the Taka."

Yamabuki's heart started pounding. Of course, she had known this was the likely outcome; after all, she was the eldest and only surviving child, and it was not unheard of for a woman to rule a prefecture. And had not Yamabuki trained hard all these years? Still, to hear him say it so plainly came as a shock. She said, "Even though I am a woman?"

"You are a woman, but you are no fool. Many people said *I* was a fool to train you and teach you, but if you had not had *it* within you, that inner strength that cannot be taught, then you would not be here at this moment. You would have found a hundred excuses for why you could not rise to the challenge, other things to divert your attention, and as princess you would not have had to look far. Your facility with the language and script of the Yellow River Delta, for example. You could easily and rightfully have buried yourself in such studies. Yet you devoted yourself to martial skills with equal determination. Plus training up Mochizuki. This shows character."

Yamabuki flushed with some pride. It was not every day that Lord Taka heaped praise upon his daughter. But she was not unaware of how family dynamics could play out in lines of succession. She asked, "What of your brother's son?"

Moroto let out a deep belly laugh. "Atsumichi? Our men are unlikely to follow him, much to my brother's dismay. Yes, he's a male Taka and son of a master swordsman, but Atsumichi is more interested in seducing girls than being a warrior. Jabbing with that tiny blade of flesh between his legs is all he seems to care about."

Yamabuki couldn't help but grin at the bawdy description, for it suited her cousin perfectly.

"I speak roughly, but you must accept the fact that warriors speak their thoughts in a different way. At times, you must speak roughly as well, without ever surrendering your status as Taka Princess. Like earlier, when you upbraided the stable boy for being unable to control Mochizuki. You know the men were watching you."

She forced a smile.

"How would you deal with an inept boy? Would you be his wet-nurse or his warlord? Who they saw was a leader who would ask much from them, and in men this brings out their best."

She realized her father was looking at her. Watching her. She said, "There were no intruders, were there?"

Moroto smiled as if he'd been waiting for this question. "There were unexpected visitors, but that was several days ago. A group of envoys."

"I had not heard this."

"No one did. They traveled as *sōhei*—presumably to avoid the wrong kind of notice. There's always some pilgrimage that monks can be on, no? They met in private with me, Prince Tachibana, and Lord Nakagawa. Your mother listened from the blind."

"They were monks?"

He grinned. "In fact the six were warriors, envoys looking to rally support for a dispossessed warlord who has ambitions on the Imperial throne."

Yamabuki snorted.

"Don't underestimate the discontent among the kuge. Ambition and conquest are ever on their minds."

Yamabuki said, "I just thought they would have learned from the Hōgen and Heiji rebellions."

"*Heiji Ran* failed, yet it enhanced the power of some people, including Taira no Kiyomori, who now acts with Emperor Masahito's backing. Someone always benefits."

Yamabuki frowned, not liking where this was going. "You're not joining this foolish cause, are you, Father?"

Rather than scold her for questioning his leadership, Moroto laughed. "I will not tangle you up in a war for the throne!"

He laughed some more. Gradually he stopped, wiping tears from his eyes.

"What is of special interest to us is news from Higo"—the province to their immediate north, ruled by the Kikuchi, one of the largest clans on the Isle of Unknown Fires. "Kikuchi Daimyō has joined his ancestors."

"Lord Tsunemune is dead? When?"

"Ten days ago. His son immediately assumed rulership and took Takanao as his daimyō name."

Yamabuki gave her father a hard look. "'Peace with one, then war with his son,'" she recited.

Her father nodded. "Takanao is of your years and ambitious, and it is said Takanao holds no affection for the Emperor. That could make things around here . . . interesting."

Yamabuki said, "You're expecting he'll be trouble for the Mikado."

"Kiyomori, perhaps."

"Does not Kiyomori serve the Emperor?" she asked, sensing there was a truth hiding behind the truth.

"Kiyomori is the real power. He masks it, pretending he acts in the Emperor's name, but he makes sure the Emperor's interests always align with his own. Our best course is to stay out of any Imperial conflict, even if it reaches our borders. We would have nothing to gain and everything to lose."

Yamabuki shrugged confidently. "No enemy would dare attack us. From the sea, they'd have to scale these cliffs, and our archers would annihilate anyone trying to approach through the Trap."

"And yet, Ō-Utsumi is a valuable holding," Moroto said. "When you come to rule, people will want to encroach, manipulate, or topple you— and not just because you are a woman. However"—he paused, searching for words—"conflicts are sometimes not settled through battle but avoided through"—he cleared his throat—"marriage."

Yamabuki stopped walking, holding the reins tight as Mochizuki lifted his head. "I hope this has nothing to do with me."

"Yes and no."

Was he to revoke her musha shugyō? Force her to marry someone?

Moroto said, "I take it your mother delved into your interest in marriage?"

She tried not to show her discomfort.

"Your face says she did."

She adopted a grim countenance. "We talked about killing."

Her father laughed softly. "I suppose that's what happens when your wife and your daughter are trained warriors—they discuss killing."

"Mother reproached me for being"—she took a deep breath—"'a willful wanderer' and all but said musha shugyō was a dalliance that would endanger the Taka." She looked into her father's eyes, hoping for escape from what sounded like a nightmare. "She says my karma is to bear sons."

Kage snorted as if in response. Moroto stroked his neck to calm him. "Karmas are complicated. Your mother loves you. You know women's ways. You know it is to protect her young."

"Mother went on musha shugyō!"

Moroto laughed. "Of course."

"You were married afterward."

Moroto nodded.

"Then why can't this wait? Takanao already has wives!"

"I believe the envoys confirmed he has three."

"And now he wants to make it four?"

Moroto gave a sardonic snort. "You mean you? Hardly. I would never sanction a match with him. He would use such a marriage to weaken Taka rule and claim Ō-Utsumi Prefecture as his own. And you would languish in some shinden far away from everything and everyone you love. That will *not* be the fate of Taka-gimi. My daughter. My only heir."

The wind picked up, sending ripples through the grass. The horses grew restless. Mochizuki put his nose against Yamabuki's shoulder, nudging her. Kage, hooves dancing, swung around as Moroto held fast the reins.

He said, "But this does not mean in the future a marriage might not be advantageous. As Taka-gimi and as Daimyō, you must do what is right for you personally, if you are able, but always what is right for the Taka."

Both mounts snorted, exciting each other, eager to move, eager to run. Yamabuki welcomed the intrusion, not at all caring for this conversation. She'd not even left on musha shugyō and her father was talking about advantageous matches! "Should we ride?"

Moroto jerked down on Kage's reins to hold him still, and reached into his sleeve. He pulled out a scroll wrapped in green-and-blue silk brocade. The whole thing was about as long as her tachi's hilt, and not much thicker. His eyes fixed on hers. "As soon as you reach Heian-kyō, go to the Palace of Black Plums and deliver this scroll to my brother, Nobuyori."

Yamabuki solemnly accepted the scroll and tucked it safely into her sleeve. "I will do as you say."

His eyes grew fierce. "Be watchful in the Imperial City, Kouma. The *miyabi*-obsessed kuge of the Emperor's Court claim superiority by tracing their lineage back hundreds of years. To them, we Taka are lower order. They will toy with you like a cat toys with a mouse. You know the Tale of the Taka."

She recited from the opening:

> As always, and in ancient times, before any place else,
> The Sun Goddess shined Her first light on the land of the Great Bay
> To grace the people called the Taka.
> When man's time dawned, Taka ancestor Great-Hawk-Fire-Wind-
>   Seeker drew his bow
> Shooting a single stone arrow into the High Plain over the Autumn
>   Creek Land.
> Weeping-Maiden-of-the-Milky-River-of-Stars then caught the
>   arrow
> She threw down the first grains of rice like tears from Heaven.

Her father narrowed his eyes. "What do you make of those words?"

"They are beautiful."

"Look behind the poetry for the entire truth. According to the *Annals of Ancient Matters*, of which I have a copy from the second original, the founder of the Taka, Great-Hawk-Fire-Wind-Seeker, was known by another name—Jinmu Tennō."

"The first Emperor," Yamabuki said softly.

"The *Annals* record that he led a great army that sailed from Mimitsu. What it omits is a story handed down amongst the Taka, from generation to generation: There was a split. Some of our ancestors opposed the expedition to annex the isles of the north. They remained, and we have been here ever since."

"I never heard this."

"There is more. The Taka can trace their ancestry back before Jinmu, back thousands of years, across the Leeward Sea."

"To Zhou?"

"No. To Chōsen."

Yamabuki stifled a gasp. Throughout her studies, Goryeo, the peninsula across the Leeward Sea—where it was said the Toi who had raided Ō-Utsumi and neighboring prefectures came from—had fascinated her. She'd read about the dynasties that rose and fell, and the wars that were fought. The confederated Chōsen kingdoms had grown to control the entire peninsula and ruled for thousands of years. To think, her ancestors lived there!

But while Yamabuki's whimsy carried her to distant and ancient lands, Moroto remained in the present. "On your travels, especially in Heian-kyō, remember who you are, Taka-gimi. The Fujiwara, the Minamoto, now the Taira—they are powerful, but they are not better than us."

Yamabuki had never seen her father so distraught. "I will be cautious."

Moroto laughed at himself. "Look at me, the nervous father. Let me just say this: As princess, as shōgun, as daimyō, the challenge is knowing whom you can rely on. Some men, they put on armor and *look* like warriors but let you down when you need them most. You will meet many of those in the Imperial City. But others"—and his eyes glistened as he spoke—"the armor is not what they put on, it is a part of them. *They* are true warriors." He clapped a hand on the plated green-lacquered *sode* protecting her shoulders. "And they'll always be warriors, armor or not."

TWENTY
MISCONDUCT AGAINST SAKIMORI

Second Quarter of Hour of the Snake
Two days past Full Moon of Unohana Month
11 May 1172

Minezaki

THE TUGGING ON HER YOROI CEASED, and Taro's calloused hand patted Yamabuki's heavy sode. "All fastened, Samurai-sama." Perhaps
realizing he might have transgressed protocol, he stepped back and bowed
low. "I hope my humble skills prove adequate."

Yamabuki paced about—stretching, moving, making sure of the bind-
ings. "Fine. Fine," she murmured. And it was fine. It felt good. Heavy.
Formidable. As much as the evening before she had relished melding in
with the common people, she felt better wearing her Taka armor.

Eiji bowed, handing her Tiger Cub, and she fastened its *sageo* to her
waist sash. Fuyuki approached, bearing her kabuto, but she raised a hand
for him to forbear. The helmet would have required her to bunch up her
hair and stuff it into the cap-top. The kabuto could wait.

The distinctive squeaks and clatter of several men in armor drew everyone's attention to the front door. A moment later, an Ōe warrior in
full armor strode in, helmeted, holding his tachi scabbard as if ready to
draw his sword. Squinting, glowering, he scanned the armory, pausing
only briefly on Yamabuki before spotting Taro.

"Taro-kun!" he roared. "You are holding my men?"

The armorer bowed repeatedly. "Hai, Sadamasa-sama! Hai."

Obviously the two men knew each other. Taro led Sadamasa to where
Misaki lay under blankets next to the covered dead warrior.

Taro spoke softly. "Misaki-sama told us that he and several others
were caught in the mountains. Two made it back down in the dark." He

lowered his eyes, shaking his head. "This one wasn't so lucky. The Yuki-onna took him. But Misaki survived."

Misaki opened his eyes and said in a weak voice, "This is true."

Sadamasa called out, and several Ōe warriors entered, some wearing black armor, some clad only in black tunics, all armed with swords. Yamabuki saw there were at least three others just outside, bearing naginata.

Sadamasa gestured at Misaki and the dead body. The sakimori lifted them both and carried them outside.

Curious, Yamabuki walked over for a better angle to watch.

The guards carefully laid the victims in the bed of a primitive two-wheeled cart that sat tipped back, its pull handles jutting up in the air. These men who had been so gruff at the border now demonstrated such tenderness toward their own.

Silence drew her attention back inside, where she saw Sadamasa eying her with suspicion. She placidly returned his gaze.

He grunted and turned to Mari, who shrank back. "You! Last night, my men encountered trouble at Saké House from a *kyojin* yahochi wearing an orange kimono."

Mari hunched into a subservient bow.

The sight of an armored warrior berating such a sweet young girl barely in adult clothes triggered Yamabuki's ire—especially since this pertained to her own actions the night before. "Does she look like a giant to you?" Yamabuki challenged.

But Sadamasa ignored her, his gaze focused on Mari. He called out, "Bunzō-kun!"

A young warrior ran in. "Ha!" He stiffly held his head to the side, as if unable to straighten his neck. Yamabuki recognized him: one of the drunkards from the night before—only now, instead of rage, his face betrayed timidity.

Sadamasa gestured at Mari. "Her?"

The man called Bunzō stared at the girl, winking one eye as if trying to focus. "Too small."

Sadamasa growled, "You're just afraid to admit it was a little girl! What about the kimono?"

"It looks similar."

Sadamasa bellowed at Mari, "You attacked sakimori last night!"

The girl stared at the floor. Yamabuki could see her trembling and was about to intervene when Taro stepped forward and bowed low. "Apologies, Sadamasa-sama. This is my daughter. She was here with me. We were up working through the night."

Sadamasa scowled. "Don't lie!"

Taro's head bobbed. "It's a common enough kimono. It's our clan kimono. All the Kōno women wear it."

"And are there any other Kōno women here?"

Taro almost melted. "No."

Bunzō mumbled, "It's not her, Sadamasa Kashira. She's too small."

Obviously disappointed, Sadamasa turned away from Mari, and his eyes fixed upon Yamabuki. "What about her?"

Unable to move his neck, Bunzō turned bodily to face Yamabuki and stared, again winking. Then both eyes widened. "Ahhh—!" He tried to nod but winced in pain.

Sadamasa bellowed, "Guards!"

Four men wearing full yoroi rushed in. "Ha!"

He pointed at Yamabuki. "Arrest her! Misconduct against sakimori!"

Yamabuki stiffened. "You have no authority."

"I'm in charge here!"

"I am Taka-gimi and answer only to my father, Taka Daimyō, and the Mikado Himself."

"Impudence! I act in the name of the Mikado. Take her sword!"

The black-armored guards surrounded her. They did not seem all that capable. Despite their yoroi, they looked more like commoners who had been recruited to fill their ranks. Likely she could kill them all, even with only her short sword. But this was not a time to fight. She remained still as they removed Tiger Cub.

Taro approached, bowing. "Sadamasa-sama, if I may—"

"Enough!" Sadamasa roared. "Or I'll arrest you too! All of you!"

Bent and cowed, Taro retreated.

Two men roughly her age and nearly her height grabbed Yamabuki's arms and guided her out the door into the bright sunlight.

Misaki, sitting up in the back of the cart, scowled in confusion. "What's this?"

"She attacked our men last night," Sadamasa said. "Misconduct."

Misaki stammered, "Sh—she saved my life!"

"*Baka!*" Sadamasa waved his arm. "Tie her hands!"

"No!" Misaki said in a clear voice. "I'm alive thanks to her."

Sadamasa's mouth opened and closed, saying nothing.

Misaki lowered his voice. "You cannot arrest the Buddha of Mercy!"

Sadamasa glared at him, but Misaki glared back.

They locked each other's glare.

Then Sadamasa broke away, muttering, "Baka." He flicked his wrist. "Release her."

The hands holding Yamabuki's arms let go.

"My sword," she said.

The guard holding it—hardly old enough to have celebrated gen-puku—hesitated, glancing at Sadamasa, who nodded. The boyish man presented Tiger Cub to her.

She accepted it without a word and tucked the sheathed weapon into her waist sash.

"Go!" Sadamasa commanded.

Two men up front seized the cart's handle shafts and tipped it level. Misaki gave a slight nod to Yamabuki before lying back, and the cart rumbled off, squeaking and creaking over the broken snow. Out front, eight Ōe guards led the way, stomping down the drifts ahead.

As the procession moved away, Sadamasa stepped close to Yamabuki. In a low voice he said, "Last night, my men were drunk and foolish, Taka-*gimi*"—and he put extra emphasis on *gimi*, as if mocking her—"but they will not be drunk and foolish next time."

Yamabuki felt quite certain that nothing could be done about his guards' foolishness, as all the fools she'd known had seemed to be of consistent character in that regard. And as for their drunkenness, the availability of saké seemed to be determinative. But she elected to say nothing.

He marched away.

The guard named Bunzō, who had been lurking, glanced sheepishly at Yamabuki, then with a grimace and bent neck, ambled away behind the procession.

Yamabuki stood in the daylight as the Ōe made their way down Ledge Road. Before long, they disappeared around the bend. Only then did she realize that her heart was still pumping hard, and she opened her mouth to take in a deep breath of cold refreshing air. No, clearly she was not safe in this town. Not with it crawling with Ōe guards who didn't know their place.

And there was a shinobi after her—somewhere.

She went back inside. Taro was already at work, kneeling at a low bench surrounded by tools, stones, and cloths, working something up and down the length of Tiger Claw's blade. His sons meanwhile were busy in the back of the armory, focused on piecework that no doubt had been set aside during the morning's disruption. Mari was nowhere to be seen, perhaps off in her own bedchamber, recovering from the violent accusations Sadamasa had directed at her.

Unobtrusively and silently, Yamabuki moved to the box where she had secreted her dispatches. Nobody so much as glanced in her direction—not that it mattered. It was more for their protection than hers; the less they knew, the better it was for them.

She reached into the box, slipped her hand under the half-finished kozane, and one by one retrieved the three scrolls, sliding each into a kimono sleeve pocket. A nagging anxiety faded away and she let out a small sigh. Now all she had to do was pack her things into her saddlebag in the guesthouse and saddle up Mochizuki. Then as soon as Taro completed his work, she could resume her journey up the North Road and cross the Pass of the Setting Sun.

She knelt a respectful distance from Taro and watched him work the waterstone along Tiger Claw's lethal edge. Every now and then he wiped the tachi's full length, turned the blade, and resumed. The otherwise loquacious armorer said nothing. Of course, Yamabuki knew how to polish swords. Every warrior worth the title swordsman knew how. But just as a master sword polisher was rarely a master swordsman, similarly it was a rarity that a master swordsman proved a master polisher. Back home in Ō-Utsumi, master swordsmith Yukiyasu insisted on polishing swords alone; and as for Yukiyasu's ten helpers who polished the bulk of the Taka weapons, these apprentices were far too intimidated by and ingratiating toward the princess to get anything done in her presence. Now she had an opportunity to observe this so-essential practice. So interesting. So mysterious.

Though Taro had disparaged his skills as polisher of swords, polisher of their very souls, it was out of modesty. He slid the waterstones carefully, yet fleetly, nimbly. At several points, when he changed stones or used a shimmering cloth, she thought to ask a question; yet Taro's intense concentration convinced her to watch without asking about the nuances.

She let her attention wander to the rest of the armory, and admired the tidiness of the Kōno's operation. Already not a sign remained of the morning's events. The blankets were gone. The nabe were stacked along the wall near the forge. The puddles on the floor had all dried away.

Her knot of anxiety returned. The Ōe were arrogant, even belligerent. But they were not known to be fools. They had commanded vast swaths of territory for hundreds of years. Yet an entire group of Ōe warriors, including a kashira, had been fooled into attempting the pass in this snow, and met with only death and suffering. Did she dare attempt the mountain pass today? It was already midday. By the time Taro's work was done, it would be approaching dark. To cross at night? Even with Mochizuki, she was not immune to freezing to death—or worse, suffering tōshō, dying slowly from blood sickness or surviving with amputated limbs.

No. Better to wait until morning, when she could cross in full daylight, perhaps even sunshine. It was either that or give up on the North Road altogether and take the roundabout route back along the coast, which would add several *more* days to the journey. She was not prepared to accept that.

A melodious voice interrupted her musings: "*The warrior watches her flower bloom.*"

TWENTY-ONE

THE EMBODIMENT OF MIYABI

YAMABUKI SMILED TO HERSELF and turned. Yoshinaka stood just inside the front doorway, his eyes sparkling, his white kimono almost glowing in the light. His long raven-black hair hung to his waist. He had just now recited an opening line of a poem, initiating a game played among kuge of refinement. In high court society it was sport to finish the couplet on the spur, going back and forth.

Before she could reply, he put the back of his fingers to his lips and nodded at Taro—who never looked up. She left Taro to his work, and joined Yoshinaka at the doorway. "*For spring light drives off winter's gloom.*"

Yoshinaka laughed, dark eyes bright. "You have dash."

"And only now you realize that? I took you for someone with far more perspicacity."

He studied her as carefully as she studied him. "You disguised yourself well last evening, the first, last, and only time I saw you. Moving in flowing orange robes, hair tied in ribbons. You had cloaked your face in oshiroi. You were quite fetching. And you are even more lovely now, without courtly makeup."

Yamabuki threw a sly glance his way. *Oh a charmer, this one. He doesn't need saké to turn his tongue to seduction. And he is as pretty as a girl.* She glanced at his shoulders and legs. Grinning, she turned her cheek. "My face looks better when it's not rice-white, you say? What do you think of the gash, which the oshiroi hid?"

Yoshinaka gazed at her as if she were the only thing in the world. "I did not notice." She felt herself blush.

In the morning sunlight he looked younger, more handsome and powerful than he had appeared under lamplight—and usually that went the other way around, or so it was said. To be beautiful, this man did not need dim braziers. No. Early daylight.

This morning's poetry challenge remained unfinished, for it was now his turn to supply the next line. Unfinished business. *More* unfinished business. Unfinished business before getting on to the subject of intimate names. Intimate names? Was that where this was headed? Her stomach fluttered at the idea.

He glanced away. "I noticed you had some excitement here."

Of course he would have heard something in this tiny town. But Yamabuki had things other than impetuous Ōe guards on her mind. Nor did she wish to speak of Misaki. None of that fit the romantic mood taking shape in her thoughts. She deflected. "Not excitement. Simply a misunderstanding of my disposition."

"Dissatisfaction with dispositions is so often the root of unrest."

Not quite sure what he meant by that, she changed the subject, bowing slightly—the bow of an equal. "I received your kind gift and calligraphy. *Arigatō gozaimashita.*"

Yoshinaka bowed in return. "So formal? I hope my poor hand did not disrespect the poetry."

Such modesty! She said, "The embodiment of miyabi."

"Now you flatter me."

"Flattery deserved is but description."

He bowed in thanks and stared into her eyes, his mouth bent in a slight grin. "Should we perhaps drink the saké to determine if it too deserves flattery?"

Until that moment, Yamabuki had been enjoying their banter, but now she felt a twinge of guilt. "Alas, the saké was used as omiki to the Gods."

Yoshinaka waited, but Yamabuki offered no explanation. He finally said, "May the Gods describe the offering to Them accurately."

"The Gods did not seem displeased." No need to say more to him, the one man who would understand what she felt.

Yoshinaka grinned and pulled a small flask of saké from his sleeve.

She smiled. Breath shallow. "Come." She led him through the armory, out the back, toward the guesthouse. "We can drink in privacy here."

"And talk," he added.

"At least that."

Twenty-Two
Armor Removed

ONCE INSIDE THE GUESTHOUSE, Yamabuki felt a burden lift from her shoulders. The irori fire warmed her. She and Yoshinaka placed their fur boots next to the mystery pair made of woven straw, which still awaited an unseen owner.

As they stepped up from the genkan, Yoshinaka said, "Nice lodging."

She bade him to sit next to the lively small fire. He placed his two swords on the floor. Yamabuki put Tiger Cub next to her.

They sat for a moment in silence taking in the warmth. Then Yoshinaka held out the stoppered flask. "The same Shinano saké as last night."

Yamabuki cast a look around the room. "Mari must have already cleaned. I have no bowl to pour it in."

He said, "No need"—and he reached again into his sleeve—"for I brought two flasks."

The saké warmed her, and it also went straight to her head. Of course it did. *I lost the morning meal.* She gazed at him, studying his face, and then she decided. *Yes. This is going to happen I will let it happen.* She let herself smile. "Are we going to go into battle?"

His eyes grew serious. "Battle?"

She brushed her hand down her armor. "I'm the only one who's wearing full yoroi."

"I hope this is not a signal of something ominous."

"Where did you leave yours?"

"Not very far. Still on Kōno's trellis. Do I need to don armor?" Yoshinaka sounded dismayed.

"No," she said flatly. "If you aren't wearing yours, then please help me doff mine." She rose and stretched out her arms.

He hesitated. "You know this means I will have to touch you like an armorer or handmaid."

"Hai," she said. "I am not concerned by this. Are you frightened of me?"

Without another word, he stood up, coming around behind her. "The sode go on last and come off first." He moved ever closer. He smelled of saké . . . just barely. She felt the sode shift slightly. So he has touched my shoulder. She smiled to herself. She felt the armor piece lift away. He put it down on the floor near her bedding. He rose, and again his hands touched her. She liked this. Different than when a handmaid or armorer undressed her. His fingers lingered, though she could hardly feel them as he slipped loose the leather fastening and stacked the second forest-green piece atop the first.

"Taka Shōgun, would be so kind to get down on one knee? I need to untie your dō."

"*Taka Shōgun*, is it? You are so formal with me."

"Ha! I have never had the pleasure of helping a future daimyō out of her armor, and so beautiful at that."

Was he saying her armor was beautiful or was it she? Did he know where she wanted to take this next? She thought about it as she dropped to her left knee.

He came around to undo the fastenings which were on the right side of the chest protector. When Tomoko and Hana-ye untied the corselet she was only vaguely aware of their presence, always too busy in conversation with them to pay much notice to the mechanics of unfastening ties. Now in silence, with only the crackling fire and the occasional gust of wind, she heard herself breathing heavily. She listened to the soft sound of his kimono. His movements were not those of a server, more of a courtly dance—like the one she had performed for everyone at the Inn of Young Bamboo. Each movement measured. Each turn of the hand studied. Gentle. Subtle.

He lifted the chest protector away and placed it next to the sode.

Wordlessly she stood, and he carefully removed the kote from her arms. Neither of them said anything. For Yamabuki, the silence only added to the growing sense of excitement—the intensity which she felt building between them. To anyone coming upon the scene, it would have simply appeared to them like what it was, one person helping another take off armor. But the quiet, intimate process caused her pulse to race—anything but mundane.

He unfastened her kusazuri and laid the heavy armor skirt aside. Finally came the suneate off her shins, and the last pieces were stacked.

With the armor removed, Yamabuki stood in her kosode under-kimono. Her hakama riding skirt bloomed. The dance, their proxy for passion, had come to an end. But Yoshinaka did not say more, nor did he sit back down, but stood silently, gazing at her with the intensity of a warrior, but she felt no fear. If the dance was over, she knew she had to sit down. If not, she had to take it to the next step. She smiled. "My handmaids could not have done better."

Yoshinaka's eyes flashed with something akin to relief. "Oh to have such a position." He affected the voice and expressions of a maid. "Though I would not know what to do in the presence of a lovely woman."

"It's not very difficult. Next, my handmaids would help me out of my hakama."

"I am not sure I know how I could do that." Yoshinaka put his hand over his mouth, but his eyes were anything but innocent.

Yamabuki sensed he was waiting for her to encourage him. She had decided, but he was being exceedingly polite. Then again, she had made it clear the prior evening that there would be no touching. It was now up to her to modify that rule.

"Like this," she said, stepping closer. She thrust her hands toward his own hakama's belt and pulled. She reached behind him, letting her hands touch his body for the first time, and pulled the back knot loose and the split riding skirt fell away. "Now you," she said, her voice growing husky.

Yoshinaka, no longer feigning affectation, pulled the front and back ties on her hakama, which likewise floated to the floor. Not waiting, she untied his obi and pulled his kimono off his shoulders. Almost as quickly, he then did the same with her kosode.

Both now stood only in their shitagi.

No longer smiling, Yoshinaka's eyes grew intense. He placed his hands on her shoulders. She gazed back into his eyes and nodded hard just once. With that, he slipped his hands under her shitagi and slid it over her shoulders, pulling the undergarment halfway down.

He paused, gazing at her breasts. Awestruck.

She waited. It was up to him to take this further.

His fingers grazed her there. Her breath caught as her nipples grew hard, and it thrilled her down her body to her center. He released her *shitagi* and it slid down to her feet.

He looked at the cloth around her hips, and his eyes widened. "A *fundoshi*?"

"You think it inappropriate? It's for all warriors, *ne*?"

"I did not know women, even women warriors, wore them."

She pulled the cloth down a bit. "Then you do not know Taka warriors." She did not add that during her time of month, she absorbed her flow with the *little saddle*, and that the fundoshi was very useful for such circumstances.

He put his hands on her loincloth and gently pulled it down, leaving her in her nakedness. His own fundoshi was still in place, and it had developed a sizable bulge.

Yamabuki fell onto the bedding. Yoshinaka moved onto his knees and lowered himself over her. She pulled his fundoshi off with a flourish, touching his hardness, letting her fingers move down its length.

"Be gentle when gripping the *tsuka*," he said melodiously.

"I am gentle with everything I put in my *saya*."

"Putting a sword in its scabbard happens at the end of a battle." He breathed hard. "This battle is just beginning."

She exhaled, smiled, and moved her legs apart.

Twenty-Three
Omamori

From his uncomfortable but reasonably dry hiding place within the trees, Saburo gazed up the Ledge Road at the armory. Its front doors were thrown open, leaving an opening wide enough for two horses, but most of the interior remained out of view. Yet he saw them together—the Taka woman and the Minamoto samurai.

After nine days of hunting her, he finally had the perfect circumstances. The armory was far from the main parts of town, a side road. This was a perfect place to attack. Kuma, the bear-like man who had shown up unannounced at Saburo's secluded sanctuary, had paid him handsomely to retrieve the two scrolls and kill her. "No witnesses and no trace." In the days since, Saburo had not wavered from this commission.

But now things had changed. For only the second time in his life, he intended to kill for personal reasons. Punishment. Revenge. He was going to slay the Taka girl right here, in broad daylight if need be. Kuma's instructions were now secondary.

Saburo looked at the *omamori* in the palm of his hand. The amulet bore the image of a *tako*. Its eight outstretched silk-embroidered tentacles enticed luck, for it was a talisman of whispers, assassinations, early death, intrigue by generals, and greedy fishermen, yet also an amulet of good fortune—one of safe return, especially from a journey over water. Takō. Octopus. A play on words:

多幸

Ta Kō

Many Fortunes.

The omamori had been his gift to Shima, a blessing before the Gods, a token of love for the sword master who had given him so much.

When he had glimpsed Shima the morning before, as the sword master stomped his way down Foot Trail before vanishing all to quickly—as had the Taka princess—Saburo did not fully apprehend how much Shima had aged.

But later that day, when he had come upon Shima's body lying dead on the muddy North Road, Saburo saw the cruel marks of time.

Shima's hair had turned white. He had shorn it completely, and also his beard. Mere stubble remained—all that was left of the soft hair that had once caressed Saburo's skin.

TWENTY-FOUR

YOU HAVE MEAT?

Third Quarter, Hour of the Bird
One day past Last Half Moon of Utū Ninth Month
First Day of Rittō, Beginning of Winter
First Year of Hōgen, Year of the Fire Rat
7 November 1156

Iwakawa-jiin, Tajima Prefecture, Main Isle

T HE MONASTERY LAY HIGH in the mountains and thus far from everything. For a young priest wishing to be alone and not think upon the tragedies that burdened him, gate duty was the perfect assignment. Nobody to talk to, nothing to do but meditate on the leafless trees and the expansive skies, no obligations but to wait for travelers—a rarity this late in the year.

So when in the dying fire of the first day of winter, Saburo saw the lone samurai approaching the west gate, it took a moment to register that this wasn't a trick of the shadows. As the sun at last slipped behind the hill-crest of the valleys, the young priest watched the stranger move through the fading light.

Saburo reminded himself that it was the custom—nay, the duty—of temples to welcome travelers for the night. Likewise, travelers understood that a small donation of money, or something of value paid in-kind, would help ensure the visitor a warm place to sleep and a share of the meal. Only the foolhardy, or those running away from something or someone, would trek on down from the summit in waning light.

As the lone warrior drew nearer, Saburo could see that the stranger hefted a naginata over his shoulder. A tachi swung from his hip. A tall and imposing man, the traveler wore a field coat, but he walked under the weight of full yoroi. No lowly spearman, this. The samurai was perhaps ten years older and at least a head taller and certainly wider than Saburo. He did not wear a kabuto. His wild mane of black hair fell to his shoulders, framing a noble face—bearded, rugged, and handsome in the way of men, with pronounced, yet well-proportioned, masculine features.

The samurai paused before the temple gate. As custom dictated, he scooped a handful of water from the *chōzubachi* and rinsed his mouth in ablution. Then he clapped his hands several times to alert the Gods, as well as everyone else, that he had arrived and intended to enter.

Saburo could no longer avoid the man by lurking in the shadows. The young priest stepped forward and opened the entry.

In the fading light, the samurai's dark eyes, like a tiger's, scanned Saburo, but not with hostility, nor malevolence. More, they were curious, looking for something—perhaps an indication of what sort of order he had encountered, what kind of priests lived here, and what customs would be observed.

"How did you get *that* duty, squinting into the setting sun?" asked the warrior, his voice deep and sonorous.

Saburo frowned, not sure what the man was asking.

"I saw you lurking behind the gate," the warrior said. "The sun was at my back. My advantage. It lit you up. The sun was in your eyes." He sniffed as he set his naginata down. Then he sat down on a smooth rock at the threshold to remove his traveling shoes—bearskin boots, at that. The first snows of winter had already fallen in the higher summits. If travelers were wealthy enough, they wore straw boots. Most commoners, however, wore straw sandals, even in winter, and if they were lucky, socks or makeshift gaiters to shield their toes from the cold. Very few had fur boots.

The man smiled. Had the warrior noticed Saburo's awe at something so simple as footwear? Saburo felt himself flush. A first-level priest was not supposed to feel this sort of admiration. Priests were men of peace, while samurai were men of combat.

The samurai finally broke the silence. "You have a name?"

"I'm Dankotaru," Saburo said, giving his formal priestly name—one he rarely used.

"Are you?"

"Am I what?"

"Resolute. The meaning of dankotaru."

Saburo shifted uneasily. There was something about this winning man that drew Saburo to him. He was powerful, yet calm. Likely he could be fierce if needed, yet he spoke with an unruffled coolness.

"I'm called Shima Sa-me," the samurai offered. This was uncharacteristic for a samurai to offer his name to someone not at least of the buke class. Perhaps he respected Saburo's status as a priest. "You always called Dankotaru?"

Saburo shook his head.

"I didn't think so. Long name." Shima removed his haori, revealing battle-worn armor that had been patched and repaired. Saburo tried not to gape. The mending meant that the stranger had seen the thick of combat and had survived. But something else impressed Saburo even more: Shima's insignia, the Imperial symbol—the chrysanthemum mon. No question. He had fought in behalf of the Emperor, the Son of Heaven himself.

"What did they call you before you came to the temple?" Shima asked.

"Gankyū," Saburo said, unsure why he even admitted it.

"Eyeball?"

"Hai."

"On account that you have one eye that wanders?"

So! Shima had noticed and spoken of it—but in such a matter-of-fact way that Saburo found himself grinning, as if they were sharing some special secret. Saburo said, "Our new bettō can't seem to remember my name, so he started calling me that"—as had Saburo's father, but he did not want to volunteer that much.

"Priests," Shima said, standing up. "They have an odd sense of things. My name means island shark, but I don't know where my father came up with that. Where can I find something to eat? You have meat?"

Saburo shook his head. "We have taken vows not to kill, so we eat only grains and vegetables. Sometimes fruit. Mostly we have dried fruit."

"Hmm." Shima sighed. "Religion means you have to give up a lot."

"Actually, even if meat were allowed, we're too poor to afford it, so if we make it a religious rule, like the Buddhists do, it comes out righteous."

Shima laughed—a bellow that resonated from deep inside. "I like you, Gun-kun."

Saburo pondered. Gun-kun, a complete mispronunciation of the hateful name Gankyū. Shima had turned Gan into *Gun, soldier*, and kyū into *kun*, a form of respect usually shared among comrades. Saburo felt flattered. Gun-kun—fellow soldier.

"Gun-kun? Any saké?" Shima asked slyly.

Saburo considered the risk of taking saké from the storehouse—saké used for sacred rites. He wanted to please this warrior who was being so friendly. "I think I know where I can find some."

"Where are the other priests?"

"At prayers. It's the observance of the first night of winter. We're all fasting. I think I can find some roots to eat."

"Roots!" Shima almost spat the word. "Roots and saké?" Shima shuddered. "How about fresh rabbit?"

"Rabbit?"

"You think these are only for war?" Shima tapped his ebira holding his arrows. "Is there a place we can set up a fire, away from all the prayers? Bring something to cook in. A small pot or iron plate will do. We'll eat rabbit and drink saké. And I'll talk. You were looking at all the scuffs on my armor. I can see you want to hear about the *Ran*."

"You fought in the *Hōgen Ran*?" Saburo bit his lip, trying to quiet the excitement he felt.

"Let's find that quiet place, and if eating rabbit offends your religion, you can just drink the saké. I'll tell you about the battles last summer."

The two went to a place far up the hill behind the temple where the smoke and smell of the fire and cooking rabbit would not drift down to the priests' noses.

Twenty-Five

A Hero Goes Unsung
in His Own House

As they ate and drank, Shima regaled Saburo with tales of glory, fear, excitement, boredom, sudden horror, unexpected turns of fortune—and death. Lots of death. "Combat does not know rank," Shima said. "Someone lower in the social order, if he's trained or just plain lucky, can defeat someone of a higher station. Young men no older than yourself distinguished themselves in single combat. It's said, 'A man can come to battle as a farmer and leave as a general.'"

Saburo hung on every word.

Shima quaffed more saké. "A thousand fell. And by the end of the fighting the heads of at least fifty enemy leaders found their way to the points of pikes and were put on display—six of whom I personally defeated."

Saburo asked, "Why did such an illustrious warrior not stay in Heian-kyō?" As soon as he'd said it, he worried that his question might have insulted the samurai.

But instead, Shima's voice grew soft. "The trouble with winning is that there is never enough reward to go around for the victors, and everyone is a hero. Heroes who fight for no pay, but just the glory, end up with nothing. And no money. And as for the glory, no one remembers it except you yourself. There's a warrior saying: '*A hero goes unsung in his own house.*'" Shima laughed. "The wise ones"—he patted his chest—"take their skills to places where their abilities are rare and will be appreciated." Shima grew more serious. "I plan to take what I know and go to the Isle of Unknown Fires. The Ōuchi are looking for a sword master to teach their warriors. I'll be leaving in the morning. But first I need to go and lean"—meaning Shima, now filled with more than his share of saké, had to relieve himself. "Gun-kun, want to help me with my armor?"

Saburo nodded and guided Shima, steadying the bigger man just a bit, as they made their way into the nearby brush. Saburo did not feel the slightest bit drunk. The fleshy and succulent rabbit and Shima's stories had blunted any effects of the saké, except for a feeling of great well-being. Of clarity. Of release. Something about the stories of the Ran had changed Saburo's thinking about his own powerlessness.

The warrior, having had far more to drink and weighed down by the armor, staggered a bit as the two found a quiet spot on a slight hillside where the rising moon provided enough light to see. Saburo helped untie and remove the lower armored apron below Shima's corselet. Saburo did not know precisely how to undo all the fastenings, but Shima's instructions were clear.

When Shima guided his *daikon* out, Saburo realized that this man was huge in every way. Shima let loose a deep sigh of release. Saburo stood by, watching while not watching.

"So tell me, Gun-kun. What is your story? How did you end up here so far from everything, eating roots?"

Saburo hesitated, not sure where to start.

Shima said, "Death has touched you. I can see it in your eyes."

A deeper darkness crept in amongst the trees under a sky that had turned absolutely black. A cloud moved across the moon. In the corridor of recollection, Saburo saw himself standing before a weather-beaten door to one of his father's silk farm's rundown sheds.

Twenty-Six
Jingling Coins

Third Day after Full Moon of Poem-Composing Month
First Day of Shosho, End of Heat
Fifth Year of Kiūan, Year of the Earth Snake
23 August 1149

Inaba Prefecture, Main Isle

T HE SHEDS WERE NUMEROUS and almost identical; each shed lined
with rows of racks; each rack crammed with shelf-trays; each tray
packed thick with mulberry leaves. It was among these leaves that the
pride of the farm, bone-white silkworms, hatched and thrived.

In memory, and alone, Saburo entered the shed, wandering deeper as
the scent of tart-but-sweet leaves filled the airless rooms. Like crackling
fire, the sound of thousands of munching larval mouths surrounded him.

He heard a moaning, unearthly voice of agony. His mother! He ran
into the darker end of the shed, chasing the sound though it frightened
him, where he came upon a vision of horror: his mother, her flesh rotting, silkworms consuming her.

His howl filled the shed.

His mother reached toward him. He recoiled—an act that filled him
with shame for years after, for she was not an unclean thing from the
underworld. She was his mother, the only person who ever loved him, if
only a little. She was covered not in silkworms but the blistering sores of
tōsō. He cried in despair for her and for himself.

He turned to run, then froze, for his father loomed in the shadows.

As far as Saburo could remember, his father never beat him. And yet, he
feared his father. And not only feared him, he loathed him. Loathed him
for his obsession with his undulating worms. His obsession with silk. His
obsession with money. But most of all, he loathed his father's dotage for

the new wife he took the very next spring. A new wife who stood above everyone else. An empress among commoners.

Saburo was still too young to question the way things were. His entire world consisted of mulberry leaves, worms, cocoons, silk, dye pots, gold, and mock titles. Saburo's father, whose given name was Mika-geishi, trained all his sons and all his daughters, one after the other, as soon as they could make words, in the art of silk making, silk dying, and silk selling. And what better way was there for children to learn a trade than to become apprentices, for that was how commoners schooled the young. Yet even as a child, the idea of following his father, and brothers, and sisters into a life herding crawling caterpillars filled Saburo with disgust and despair.

When Saburo reached about eight summers in age, he admitted to his father that he felt a bit of an aversion for the worms. A small confession, softly said. "Worms just eat and eat and they do nothing else." He said he found their endless munching disgusting.

"Fool!" Mika-geishi roared, almost beside himself with rage. "Draw pleasure from the sound, idiot!" he yelled, waving a stick. "It puts food in our bowls."

And indeed his words were literal. As the worms finished their spinning, everyone gathered the mature cocoons and boiled them before the larvae could break out and damage the silk strands. Once boiled, the silk could be unwound. And as for the dead larvae, they were there for the eating. Everyone in the family found them tasty—all but Saburo. But no matter, as that meant there was all the more for the rest of the family. For Saburo, trees provided him with more tasty fare—apricots, peaches, plums, apples and cherries. And of all of these, cherries were his favorite.

At the marketplace, Mika-geishi's role was the collector of monies. The sons copied his method, acting outwardly obsequious, but shrewd beneath. Usually Saburo stayed at the farm to tend the silkworms—after all, someone had to be there to make sure the worms were perpetually fed. But occasionally Saburo was expected to help at the market, and though he never looked forward to it, he tried to make the best of it. He distracted himself by being useful, taking on the physical tasks having to do with the cart and goods: loading, unloading, and grouping the festively colored silks, making sure they were meticulously folded and arranged.

While some might have said such womanly tasks should be left to his mother and sisters, the women were otherwise engaged in the selling of silk. And though Saburo did not particularly enjoy the work, he welcomed anything to avoid the bartering and the inevitable shouting that filled the air when people started haggling—and shouting was something his father relished. Young Saburo found his father's inane cawing to be embarrassing. Everyone knew what the prices were. During any season, they hardly ever varied. Why pretend things were otherwise?

Yet Saburo saw that the wrangling brought something out in Mika-geishi. Animated, his father no longer was the dour and brooding man of the silk sheds. And by the end of a market day, Mika-geishi led his family back to the farm with the cart empty and his purse full, jingling with coins.

It was only later in life that Saburo came to understand that his father's obsession with money was actually a means to an end. His father's true obsession was to live up to the expectations of Himeyo, his new wife who was nothing like Saburo's mother had been. Himeyo, whose name meant *excellent princess*, was the one-time daughter of a now-impoverished minor samurai, so she never stooped to enter the worm sheds, let alone work there. Her role in the family centered on showing off the silk finery. Mika-geishi impressed his children with this truth about the silk trade: When customers saw the fine silk garments worn by someone as lovely as their new mother, customers would surely buy. Seeing the comely Himeyo wearing silk fabric would whet their appetites—and perhaps even their lusts—and they would imagine their own wives looking as fetching.

Festively dressed to confirm the family's opulence, the daughters attempted to emulate their new mother's banter with the silk buyers at market. While it came naturally to Himeyo, try as they would, the daughters' efforts were mere mimicry. Himeyo always had to immediately step in when a potential buyer, even innocently, seemed taken with one of the daughters. After all, what were they but girls? Unrefined farm children. Everyone in the family knew refinement came from a birth higher than theirs, for their new mother always stood higher and always would— higher than their father even, standing maybe just to the right of the Buddha. Perhaps she was a bodhisattva, an embodiment of the beauty mere mortals could only worship, a divinity that revealed itself as Kannon, a woman of thirty-three earthly manifestations, each of which at one time or another she was said to express. Saburo's brothers and sisters either foolishly or instinctively out of a sense of self-preservation knew that they were to revere "her majesty."

This deification did not go unnoticed outside of the family. At the central market, the other tradespeople, mostly the women, took to calling her "The Empress." At first, Saburo believed it was out of respect. Only as he grew older did he realize this sobriquet also carried a barb in its tail. Himeyo had her own thoughts on the matter. After all, shrewish words came from shrews who still had field dirt under their fingernails.

One season, after Mika-geishi had acquired enough wealth—no one quite knew what that threshold was—he assumed a formal clan name: Kinu, *silk*. This was quite a presumption for a silk maker, a commoner by any reckoning, and was not officially recognized by the authorities. Nevertheless, Saburo's oldest brother came to be called Kinu Ichiro, first son, and the next oldest was Kinu Jiro, second son. Both were said to be handsome, which meant they had physical strength, had good teeth, could see well enough to spot the faintest of stars in the night skies, and were charming, which in a farm boy was a kind of easiness.

But Saburo, the third son, never came to be called Kinu Saburo. From the time the child learned to form words, he understood that his name was not Saburo, but Sakana Gankyū, *fish eye*. Without a doubt, fish were lucky. They were bringers of money. Did their scales not look like coins? But in Saburo's case, the name suggested a witless and homely boy, for Saburo was malformed from birth. His right eye socket was slightly indented and thus the eye appeared to wander, giving him a vacant look. And so although, by all accounts, Saburo could see the same faint night stars and had wits at least as sharp as his brothers, and with more mental acuity than most, the odious name given him did not change. Gankyū. The boy with eyes of a fish.

Eyes of a fish or not, one day, when he had reached twelve summers, Saburo noticed a girl at the market.

Twenty-Seven
So You Like Girls

First Day of Long Month
Fourteenth Day of Hakuro, Descent of White Dew
Third Year of Nimbiō, Year of the Water Rooster
20 September 1153

Inaba Prefecture

S HE WAS ABOUT HIS AGE and always accompanied a seller of straw
goods—baskets, hats, cloaks, and sandals. She had a sweet smile,
kindly eyes, and an innocence Saburo found attractive. He was not yet of
that certain age when boys' interests in girls drive them to distraction, yet
he could not keep his eyes off of her. He always watched her from afar.

On two occasions she smiled at him, shyly, if only fleetingly, and each
time Saburo found himself blushing and reflexively looking away, feeling the fool, and though he immediately looked back up, she had already
turned away. After the second time, he never managed to catch her eye
again.

With autumn upon them, the markets already started to quiet down,
and he worried if he would ever get a glimpse of her again.

His thoughts were of her as he helped his brother gather leaves. The
two brothers worked quietly, grunting as they hefted the carriers. The
day could not have been warmer, the sun no brighter. The breeze carried the scent of grass and leaves and animals. The silkworms that had
not been boiled but rather selected to parent the next generation of larvae now emerged from the torn filaments of their cocoons. Strangely
deformed things. No longer larvae, yet not yet moths, the hatchlings
crawled out, pushing, pulling, drawing themselves into the sunlight to
let the heat dry their wings. The reborn insects, taking final form, were
now ready to mate.

Saburo slowly hatched an idea of his own. After a while, he spoke. "Could you pretend that you are too sick next market day?"

"Sick?" Ichiro sniffed. "I'm not sick."

"I mean *pretend* you are sick."

"Why should I? Besides, the old man will be angry and lose his temper and you know everyone hates that." Ichiro looked skyward to emphasize his point.

"But if I can take your place, he won't be mad," Saburo looked hopefully at his brother.

Ichiro shook his head. "I feel well. Besides, I like the marketplace and you don't. Why do you suddenly want to go to market?"

"I just want to go, that's all."

"You never talk to the customers. You just hang back and sulk, or maybe you're shy, I don't know. And you're always glad to leave. I can see it on your face."

"I'm liking it more."

His eyes narrowing, Ichiro cocked his head. "Is it because of that girl?"

Saburo felt himself flush. "What girl?"

Ichiro smiled knowingly. "The one at the straw weaver's."

"I don't know who you mean."

Ichiro smiled even more broadly. "You know the one. The one you keep looking at, but who never looks back. That one."

Saburo wanted to run away, but Ichiro was faster. If he tried to run, Ichiro would catch him.

"Ha-hah!" Ichiro laughed. "So you like girls. Nothing wrong with that. I like 'em too." He nodded. "My daikon gets hard just thinking about them. Bet yours does too."

Saburo started to protest.

"Ha!" Ichiro pushed him. "Don't lie. I know you do. Everybody likes girls. But you can't do anything unless she lets you get close." Ichiro wrinkled his nose. "You know her name?"

Saburo gulped.

"Ha! You don't. You pine for a certain girl's *omeko* and you don't even know her name."

Flustered, Saburo grabbed the first thing that was near him, a small log, and with all his might flung it at his brother's head.

Ichiro was fast and dodged it. Saburo leapt at Ichiro, snarling, but laughing wickedly the older boy pinned him, knees against Saburo's shoulders. Saburo thrashed, but it was no good.

"Calm yourself, Saburo." Ichiro's voice grew soothing. "If you care that much," he said with a smirk, "I will let you and your daikon chase after her."

Saburo stopped fighting and yielded. Ichiro rolled off Saburo and stood up, shaking his head. "All this for a girl whose name you don't even know." He looked down at Saburo. "It's Sairyū. She's called Sairyū. Everyone in the market place knows her."

"Everyone?"

Ichiro laughed. "No. Not *that* way. Her father watches over her." Ichiro grinned cunningly. "I'm sure you'll be the first to have your way with her."

Saburo sprang to his feet, pushing out his chest. Ichiro put out his hands in surrender, palms up. "Stay calm. You will never win her if you don't talk to her."

"How can I?"

"I have an idea."

TWENTY-EIGHT
TEN RED CHERRIES

Third Day of Long Month
22 September 1153

O N MARKET DAY, WITH Ichiro feigning illness—which he substantiated by managing to vomit when he stuck a finger into the back of his own throat—Saburo took his brother's place with the cart. He brought ten perfect cherries that he had fresh-picked from the family orchard. He planned to walk up to Sairyū the moment he arrived and offer her the cherries, but when the Kinu clan arrived, Mika-geishi immediately put Saburo to work unloading the cart. Saburo carefully placed the cherries away from the dust that was kicked up in the market area, and there they would stay until he was free. Then he would go talk to Sairyū.

Once the silk stand was set up, Saburo saw that a crowd of buyers had descended upon the straw weaver's stand. Sairyū was busily selling hats, baskets, rain jackets, sandals, mats, and all manner of straw-woven things. It was not the time to barge in. Then the Kinu stall got busy. Saburo's father barked orders. His mother chided him to work harder. The gulf across the road to her cart grew as wide and turbid as a river, overflowing with people—a flood which Saburo would wait to ford.

For most of the day, Saburo kept waiting for a right moment, but when was a right moment? And when he approached her, then what? What if she were to say she did not like cherries? What if she said she did not like *him*? What if she said nothing? What if she ran and hid? As he thought of all these possibilities, his legs grew too heavy to cross to the straw weaver's stall.

By day's end, most of the silks were sold. The sun had already moved low into the west. Realizing there never would be a right moment, Saburo, his mouth dry, gathered himself and went to get the cherries. But now, with them in hand, only he himself could prevent himself from going up to her. *I can do this. I can do this. It's just putting one foot in front of the other.*

The once-teeming road now held just a trickle of people. He could clearly see her. Pretty. Plain—nothing like the fancy woman his new mother made herself out to be. Sairyū was everything Himeyo was not. Unpretentious. Innocent. Humble without ever being low.

His knees wobbling, Saburo took the first step across the road. One step and then the next. And the next. Saburo made his way across the road, fifteen steps, if that, a short distance to the straw weaver's cart.

Sairyū stood there alone. She looked up at him. Without saying as much as hello, nor volunteering his name, he thrust his palm out to her and said, "Would you like some cherries?"

She gazed into his palm, looked up, smiled sweetly, nodded, and then to his utter amazement took a single cherry from his open hand.

"You can have more. They're all for you." He grinned.

She smiled again. Their eyes met.

She smiles with her eyes.

"I'm Saburo," he said, suddenly beaming so broadly he thought he might look foolish, but she just looked back, mirroring him.

"Ha! Fish Eyeball! There you are," his father called from the silk cart.

Sairyū giggled with embarrassment.

Saburo flushed.

"What are you doing there, Fish Eyeball? Get over here!"

He realized she was staring straight into his eyes. Was she laughing because of his eye? Maybe that was it! Saburo dropped the cherries and ran as hard and as fast as he could back to the silk cart.

"What are you doing?" his father thundered as Saburo ran up. "Talking to a girl? You're lazy. Stupid. Get to work. That girl's not for *you*. She's laughing at you. Can't you see?"

And indeed, Sairyū stood at the basket vendor's stand, looking down at the cherries spilled onto the dirt, her hand over her mouth.

"Those cherries were from *our* orchards, weren't they?" Himeyo snapped. "And you are giving *our* food away to some basket maker's brat? Get to work!"

"But there is no work to do," Saburo said.

"You dare speak to your elders in this way!" Mika-geishi grabbed the boy by the scruff. "Show respect!" He pushed Saburo hard against the cart.

"Associating with a common weaver of straw!" his mother hissed. "You are of the Kinu! How do you *ever* expect to rise if you put your snout in the mud with the lowly!"

Saburo looked to his brothers and sisters for help, but they silently went about their work.

Needless to say, on the Full Moon of Long Month, when the next market day came, Saburo was left to tend the caterpillar trays. "Make sure they get their fill" were the last words Mika-geishi said as the family rolled off to market with more bolts of silk. His brothers did not look his way. His sisters giggled. The parents looked ahead. The cart rumbled on until Saburo could hear it no more. Left alone, he listened as the shed filled up with the soft sound of the greedy, munching larval mouths feasting in the leaf trays. He remembered his mother standing before him, covered in yellow-green pustules. To him, the silkworms forever sounded like approaching death—soft and imperceptible, and whose horror did not reveal itself until it was too late.

Saburo had already decided he would not tend to the caterpillars as he had been told. Instead he donned a nondescript cotton traveling kimono, one which would not identify him as a merchant's son, stuffed a few personal belongings into its sleeve pockets, along with some fruit, and left the silk farm at a brisk walk, forever.

TWENTY-NINE

WHY ARE YOU HOLDING BACK?

Full Moon of Long Month
4 October 1153

L IKE MANY A YOUTH who leaves home, Saburo had no plan beyond
his flight. He had the foresight to bring ten fat plums along. Well
before dusk, ten plum pits littered the road behind him.

Soon, no doubt, his father and brothers would be out on the road looking for him. He avoided settlements and hurried past farms, fearing the
locals might be turned into informers by the Kinu family when they made
inquiries. "Did you see a boy with a deformed eye?"

However, once the road headed into the mountains, farmhouses were
less frequent and settlements nonexistent. And as the land grew ever
steeper, even the random dwellings disappeared altogether. When night
fell, his family had not as yet caught up with him. In fact, he saw no sign
of human activity along the mountain road. He smelled no smoke from
cook fires, nor the scent of farm animals or tilled fields.

Benighted along an isolated stretch of road as empty as his belly, Saburo
stole into the brush and down a slight ravine, where he found a dry mossy
tree. He leaned against it and slept propped upright with one eye open,
regretting that he did not bring the small dagger with him. He passed the
long and lonely night wrestling with the thought of returning home. It
was his wish for food more than anything that set him to think in this way.

The dawn was cold in the mountains and, having shivered most of the
night, he waited for the sun to rise and warm the land before setting out.
He pondered. The mountains were much more lonely than he had pictured. He weighed whether he should head up over the pass or turn back
toward the settlements and see if he could find something to eat.

Maybe he could find a farm where they needed help, but then again what skills did he have that anyone would want? All he knew was how to put mulberry leaves into trays. That and boiling cocoons. Besides, that was what he was running away from.

He straightened himself out and made his way out of the brush. He decided that when he got to the road he would throw a stick into the air and, depending on which way it pointed when it landed, he would strike out in that direction. Had he asked his stomach, it would have pointed him back down the hills to the settlements, irrespective of the throw.

He heard someone coming. A light step. Not trudging. He squatted down, hiding behind the rise. Was it his father? His brothers? Maybe they were coming to beg him to come back, sorry for what they had done. Sorry that they had made him run away. But then another thought crossed his mind. Maybe they were here to drag him back. Laugh even more. Torment him. Beat him.

Saburo held his breath as the sound drew nearer. The stalks he hid behind made it hard to see clearly, but that was good, for they hid Saburo equally well.

He saw a shape. Just one person. Another boy. Someone about as young as he. Not anyone Saburo knew. Dressed in fine clothes. Saburo saw a flash of indigo. *Expensive kimono lining.* The boy had a short sword tucked through his sash. And he walked with purpose, seeming to know where he was going. A confident step. It wasn't long before the other boy disappeared up the road.

Forgetting all about throwing any sticks in the air, Saburo slipped out of the scrub and followed, but back far enough that he would not be seen, ducking now and then into the weeds and brush or hiding behind trees. Every once in a while, the other boy would pause in the road and then resume walking.

In the thick upland woods, the boy with the sword stopped at a small roadside Shintō shrine. He turned, looked in Saburo's direction, then called out loudly to no one in particular, "There's sweet water here!"

Saburo ducked his head down.

"Why are you holding back?" The boy with the sword waved his arm. "I know you've been following me since the Hour of the Dragon. What are you afraid of? This?" He pulled the sword, still in its scabbard, and set it down on some grass. He then opened his arms in a gesture of peace.

Saburo hesitantly stepped out into the road, but he did not go any closer.

"It's fresh-running and cool." The boy cupped some of the flowing water in his hands, but it dribbled out from his fingers. "Looks like you'll have to get it for yourself."

Saburo thought about it. *Water.* His thirst was strong, and though he could have waited for the other boy to move on, something about his smile and easy manner helped Saburo overcome any doubts.

As Saburo approached, the other boy stepped away, extending one arm toward the spring in a gesture of invitation, as if the spring belonged to him. The first sound other than Saburo's own feet in the dirt was the sound of gurgling water. The first scent other than the road dust was the fragrance of moist earth.

Honoring the spring was the entire purpose of the small Shintō shrine. Saburo took it in at a glance: two red-lacquered uprights and a crossbeam painted the same color, all finely made and maintained.

The boy said, "Put your mouth to the crack in the rock and drink from the *sairyū.*" The *rivulet.*

Without ceremony, Saburo put his lips against the opening. Delicious! He drank his fill, then turned to look at the boy.

"Good?" the boy asked.

"Good," Saburo answered with a nod.

"You're headed over the pass too?"

"Hai."

"My name's Aka-rui."

"I'm Saburo."

"There's a temple at the summit," said Aka-rui.

"You have traveled over this road before," said Saburo, now sure why Aka-rui walked with such confidence.

"No."

Saburo frowned, puzzled.

Aka-rui pointed uphill at a roadside wooden post with calligraphy. "It says so there. Mountain River Mouth Temple."

岩川寺院

"Oh?" said Saburo.

"Ha!" Aka-rui brightened. "You don't know the scripts?"

Saburo looked down.

"But it's easy," Aka-rui said, and he pointed with his fingers. "Focus on each piece. First, See the wavy lines? *Kawa*, just like a river:

川

"See how it flows between the banks? And *mouth*:

口

"Or round thing. And above that, *mountain*:

山

"So put it together and it's *mouth of a river under a mountain cliff*:

岩川

"Easy!"

Saburo nodded, understanding for the first time. Aka-rui had broken down the calligraphy into three parts. His abilities impressed Saburo, who had been taught nothing of reading the symbols.

"The next one's hard," Aka-rui said, frowning, "so at first you'll just have to remember it. *Temple*:

寺院

"Once you memorize the kanji, you'll see it everywhere."

"Mountain River Mouth Temple," Saburo recited.

"Yamakuchikawa-jiin," Aka-rui repeated. "I really don't know many calligraphies." He snorted. "Just a few. Come on. Let's go see this temple." Aka-rui grabbed his scabbard and stuffed it back through his sash.

After walking together in silence for some time, Aka-rui asked, "You leaving your family?"

Saburo wondered if it was so easy to see. *Do I wear it on my face?*

Aka-rui said, "Me too." He added, "My father's a drunk."

Saburo's mouth hung open.

"Actually he's a warrior," said Aka-rui. "Yours?"

"Silk maker."

"Mine's always angry. Beats me with fists. Your father beats you too, no?"

"Yes, but not with fists."

"With a stick? That hurts too. I know."

"With words."

"Hmm. Is that worse or better?" Aka-rui asked only himself, for he was now not really looking at Saburo.

Saburo answered anyway. "Different is all, I guess." He was surprised to find himself speaking so openly. "When you're little, you believe that that's the way the world is for everyone, but when you get older, you see it's only that way for *you*. They only hate and hurt *you*."

"My father was far more generous," Aka-rui said. "He beat my brothers too. Sometimes even my mother. There was plenty of beating. Lucky for us, he was away with the armies a lot." Aka-rui laughed darkly. "But he made up for it when he got home. See?" He pulled back his right tunic sleeve and flexed his arm. "It doesn't go all the way anymore. He did that when he threw me one time. I landed against a boulder. Never healed right."

Saburo did not have words.

Aka-rui studied Saburo's face. "You said he didn't beat you, but . . ." He pointed to his own right eye like a mirror indicating Saburo's imperfection. "Did he do that to you?"

Saburo gulped. He had never considered it. He had always been told the Gods had made him this way in the beginning.

Aka-rui went on to describe one of his own brothers who looked much the same as Saburo. "Maybe that's why I feel I can speak to you. You resemble him, except he lost his power to make words. Something happened inside after his head was dented."

Saburo looked deep into Aka-rui's eyes. Indeed, they were without malice.

"All I want now is to be free," Aka-rui concluded. "You? What do you want?"

Saburo said nothing. His thoughts were racing back to the mulberry groves. Then he thought about himself. Had he always looked this way? Was his right eye always slightly sunken in, the side of his head slightly deformed? He could not remember. He finally said, "I'm not sure. I don't think anyone ever hit me. Not like that."

Both boys again fell silent as they walked up the steepening road.

Saburo slowed. "Look."

He pointed at what he saw ahead—a white-haired man pulling uphill a small two-wheel cart filled to the brim with large sacks of fresh late-summer vegetables and grains. The two boys shot looks to each other. *Shall we help?* It was not in expectation of payment, or even the promise of a peach or plum. It was something rural boys simply knew they had to do when they saw an elder who struggled.

"Oji-san," they called out as they increased their step. "May we help?"

The old man looked over his shoulder, continuing to pull the cart along. He was dressed in a simple workman's tunic.

"We're headed for the summit," said Saburo.

"So am I," the grandfatherly man said with a short laugh. "Where else would any of us be going?"

Aka-rui moved behind the cart to push it. Saburo grabbed one haul-pole. Immediately the cart picked up speed. It wasn't long at all before the sun was directly overhead, and the old man, the boys, and the cart came to a place where the road flattened out—a passage, a cut, actually, wedged between steep hills in a wooded area.

A Shintō temple and monastery sat perched on the northern slope. Ten to fifteen buildings painted red or left natural wood rose along the hill, one behind the other, each structure having a commanding view of the western valleys. The roofs were milk-stone green. A wooden-slat frame wall filled in with thatching surrounded the temple's perimeter. Vivid blue, green, white, red, and yellow prayer flags flew prominently. The smell of pine fires mixed with the mountain air. Thick forest filled the land all around. A waterfall dropped from a high vertical wall, no doubt the primal source of the spring waters they had drunk earlier.

"It's *beautiful* here," Saburo said.

"Some think so," said the old man.

"This is Mountain River Mouth Temple!" said Aka-rui.

"Not quite," said the old man. "Rock River Temple. Iwakawa-jiin. But maybe this place is good. Maybe the Buddha put you on this road, on this path, on this day." He eyed the boys. "You brothers?"

They shook their heads.

"Didn't think so. You don't look very much alike. Where're you headed?"

"To Heian-kyō," said Aka-rui.

"Oh?" The old man sounded genuinely interested. "Why's that?"

"It's the Imperial City," said Aka-rui. "The Son of Heaven lives there. It's the most beautiful city anywhere. A city fit for the Emperor."

"You've been there? Either of you?"

The boys shook their heads.

The old man looked at them closely. "Parts of the city, where the kuge live, are filled with many comforts, if you are kuge. Other parts aren't even finished. There are robbers who run freely. Even the law is afraid of them, and when the law does come out in number to catch the thieves, the ruffians disappear like rats. That is until the soldiers go back, and then the robbers come out and go back to robbery."

The boys looked at the old man in surprise.

"Yes," he nodded. "I was born there. I left long ago. You boys leaving to go to a place you know nothing about?"

The boys said nothing.

"Two runaways?"

Again, they said nothing. Saburo lowered his head. This old man seemed to know everything about them.

Aka-rui's stomach suddenly growled. He laughed at himself.

"You hungry?" the old man asked.

"I just ate," said Aka-rui in samurai fashion.

The man nodded and pulled his cart toward the side of the temple. "This is where my load is bound." He pointed in the other direction, toward a series of stone steps some distance away. "If you are hungry, perhaps the priests will feed you. That's where you enter. You know what to do?"

"Rinse our mouths," said Aka-rui.

"Clap to let the Gods know we've arrived," said Saburo.

"When you're greeted at the gate, tell them you are here to see the bettō, Abbot Nin-tai. Maybe you'll even get fed."

With that, the old man pulled the cart along the fence toward some undisclosed gate.

"You think we should go inside?" Aka-rui wondered.

"The old man said we should."

The two runaways climbed the stone steps.

Thirty
The Bettō

One day past Full Moon of Long Month
5 October 1153
Iwakawa-jiin, Tajima Prefecture, Main Isle

S ABURO AND AKA-RUI CROSSED through the temple's threshold gate, which revealed an open-air courtyard. A white-robed priest scurried up across the large slabs of rough paving stones. He bowed, welcoming them. "You are travelers?"

"Hai." The boys bowed nearly in unison.

"Are you Abbot Nin-tai?" asked Saburo.

The priest smiled. "I am called Daimaru. You are both pilgrims?"

The boys looked to each other, not sure exactly how to answer that.

Daimaru shook his head. "He doesn't give audiences, even to pilgrims."

"The old man with the cart said we're to ask for Nin-tai by name," said Saburo.

A look of surprise crossed the priest's face. "Ha!" he gasped and then scurried away.

The boys looked at each other. "Do you think the old man was wrong?" Aka-rui asked.

"Laughing at us, maybe?" wondered Saburo.

"Maybe they were going to only feed *him* for bringing the cart up the hill. They didn't see us help."

"We didn't do it for the food."

"True enough." Aka-rui nodded. "Still, did you hear my stomach growl back there?"

"At first I thought it was a mountain demon." Saburo made a face.

Both boys laughed.

Daimaru came back with a deliberate step. "Come with me," he said, bowing slightly.

They were led to an eating hall. Taking off their shoes, they entered. Inside a group of men and boys sat around the perimeter. The group was composed of six green-robed elders, fifteen white-robed priests, and the remaining thirty or so were ordinary boys, likely the novices.

"Sit," Daimaru indicated.

One of the elder men in green robes, likely Nin-tai, raised his bowl and everyone proceeded to eat. It was a simple meal of slick and smelly soybeans on a bit of rice with a small cup of kelp broth, but Saburo could not remember having ever eaten anything more delicious. He had supposed that in a monastery the holy men would be somber and eat while muttering prayers between bites or speaking of things religious. Instead they were friendly and engaged the boys in polite conversation, asking where they were from and where they were going and what wonders they might have seen on the road.

The meal soon ended and the crowd dispersed.

The boys asked if they could help in thanks for the meal. They were told, "Nin-tai will now see you."

The priest Daimaru now led them up a hill within the monastery toward a low-roofed building with closed doors. "Wait here," he said and stepped away.

Alone, they stood outside.

"We've been fed, just like the old man promised," said Aka-rui.

"Maybe they'll want something in return now," Saburo said. "The man in green robes at the meal, Nin-tai? I wonder if he'll want us to help the old man push the cart back."

"I don't want to go back."

"Neither do I." Saburo shook his head. "Our parents could still find us."

Daimaru returned and opened the doors to the low-roofed building. "Please go inside."

The boys bowed and entered. They had expected to see the fat priest in green robes, seated like a Buddha, awaiting them. Instead a taller and thinner man in green robes stood at the far end of the room, looking through a portal out at the valley far below.

The boys came forward and bowed again.

The man in green robes said without turning to look at them, "I can never get enough of the view from the temple."

The boys knew the voice. *The old man with the cart!* They shot looks of surprise to each other. He turned away from the window. It indeed was he.

"Bettō Nin-tai," the boys more or less said in unison, bowing again.

He returned their bow.

"We did not know you were the bettō," said Saburo.

"Why didn't you say anything?" asked Aka-rui.

"That I am Nin-tai?" He smiled enigmatically. "When I am away, I am not the bettō of the road nor of the cart, nor of anything or anyone, save for myself. I am again just a man. It is good to be just a man, Nin-tai the man, again, if only for a time. Can you understand this?"

The boys, faces sober, said that they did.

Nin-tai laughed softly. "We are a syncretic order. Do you know what that is?"

Neither boy did.

"The myriad Gods are everywhere, yes?"

They agreed.

"Well, if one of the kami tells you about Himself, though He speaks for all, we hear Him using the words He chooses in His manifestation at that particular moment. Another time, different words are used in a different manifestation. Both are true, but to choose one set of words over another set of words is simply to not listen. *Laziness.* Words of enlightenment are uttered by God because God has many faces He shows us. And sometimes a God even comes in the form of a woman."

Saburo had never heard of such an idea.

"Enlightenment is not just understanding one tradition. It is listening to *all* traditions."

The boys stood silently.

Nin-tai continued, "I notice you have good manners."

Saburo could not exactly remember what he did that was so mannerly.

"You helped a stranger. Cheerfully. Without asking for something in return. You conversed respectfully with the others at the temple during the meal, taking no more than your share, though I could see neither of you have eaten for quite a while. Stomachs speak when they are empty." Nin-tai laughed, pointing at Aka-rui, who grew slightly red. "You both offered to do chores, without being asked." Nin-tai looked at them care-fully. "What are you looking for in Heian-kyō?"

The boys said nothing. Nin-tai waited. He was not going to let them get away merely with shrugs. But they still said nothing.

"Reading and writing. Are these valuable skills?" asked Nin-tai.

The boys agreed they were.

"Will anyone teach you to read and to write in Heian-kyō?"

They didn't know.

"I can tell you, they won't. They'll teach you to be thieves and worse. You'll learn how to rob and steal to get food. How to live in an abandoned building. To be worse off than from whatever you are running from, re-gardless of how bad you think that is."

Saburo gulped. *A thief? A robber?*

"Is either of you a daimyō's son?"

Both shook their heads.

"Either of you commit any murders lately?"

The boys looked shocked and again shook their heads.

"Probably no one will want to find you. But if you want, you can stay here until the next Full Moon before you leave. By then they will have given up, if they bothered to follow you at all. And by then you will get an idea of our lives here at Iwakawa-jiin. And maybe, you just might . . ."

With that, Nin-tai bowed and left the chamber.

And if anyone from their families ever came looking for either of the runaways, the boys never heard so much as a whisper of it, for indeed neither was a daimyō's son, nor had either of them ever killed anyone. They were of little interest to anyone but themselves and the priests who took them in.

The idea of killing someone had never occurred to Saburo. He never would have believed—even if a soothsayer came to him and divined his future—that by the end of his journey away from the silk farm he would become a *shinobi*, a ninja, a man operating in the shadows who killed for money. The utterly profound change in his heart happened after he learned, firsthand and brutally, more than a few things about the nature of the world and the limits of human kindness, even amongst those who postured as upright holy men.

THIRTY-ONE
MY FATHER, THE HOLY MAN

One day past Full Moon of Gods Month
26 October 1153

Iwakawa-jiin

T HE FULL MOON CAME AND WENT, and Saburo and Aka-rui stayed, and it was for more than just the food and a place to live. Nin-tai's words had ignited the boys' imaginations. He taught that imperfection resides in all people. Perfection was an aim for all to strive for. The abbot was a man of honor, goodness, wisdom, and above all, kindness. As far as Saburo was concerned, he had none of Mika-geishi's flaws and failings. The abbot proved to be the perfect substitute father.

In their work tunics, the boys joined the novices in making sure the temple was well tended so that after their work was done they could concentrate on spiritual matters. The celibate men in robes spent their earthly days pondering life.

Nin-tai spoke at length about a Zhou Dynasty tenet that was rooted in the teachings of the philosopher called Kōshi, who taught the virtue of filial piety: love, courtesy, respect, obedience, humility, and duty, as well as care and protection of one's elders. Saburo lavished that on the abbot. For Nin-tai's part, in return for Saburo's filial piety, he responded in the manner of Kōshi's teachings by offering fatherly love.

To young Saburo, in many ways the abbot resembled the drawings and statues of the great Kōshi: a wise-looking man, usually depicted with a long, thin white beard and dark, bushy eyebrows. These representations made it easier for the boy to adore the bettō almost to the point that Saburo began to believe that Nin-tai was the living reincarnation of the Zhou Dynasty's greatest philosopher.

The bettō taught that during meditation, enlightenment came after the mind was clear of clutter. *Empty your mind. Think of nothing.*

Saburo eagerly went to sit quietly. He found he could not keep his mind still. No matter how hard he tried, his thoughts raced around, swinging from lesson to lesson, grabbing onto ideas and discarding them, screeching in frustration and confusion. He scolding himself for not succeeding, took a few deep breaths, and tried again. And again he failed.

At the end of the day, Nin-tai asked Saburo if he had any questions.

Saburo burst with despair. "I can't do it. How can I think of nothing? When I think of nothing, I'm thinking about something, and then other things, and it's like my thoughts are running in circles."

Nin-tai surprised Saburo by laughing. "I see you have met Shin-en."

"Shin-en?"

"The monkey everyone has encountered during meditation."

The hurt inside Saburo began to fade, if only because at least he was not alone in this.

Nin-tai said, "The best way to deal with the monkey is to first notice its presence."

Saburo snorted. "That's not hard."

"Then gently bring the mind back to a state of emptiness."

But how was he to do that? He wanted to ask, but the bettō just smiled benevolently and walked on.

Over the next several days, Saburo meditated, this time focusing on noticing the Shin-en. That part was easy. What Saburo struggled with exactly was how to get rid of Shin-en. "I don't know what to do," he confessed to Nin-tai.

The bettō smiled. "That's fine, for doing is not the way. Practice not doing." But that left Saburo with even more thoughts for the monkey to ponder.

As the months passed and the weather turned cold and snows blanketed the mountainsides, Saburo eventually mastered his mind enough to force the monkey out—a shoving contest in the manner of sumo wrestling. And though Saburo privately congratulated himself on this level of mastery, Bettō Nin-tai said that this was not quite to the point. "Emptiness is not the goal, it is but the means. We don't achieve emptiness. Emptiness is what we practice."

"So I should practice pushing Shin-en out so I can get better at it."

The bettō was far too wise to say that Saburo was *wrong*, a word that was hardly ever helpful, but rather that Saburo's approach to enlightenment focused too much on overpowering something. "We seek harmony, not battle. Shin-en loves battle. When you fight, you give the monkey what it wants."

"So you mean, do not fight?"

"Fighting is not emptiness."

"So let the monkey win?" This was the one teaching Saburo could never quite fathom. How by surrendering could he ever win?

These conversations with the bettō became less frequent over time. Saburo learned, if not how to empty his mind, at least how to sit still and wrestle with the monkey in silence. Shin-en had many interesting things to say and ideas to think on, and it did not want to leave until it had its say, which in the end proved unending, and in truth often fascinating. The monkey loved Nin-tai almost as much as Saburo did, for the bettō's teachings introduced the novice to so many ideas. Shin-en and Saburo thrived.

After three years of study at Iwakawa-jiin, having learned to read and to write, Saburo was elevated to first-rank priest, the initial level. He had also learned numbers and to calculate, for first-level priests were responsible for the ōgane that marked the times of day and night, tolling every quarter hour: Bells that called people to prayer. Bells that marked the beginning of the day, midday, and the evening. The passing hours of the night divided into the five watches that ended at dawn. It was the priests who announced the months, and proclaimed the festivals and holy days, and knew in which years and on which moon a thirteenth month had to be added to the lunar cycle to bring the calendar into balance and alignment with the sun.

Saburo and Aka-rui were no longer mere boys. Aka-rui had grown into a large and strong youth, probably resembling his warrior father in size and strength. Handsome, in fact. Aka-rui also had a fiery temper. Saburo never said anything to him about it because Aka-rui never let it get out of control, neither raising a hand nor striking anyone—so far as Saburo knew. Aka-rui turned his temper instead into passion.

As for Saburo, he did not fill out in the way that Aka-rui did, though the two matched each other in stamina and fervency of prayers. As far as the injury to Aka-rui's elbow and Saburo's disfigured eye, no one seemed to notice or care.

Logic would suggest that the son of a mere silk maker would eventually die, while the God-Emperor would not. After all, if a God wasn't immortal, how could He be called God? And yet, in the Second Year of Kyūju, the young Emperor, whose personal name was Narihito, died just six months short of His fourteenth year of reign.

The death of this Emperor would not change Saburo's life—at least that's what Nin-tai said. In the way of things, the death of an Emperor was something to be observed and mourned, and then life went on. Little ever changed in the Imperial City or countryside.

Narihito's older half-brother Masahito ascended to become Emperor. However, there was a dispute about succession. Rival factions within the Imperial family claimed right to the Chrysanthemum Throne. Tensions built over the next year, until the conflict came to arms. Both sides beckoned allies from other clans. Mounted warriors of the different factions filled the roads going to and from Heian-kyō, including the normally quiet highway that passed by Iwakawa-jiin.

Although he admitted it to absolutely no one, especially not to Aka-rui, Saburo admired these men and the lives that they had chosen for themselves. In their magnificent costumes of vivid color, no creature of nature could match them in their lavishness. Armed with naginata, swords, bows, and arrows, they moved in martial magnificence—as did the sōhei, the fractious warrior-monks who numbered in the thousands and who had fluid loyalties.

Battles broke out within the Imperial City. The old Imperial Palace was burned. After a mere nineteen days of fighting, the events that came to be called Hōgen Ran ended, Masahito retained his claim on the throne. And Saburo's life would be changed forever.

THIRTY-TWO
THE IWAKAWA-JIIN INCIDENT

Three days past First Half Moon of Rice-Ear Month
Second Week of Taisho, the Great Heat
First Year of Hōgen
30 July 1156
Iwakawa-jiin

O NE WARM, SUNNY, AND QUIET DAY, a small contingent of sōhei
    arrived at Iwakawa-jiin. A commotion erupted at the gates. The
ōgane boomed in rapid rhythm. *Alarm!* Aka-rui ran through the inner
courtyard, shouting, "Everyone to the front. Help the bettō!"

Saburo immediately set down his calligraphy brush, grabbed his walking stick, and ran toward the front. Nin-tai already stood just outside the
gate, as priests, postulants, and novices folded in behind him. Aka-rui and
Saburo made their way to the front of the assembled as the temple bell's
last toll echoed from the bluffs.

Saburo found himself facing eleven heavily armed warrior-monks who
were irate about something, he was not sure what. They stood no more
than five paces from the bettō, so close that Saburo could smell their rank
sweat. One look at them and Saburo's heart turned into ice. His breath
caught in his throat.

The sōhei stood larger than any of the priests. Most had huge hands
with which they gripped their sword-tipped polearms. Although their tunics were not all that different from those of the priests of Iwakawa-jiin,
they wore mailed cowls and hoods. Only their eyes provided clues as to
their expressions and thus their emotions. It was eerie how their eyes ag-
itatedly darted back and forth as they looked to one another.

Perhaps seeing Saburo's fear, perhaps to reassure, Aka-rui opened his
robes just a little, revealing the leather-wrapped hilt of the short sword

he had brought with him when the two of them had first arrived at the monastery.

Saburo almost gasped.

"Don't be afraid," Aka-rui whispered, flashing Saburo a knowing look.

Nin-tai, who saw nothing of what was happening between the two boys behind him, remained calm, not moving. "Iwakawa-jiin is not a martial order," he said to the warrior-monks. "We do not carry weapons. We aren't interested in proving anything through the force of arms."

"Ha!" said the leader of the "Eleven," as Saburo later came to call these particular men. The leader had a deep voice, as well as a faded scar, likely from a blade lick, that crossed over one eye. "And those hardwood walking sticks?" He thrust his finger at the syncretics. "Are you not armed? That bunch behind you is here to back you up, or are you saying they're here to meditate!"

"These?" Nin-tai swept his arm. "They're unarmed. The walking sticks help the old men and children climb the steep trails in the mountains," he said in a soft but commanding voice. "All we want to do is go back to our prayers. This temple has nothing you want or need. Please leave us to our meditations."

The scarred leader raised his naginata. "*We'll* decide when and where to go, not you, old man." For emphasis, he flicked the naginata, and the blade-sheath flew away, exposing the shining blade. He lowered the polearm and slid into a low stance from which he could strike with speed and power.

"This is too much," Aka-rui hissed and started forward.

"No!" Saburo seized Aka-rui's sleeve, but Aka-rui twisted, and Saburo's fingers lost their grip.

Aka-rui jumped out from the assembled priests. "You've dared speak to the bettō in such a disrespectful way," he shouted. "Apologize now! Prostrate yourselves before the holy man! Immediately!"

The sōhei leader's eyes brightened in amusement, and he laughed wickedly.

Nin-tai put himself between the Eleven and Aka-rui. "Go, Aka-rui," he whispered. "Go. Leave now."

The man with the naginata mocked, "Listen to the *yamazaru* who is certainly *brighter* than you, Baka-rui"—a deliberate mispronunciation of the young priest's name, twisting Aka-rui, *bright*, to mean *common fool*. "An idiot disciple follows a mountain monkey!" The leader laughed, looking at his fellows, who burst into laughter along with him, adding rude simian noises and making monkey-like gestures.

Nin-tai turned and guided Aka-rui away.

The leader of the Eleven muttered, "Shove your walking sticks up your backsides."

Aka-rui looked over his shoulder and pulled open his tunic to reveal the short sword's hilt. "I'll shove this up inside yours, if you like."

"Not a martial order? Ha! Liar!" the scarred man howled. His naginata flashed.

Aka-rui pushed Nin-tai clear. There came a terrible sound as the blade tore flesh and bone. Blood spurted. Aka-rui fell instantly.

Dead.

Never had Saburo seen anyone killed, let alone be cut down in this horrid way. Nin-tai bent over the boy-priest whose white robes were soaked red.

Saburo stood stock-still in horror as the naginata swept again.

Nin-tai fell. His blood flowed and pooled with Aka-rui's.

The temple priests shrieked and shook their walking sticks—and then, as one, all eleven warrior-monks moved their polearms into fighting position.

The deputy abbot, Dayu-suke, turned to the priests and waved his arms over his head. "Everyone hold!"

Though the priests followed his order and did not advance, they continued to raise their staffs and shout angrily at the hooded men, but it was in vain. The Eleven marched right through the gate, shoving aside anyone who got in their way, and swarmed through the temple, throwing open cabinets, ripping down banners, apparently searching for objects of value. But Iwakawa-jiin, though a proud order with roots in both Shintō and Buddhist traditions, was not a temple filled with riches. There were no jade Buddhas or gold shrines to pillage.

The leader shouted, "These mountain monkeys live like monkeys!" And he led his warrior-monks back out the gate and toward the road beyond, leaving the hapless priests to deal with the dead.

THIRTY-THREE
MOURNING

T HE BODIES OF THE BETTŌ and Aka-rui were interred in the graveyard next to the temple, where abbot, priest, and novice alike lay
under tall upright stone pillars, each carved with the name of one of the
deceased. In this sect, unlike the Buddhists, the dead were not given post-
humous names to carry into the afterlife. The Buddhists said *kaimyō*, a
death name, prevented the deceased from being called back from para-
dise by the living whenever the living prayed for the dead. But Nin-tai did
not believe the spirit went away; instead, it went back into all of nature,
to be at one with it forever. Nin-tai had once said, perhaps lightheartedly,
"It might be enjoyable to be called back and see what everyone was doing, even if it was only at O-Bon"—the one celebration festival when the
spirits of the dead ancestors were welcomed to visit the living.

To commemorate the departed spirits, Saburo and some of the other young priests planted a small camphor tree near the grave of Nin-tai.
Camphors were said to grow large and have lifespans of centuries, and
so as long as the tree grew, generations to come would see the priests'
tribute and thereby remember the fallen bettō, even if they never knew
him in life.

Saburo could, of course, pray for the souls of Nin-tai and Aka-rui at
the small memorial tablets within the temple, but he preferred going to
the cemetery to walk out under the tall pines that stretched skyward. He
looked down at Aka-rui's gravestone. The remains of a man he'd called
his friend lay beneath. He felt a singular loss of the bettō. He missed Nin-
tai's insights. All the teachings of the master flowed through Saburo's
mind, the same as the stars in the river of heaven flowed across on their
annual journeys. Some of the bettō's ideas revolved in the young priest's

mind like the constellations, slowly weaving their way through the heavens. Others were quicker, like comets. Still others were immobile, like so many spots of light. Stars immutable.

Every evening, Saburo would stand before the markers, uttering the prayers he was told were correct and proper for the dead of their station—abbot and priest. He tried to feel their spirits soothing his injured heart, but no spirit came within him to do any healing. They simply were dead. Dead and gone.

Not too long after the killings, the deputy bettō, Dayu-suke, took over Nin-tai's duties, and slowly Rock River Temple returned to its routine.

The new bettō? Saburo sighed. While Nin-tai looked like Kōshi, the new bettō, Dayu-suke, resembled Daruma: so round that he almost seemed armless and legless. But worst of all, the new abbot was humorless. Humorless and uninspiring and bland. Dayu-suke droned on about the deaths of Nin-tai and Aka-rui being sad. Regrettable. Terrible. Unfortunate . . . a spring of words that all meant pretty much the same thing: the priests were powerless. The new bettō admonished the priests to accept things as they were. Accept what had happened. Some kind of power outside of themselves had set the world to tumble until it came to this state. Dayu-suke said that prayers would heal, and that, when saying the prayers, everyone should remember those who had died, but above all they should not bring darkness into their hearts.

Saburo was to pray and look for peace in his heart, but it was not long before Saburo saw that in the place where his heart had been there was now a granite stone.

THIRTY-FOUR

THE SWORD

I T WAS NOTICED THAT Aka-rui's short sword had gone missing—the sword that not even Saburo realized Aka-rui had kept. "Hadn't Aka-rui disposed of it once he joined the temple?" And though the blade was of no use to the priests, the mystery of its disappearance piqued their interest. "Did anyone see what happened to it?" The elders and priests searched for the blade but turned up nothing, and in the end, the new bettō concluded that one of the sōhei had probably made off with it as a prize—the only prize from the renegade monks' fruitless raid.

Of course, Saburo knew its whereabouts, though he was not entirely sure why he had taken the sword for himself. During the pillaging of the temple that day, the remaining priests had followed the warrior-monks, pleading with them, explaining that the monastery contained nothing of value, begging them not to destroy what little they had, while the novices had barricaded themselves in the pantry.

In the ensuing chaos, while no one was looking, Saburo had picked up the sword. Knowing he could not get far without being seen with it, and given that the rampaging monks likely would have set upon Saburo for the same reasons as they had set upon Aka-rui, he slipped the sword and scabbard into a crevice beneath the stone-and-wood steps not far from the putrid pools of blood that still soaked the ground. It was at best a temporary hiding place.

During the ensuing all-night prayers and chanting of funerary rites, Saburo snuck back to the main gate to retrieve the weapon. He knew he had to move the sword and scabbard further away from the scene. He got it as far as some fallen pine needles at the fence line. That was all he dared the first night.

Some days after the funerals, he moved it again, this time much further—to an outcropping of rocks in unfrequented woods along the hill behind the temple. Wrapping the scabbarded blade in dark cloth, he placed it deep inside a rocky hollow.

Unlike the gravestones, the blade was something Saburo could keep that was undeniably Aka-rui's. Though his friend's decomposing body was slowly merging with the earth, the sword, like the stars, was immutable. In dark secrecy, Saburo visited the sword, briefly removing it from its hiding place. He marveled at the blade as he pulled it from the scabbard. Like all fine swords, Aka-rui's sword was so perfectly polished, it was mirror-like. Sometimes he saw Shin-en staring blankly back at him from the polished-steel—a mirror both in reality and within his mind. When Saburo wanted to weep, the monkey wept. When Saburo wanted to scream, the monkey screamed. When Saburo gnashed his teeth, the monkey likewise obliged. After a while, the mimicking was replaced with whispers, for the monkey knew in what manner to speak and which words would strike Saburo to the quick, for it saw what was in his heart.

Saburo started to brood over what Aka-rui would have thought of his part during the battle with the Eleven. It was clear his friend had been a hero, while Saburo had stood as still as a stone grave marker. *What about the Eleven? You could kill them*, Shin-en whispered. *Kill allll of them. The* ōryōshi *will be happy that you have done their work for them*, it hissed. *The lawmen will be pleeeased with you. So will the other priests, even though they dare not confess it aloud.*

Saburo went to Nin-tai's headstone to talk to the abbot about the role of revenge in relation to filial piety, but the granite said nothing back. The stone formation in his heart could not converse with the stone of the monument.

Shin-en began to pester Saburo with one question: *Why?*

At first Saburo did not understand. *Why what?* He asked the monkey, but an answer wouldn't come. Finally, after a month went by and Saburo progressively found himself unable to stay asleep, the monkey came to him in a semi-dream and wailed, *Why are the bettō and Aka-rui dead while the renegade monks are still alive? Why?* The monkey screamed woefully, its shrieks so loud they woke Saburo. The sound still pierced the room as he opened his eyes, for it came from his own throat.

THIRTY-FIVE

You Are Taking on Obligations

Eight Bell Strikes, Hour of the Ox
One day past Last Half Moon of Utū Ninth Month
First Year of Hōgen
7 November 1156

Iwakawa-jiin

S ABURO TOOK A DEEP BREATH, feeling the keen agony of loss, but also a liberating relief from releasing what he had held so tightly wrapped around his stone heart. Shima nodded, and they sat in silence by the waning fire for a while.

Finally, Shima said, "What did the authorities do?"

"The ōryōshi were useless. They asked if we'd seen the faces of the attackers. We told them that the Eleven wore cowls. Then the authorities said they would not act, because they did not know who to arrest. But it was obvious the ōryōshi knew exactly who we were talking about."

Shima said, "Ōryōshi are good for handling theft or a raving madman or even a dishonest official, but they won't touch warrior-monks unless it's ordered by the Emperor. The sōhei are their own law. There are thousands of them. Scores of monasteries, all filled with young, armed, and brash holy men. They're not even all that holy."

"I wish I could have done something."

"What would you have done?"

"Aka-rui was brave. He stood up to them."

"And where is Aka-rui now?"

Saburo sighed. "Dead."

Shima raised his brows.

"But I should have done *something*." Saburo felt his voice quavering. "Stood up to the sōhei." He held back sobs.

Shima's voice expressed no emotion, nor did his face have any definite expression. "You are alive. The saké lets you feel what you have kept inside of yourself."

"I should have died." Saburo wiped his eyes with his sleeve. "But I was a coward."

"Oh?" Shima said slow and low. "In warfare, if a unit encounters vastly superior numbers, it does not stand there to be slaughtered or hurl itself against an enemy in a suicide attack."

With questioning eyes, Saburo looked at Shima.

"Stories of fighting to the death were invented to rally fools. Fighting to the last man is futile. A wise commander and wise troops know when to withdraw, regroup, and attack another day. Maybe you have saved yourself for another day?"

Saburo mulled this over. With Nin-tai no longer alive to guide his meditations, leaving him alone to wrestle with Shin-en and the confusion it wrought, perhaps the warrior's wisdom was exactly what Saburo needed right now. "I have something to show you."

He walked only a few paces, reached into the outcropping of rocks, and pulled out a large dark bundle.

"I have this," he said, unwrapping the blanket, exposing the short sword hilt. "This was Aka-rui's." He dropped the blanket and cradled the scabbard between outstretched palms.

Shima looked him in the eye. "You do know that by taking his sword you are taking on obligations."

Saburo felt the weight of the words, though he wasn't sure what Shima was implying.

"Where did he get this?" Shima asked.

"Aka-rui never told me."

"Have you looked?"

Saburo did not understand.

"May I?" Shima put out his arm.

Saburo obliged and Shima received the weapon almost reverently.

"Hmm. Blood stains on the hilt." He pulled the blade from the scabbard, eyeing the cutting edge. He nodded. "Beautiful *sugata*." His finger reverently caressed the angle at the tip. "*Chū-kissaki*. See? Longer than most." He traced a finger along a slightly rippled coloration that ran the length of the blade. "Masterful. Look at this *hamon*. I've seen this style before. Who made this *ko-dachi*?"

Saburo shook his head.

"Time you learn this. I will show you the maker's name."

His hands unusually steady for someone who had drunk so much saké, Shima took a small tool from his sleeve and proceeded to knock out two round pegs that up to that point Saburo had thought were merely ornamental. In a moment, he pulled the hilt away, exposing the tang. Shima turned the tang against the light, revealing two kanji engraved in the metal. "Arinari." Shima looked up, eyes twinkling. "Swordmaker to the Imperial House. Your friend, Aka-rui, was likely more than he seemed."

"He said his father was a warrior."

"Well, if this belonged to him, he was no ordinary warrior. You think Aka-rui was a thief?"

Saburo shook his head, wanting it not to be so.

In moments, Shima reassembled the blade and handed the weapon back to Saburo. Unsure what to do with it, he rewrapped it in the blanket.

"Is there a place I can sleep?" Shima asked. "My head's spinning."

"Mine too," said Saburo, though he was sure it was not from the saké, for the information about the sword, the ko-dachi, Shima had called it, revealed a new beauty to him. In his hands, he felt a power coming from the sword wrapped in its blanket. Was he feeling the warrior's soul? Or was it just the saké inspiring ruminations of fancy?

Shima hefted his chest protector and weapons. Saburo picked up Shima's shin and sleeve guards and led him into the temple, back to a sleeping alcove offered to guests.

Shima said, "I like you, Gun-kun. You have Yamato spirit." He sat down on the bedding. "I'm drunk, but not so drunk I don't know what I am saying. You get seasick easily, Gun-kun?"

Saburo shook his head.

"Experienced sailor, are you?"

"Never been on a boat."

Shima laughed. "Buzen is the Ōuchi stronghold and the only way to get there is to cross either the Barrier Strait or the Bungo Strait. The Ōuchi control the eastern half of Nagato. The Ōe rules over the western half and the two clans are skirmishing for the middle."

"I didn't know that."

"No one's supposed to know, or the Emperor would send troops, and neither side wants that. But the Ōuchi do want to increase their skills. That's why they are looking for an Assistant Chief of Weapons. I intend to become that man."

"Why not the Chief Instructor of Weapons instead of Assistant?"

"The Chief Instructor's eyesight's deteriorating." Shima moved the palm of his hand over his eyes like a veil. "Cloudy eyes. They say his mind's still sharp, but—" Shima broke off.

"If he can't see, why does the daimyō keep him?"

"The daimyō is a wise old man. Knows not to strip a retainer of dignity. Wise, and maybe a bit sentimental." Shima grew cheerful. "The Assistant Instructor of Weapons can have an assistant. That person is responsible for keeping the training hall in order. This means putting away weapons, polishing the floors, and generally doing as he's told." Shima looked up. "Interested?"

Saburo broke into a grin. "Yes!"

"Tomorrow, I'm leaving. If you want to come with me, you can. Then you, too, can learn to be a warrior."

Saburo gasped. Was this possible?

"Now," said Shima with a wave of the hand, "let me sleep this off. I've got to be on the road in the morning, early." He rolled over, his face down, and mumbled, "Oh, and bring your ko-dachi with you. You'll need it."

Saburo practically walked on air as he found his sleeping roll. Had Shima been there the day the bettō fell, the Eleven would also have fallen—and quickly. Maybe the warrior-monks would have been killed before they could hurt anyone. Saburo pictured himself in armor and with a sword, cutting down the sōhei. He even imagined a look of gratitude shining in the faces of Nin-tai and Aka-rui, who would owe Saburo their lives.

Saburo, too, could master weapons and bring justice where no one else had—not the priests, not the ōryōshi, not anyone. All the priestly vows and all of what he had once held sacred ceased to hold any sway.

With the windows open, the forest smells became more intense. Saburo still recalled Shima's scent. His sweat was not at all rancid, but pleasing. Everything about the man was something that Saburo suddenly came to desperately admire. He would follow Shima to wherever that would lead.

Thirty-Six
It's All War

Full Moon of Gods Month
29 November 1156
Ōuchi Compound, Buzen Prefecture, Isle of Unknown Fires

SEVENTEEN DAYS AFTER THEIR DEPARTURE from the monastery, Shima and Saburo crossed the Bungo Strait and docked at the rocky eastern shores of the Isle of Unknown Fires. From there they followed the Upland Road for another four days. The road took them along the coast of Bungo Prefecture and then into the foothills of Buzen Prefecture. On the early afternoon of the Full Moon of the Little Snow, the Ōuchi compound finally loomed in the distance.

"This must be as grand as the Emperor's palace." Saburo marveled at what he saw in every direction.

Shima laughed loudly. "Hardly. The Emperor's attendants live in buildings bigger than any of these estate houses. His palace is the size of this entire complex. Look close. Despite its ornateness—never forget—we are in a military compound."

Shima announced himself at the gates to guards who seemed to be expecting him. "This is my hand-man," Shima told them, and the guards bade them both to wait.

Everyone in sight, save for Shima and Saburo, wore the fire flower insigne, the hanabishi. Saburo was not familiar with clan mon, but he soon realized that his simple tunic with no emblem at all did not impress the sentries, while there was no question they noticed Shima's chrysanthemum mon of the Imperial House and were duly impressed.

It wasn't long before a seemingly important man in courtly robes arrived and instructed them to follow. Shima followed a stride behind, looking lordly in his battle gear. Saburo trailed them both. Once inside the gates, Saburo started to appreciate the nature of the compound. He had never seen so many military men in his life. He tried to take in everything, but comprehended little of how it all fit together.

As they crossed the central yard, Shima said so only Saburo could hear, "This is where it will be, Gun-kun. There." He pointed to an outdoor dais. "Tomorrow the warlord will sit there, surrounded by his generals and his personal bodyguards. Any one of his bodyguards is worth thirty regular warriors."

"Why will they all be there?"

"To test me."

They were shown to a chamber near a training area where they were to rest and eat. Saburo noticed how quiet Shima had become. Was he meditating?

Of course he is, whispered Shin-en inside Saburo's skull. As Shima continued to sit quietly, Shin-en filled Saburo's head with grand plans to become a warrior. *You will learn how to kill. You will be strong. You will be able to kill the Eleven.* Saburo tried not to listen, but he could feel truth in Shin-en's words, and it made him both sickened and excited. Troubled dreams visited Saburo that night, but the next morning he could remember none of them.

Late in the morning, just before the Hour of the Horse, Shima strode to the middle of the central courtyard and bowed before the assembled. The daimyō, in the most elegant kimono, sat at the dais, flanked by six men wearing dark robes and grim faces. Another twenty men in armor, likely the royal bodyguard, extended out on either side.

The appearance was daunting, and Saburo immediately worried that Shima might be outmatched. And unlike when they had first met, at dusk at the monastery, when the sun had given Shima the advantage, Amaterasu now stood high overhead. Under cold clear skies, no one would have the advantage.

Nine bells sounded, and a tough-looking warrior pulled his sword with menace, approached Shima, and struck. Without any words, the test began in earnest. Three quick moves—strike-parry-counter-strike—and the opponent stopped and bowed, admitting defeat. One after the other, three more opponents engaged Shima in single combat.

The challenges quickly grew more complex, and Saburo's concerns for Shima's welfare were forever dispelled. Ōuchi warriors set upon Shima from all sides in a series of mock battles and skirmishes. Barely holding back, multiple opponents rushed Shima with a variety of weapons. On foot, he had to unhorse and defeat samurai who tried to run him down while they swung naginata. Bowmen shot volleys at Shima, but before the arrows could reach him, he cut them mid-flight with his blade. Barehanded, he grappled with and disarmed oncoming attackers. The attacks came in wave after wave, and while the attackers themselves were allowed to rest before re-entering the fray, Shima had to defend without respite.

Finally, eight bells sounded. Lord Ōuchi raised his war fan, and everything came to an abrupt stop.

Shima, drenched in sweat, stood in the center of the yard, undefeated. The Ōuchi he had fought stood along the yard's perimeter, near the warlord. The retinue now looked to one another, nodding slightly in acknowledgment. Shima had carried the day.

More than satisfied, the daimyō made a speech and, as Shima recovered, catching his breath, redness leaving his cheeks, appointed him the clan's Assistant Instructor of Weapons. Then Shima was dismissed.

Saburo accompanied Shima to his quarters. "I thought they were trying to kill you," Saburo blurted, once they were out of earshot.

Shima sipped water, for if he drank as much as he actually desired, it might have killed him. "Ah!" he rasped, then swallowed another small amount. "They would have liked to," he said, wiping his mouth with his sleeve. "They are suspicious and resent outsiders. They won't accept just anyone. These fellows are at war and it's a serious business with them."

"War?"

"Every clan that holds territory is always at war. Whether they're fighting or ready to fight. It's all war."

Thirty-Seven

The Third Kind of Student

I N TRUTH, SHIMA DID NOT WANT a servant as much as he wanted a worthy student. He knew the ways of young men and had grasped the secret longings in the youthful priest's heart the night they first met, and so it wasn't before long that Shima let his "servant" take a place among those training—provided Gun-kun finished all the physical work in the studio.

This suited Saburo perfectly. Not being an Ōuchi retainer, he had no other official duties or outside obligations taking him away from the training hall. This enabled him to practice from the Hour of the Rabbit to the Hour of the Bird, studying sedulously for a year, then two, then three.

To Saburo, the training represented a confluence of disciplines. One priestly, the other martial, they flowed into a unitary emotion within. As Nin-tai had instructed Saburo in meditation to empty the mind, Shima concentrated on the body; and meditation, if it could be called that, came about only as the body was pushed to exhaustion.

In fact, Shima's training proved more demanding. The mind of a student-priest might wander during meditation, and back at Iwakawa-jiin, who among the instruction leaders truly knew if a student's meditations were going well or not? If a priest noticed a novice beginning to slouch, the wandering mind was brought back by a gentle touch on the student's shoulder. But under Shima's sharp eye, lapses of concentration were more easily recognized. An initial mistake earned a smart rap by *bokken* to the wrist, the hand, the thigh, the rib, the shin, or chest, reminding the student where an enemy's blow would have landed. Repeated bruising piled up for repeated mistakes. Shima would thunder, "You think *this* is terrible! Wait until you meet a man who actually wants to hurt you! If you should survive, you'll return and you'll grovel at my feet to thank me for my loving harshness."

In theory, broken bones would result from incessant mistakes, but it never came to that. The daimyō insisted students were to be dismissed before they were seriously injured. He could not afford to have his subjects perishing in the training halls—especially not the young royal ones.

For Shima, this was the source of his greatest frustration. In private, he confessed to Saburo his displeasure with the laxness toward the highborn students, and explained how there were three kinds of students. The first kind, the unschooled ones, attended to find glory, or status, or to inspire fear, or simply because royal duty demanded it, for the destiny of the students, particularly the younger ones, was to become Ōuchi warlords or generals. Under his tutelage, they faced grueling physical training and thereby attained a singular sort of enlightenment. He would tell them, "There is skill and there is will. Both are needed. Just one won't do." Did the students possess an inner desire? If not, such students soon fell by the wayside.

But what gave Shima the most satisfaction was the second type of student, who emerged from the first type. Like hammering strength and flexibility in a sword's tempered line, Shima worked their bodies to the peak of fighting skills that became instinctual—as reflexive as pulling a hand away from hot steel. And it pleased him to watch over three years how Saburo became an exceptional example of this second kind of student. At almost eighteen summers, Saburo had become strong and well built, skilled, and filled with resolve. In fact, his natural youthful strength and dexterity would never be greater.

But most prized of all by Shima was the third kind of student—the grizzled ones, dark of eye, who stood ready to kill anyone at any moment, and could move their swords faster than a blink. The masters. Ones like himself. Shima could see that, in practice with the weapons, with every stroke, and with every move, Saburo was picturing how he would deliver a blow to each one of the Eleven. It became clear how close he was to becoming the third type of student. Armed with Aka-rui's sword, Saburo was on an inner journey that Shima would have to watch as an outsider. The final test had yet to come.

Thirty-Eight
The Zodiac

DURING HIS THREE YEARS in Buzen Prefecture, Saburo uncovered a great deal of information about the warrior-monks who had killed Nin-tai and Aka-rui. It turned out they were not monks at all, but had risen up from being low-level enforcers, likely *hinin*, the bottom of the social order. Their group was known as the Zodiac, and they were notorious.

Originally there had been twelve of them, and each man had taken delight in adopting the name of an astrological beast: Dragon, Viper, Stallion, Ram, Monkey, Hawk, Wolf, Wild Boar, Rat, Ox, Tiger, and Rabbit. How or why they decided on these names—either through birth year, by lot, or by other means—was not exactly clear, but it was known that Ram had died sometime early on, just before their murderous raid on Iwakawa-jiin.

Actually, their names did not precisely match astrological beasts; they were embellished to live up to the men's grand senses of self. For example, the one who should have gone by the sign of the dog called himself Wolf. Horse became Stallion, snake became Viper, and sheep became Ram. Even mouse became Rat. Alas, poor Rabbit—not much could be done with that name, though those born in the Year of the Rabbit were said to possess good qualities. The man named Rabbit, like many born under that sign, had the qualities of an artist, and it was because of his skill with colored inks and the needle that all of the Zodiac had ended up with beautiful designs scratched into their skins—*irezumi*—at least so it was said.

Criminals were often marked with ink on skin so that the innocent and all law officers would know with what and whom they dealt—a petty thief, a swindler, someone who had maimed, molested, or whatever.

The list of offenses was long. Each offense resulted in a mark. And those who had run afoul of the law would hide the incriminating marks, for five marks usually earned a death sentence, regardless of the severity of the crimes. In defiance, some criminals embellished the marks with additional inking and made a show out of them, holding them up high and proud and thereby intimidating the meek. Throughout the land, drawing pictures on the skin became a sign of a certain kind of manliness and beauty.

And this is what the Zodiac were said to have done, though because of the sōhei robes they usually wore, only hints of the body art had been observed.

Initially, when the Zodiac had first gathered as a group, they had been welcomed by many of the common people—mainly because one of their first orders of business had been to depose a gang of small-time thieves. The grateful populace had praised the apparent monks for their great act of courage. But soon the commoners discovered that these warrior-monks were harsher and more capricious than the former gang had ever been.

As a result, the Zodiac tended never to stay too long anywhere. They were constantly on the move, stopping at local settlements to demand "holy offerings" that were little more than extortions. Since no one dared withhold a religious offering to armed sōhei, the farmers could not exactly claim that they had been robbed. As such, the Zodiac, despite their colorful irezumi that suggested criminal pasts, were never accused of any crimes, let alone brought to justice. It was easier for the authorities to just look the other way.

It would take someone else to right the wrongs of the Eleven.

And that's how Saburo came to decide that he would die in the First Year of Heiji, seven nights after the autumnal equinox, on the Full Moon of Leaf Month, placing his death on the seventh night of the sixteenth solar stem of the Year of the Earth Rabbit—just days before Kanro, the time of dew, the time of tears. A fitting time to leave the earth. All the astrological indications pointed to it being a particularly auspicious day— that and the fact that Saburo knew where the Eleven would be that night. They would be in the mountains of Nagato. In Ōuchi territory. At an isolated shrine temple.

From rumors and random tales—of which there were plenty, for wherever the renegade monks went they left mayhem in their wake—Saburo, with the help of Shima, had pieced together the Zodiac's cyclical travel patterns. For the past three years, during Shūbun, the Eleven had lodged at the Yawara-kaikaze-gū. Perhaps they liked its name, Soft Breeze Shrine. Perhaps they found security in the rugged rock terrain of the Chūgoku Mountains. Most likely, one of the men was from the area and had suggested the shrine as a pleasant location high above the heat and far from the eyes of ōryōshi. It was especially convenient that the Ōuchi held influence over the area—no frontiers to cross.

Saburo announced to Shima that he would travel to the temple and, under Full Moon's light, kill as many Zodiac as possible, though undoubtedly it meant dying in the process.

Shima was not even slightly surprised at Saburo's readiness to go to his own death. In fact, he agreed. The time had come. But Shima's reasons had nothing to do with knowing where the Zodiac would lodge. He had watched how Saburo's desire to settle scores had not slackened. If anything, it had hardened. And Shima understood that further training, without experience, would become a student's undoing—just as continually polishing the same edge of a fine sword over and over eventually led to dullness. Even the hardest steel that ran along the outer cutting edge would eventually wear away. Though sharp, an over-polished blade was soft and would not endure many blows before breaking.

Short of actual combat, Saburo was as sharp, hard, and as ready as he ever would be. And Shima knew that it was better to die in battle than to live with a festering heart.

THIRTY-NINE
TO DEFILE A HOLY PLACE

Full Moon of Leaf Month
Seventh Night of Shūbun
First Year of Heiji, Year of the Earth Rabbit
29 September 1159
Soft Breeze Shrine, Suō Prefecture, Main Isle

UNDER THE BRIGHT GLOW of the Full Moon, walking by himself, Saburo arrived at Soft Breeze Shrine.

Shima had offered to accompany him into battle with the Eleven, but this was something Saburo had to do himself. "I must kill them," he had replied. "For others to do it would deprive me of the satisfaction." And so Shima waited below with the horses.

The shrine itself was located up a steep crag, cradled amidst a natural ring of enormous stone pillars—a veritable fortress that could be reached only by trekking up a long series of very steep steps carved out of a sheer cliff. Once near the top, the path wound its way around boulders taller than three men.

At first Saburo heard nothing but insects and the rustle of wind through the trees, but as he worked his way through the ring of granite, raucous singing reached his ears. Bawdy songs. The shrine's priest no doubt had run away.

The shrine itself was quite small—one building that served as shrine and dwelling for the priest. It stood unguarded. No sentry. Likely the Eleven were confident. Anyone approaching enemies would have to take the steep rock path and come in single file.

Saburo's tachi and Aka-rui's short sword were sharp, polished, and pristine. He did not wear armor, just a simple-looking riding kimono and hakama chosen for him by Shima from among the Ōuchi martial

gear—but which was specially designed for assassinations. Though
it looked ordinary enough, the kimono had inner sleeves with clever-
ly sewn-in pouches for weapons. Four *tantō* daggers and two throwing
stars were tucked away. He gave one last check of the inner flaps to make
sure that they were properly folded back. The weapons had to easily slip
into his grasp when the moment came. There would be no allowance for
fumbling.

He had rehearsed the battle countless times at the Ōuchi Compound,
but in training he knew his opponents, fellow students who played the
parts of the Eleven, so he always had a pretty good idea where they
would be sitting, and their combat skills, along with their favorite tricks.
But this would be different. He had no idea of what he'd find, no way
to know how matters would unfold, except that the Eleven were experienced killers, and that once engaged in a fight, they never held back. The
only important question was how many of the eleven men he would take
down before he himself fell.

*Is there a life after, or is that merely a story we tell ourselves to push away
the anguish of death?* If there was a life after, then he'd find out. If there
wasn't, then there was nothing to worry about.

Saburo uttered his final prayers, certain that he would not emerge alive.
Three years of preparations would end in this rocky arena with walls so
high that they all but blocked the glow of the Full Moon. After Nin-tai's
and Aka-rui's deaths, he had pictured his own tall stone grave post in the
burial ground somewhere near theirs. But likely when people found his
body here—*if* they found his body—no one would know who he was.
No name would be inscribed in stone. His grave marker—whether his
name was inscribed there or not, whether his body was buried or left for
the scavengers—would be the high stone pillars surrounding him now.

Fitting that they were so tall. An Emperor could not wish for a more
grand memorial, though Masahito's name would at least be remembered.
His would not.

He huffed with amusement at this thought. Strange that at a moment
like this he could feel amused.

The singing, laughing, and carousing continued unabated from inside.
Saburo adjusted the eyepatch, took a long, deep breath of fresh autumn
air, and walked through the dark red uprights and crosspieces of the *torii*

gate. He was crossing from the profane to the sacred. But what he planned to do to the men inside was anything but sacred.

I will now defile a holy place.

Saburo paused before the doors of the shrine that were guarded by a pair of stone-carved lion-dogs, their granite mouths cut into perpetual snarls, their fangs and hungry tongues showing. He gazed into their frozen stone eyes that returned only their terrifying countenance. Was he, too, like one of them now? A granite lion-dog.

His mouth was dry. He had looked forward to the ritual of clearing his mouth out with water before entering the shrine, but the chōzubachi by the entry door was empty. Without the actual priest around, who would fill it? Obviously none of these "spiritual" men. But that did not matter now. As soon as the door opened, he would strike.

My last night on earth.

His heart beat so hard that his ears throbbed. Saburo raised his hands to announce to the Gods he was coming into the shrine. And if the Gods stayed to watch, what wouldn't they witness now?

He clapped his hands together.

Forty

In the Pure Land,
They Await Us

T HE MIRTH INSIDE THE SHRINE suddenly died down.

"See who that is!" a voice growled from inside.

Dragon!

The shrine door opened. A man with a shaven head, reeking of saké, and wearing nothing but a loincloth, snarled, "What?"

Saburo stood frozen, gazing at the unexpected sight. Never had he seen anything like the drawing that decorated the man's body. From abdomen to chest, a giant white snake illustration coiled, ready to strike—mouth open, fangs bared, yellow eyes with slit-like black pupils staring straight at Saburo. There was no question as to which of the Eleven this man was. Viper.

"What do you want?" Viper hissed.

Before Saburo could answer, a voice from inside said, "Send him away."

Another said, "See if he has anything worth taking."

"Does he have saké?"

Viper turned his attention back into the shrine. "He doesn't look like much to me." Saburo knew he should strike now, but something held him back.

Yet another voice said, "See if he has any money on him."

Viper turned back. "You have any money?"

Slowly Saburo reached into his sleeve pocket and produced a gold coin.

Viper's ink snake had yellow eyes, but his own eyes were red—bloodshot—and now they grew round. "He's got gold."

Another man joined him at the entry. Wolf. On his naked body was inked a black wolf, ferocious, baring yellow teeth. Its lower legs stretched down the man's thighs, while the top of the beast's head ended just below the man's neck. But it was Wolf's *chinko* that was most remarkable: where the organ belonged on the wolf was the man's own; and as the man moved, it moved. Wolf smiled slyly. "See something you like?"

It was probably not the first time anyone had stared. After all, wasn't that the purpose? But Viper laughed as though he'd never before heard that jest.

Wolf leered at Saburo, looking him up and down. "That sword, where'd ya get it?"

"Took it off the dead," Saburo said measuredly, and added, in a commoner's mode of speaking, "Dead don't need swords."

For the first time, he sensed everyone inside fall quiet.

"Open the door wider," a deep voice said.

Viper pushed the door aside, revealing a small room brightly lit with several braziers. Saburo quickly surveyed the scene. High ceilings without low lintels. Long swords would work in there—but the Eleven's naginata were too long.

He took a step forward. Viper backed away. Saburo stopped just inside the shrine and looked around.

All the men had shaved heads and were either naked or stripped to their fundoshi. Saburo's presence didn't seem to bother them one bit.

Though it had been Saburo's intent to immediately start killing, there was something enthralling about being in this room with these men in all their naked glory. For the first time, he saw them not as eleven phantasms, not as eleven anonymous figures, all alike, hooded, with eleven pairs of eyes and eleven polearms, mighty warrior-monks who had killed Nin-tai and Aka-rui before disappearing in billowing celestial mists.

Now they were merely men, with real bodies.

Bodies that could break.

Bodies that could bleed.

His gaze paused on a man sitting on the floor near the front.

An emerald green dragon decorated his body, scales outlined in orange, its head poised on the man's right breast. Its arched razorback body spanned his chest, and its long tail slithered down his left arm. The eyes were red as rubies. Its mouth hung open, revealing a burnt-orange tongue. If the illustration wasn't enough, the man's facial scar skipping from forehead to cheek confirmed his identity: Dragon, the murderer of Nin-tai and Aka-rui.

He would die first.

Dragon asked in his resonant voice, "Where'd you get the coin?"

"Stole it," Saburo said calmly.

"Pickpocket?"

Saburo shrugged. "Maybe." He took a deep breath. "And maybe not."

"He talks in riddles, this one," said someone else.

Saburo looked at the man who spoke—a reedy man toward the back, needle in hand, his torso inked with a dagger-toothed rabbit that probably did not look as menacing as intended. What rabbit could?

Rabbit refocused his attention on stippling an ox image on the back of a man as big as an ox who studied Saburo while trying not to grimace from Rabbit's needle.

Closer to Saburo squatted Tiger, Rat, Monkey, and Hawk—each identified by his own irezumi—around a dice cup, cloth, and heaps of coins. The four of them appeared quite drunk, but their weapons lay next to them on the floor, within easy reach.

Tiger rattled the bones inside the dice cup, softly laughing, as if he were encouraging the dice to do his bidding. His tiger body art showed the most perfect golden-yellow coat with coal-black stripes, its tongue licking one paw, its back haunches high, gazing at him with innocent eyes.

The drawing of the rat held unsavory eyes, identical to Rat's own, which he kept trained on the dice cup as though Tiger's laughter was influencing the rolls.

The monkey's smile was as much a vicious sneer as it was anything as its hands stretched out, ready to grab. Monkey himself concentrated on the upcoming dice throw, paying no attention to the lone man at the door.

Hawk shot a quick look over his shoulder at Saburo before going back to the fascination of the game, but the inked hawk on his back seemed to glare at him.

The last two of the eleven men, Wild Boar and Stallion, lay passed out in each other's arms amidst empty saké flasks along the south wall of the shrine. The illustrated wild boar seemed poised to leap off Wild Boar's back as the man snored. His head rested on Stallion's shoulder, obscuring all but the horse's head.

Saburo had caught them mostly unprepared. But as the tension of the moment grew, he relished the increasing calm he felt.

"Why are you here? So we can rob you?" asked Rat. He feigned a laugh. Others joined in with forced laughs without humor.

"Maybe I've come to join you," Saburo said.

"You? Join us?" Some of them snickered.

"Yes. I've been looking for you for some time now."

They fell silent. Dragon cast a sideways glance at his own sword. Tiger squinted intently at Saburo, perhaps wondering if there was something familiar in the stranger.

Viper stepped close to Saburo's side, and Saburo could sense Wolf somewhere behind him.

Dragon said, "Looking for some time?"

"I'd like to be one of you."

"Pah!" Viper spat.

"One of us?" Wolf growled. Saburo half-turned his head to see Wolf leering at his body. "Not much to look at."

"We're holy men," Monkey said with a sneer, dice cup in his hand. "What'd you know about a monk's life?"

Saburo's voice took on a hard edge. "I have as much religion as any of you."

"You want to join us?" said Hawk, turning to regard him with his own eyes. "Come on over here and drink some saké and get to know us better. Have a little fun, and depending on how you do, we might consider whether you can join us."

"Yes," said Wolf, standing very close, his daikon thick and twitching.

Saburo said, "You're all holy men. Warrior-monks. So am I."

"Humph," Rat grunted.

"You have to prove yourself," said Hawk.

"Let's hear a sutra," Dragon said, eyes narrowed.

Saburo turned his head, speaking to all of them.

> Let all vows be attained
> So the universe can be rocked in ecstasy
> And release the heavenly beings
> To fall to earth like blessed rain.

Rat looked at Tiger and muttered, "Pure Land prayer."

Tiger nodded once, hard.

"Probably all he knows," said Wolf. "Memorized it just for the occasion."

"More than you've memorized," Rat sneered.

Eyes fixed on Saburo, Dragon said, "Recite Buddha Flowers."

Saburo held his gaze.

> *Bring flowers so all the Buddhas*
> *May return to their origins*
> *Though far away, their compassion flows*
> *Pray for those already there*
> *In the Pure Land, they await us.*

"A prayer for the dead," Rat said softly.

Tiger nodded. "That's not a common one."

"Ha!" Monkey shouted—but not about what Rat said. He scooped up winnings from a dice roll.

"Ahh!" Hawk moaned, not happy.

"What's your name, upstart?" Ox demanded.

Saburo restrained a grin and said in a quiet voice, "You could call me Ram."

Several of the men flinched. "RAM?" Ox growled. "Ram's dead! Killed in battle."

"But isn't Ram the twelfth?" Saburo asked, feigning innocence. "The missing member?"

Wolf pointed down at his exposed manhood. "No members missing here."

The room erupted with laughter. Saburo regarded them with utter calm, even as anticipation built within. "You don't remember me."

Tiger sneered. "Remember you? Pah! Who'd remember you?" He shook the dice cup.

Saburo said, a quiet edge to his voice, "I was younger then."

"Weren't we all," Wolf said, laughing.

Hawk quipped, "Back when your daikon could still get hard."

"Ahh! Hard enough." Wolf faced Hawk, turning his back to Saburo. "Just come over here and I'll show you what I can still do. I'll have you screaming like a maid."

Everyone broke into laughter. Even Saburo grinned. But the calm within him was threatening to burst. He realized he had lingered too long. Already their guard was up from when he had first arrived. He reached into his tunic sleeve.

"What? More gold?" Everyone laughed.

Saburo's hand shot from his sleeve. A flash—something glimmering flew across the room.

Dragon screamed, a throwing star lodged in his eye.

Stepping forward, Saburo spun, drew his tachi and struck one-two. Viper and Wolf collapsed, blood surging from gashes in their bellies.

Ox and Rabbit fumbled. Dragon writhed, clutching at his eyes. Tiger and Rat reached for their swords.

In one smooth motion, Saburo pulled and threw a knife. It struck Rat in the chest. Rat pulled the dagger free—a mistake. His blood gushed from the wound and his knees buckled.

Tiger rose to his feet, sword in hand. Saburo let fly a second tantō, hitting Tiger in the neck. Blood spurted everywhere as he fell forward onto the dice game, splaying across Monkey and Hawk's swords even as they tried to draw them.

Saburo leapt forward, and with two quick strokes he cut Monkey and Hawk down. They toppled onto the other bodies.

Eyes wild with rage, Ox shrugged off Rabbit, yanked his blade out of its saya, and lumbered toward Saburo. But the pile of the four fallen gamblers blocked his way, and he had to stumble around them.

A roar came from behind.

Saburo without looking thrust his blade back and into the belly of someone—Wild Boar, who gagged, coughed blood, and crumpled to the side, landing on Stallion's head, waking him from his stupor.

Saburo shuffle-stepped and brought his blade down hard onto Stallion's torso, which erupted with blood.

From his other flank, now clear of the piled bodies, Ox and Rabbit approached quickly.

Saburo tried to bring his sword up to defend, but his blade had wedged into Stallion's ribs. He released it and threw his third dagger hard. It hit right between the ox eyes on Ox's chest. Blood coursed out around the hilt. Eyes vacant, Ox staggered and twisted as he fell.

Rabbit, true to his name, quickly and nimbly leapt onto the pile of bodies, ready to pounce. The fourth and final dagger flew from Saburo's hand, but Rabbit parried it, sending it uselessly into the ceiling, and lunged at him, sword swinging across.

Saburo dropped, rolling to the side to avoid the strike.

Rabbit spun and lunged again at him.

Hand scrambling, Saburo grasped a fallen sword and brought it up just in time to point the blade into Rabbit's belly. Under Rabbit's falling weight, the hilt ripped from Saburo's hand and jammed against the floor, driving the blade even deeper into Rabbit, spearing him. Blood spewed out of his mouth. Saburo shoved him to the side, toppling him over, and rolled to his feet.

Ten men down.

The only one remaining was Dragon who stumbled about, blinded by the throwing star and the blood gushing from his face.

Calmly, hands empty, Saburo walked up to him. "You remember Abbott Nin-tai! You remember priest Aka-rui?"

Crying in pain, Dragon waved his sword blindly.

Saburo pulled Aka-rui's sword from its saya. As Dragon swung, Saburo brought the short blade hard across the man's shoulder. The arm inked with the dragon's tail fell from its body, hand still clasping the sword.

Saburo's second strike severed the man's neck. Dragon's head fell with a thunk. His body, spraying blood from the neck, crashed to the floor.

Stillness fell over the shrine.

Saburo listened. Four men moaned.

With Aka-rui's sword, Saburo went to each of the fallen and methodically plunged his friend's blade into them one final time.

When he came back to Dragon's headless body, Saburo raised up the sword and drove it down hard, point first, clear through Dragon's chest and into the plank floor underneath.

He left it there.

The silence now truly was profound.

He stood, gazing at the carnage. He himself was uninjured. The blood that covered him was not his own. The trove of Zodiac coins were scattered everywhere, covered in gore. The stench of sliced-open bodies and released bowels filled the room.

Using his foot to apply leverage, he extracted his tachi from Stallion's chest. With a discarded robe he wiped the blade clean and sheathed it, then walked to the open door, leaving the throwing daggers, throwing stars, and Aka-rui's sword with the dead.

As he stepped into the chill of the autumn night, Saburo realized he was soaked not just with blood but his own sweat. From the porch that circumscribed the shrine, he took one last look into the building filled with dead men.

As he made his way out of the rim rock, the Full Moon once again shone down upon him. A breeze stirred the leafless trees. A nearby owl hooted, bringing luck and announcing death.

Saburo descended the stone steps.

He took three deep breaths.

And then broke into a run.

He sprinted back down the road by which he came. He ran as hard as he ever had in his entire life. He ran until he came to the place in the woods where Shima waited with Raiden and Gaki, their mounts.

The two men stared at each other. Shima asked, "Did it feel good?"

FORTY-ONE

MALE COLORS

THE TWO MEN STOOD facing each other, both knowing that everything had now changed.

Shima asked, "All dead?"

Saburo nodded hard, completely out of breath, yet not feeling even slightly tired. If anything he felt giddy . . . and dazed . . . and elated. "It happened so fast."

"But you remember it," said Shima. "Not a blur?"

"I remember it perfectly," Saburo said to his own surprise.

"One thing moving to the next?" Shima nodded. "Like a dance?"

"Hai. Like a wild dance."

"And no fear?"

"No. Not once it started." Saburo shook his head. "I was never so *alive*."

"You're a man now." Shima's voice was silky, his smile both humorous and wicked. "Let's celebrate with saké." He retrieved an ample flask from a saddlebag. Without ceremony, he pulled open the stopper and swigged directly from it, then wiped his mouth with his sleeve. He handed the saké to Saburo, who drank and drank and drank in a series of long gulps, like a man who had been without water for days.

"Strong," Saburo gasped as he came up for breath, then belched. He laughed at himself.

Shima's eyes twinkled boyishly. "You did it," he said, putting his arm over Saburo's shoulder, touching Saburo tenderly perhaps for the first time ever, and pulled him close. Standing side by side, he said, "You're a man."

Saburo began to grow hard. He turned his head, letting go of the empty saké flask, which tumbled to the ground and rolled away. He took a prolonged look at Shima, and he turned fully him so that now the two men faced each other.

The moonlight made it all bewitching. As the owl started hooting, Saburo put his own arms around the taller man. Shima put his other arm around Saburo's back. The men each let out a sigh, embracing slow and hard.

There was a long moment of silence, punctuated by only their breathing.

And though the mouth was considered a vile and unclean thing, Saburo had drunk from the same bottle. He could smell the saké on Shima's breath. His sweat. He felt himself grow even harder. He had thought his heart had been beating fast during the battle, yet now it beat as hard as ever. He reached up to caress Shima's cheek. "I'm sorry. I smell of blood . . . all over my clothes."

"Then you should get out of them," Shima said. "I'll join you."

Efficiently, yet unhurriedly, they removed their kimono. Saburo looked at Shima's more massive body. Broad and solid like a bear.

Shima likewise allowed his gaze to linger on Saburo, the well-formed young man whose physicality was at its peak.

They looked into each other's faces, the two men, like two virile moons under the real moon's glow.

"Do you want to do this?" Shima whispered, his voice slightly hoarse.

"Yes."

Indeed, Shima's daikon was large. Saburo let out a sigh, a gasp, and without any real effort lifted Shima off the ground.

Shima gave forth a deep laugh. "You're much stronger than you look."

"I'm a lot more things than you know."

The men demonstrated their strength in crushing embraces, wrestling each other in a sensual way. Hard caresses and scratches that did not break the skin. Slapping and hitting that left no bruises, marks, or damage. It did not matter that Saburo was the smaller of the two. He hefted the sword master and pressed him against his body, jumping on top of him, and with sheer strength pushing him down.

Saburo was aware that physical love, *nandō*, was well-known among warriors and had its own special rules. There was no "woman's role" when male warriors gave themselves to each other. Both men had to be forceful. Neither would yield. It would be demeaning to be submissive. Insulting to try to govern the other. They would thus wrestle and let hardness rub against hardness.

The trees hissed in the slightly cool breeze. As the moon moved behind the trees, shadowy light shrouded them both, creating a world which held only the two of them. They pulled even closer together. They embraced even more deeply. Their bodies seemingly fused. Their breathing grew heavy and in tempo. They whispered. They exchanged words with each other that no one else could hear—only things that men of battle could possibly celebrate, let alone understand.

Shima and Saburo, feeling, touching, smelling, growling, and grunting—almost like they were in battle, yet not. There was no relaxing, except at the final spasms, and then it was mutual gasps when the excitement reached a peak. Until they were sated. Exhausted and fulfilled.

They lay on top of their clothes in the tall grasses, recovering until sleep took them both.

Some time later, when Shima awoke, he saw Saburo lying on his back next to him, gazing into the sky. Their two horses stood nearby, asleep.

"I would have thought you'd sleep more soundly after all *that*."

"I'm too excited to sleep," Saburo said.

Shima smiled knowingly. "You cold?" he asked softly.

Saburo shook his head.

"I'm not either, but I'm thirsty." He rose and retrieved another flask of saké in Gaki's saddlebag. The men shared the flask as they both lay back looking into the night sky.

"Were you and Aka-rui lovers?" Shima asked.

"You asked me that years ago, and I said no."

"Why weren't you?"

"It would've been the love between boys, something I do not care for." Saburo scowled. "Why'd you ask about him again?"

"Because of how you were . . . just now. Like you'd done this before. You were perfectly at ease."

"At ease?" Saburo laughed. "I am sweating, and I know my muscles will be sore in the morning."

Shima joined him in laughter. "So the other boys didn't court you?"

"No one there could ignite my heart," said Saburo. "Boys aren't manly."

"And the elders?" Shima asked.

Nanshoku, male colors, often happened in monasteries, as well as among the warrior-monks. It was repeated by some that any number of men were drawn to religious studies precisely for the all-male environs where passions could run wild, especially among youths who found one another enticing.

Saburo grimaced. "I was no *chigo*, if that's what you're asking. It wasn't tolerated at our monastery, and I am glad for it."

Shima looked into the sky. "So you learned, then, from being with women?"

Saburo thought of Sairyū and the cherries he had offered her that day at the market six years before. "No woman has ever given me her skin," he said, using the common expression.

Shima turned and gave him a hard look. "Though I believe you, it's hard to believe a woman would not offer herself to you."

"You know from the ancient texts the story of the Moon?" Saburo said, stroking Shima.

"The brother of the Sun Goddess."

"But you know how He came into being?"

Shima shook his head. "When I grew up, there was no time for such stories. I never attended a monastery, but maybe *you* know?"

Now it was Saburo's turn to laugh softly, and he began to tell a tale. "Tsukuyomi is the brother of the Sun Goddess. He was born out of the right eye of the Creator God, Izanagi, *male-who-invites*."

"Male-who-invites?" Shima repeated. "Maybe this story has something to do with us."

Saburo smiled knowingly. "Izanagi had to cleanse Himself of sins after He escaped from Ne-no-Kuni, the Land of Roots, and He immersed himself in water to wash all bad things away. As He washed, the Moon God fell from His right eye."

"Sounds like an interesting God, and maybe a good one."

"Well, actually not. He killed the Goddess of Food. Would you like to hear about that?"

"No," Shima said simply. He rolled toward Saburo, and once again the two men proceeded in their sport.

Only as the dawn broke peach in color did the two men, exhausted from their night together, stand side by side, naked, ready to face the day.

"I want you to have this," said Saburo. "It's a trifle." He held out a small blue-beaded pouch with a black silk drawstring.

"An omamori. Good luck for travel over water." Shima looked sharply at Saburo, taking the prayer amulet into his hand and gazing at the takō image. He said nothing more.

The bond had been sealed.

Forty-Two
Banishment

A s the sun rose, Shima and Saburo prepared to head back to the home province. Smiling, yet serious, they went about saddling Raiden and Gaki.

Shima paused to look toward Soft Breeze Shrine, which stood as peacefully and undisturbed as ever. "Did those men have money?"

Saburo nodded. "They had loot, but I came only to kill them. If I now took their money, it'd make me no better than them. Killing for money."

Shima scoffed and went about checking and tightening Gaki's tack.

Saburo continued, "Whoever finds the bodies is welcome to the blood money. Leave it for the shrine priest, I say. He'll have to restore and cleanse a desecrated shrine. Maybe the money will help him do that."

"I'm sure. After all, that's exactly what I would do." Shima laughed darkly and shook his head.

And with that the two men rode into the rising sun.

But if the shrine priest ever found the loot, Saburo never heard about it. After all, wasn't that the way of booty? Bragging only invited consequences. Booty, like omeko, was something secret and best hidden, lest it became profane. And in keeping with discretion, no one ever spoke of any blood-drenched money found at any shrine.

What was widely repeated, however, was that eleven "holy men" had been murdered. Their decomposing bodies were discovered some time after the Dark Moon.

Holy men indeed!

The first stories, mainly speculation, painted a picture of superior numbers rushing into the shrine and massacring the unsuspecting monks while they were deep in prayer and meditation. However, a certain former priest who gave up the holy life and ended up in Heian-kyō after he mysteriously came into a sizable sum of money, his tongue loosened with sufficient saké, told the story of the night he "saw something." He "just happened to be traveling" the night of the killings. He said that one man and only one man "entered the shrine and then left after a great commotion." It was hard to see through the brush, even though the night had been brightly moonlit. The former priest told of the massacre in a general way—after all what could he see behind closed doors?—but then proceeded to repeat with unconcealed relish how afterward the lone man met another man and together celebrated the battle by sharing "out under moonlight, no less," each other's body. Likely the former priest had observed this better than what had happened within the closed walls of the shrine. Thus, a second rumor began to spread that a certain man, young, talented, and most powerful, had traveled to Nagato to kill the Zodiac.

Over time, as more facts leaked out, the Ōuchi conducted a quiet investigation within their ranks. Many of the retainers were called out and asked who of their number were away during the autumnal equinox and what clothing and weapons had gone missing right before the killing of the Zodiac. Everything pointed to Saburo.

This put the Ōuchi in a predicament not to their liking, nor of their choosing, and it came as a surprise only to Saburo that he was summarily ordered to leave the Ōuchi compound. Moreover, the Ōuchi disavowed all affiliation with him. He was never any kind of Ōuchi retainer, merely a runaway priest, a lapsed priest, a straggler of dubious character. The clan did not want to run afoul of the powerful sōhei. Even though the Zodiac were regarded as renegades even by their brethren—and more than a few branches of warrior-monks were glad to see the last of them—the Ōuchi did not want it said that any contingent of their retainers had engaged in battle with anyone at all connected to the sōhei.

Saburo, not an Ōuchi retainer, had acted alone.

Shima's part in the episode was never spoken about, nor was the sword master ever punished, for it would have been an admission of a conspiracy. Besides, there was never even a hint of Shima having lifted his sword against the Zodiac. And thus, Shima, caught in the middle, was told to separate himself from his one-time protégé.

The Ōuchi said they would not personally escort him out of their prefecture, but if he did not leave of his own volition, he would suffer punishment—a euphemism for execution. Saburo was stripped of all insignia, though he was permitted to keep his swords. As for his mount, Raiden, the Ōuchi kept the stallion.

And so, Saburo was unceremoniously expelled from the Ōuchi compound on foot and told to leave Buzen Prefecture at once.

Forty-Three

A Hundred Heartbeats

Four days past first Half Moon of Long Month
First Day of Sōkō, Descent of Frost
25 October 1159

Buzen Prefecture, Isle of Unknown Fires

S ABURO WALKED EAST, out of the high mountain basin valley and toward the Windward Sea. Shima, his teacher, his friend, and much
more than that, had not so much as deigned to see him off on his journey. As promised, he had no escort, yet he had a feeling that he was
being followed as he walked mountain trails through the folded valleys.
He saw nobody.

Saburo knew he was supposed to feel sad about leaving, but surprisingly he didn't. He felt empty. In all the time since arriving in Buzen, and
maybe even going back to the day Nin-tai and Aka-rui were murdered,
he had focused on nothing other than killing the Eleven—picturing the
deaths of each in exquisite detail. His imaginings had filled endless hours.
Always different. Always exciting. Unique. In his fantasies within the
training hall, the battle with the Zodiac had gone on in all its variations,
all day, every day. Now he had real images to remember, and what had
happened so very quickly. Ten blade strikes, if that. Four dagger throws.
One throwing star hitting Dragon. A hundred heartbeats later he stood
over the bodies. Three years of training and it was over in barely a blink.

That night he'd felt such release! Such freedom he felt having survived
what nobody should have survived! Shima was there to celebrate with
him in the nandō way. And for the first time in his life, Saburo had felt
love.

But after that, Saburo felt adrift. He had watched the Ōuchi investigation into the crime with remote indifference. Shima had said little. Even

Shin-en had gone silent. By the time the final decision of exile arrived, Saburo was relieved. *Now at least I can find something new.*

After two days of walking the hills, Saburo climbed up a rise and came upon the great waters. The Inner Sea. He stopped to look at the shimmering waters in the late morning's light. Though the sun blazed bright, a light fog shrouded the horizon.

As a child, when he first saw the vast Leeward Sea, Saburo had asked what lay beyond its edge. He was told that there were only strangers who spoke in strange tongues and had strange ways. To Saburo, that had sounded unbelievable. But it had captured is imagination. An entire world, unknown, just beyond the horizon! Since then, Saburo had always seen a horizon toward which he sailed in his imaginings—to get away from his imperfect father, to seek spiritual perfection through Nin-tai, and, under Shima's guidance, to deliver a perfect attack on the Eleven.

Was there any horizon for him now that he had killed the Eleven? Or had he, by killing them, ended all purpose in life so that he too sailed on, doomed to be lost in the uncharted monotony of a changeless sea? Was the undiscovered country a place he still had to sail to, or had he unknowingly already landed on the shores of that country from which he could never escape, surrounded by unending ocean on all sides flowing off into eternity? He feared this might be true, for what else did he really know? What had life taught him in his eighteen years? How to place leaves in silkworm trays? Closing his eyes and emptying his mind? Killing the wicked? In each of these incarnations, he had a father, either real or a proxy. Each had taught him a profession—tradesman, priest, warrior.

And the only one he had truly mastered was the one Shima had taught. How to kill men.

Saburo walked on. It wasn't until the third day that Saburo finally left the Ōuchi domains, crossing into the lands governed by the Ōtomo. The sakimori on the border leading into Bungo Prefecture only asked him a few questions. He told the border guards he was headed across the Bungo Strait to cross to the Isle of Two Kingdoms, and this satisfied the guards, who allowed him to enter without further challenge.

Three days later, as the sun stood overhead, Saburo arrived at landing docks at the Bungo.

A lone mifune awaited at the reed-sprouted rock shore.

Its *senchou* looked up as Saburo approached. "Greetings Kinu-sama," he said, as if Saburo were a noble. And what's more, he knew Saburo's long-abandoned clan name.

Saburo darkened. "Why did you call me that?"

"We've been waiting for you."

No passengers were on the boat. He looked around, but nobody else was in sight. "Is there no one else sailing across?"

The senchou smiled. "The mifune awaits."

So, the Ōuchi had let him go, but they intended to kill him after all, only not within their own territory. They had waited until he was out of their province to strike.

FORTY-FOUR
PASSAGE

Hour of the Horse
Full Moon of Long Month
30 October 1159
Bungo Strait, Isle of Unknown Fires

"HOW MUCH FOR PASSAGE?" Saburo asked.

"A copper should do, I think," said the senchou.

"A copper?" A suspiciously low price. Crossing the Barrier Strait just a month before had cost a piece of silver, and that was a much shorter trip.

The senchou bowed. "The wind is with us." He smiled. "And the load will be light. Only one other passenger, along with the horses."

So. They mean to get me out in the middle of the Strait, kill me, throw me overboard, and let the currents take my body out to sea. He laughed grimly to himself and stepped aboard. Of course he was walking into an ambush, but better to have it out now. He loosened the sword just enough that it would slide easily.

The bright daylight glinted off the water, dazzling his eyes, so at first he did not see his own dun in the horse blind. But there was no mistaking his stallion. "Raiden!"

"I thought you might need him."

Shima?

Saburo spun around. Standing on the shore, Shima wore no armor. A disguise. A dark cloak and wide *amigasa* hid most of his face and features. He had ridden out on Raiden—good way for him to further cover his trail. *Just like the Ōuchi: sending Shima to kill me, and thus punish us both.*

Saburo slowly moved his hand toward his sword hilt.

"Hardly the way to greet an old friend." Shima's smile was pleasant, not menacing.

"I thought someone would come looking for me."

"No one's looking for you. Lord Ōuchi is satisfied, as long as you're gone."

"And the authorities?"

"You mean the ones who would not take on the Zodiac in the first place? They're just as busy now with other things as they were when the monks killed Nin-tai and Aka-rui."

Shima stepped onto the mifune. It rocked from his weight. "Likely the ōryōshi are glad the gang is dead and they can be done with them." He sat down on a bench built along the boat railing. "I disagreed with Lord Ōuchi," he said, stroking his beard. "The sōhei won't lift a finger to avenge that scum."

What Shima said made sense. Saburo felt regret. "I let my tongue wag too much after the battle. If I'd kept my mouth shut, no one would have known it was me."

Shima shrugged. "I didn't tell anyone about what happened. Not about anything, but someone did. Everyone loves a good story, especially when it's true. We'd been asking around about the Zodiac. I'm sure that's how somebody put it together."

"I'm sorry I got you mixed up in this."

Shima shook his head with a small nod of admiration. "That night? I wasn't entirely sure you're going to come out alive."

"I was *certain* I wasn't." Saburo drew in a deep breath. "It never occurred to me that there would be any afterwards."

"No afterwards?"

"I have been thinking about that since I left."

"Thinking of?"

"Afterwards."

"Ah."

"I thought everything would end that night. At Iwakawa-jiin, they were formidable."

"The night you went in after them, they were into their saké. Not like when they raided your monastery. But," Shima said, his eyes menacing with resolve, "if you hadn't come out, I'd've gone in and finished them."

"I think it's easier to fight when you don't think you're going to live."

"You going to fight again?"

"I think I killed everyone I set out to kill."

"What do you plan to do now?"

It was a simple question. Saburo answered simply, "I don't know."

"You've been walking at least four days. No ideas in all that time?"

"Mostly I've been thinking what I'll do in order to eat."

"Going back to the monastery, maybe? Be a priest again?"

Saburo shook his head. "Not after what I've done. I can't ever be a priest—" He broke off with a hiss. "Before I went to the monastery, I was headed to the Imperial City. Maybe that's where I should go."

Shima grunted. "Just because the Ōuchi are distancing themselves doesn't mean there aren't others who would in fact appreciate a man of shall we say . . . talent?"

"I'm no samurai. I was a priest. A farm boy before that. Nobody will bring me in like you did."

"I brought you in because you had *will*."

"But that was you. I'm not sure any clan will have me. I'm not buke."

"My beginnings are as lowly as any." Shima's voice rumbled darkly, twinged with humor. "At least you were a priest."

"You served in the Hōgen Ran—for the winning side. The Ōuchi had to accept you, no?"

"No," Shima said flatly. "But the strange thing is that, for all the buke and kuge who descend from fancy parents and high titles, there are even more who come from simpler roots. As I have told you over and over, battle knows no pedigree. A farmer with a tachi can cut down a noble with a tachi with but a single cut. The battlefield remembers only who wins. You've established yourself. Your talents could prove useful. There are rewards, so long as you don't end up lost inside some army. Pick your battles carefully, and make sure there's enough gold at the end to go around."

Saburo scowled.

"Don't look so skeptical."

"To kill for money?" He shook his head in disapproval.

"There are others just as foul as the Zodiac and whom the ōryōshi ignore. Raiding farms. Terrorizing innocents. Robbing. Maiming. Raping. Killing. If people want to give you gold to rid the world of vermin, should you look away from payment?" Shima sniffed. "Even priests accept alms."

"Nin-tai would say that road is wide and slippery."

"And you are far down that road. Afraid you'll slip now? There are other Nin-tais in this world—with different names. It's just you've never heard of them . . . yet."

Saburo looked away.

"Or do you could go back to being a farmer or maybe take up a trade or perhaps marry a rich woman—or maybe even become the lover of a handsome samurai and travel together?" Shima was silent a moment. "You remember that night?"

Saburo did remember. He remembered it very well. The exuberance of having survived and the plentiful saké. He had permitted himself to share the love he had always denied himself. And so even as the last echoes of his human innocence dissolved into the earth, he and Shima had embraced, coming together in open intimacy of nandō.

He also remembered the night at Iwakawa-jiin when they first met. When his attraction toward Shima was the honest and true admiration and affection of a young man suffering loneliness and heartbreak, who sought reassurance and strength and, yes, love from a man of strength and action—the opposite of Dayu-suke. And Shima had responded generously, giving Saburo whatever he asked for.

But only now did Saburo realize that Shima had wanted something in return: for Saburo to become a man who could wreak vengeance with a cold heart. In this, Shima had succeeded. Since the massacre, Saburo drew away from Shima. Their last moment of true closeness was when Shima's student had crossed the vale from human to monster.

Saburo had been changed into someone else, something else.

Not the person he had been before.

Not a priest, not anymore.

He was now a killer. Brutal. Remorseless. Barely human. His vengeance on the Eleven had not brought his heart back, only hardened it.

Shima said, "You're quiet."

Saburo sighed and shook his head. "I remember."

"Hmm," Shima grunted. "I brought Gaki with me. He's over there." And indeed the stallion was in the shade not far from the docks. "I can bring him aboard. Strike out to the Isle of Two Kingdoms."

"We drank too much saké. So much my head spun. It was the saké that caused me not to be myself."

"Saké, ne?" Shima's eyes lost the mirth they'd had only moments before. "It was just so much saké then," he said slowly, stretching each word out. "Nothing more? Just drink?"

Saburo did not look at him.

"You don't get hard anymore for me?"

Saburo shook his head.

Shima sighed deeply. "Too bad only saké does that to you."

"I am done with saké."

Shima snorted. "Done with *it*, are you? Hmm. You may one day see that some things taste good and you continue to drink them, even if you awaken the next morning with a spinning head."

Saburo gazed across the Bungo.

Shima said, "Maybe you are one of the ones who gets hard only after using his steel sword, and that frightens you."

Saburo could feel Shima staring intently at him.

"Maybe it's why you ran away from the monastery in the first place. You were running from yourself."

Saburo faced him with defiance. "The monastery was home. Nin-tai would not abide nanshoku. Elders do not take advantage of innocent boys."

Shima's jaw set itself like stone. "Boys!"

"Boys who put their filial trust in an elder. And you certainly are elder," Saburo said, his words calculated bite like sharpest steel. "What are you? Almost thirty?"

"I may be ten years older than you, but you are no chigo," Shima said through clenched teeth. "You're a full-grown man!"

"I'd never known what physical love was, and you led me along."

"Oooh." Shima's voice was cold as a winter wind, barely more than a whisper. "You dare!" Shima flushed. "You came to take what I taught. You then killed eleven men. And you have the audacity to speak of your innocence! For three years I watched you plot your bloodletting day by day, and now you hide behind the fiction that you are not responsible for your own plot?"

"Maybe you are right," Saburo said. "Nevertheless, I do not want to follow an old man."

Shima bolted up as if about to strike Saburo dead on the spot.

Saburo decided he would not raise a hand. Maybe he did owe Shima his life. Maybe death at Shima's angry hand would be the best way to end it.

But Shima did not move. A long time passed in silence.

Finally Shima said, low and quiet, "Very well. I wish you well in your world without . . . saké."

Shima again reached toward his sword. Saburo again readied himself for the blow. But instead of drawing steel, Shima took a small satchel from his sleeve and tossed it at Saburo's feet.

It landed with a metallic clunk. "That was for us. Now the money's only for you. In the Imperial City, you'll need every coin there."

"I can't take money."

"You're a thief," Shima snarled. "You took what I taught you. You might as well have that, too!"

The mifune rocked, water slapping its hull, as Shima stepped off and stomped toward his horse. Almost at once, he was in the saddle.

Saburo lowered his eyes and watched the boat's rocking motion, so disconnected from the firmness of the shore.

Shima's voice called from the shore, "I fight because it's the manly thing. It's time for you to decide what and who you are, for I have no use for you." After a pause, the sword master shouted, "I wish I had never met you!"

A wave of hot bitterness filled Saburo's chest. He looked up, trying to catch Shima's eye, if just for a moment, but it was not to be. The rider had already put spurs to horse and was thundering out onto the road, rocks and dirt flying as hooves clattered away—as if Shima were riding Gaki off into a great battle.

Saburo gazed at the drawstring satchel at his feet. He picked it up, sat on the boat bench, and looked inside. He gasped. At least two hundred gold coins.

Saburo stood up, looking for Shima, but the only trace was dust roiling in the soft breeze.

FORTY-FIVE
FALLEN

Hour of the Sheep
One day past Full Moon of Unohana Month
Second Year of Shōan
10 May 1172

North Road, Nagato Prefecture

IN DEATH, SHIMA SEEMED LARGER than Saburo remembered. The sword master lay face down in the mud, long arms extended fully out over his head, fists still clutching the man-length nodachi. In the cold drizzle, his indigo and orange yoroi glistened, appearing polished and pristine, except for a bloody gash just under his ribcage.

Saburo knelt down next to him and gently nudged his shoulder, and it yielded slightly. The body had not yet begun to stiffen. Not dead long. He pushed harder and rolled the body face-up.

He suppressed a gasp. He had killed many targets and been in terrible battles with grisly carnage, but nothing prepared him for the lifeless face of his own mentor. Mud smeared his cheeks and jaw. Sand grains clung to his eyeballs and invaded the creases of the lids. Rainwater dribbled from his mouth.

Shima's eyes were clear. No sign of the black that swallowed the eyes of victims of fugu poisoning.

This meant the false monks weren't the killers.

What had earlier been his slight regard for a mere girl disguised as a samurai turned into bitter rage. Clenching his teeth, he poured water from his canteen across Shima's eyes, rinsing away the grit. Then closed them.

Saburo closed his own eyes. He had to compose himself. He was renown even among the shinobi for his ability to kill anyone efficiently, without compunction or remorse, and always with discretion. He always applied patience and attentiveness, things he had learned from his old mentor-father Nin-tai, in everything he did. He had never failed in an assignment. For the man of the shadows, death brought clarity

He focused now on what he knew and didn't know. The routine calmed and centered him, bringing him back to cold reality.

Earlier, as he had come up the road, he'd encountered farmers carrying fabrics. He saw terror on their faces. At the time, he'd assumed he—an unpredictable armored samurai on a lonely road—had frightened them. But then he came upon the scene and realized the dead bodies had terri-fied those pitiful farmers. Had they actually watched the battle, seen the Taka girl defeat these men? If so, she was only a short distance ahead.

He could dash up the road and cut her down. It was possible she might not expect someone to rush up so soon—or at all.

But experience had taught him that appearances could deceive and to always check for the small clues. He slipped a hand under Shima's dō. His chest, the thickest part of his body, was only slightly warm. Yamabuki could have done her killing as long as an hour before. Possibly longer.

Plus she was on horseback. Although that made her easier to follow, it also meant she was traveling faster than he could on foot—two to three times faster, even accounting for periods when she would have to walk to let her stallion rest. Unlikely he could catch her before nightfall. Yet she would have to stop somewhere for the night. He could get his chance while she slept.

He swept his gaze around. Aki lay face down, pierced by one stabbing thrust through the lung. The Taka girl surely had done that. Across the road, Ie's body lay sliced in two from a much more brutal and powerful attack. Shima's nodachi, no doubt.

Why had the fools attacked Shima? Had he tried to help the girl, only to have her turn on him? Had she caught Shima with his guard down and killed him out of spite or malice?

No. His guard wasn't down. Clearly from how he fell, she'd struck when his nodachi was raised high, poised for attack. For her to have killed Shima with one thrust in face-to-face battle indicated superb skills for anyone, let alone a young noblewoman that Kuma had dismissed as "un-tested." Obviously she had been trained to a high level. Why go through all that trouble for a mere girl?

"Taka," he hissed out loud. Such a small, secretive, and rather isolated clan, and yet his client seemed to know exactly when she'd departed on her journey and what she carried. Kuma had to be Taka. Why did Kuma want these particular two scrolls? Why did he want the warrior dead, her body never to be found? He had said she was "high rank." Could it be that she was of very highest rank? As a policy, Saburo preferred never to ponder why he was being hired; yet now the petty intrigues within the Taka clan had touched his own life.

He stepped back to take in the entire battle scene—the footprints, the trampled brush along the road's edge—and then he noticed the deep wheel ruts and trudging indentations from footsteps tracking past the roadside shrine. The fabric merchants. At the Barrier Strait, he had watched them slowly, awkwardly roll their cart aboard the kobune that carried the Taka warrior, Shima, Aki, and Ie. No doubt they came upon the scene here only once the battle was over and pushed their cart straight through, wanting nothing to do with dead bodies. They couldn't have gotten far since then.

Saburo turned to gaze uphill on North Road—and only then did he notice something inexplicable: the wheel ruts bent to the side, turning away from the road and straight off the ledge. He moved to the edge and peered down.

Forty-Six
Ninjo

A CART LAY SMASHED TO PIECES at the very bottom of a ravine. The merchants were nowhere in sight, but their footprints continuing up the road. A cart with this much silk aboard was worth a small ransom. To just dump it in a gully? Had they panicked at the sight of the murder?

The cart lay on its belly in loose dirt by a small stream, having battered trees on its way down, losing wheels and bags of cargo along the way. One bundle hooked by a pine branch had split open, revealing mostly straw inside. Other ripped silk satchels further down also revealed straw contents. The silk outer wrappings were obviously intended to deceive all but those who gave careful scrutiny.

The green tunics the merchants had worn were scattered along the hillside. Also their shoes. What commoners would have tossed aside new-made shoes?

He focused in on the cart itself. For all the violence in its demise, it appeared to be largely intact, but for a side panel that had been torn off to reveal a compartment that ran the length of the cart underneath the bed flooring. What were they smuggling in there? Something they could carry by hand. Exotic treasures from across the Leeward Sea? That made no sense. Even smugglers alarmed by dead bodies would not have discarded their own clothing—let alone the cart itself—without getting something in exchange. Even the straw would have found a buyer in any of the nearby towns. Yet everything had been cast aside—except for whatever had been hidden in that compartment. Obviously, their ruse did not matter anymore now that they had gotten past the Nagato sakimori. Now they carried what they had smuggled across the Strait and no longer felt the need to be disguised as merchants.

Being himself a master of disguises, Saburo wondered what appearance had they assumed. He took a few steps along the ledge, examining the wreckage below, and that's when he saw something he recognized even from this distance: a warrior-monk's gray-white tunic and distinctive leg-strap sandals that had spilled out of the cart. The exact kind of disguise worn by the Zodiac. Convenient for men who did not want to be bothered by local authorities.

But sōhei could not travel carrying exotic valuables without raising suspicion. But the cart's hidden compartment would have been perfect for transporting polearms—a preferred weapon of warrior-monks.

Saburo sighed. Armed or not, these men almost certainly had nothing to do with the Taka warrior and the scrolls she carried. Enough about this.

He glanced up and down the road for travelers. He remained alone, at least for the moment. The early afternoon sun broke out of the clouds. It still stood fully two fists high. Not yet Hour of the Monkey—yet with every moment, the Taka woman was getting further away.

Quickly he contemplated what had to be done. The bodies were unavoidable. Even if he dragged them into the ravine, they'd be found eventually, and that would raise questions. The last thing Saburo needed was having presumptuous ōryōshi inquiring about unexplained murders. He'd learned long ago, better than leaving no clues was to leave specific clues leading to an obvious explanation. No questions, no mysteries.

If the scene here appeared to be a routine robbery—hapless travelers who'd been ambushed by brigands—the ōryōshi would dismiss the incident as trivial, or at most focus only on local troublemakers. Yes, that would work.

Saburo rolled Aki's body over and searched his tunic, but found no coins. The fake monk stank of saké. Not just a fool, a drunken fool who spent his money on drunken foolishness.

Ie's upper torso lay facing up, his face the bloodless alabaster of the divine. But mortal entrails spilled from the severing wound that ran from shoulder to opposite hip. Saburo's probing fingers found nothing in the man's rent tunic. Saburo crept over to the lower half of the body, where the stench of kuso threatened to overpower him—the most undignified part of death, the body's release of excrement, the spirit's last gesture to the floating world. Breathing through his mouth, he found a gold coin stitched into the lower tunic hem. Quickly, yet careful not to touch the fugu, he flung the two assassins' poisoned blades deep into the ravine. Now they were just two unfortunate monks. And the weapons, if found, would be associated with the owners of the cart.

Taking a deep breath of cold air to keep his head clear, Saburo knelt beside Shima. "Forgive me," he whispered, and he probed the samurai's sleeves. His hands came away with two heavy purses, each filled with gold coins.

So much gold! More than Saburo had paid the failed assassins. Had Shima also been paid to get the scrolls? No, more likely thrifty Shima had earned and saved the coins—just as he had when working for the Ōuchi.

The clank of the coin satchel landing in the boat rang in Saburo's memory. He said, "You called me a thief."

Shima did not answer, but Shin-en began to shriek. Saburo shoved the monkey out of his mind.

Saburo couldn't take Shima's gold now. "I've already taken so much from you." He tucked the purses back into the sword master's sleeve. *Someone else can steal the money.* Even ōryōshi wouldn't pass up such a fortune.

But the girl had not taken the money. Young, blooded for the first time, she would have focused on having taken life—not unlike how he after killing the Eleven had left behind the blood-covered treasure. How else was she like him?

Another burst of rain came down in the sunshine as he felt under Shima's tunic for anything else of value, and his fingers touched a silk cord.

His heart skipped a beat. He dared not believe it. He traced the lanyard to the pouch he knew was there. He shoved the tunic aside. Saburo slipped loose the silk drawstring and removed what was inside.

The omamori.

Shima had kept it all these years, long after the talisman had lost its power. Even after their agonized parting. The takō embroidery was slightly soiled, as if Shima had occasionally rubbed his thumb across it. The sentimental sword master.

When Nin-tai had died, Saburo had not wept. When Aka-rui had died, he had not wept. Not since the death of his mother had he wept, but now his body was wracked with sobs. He cradled Shima's head in his hands, saying all the things he had wished to say to him in life, telling him how he wanted it to have been different. "I loved you."

He gently lowered Shima's head to rest. Rain coursed like tears down the dead man's cheeks, and when he saw Shima crying, Saburo sobbed even harder.

Totally spent, gut aching, Saburo murmured what Shima had called him. "Dankotaru." Resolute.

He sniffed. This was not the time to let his own sentimentality overwhelm him. He had already lingered for too long. He slipped the amulet back into its pouch and tucked it into a sleeve pocket.

Now for a weapon. The short sword he had procured in Akamagaseki surely would not be enough against the Taka warrior. Shima's nodachi was far too large for Saburo to wield, but Shima also carried a tachi.

Saburo stood and half-drew the weapon. It gleamed in the sun, polished and sharp, without a notch—as to be expected of a sword master. He shoved it back in and tied the scabbard to his waist sash.

He thought of *giri*, his duty to complete the assignment, whatever the cost. But now he felt something else, an added strength—*ninjo*, human feelings. For the first time since the Eleven, he would kill for personal reasons. For vengeance. The Taka warrior would die at his hands. Saburo would kill the Taka warrior named Yamabuki. Giri demanded it and ninjo would drive it.

He started up the road, carrying the sword of a fallen friend.

FORTY-SEVEN

THE FOX IN DARKNESS

T HE DAY'S LIGHT WANED, but Saburo maintained his brisk pace. As always, he kept his ears tuned to the sounds around him, which so far were just the unremarkable murmur of the forest. Birds, insects, squirrels. Even in the unseasonable cold, the pulsing mating chorus of *minminzemi* filled the air, each insect falling silent as he moved past, then rejoining the song behind him.

He now regretted his choice of wearing armor. *Mushi no shirase.* The bugs were letting him know. The guise of samurai had seemed perfect when he had set out on the North Road from Akamagaseki, but now its little squeaks and clacks as the platelets shifted on his body distracted him—and obstructed his hearing.

He felt the presence of Shin-en once again. *She has killed Shima*, the monkey whispered in his skull. *Why is she still alive?* And Shin-en began its shrieking and howling. Unable to clear his mind, Saburo grappled with the monkey. He had to refocus.

Focus! Details reveal events.

Saburo turned his attention to Yamabuki's large colt's hoof tracks in the mud hardening in the unseasonable cold. By their separation, it was clear that the horse maintained a steady pace.

But additional marks told him that the false silk merchants also walked ahead of him, how far ahead he could not tell. The pattern of their footprints, two abreast, indicated military training.

Well, it was no matter for him. Their intrigues almost certainly bore no connection to his task.

His mind focused on killing the Taka warrior—and immediately Shin-en returned, shrieking and howling in excitement as Saburo pictured the expression on Yamabuki's face when his sword sliced open her belly, and the sound of her body hitting the ground, her eyes empty.

As the sun fell below the trees, thickening clouds above burned blood red before ripening into smashed, bruised plums. Gloom settled upon the forest. Trees and rocks disappeared into murk. And Saburo realized that the false silk merchants' footprints had disappeared as well.

He stopped to listen. The insects had fallen silent. Gentle wind rustled the treetops. He reached out with all his senses and heard a distant voice. A laugh. A whiff of burning pine. Campfire? The men who were not silk merchants were making camp, but where? Then he saw it. Over to the left, a vague glow seeped from a copse.

For the span of three breaths, he weighed his options. The Taka warrior likely would stop in Minezaki. If so, he would lose nothing by investigating these men. It wasn't because he wished to discover the reasons of their ruse. The idea of having armed men behind him annoyed him.

Quietly he unfastened his Hayakawa armor and stacked the pieces behind a tree trunk. The cold air chilled his skin under his sweat-damp kimono. Somewhere, an owl called *oooooooo-hoooo-oooo*, sending luck and protection against misfortune through the woods. Protection for him? Or for those men?

Was this a mistake?

As if in response, the sharp blue light of the rising moon illuminated the treetops—then almost immediately was swallowed by dark clouds. The forest was giving him his answer. The blackness provided a shield more effective than any armor.

He tucked the swords into his waist sash. Then as silent as the silence itself, he slipped into the forest, becoming one with it. Wind whispered through the pines. Again the owl called *oooooooooo-hoooo-ooo*. And men's laughter, suddenly so loud in the dark void, answered.

The campfire glow grew brighter as Saburo approached. In the middle of a small clearing, several stacked branches blazed with fire. Six men moved about, casting long ghostly shadows into the woods. They wore robes of sōhei.

Individual voices began to find their way to him.

"It will be good to sleep in a bed tomorrow," said on with slightly slurred speech.

"You think Kiso will let you rest with the news we're bringing?"

"Kiso doesn't trust the Ōuchi."

"He trusts the beauty of their women."

The men laughed quietly.

"He trusts the beauty of *all* women!"

More laughter.

"Beauty visits all clans."

"And that's why in the end they will side with Kiso. He understands how to win."

Again they laughed. Indeed, these were no monks.

The voices fell silent. The sharp-sweet smell of cooked rabbit filled the air. Not the diet of religious men. The aroma brought back memories of the night he'd first met Shima. Now Shima lay dead in the road. No burial. No rites. And shinobi or not, priest or not, Saburo knew the sutras. He could have at least performed the rites before leaving.

Shin-en whispered, *You should feel guilt.*

Saburo pushed Shin-en aside. Guilt was a luxury an assassin never dared buy.

One of the men said, "The general won't like the news about her brother."

"Ne," said a deep voice. "Say nothing about it."

"We have to."

"Why?"

"Because it was *he* who convinced the Ōuchi to meet."

Another asked, "Will there be a meeting without him?"

"Let Kiso decide," the deep voice answered, and the other voices fell silent for a while.

Wanting to see their faces, Saburo floated closer, like a ghost, making no sound, a shadow within shadows, until he felt the warmth of the fire against his cheeks. A trio of intersecting skewers held the large, skinned animal roasting over the flames.

The six men, heads uncovered, did not have the shaved heads of Tendai monks but the wild black manes and beards of buke. Warriors. Large warriors at that. Their naginata leaned against tree trunks, the poles adding to the dancing shadows from firelight, but the men themselves remained armed with both tachi and personal swords. Even so, they behaved as if they had no concerns about any potential threats around them. If they had sensed danger, they would not have kindled a fire and roasted a rabbit. But they sat at their ease, tearing hunks of flesh with knives and fingers and swigging from a passed-around flask.

And unlike sōhei, who lived lives attuned to the nature surrounding them, they had permitted death—in the form of Saburo—to steal so close without challenge.

A squat man took a gulp of saké and shook his head. "They should rename it the Isle of Obstinate Daimyō. Kikuchi. Itō. Taka. Sagara. Shimazu. They think that somehow they can stay out of it."

The warrior next to him, thicker, with wilder hair, said, "The Taka brother Tachibana was interested. You saw?"

"Kiso would like the Taka woman."

"The warrior on the boat this morning? A tall sapling."

"That sapling killed the Ōuchi fencing master."

"Baka!"

"He challenged her on the boat. They obviously had a duel."

"And what about the dead monks? She killed them too?"

"Maybe her hands are fast. A killer kills."

"Give me that flask."

The squat warrior passed the saké bottle to the wild-haired man—who took a deep gulp—and reached out over the fire, tearing off more meat. For the space of thirty breaths, the men said nothing. Damp branches crackled in the fire as the men chomped, swigged, and sighed over their meal.

"I had a thought," said a warrior across the fire, whose gray-tinged hair suggested he was eldest. "What if the sapling is Taka Daimyō's answer to Kiso's entreaties?" He gazed one by one at each of his companions. "She could be with him right now."

Chewing, the squat man said, "That's not good."

The elder warrior said, "Kiso's incautious with women."

"Ha! And he has done so well trusting men. His uncle killed his father to take power of the Minamoto. I think he thinks that a woman would not do that."

"No woman could. She'd be eliminated if she so much as tried. Men won't follow a woman."

"Ne!" rumbled the deep voice again from a tall, angular man, his back to Saburo. "Respect for the general."

The squat man bowed his head.

But the elder warrior was not finished. "Taka Moroto has a daughter. His only heir. It is said she has been trained with the sword. *She* could be the sapling, ne?"

Those words nearly shook Saburo out of his cloak of shadow.

The wild-haired warrior spat out a bone. "Moroto will marry her off to Takanao for peace with the Kikuchi."

"Takanao might join us," said the squat man.

Again, the tall man sounded off in a low warning tone. "Hey. They will choose sides when they are forced to."

The squat man snorted. "The daimyō on that isle are cowards. If they had gills, they'd crawl into the sea to get away from what's coming."

"Ne! You talk too much."

The squat man sneered at the tall man. "You think Masahito is listening? Does Kiyomori have owls spying on us?"

"What I hear is saké talking."

Saburo heard a leaf crack.

Ten steps to his right stood a large fox, red fur seeming to glow in the firelight. It stared at him with uncanny intensity. Saburo's blood ran cold. Was it a God? Saburo felt a shiver. Why would a God appear now? A trickster come to toy with him? He flushed with a surge of rage. What had the Gods ever done for him? All the people he ever cared about were dead.

The fox bolted directly in front of him before dashing off into the deeper woods.

The six men turned at the noise and stared straight at Saburo.

The voice of his teacher and lover flash in his mind: "*Two equally matched swordsmen have an even chance in a duel. Two against one, it becomes one in three. Three against one, it's one in six. Four against one, survival is one in nine. Take out as many opponents as quickly as possible before the battle begins.*"

Saburo sprinted forward, drawing Shima's tachi, and struck two men down in one sweep. The remaining four leapt back, pulling their blades free of their scabbards.

Four left—one in twelve for an ordinary swordsman, but Saburo was no ordinary swordsman.

Like a fox, he feinted attack at one, then twisted around as the tachi tore through the chest of the man next to him. Three left.

They spread out, surrounding him. The one behind slid to the side, at least three steps away, his steps snapping twigs. Two other men stood in front of him. Not young. Seasoned warriors. Older hands with weathered faces and unblinking eyes that had known battle—eyes that would not accept anything but their opponent's death.

Saburo could not permit them to live, not after seeing his face. Now he would find out what the trickster God intended for him—or for them.

The taller man, the one with the deep voice, flicked glances around left and right, alert to possible attacks on his flank. Saburo grinned. Men always assumed no one would dare act alone.

The other man before him, short and thick bodied, locked eyes, holding his sword low at the ready, pointed downward along his front leg.

Approaching slowly, maintaining a balanced stance, Saburo held his own sword low and back. His foot touched a thick branch at the edge of the campfire, and now he knew what would happen next.

He slid his other foot slowly around while raising his tachi high.

He glanced left.

Both men looked.

He kicked. The branch flipped up, sending sparks flying.

To their credit, they did not lose focus even as the cinders burned their faces. The tall man took a half-step back, but the squat man, tough as he was thick, stepped forward and smashed the tumbling log in two with a hard lateral strike, splashing sparks at Saburo.

Saburo jumped forward, moving in close, driving his tachi into the man's chest, pinning him to the air.

Spinning now, he let go the hilt and drew his short sword, coming in low against the tall man, who brought his blade down with a powerful two-handed strike.

Saburo flashed his sword up—short sword met long sword, steel met steel with a loud crack. Saburo's blade vibrated more than it should have. His right hand stung with pinpricks. He kicked a leg out high, smashing the tall man's knee.

The other warrior cried out.

Saburo cut through the tall man's torso, sapping his wind. The warrior bent over, wounded. Staggering. But still on his feet.

Seeing his chance, the third man who had hung back charged with powerful diagonal strikes. Saburo barely parried them. The squat man impaled by the tachi finally fall back to the dirt—blocking Saburo's shuffle-steps. Now off balance, Saburo flung the short sword at his attacker's face, not expecting to do damage, only to disrupt his rhythm.

In the moment's hesitation, Saburo pivoted around and ripped his tachi free from fallen squat man's chest. His attacker reset his stance, eyes focused on Saburo's longer sword. Saburo dropped one arm and let his personal dagger slip into his hand. With a rising snapping motion, he flung it low. It slammed into the man's groin. Saburo's long sword sliced through the man's face. Blood spewed in an arc. The man fell in a rolling tumble.

Five of the warriors own, the tall warrior remained, still standing despite a shattered knee, bent only slightly, clutching his side wound, sword held out in one unsteady hand.

Saburo approached him slowly. The sole survivor had little left in him. He'd be dead soon anyway. Saburo considered just leaving him. But something about this man dressed as a warrior-monk brought up rage within the fallen priest. And he had no time for waiting.

His blade flashed, knocking the man's sword out of his hand. Another flashing motion and the warrior's arm came off at the elbow.

And still the tall man stood, glaring at him with defiance.

Saburo brought down his sword again, severing the man's other arm at the shoulder. Blood spurted from both wounds, but weakly. The gash in his torso had released most of it. The man's fierce eyes turned glassy. His body tipped forward. Saburo stepped out of the way, and as the man fell, Saburo swung the tachi once more, taking his head.

Breathing deeply, his heart pumping, Saburo surveyed the slaughter—and it had been a slaughter. He walked up to each one and drove the tachi point into each man's heart. Just like the Eleven. No witnesses.

The fire logs, scattered now, lost much of their flame. In the fading light, he grabbed a discarded head scarf and wiped the blood off Shima's tachi. Its blade remained marvelously undamaged. He slid it into its saya.

After retrieving and wiping down his short sword, he examined its cutting edge. Deep notches. Though the sword hilt inscription proclaimed it a Kuninaga blade, it had to be a forgery. What could he expect from a shop selling dead men's armor? He tossed the damaged sword into the remnants of the fire.

From a scabbard lashed to the squat man's waist sash, Saburo pulled a ko-dachi. This blade gleamed even in the dimness. Good enough. He slashed the sageo, tucked the empty saya into his waist sash, and slid the blade home.

A rumble in the distance. A breeze of cold gave his damp skin a chill as the distinctive clinks and clops of mounted horses grew louder. He turned his head slowly, listening. Downhill, out on the road, fives horses moved at a canter. Sakimori guards.

Would the guards see the campfire? Too late now. Scattering the logs would only kick up more sparks. He waited. The sakimori would have encountered the dead bodies of Shima and the false monks. Was this a manhunt? The riders excitedly shouted to each other. Laughter. After a few breaths, the sound shifted and began to fade.

Saburo glanced over his clothes. In the encroaching darkness, he could just make out blood spattered across his front and sleeve. Not too bad; the robes of the fallen were in even worse shape. But he did not want to encounter any authorities like this. He'd need to acquire a new disguise by morning.

If he had not killed the Taka warrior by then.

The mostly picked-over rabbit carcass lay at his feet. With hard fingers, he tore off a strip of flesh from the hind and shoved it into his mouth. Chewing on the bitter meat, he stepped back into the darkness.

Only murky shadows in the dark guided back to the North Road. Leaving the Hayakawa armor behind, he strode uphill in the strengthening icy wind. Scattered snowflakes flitted around him, touching the ground only to slide sideways in a restless dance.

Forty-Eight

Dark Fog

Hour of the Ox
Minezaki

THE TOWN BORE NO SIGN announcing its existence. But clusters of weathered and indifferently maintained *minka* homes—clapboard walls and peaked thatched roofs, ghostly with a dusting of snow, tattered with rents and holes—rose up along the road. Saburo passed the first structure, long since abandoned, with windows that gaped open like mouths to the underworld. The next home also appeared uninhabited; yet he smelled firewood and an occasional whiff of millet. Desperate people surviving after a rough winter? He walked on.

The snowfall grew heavier, now sticking to the road. His steps left footprints. *More tricks from the Gods?* He cinched his cloak a bit tighter.

A stooped gray couple squatted in the darkness against the wall of a nondescript clapboard minka more haphazard in construction, assembled from leftover scraps from finer buildings. He ran up to them, as if in an anxious hurry, and said in a weak voice, "Please, I'm looking for a samurai. I have an urgent message for her. Riding a horse? Wearing green armor so dark it's almost black?"

The man gaped at him, working his lips over toothless gums. The woman shrugged.

"You saw her? Where did she go?"

The woman touched the old man's shoulder and stole inside. The old man, confused, slowly followed her, and the door banged shut.

Saburo continued up the road. The strange summer storm intensified. Carried on the wind blowing down from the mountains, snow swirled around him, and now his footprints disappeared in an ever-restless whiteness. Surely Yamabuki could not have gone on in this weather, especially over the pass. She had to have stopped somewhere nearby for the night.

As he had in Akamagaseki, he now peered around behind each building he passed, checking for stables. Few homes had any—their tenants too poor to own horses, let alone house them in separate structures—and what sheds he found stood empty and unused.

As the density of minka increased, so did their quality. All bore peaked roofs, though most of thatched straw, not shingles.

He reached a crossroads—the reason the town even existed. A broad road extended off to the left and right: the East-West Highway, a major traveling route that reached from the Leeward Sea to the Inland Sea. But nobody was traveling on this night.

The Taka warrior likely had not taken the long way around to the Imperial City. With this weather, she had to be somewhere in this town.

He continued on North Road into the densest part of Minezaki. The minka now stood wall to wall, and many abutted bluffs or large boulders, making getting around them more difficult, checking stables more time-consuming. Often upon creeping around to the back of a structure, he encountered the stone or steep dirt of a cliff face. Twice he had to throw rocks at skeletal dogs that pestered him for food. At none of the stables he found were horses.

He crept up to one somewhat maintained structure and peered through an open window. Dark and silent but for the faint hiss of burning coals. He slid open the door. Nobody. He entered.

The entire interior was one room, deserted; yet an iron plate sat within the irori, glowing red. Someone lived here and was perhaps soon to return. Saburo warmed his hands and feet.

He tried to center himself and reflect on his next move, but instead found himself thinking about Shima. *Shima! Dead!* The cold body—so altered since that night they'd first embraced.

His thoughts wandered further back—to Iwakawa-jiin. But now the temple had turned cold and lifeless and withered priests trudged ghostlike through corridors and across courtyards. The few faces he recognized were aged. He floated through walls, past the kitchen where flavorless millet bubbled in a pot, and into a large chamber where a small deflated man, gray and hunched, sat in meditation in front of an incense flame. The light flickered across the gaunt face, and Saburo realized he was looking at Dayu-suke. The bettō who took Nin-tai's position had become a shadow of himself—no longer the fat but shriveled. Old. Barely alive. Dayu-suke's lips moved, and the words reached Saburo's ears, yet Saburo could not understand them. The old man chanted in some unfamiliar language. The only word Saburo could make out was "Dankotaru." The room dissolved into smoke and Saburo found himself in the misty graveyard, by Aka-rui's weathered marker. Aka-rui, still young, climbed out of the ground and frowned.

Loud stomping the boards outside brought Saburo out of the fog. With feet soft and silent, he moved to the corner by the door. Slowly, he slipped his sword, scabbard and all, from his sash and held it from the middle.

The door slid open. A gaunt man with snow on his black hair stepped in.

Saburo struck. The scabbard smacked hard against the man's skull. The man crumbled. The shinobi checked outside for anyone else who might have been coming along.

Satisfied, he slid the plank door shut and moved back through the dark room, looking for a pot, basket, anything that might have contained something useful. He yanked down straw-mesh sack hanging on a wall. Inside was a cheap kimono, thin material. In the dimness, it appeared rather plain. Perfect.

He kicked off his robe, walked to the irori, and tossed his blood-spattered garment onto the coals. Immediately smoke rose, thick and slow. He slipped on the new-found kimono and tied the sash. The ko-dachi's scabbard tucked in easily, but the sash seemed too insubstantial for the tachi. He couldn't leave Shima's sword behind, so he fashioned the saya's sageo into a loop and threw the cord over his shoulder to carry the sword on his back.

The man he had clouted moaned. Saburo moved to him, drew his knife, and slit open the man's throat. As blood spurted out onto the planks and seeped through the gaps, smoke from the fire crawled along the floor to caress the body. Dayu-suke's chant seemed to dance at the edge of his awareness.

Saburo pushed open the door, stepped out, shut it behind him, and continued up the North Road further into Minezaki. The snow was surprisingly deeper now. What hour was it? He'd heard no tolling. He would have guessed toward the end of the Hour of the Pig. But the chill and the snow gave him the sense it was much later. The Hour of the Mouse? Hour of the Ox? Hour of the Mouse? His mind ran in circles. And still the dark fog clung to his thoughts. Was the bettō trying to curse him? He recalled the large fox with the intelligent eyes. A God? Or was it a shapeshifting *tsukimono* conjured to possess his soul?

He scooped up a handful of snow and shoved it into his mouth. With his tongue, he worked the snow around as it melted, letting the cold clear his head. He spat out the resulting water, as if rinsing his mouth in ablution.

Possession! Bah! Gods! Bah!

He headed up the road, lifting his legs to clear the snow.

A lone brazier in front of a short, wide building illuminated a green banner marked with the word Saké. Finally. People.

FORTY-NINE

INTERESTING NIGHT

S ABURO DUCKED INTO THE Saké House. Empty. A stooped old man in a brown kimono with white stripes moved tables and picked up fallen benches. "Saké House Man," Saburo said.

Without looking up, the silver-haired man bowed stiffly. "Cost you a copper," he muttered with barely veiled disdain and shuffled by Saburo toward the back.

"I don't want your saké."

The proprietor stopped, turned, and peered up at him, his eyes flitting back and forth from Saburo's face to the kimono he wore. "Where's Ase?" he asked, eyes narrowing.

Saburo glanced down to see in the brazier light a distinctive yellow leaf pattern in the seemingly plain brown kimono he'd acquired. Not quite as anonymous as he had assumed. He laughed gently. "The man with dark hair? He sold it to me. My kimono was soiled from falling into a mud hole." He glanced down modestly. "I did not want to embarrass my lord."

The saké man resumed his way toward the back.

"I bear a message for a Taka samurai, a woman wearing dark green armor. She here?"

The old man jerked his head. "No."

"It's important I deliver this message. I can pay for information."

The man paused.

Saburo stepped forward and clapped a small Sòng Dynasty copper coin onto the counter. "Nobody by that description?"

The old man turned. His gnarled fingers scooped up the coin. He examined it closely, then looked up with a knowing smile. "Interesting night." He paused, studying Saburo's face. "But no woman samurai."

"Interesting? I think your answer is too vague to merit a Sòng copper."

The saké man slowly nodded. "Sakimori." He said the word as if it were cursed. "Drunk already. Talked about a samurai killed on the North Road. Not a woman."

Saburo held up his hand, rubbing thumb and fingers together. "That's all?"

The man spat. "With sakimori, it's never one thing. They come here already drunk. I don't know why. They tried to get a yahochi to join them. But she had a sword." He smirked. "That did not go well." He turned away.

"Yahochi with a sword? Did not go . . . how?"

The saké man jutted out his chin.

Saburo narrowed his eyes, set his jaw, and clapped another copper onto the counter.

"She was too much for them. Didn't draw her sword. Broke their bones with just the scabbard." He chuckled and picked up the coin.

"Not a warrior?"

The old man waved his hand in front of his face, fingers dancing. "Made up. A yahochi, I said. Long black hair down her back. Young. Beautiful—probably. Who can tell with all that makeup?" He shook his head. "She wore a local kimono, but she was no local. Her speech? Strange accent. Strange words. I didn't know that women who give their skin are taught to fight."

Saburo exhaled deeply. "They aren't."

The man squinted at him. "Didn't think so."

Saburo held up another coin and placed it gently on the counter. "I believe this woman might be the very lady I am to deliver my lord's message to. Do you know where she is?"

The man shrugged, sagging as if a burden were set on his back. "She left with a young kuge."

"A huge? What kuge? Does he have a name?"

The man shrugged again. "Don't know. Been around alone for several days. Easy to spot. Gentian flower on his kimono."

Saburo's heart started to beat hard. Minamoto—the man named Kiso who no doubt awaited his men's arrival. Saburo remained outwardly calm. "Where's he staying?"

"Red Banners. But I wouldn't—" The old man cut himself off.

Saburo ignored the breach of manners. "This yahochi. Wearing a lo-cal kimono, you said?"

"Kōno's. The armorer's family colors and pattern. Orange with butter-flies." He shook his head. "Sad business, that."

"Sad?"

"No use for those kimono. Pox outbreak six years ago. Dead wife. One of the twin girls."

Saburo's pushed away memories of his mother's death. This very mo-ment, the Taka woman was likely in the arms of the woman-loving Kiso. Saburo could strike now.

The old man took a seat in a corner and wrapped a blanket around his shoulders. Saburo asked, "Kind uncle, what's your name?"

"They call me Unagi."

"I need a room, Unagi-kun. Where's this Red Banners? It sounds worthy."

Unagi jerked his head. "They won't have a room for you. Only Minamoto not Minamoto."

"Minamoto not Minamoto?" Saburo repeated.

"They're the only ones. Are you Minamoto?"

Saburo shook his head.

"Didn't think so."

"Another place nearby then?"

"I have a room for you. Five coppers."

Saburo placed on the table a coin larger than the others, worth twen-ty coppers.

Unagi snatched it up, trying to hide his delight. "Out, to the right, take the alley. House banner with cherries. You want saké? I'll get you a flask to take with." He rose from his seat and quickly ambled toward a low curtained doorway to another room.

"May tomorrow be less interesting," Saburo said to his back and stepped out into the snowy night.

Hard icy snow bit his cheeks. Wind blew drifts across the road. His own footprints from before were already lost in the white. He paused at the corner as his eyes grew accustomed to the darkness away from the brazier light, then started down the alley, hand on the hilt of his ko-da-chi. He didn't put it past the old man to send out armed *akutō* to rob a stranger carrying Sòng coins. But nobody confronted him. In fact, no-body was out at all.

Almost immediately he came upon a solid building draped with red banners, snow drifts blown up against the door.

Directly across stood a more humble building bearing a weathered banner with a marking so faded it was barely visible: Sakura.

Saburo crossed over and clapped his hands.

After a dozen breaths, he wondered if anyone had heard him. But at last the door clunked and rumbled open, splashing light out into the alley. A small woman of middle age with kind eyes and sun-warmed cheeks, wearing a gray kimono, smiled up at him. "Apologies. I'm not so quick at my age."

"Unagi," Saburo said.

She invited him in. He unfastened his sandals and unwrapped his legs, then followed her barefoot around down a short hall that bent to the left twice—obviously a larger structure than it had seemed—before leading into a small room where an irori burned, warming the space. Probably where she herself slept. From a nook, she retrieved a straw-mat bed-roll. She bent over, laid it down, and with a deft shove unfurled matting with a blanket already placed. "I have no food at this hour. Apologies. I do have saké."

"Nothing," Saburo said.

The woman bowed. "Water in the pail. I will have hot water and food ready after the sun is up." Her mouth twisted. "If we can see Amaterasu in this storm. By halfway through Hour of the Dragon, in any case. Two coppers for rice. Eight if you want meat."

She bowed low and slid the screen door shut.

He suddenly felt a wave of exhaustion. Let the Taka warrior have her tryst. He would strike in the morning.

He found a wooden cup hooked on the edge of the pail and drank a mouthful of water. Then he lay down on the bedding and closed his eyes. The coals in the irori hissed.

FIFTY
AMBUSH THE UNSUSPECTING

I N DARKNESS, A FOX CRIED its laughing feminine bark. Cold wind blew up a cloud of unswept leaves and dust that stung his eyes. Squinting, he turned away and stepped through the door into the Soft Breeze Shrine.

The Eleven of the Zodiac, all naked but masked like sōhei, glared at him. "You again?" Not hesitating this time, Saburo drew Aka-rui's ko-dachi and cut through Dragon's neck—but the blade passed right through without touching the flesh. Dragon laughed. The rest of the Eleven joined in, all laughing.

Saburo stood helpless among his fellow priests and novices at the main gate of Iwakawa-jiin. Dragon lowered his naginata and moved on Nin-tai. Saburo jumped forward to block—but his ko-dachi was gone, his hand empty. The naginata blade passed through him as if he were smoke and sliced into Nin-tai, who crumpled to the ground. Aka-rui cried out and charged forward, his ko-dachi in his own hand. Saburo cried out, "Don't! Let me!" But Aka-rui did not hear or see him and ran by.

Saburo spun around. The Eleven were gone. His fellow priests were gone. The bloody bodies of his mentor and his best friend lay in the dirt.

A fox charged out of the woods and took a position over the corpses, snarling. Saburo drew his tachi—Shima's tachi. Could he strike down a God? The fox reared up on its hind legs and transformed into a large man—*Shima!*—who said in his resonant voice, "Did it feel good?" It erupted into laughter, deep laugher, and leapt into the air. It's body shift-ed, sprouting fur, twisting—and was swallowed in a mist that roiled all around Saburo.

A woman's voice as smooth as the silk his mother wore whispered all around him, "Help me." The most lovely woman he had ever seen emerged from the mist. She gazed at him in a most forthright way. The feral intensity of her eyes terrified him, yet he couldn't look away.

"What are you?" he asked.

"I am of Bùxiû, I am called Rènxìng." Her words echoed inside his head.

"Why are you here?"

"Because of Qiānnián."

"Who is Qiānnián?"

"You do not know Qiānnián, you will help me."

"Help? How?"

"Kill Yīng Shānchuī."

"I know no such person."

Rènxìng tittered and her eyes turned black and she laughed hysterically, dissolving into the mist.

Saburo snapped awake, twisted in the blanket.

The room of the inn felt hot. His body dripped with sweat. Daylight streaked in from cracks between the window screen slats. Children's excited high-pitched voices squealed just outside. Calming his breath, he listened as they laid out plans to creep up on one of their number and pelt the unsuspecting victim with snowballs.

Yes, and so it begins, Saburo thought to himself. *Sneak up. Ambush the unsuspecting. We all learn this lesson.* With a whoop, the children ran off. But then something distracted them. "Look! Look!" they screamed.

Saburo's curiosity was piqued, especially as he heard the crunches of many footsteps in the snow and the grumble of men's voices. Pushing himself to his feet, he put an eye up to one of the slits to peer outside.

The view looked out on Saké House from the side, where the alley intersected with the road. Some thirty townspeople gawked at the spectacle of a jun of Ōe guards escorting through the deep snow a hand-drawn two-wheeled cart. In the cart's bed, two people lay under blankets—one, feet hanging over the end, pointing downward; the other, supine, face staring at the sky.

Saburo grabbed his weapons and found his way to the front door, where he wrapped his legs and tied on his sandals. The bright morning sun was higher than he'd expected. Hour of the Snake at least. Snow had piled high in the alley, but a narrow path had already been packed down near the buildings. The farmers and other townsfolk warily made way for him as he walked up to look.

A wide-eyed farmer said to his fellows, "They had no chance."

Saburo asked him, "A duel?

"No, the snowstorm on the pass. Many died. One survivor."

For an instant, Saburo feared that Yamabuki was among them and he had missed his chance to kill her himself. But then he dismissed the idea. A Taka warrior was unlikely to travel with Ōe.

The cart stopped in front of Saké House. Some guards went to the back of the cart, gently lifted one man, and carried him inside. The other body was left in the cart.

Five Ōe warriors milled about in front, ostensibly standing guard. To Saburo they looked like young rustics, likely drawn to the adventure and status of soldiers. They did their best to affect grim countenances, though given their relaxed confidence, they obviously did not anticipate trouble.

Perhaps sensing this, or simply too foolish to be frightened, one daring boy of no more than eight summers ran up to them, giggling, and in their manner marched back and forth through the snow, bearing the child's version of a scowl. The child came only waist high to any of the men, but what he lacked in size, he made up for in mimicry.

The guards could not help but laugh. Two of them added to the fun by joining in the boy's imitation. Their scowls grew severe, though their eyes remained mirthful.

That fun accomplished, the boy grew curious and approached one of the young men, the one amongst them with the most kindly expression, and extended his hand toward the man's hoko yari.

"Ah," the man grunted and moved the polearm's shaft within reach. The boy stretched his hand and let his tiny fingers caress the wood. The man said with a smile, "One day you may walk among the sakimori in the service of the Ōe clan."

The boy beamed.

Suddenly a woman rushed up, plowing her own path through the snow. She scowled at the guards like a wolf ready to fight, her mouth frightened and angry, and grabbed the boy's wrist, practically lifting him off the ground. "You worthless child!" With an open palm, she slapped him across the back of his neck.

"Ow!" the boy moaned and burst into tears.

"Quiet!" She delivered another slap and yanked up by his arm. "You have work to do, you shiftless boy!" She led the sobbing boy away. The young guards glanced at one another and resumed their show of grim demeanor.

Saburo considered returning to the rooming house for the food the old woman had promised—but a young man in finely made white kimono caught his attention.

FIFTY-ONE

THIS MAN COULD HANDLE HIMSELF IN BATTLE

Third Quarter of Hour of the Snake

THE YOUNG MAN HEADED AWAY from North Road, following a broken path through the deep snow toward the high cliffs beyond. His silk kimono's delicately woven blue mon of gentian flowers over bamboo leaves confirmed his class and identity. No doubt this was Kiso. Perhaps he was seeking a rendezvous with the Taka princess. He was smiling— the smile of a man in love.

He strode across the snow with the confidence of a fighter. Strong. Loose. Balanced. Connected to the ground. Young men unfamiliar with weapons often carried their swords in hand as they walked to prevent the scabbard from swinging wildly and striking them in the arm or even the face. But this man's deep *ajisai*-blue tachi saya, hanging by its matching sageo, seemed to float alongside his thigh. Saburo knew: this man could handle himself in battle.

Feigning the purposeful hunched walk of a farmer—not much he could do about his swords—Saburo followed from twenty steps behind. A few common townspeople glanced at him, perhaps recognizing the distinctive pattern on his borrowed kimono or the sword strapped to his back. Good. Let them remember the sword and kimono and forget his face. No one dared speak in challenge.

The buildings and trees on one side of the road gave way to a sheer drop, where wind eddies roiled up frost to sparkle in the sun. The tracks veered up a side road along a ledge. A group of buildings came into view. Kiso walked directly toward them.

Saburo dashed to a stand of trees, ducked under snow-laden branches, and crouched on the damp soil. From this vantage, he held a clear view of the buildings.

The young kuge walked right up to the largest building and paused in the wide-open double doorway. A moment later, the Taka warrior stepped into view, smiling. Flirting. Yes, there was definitely affection between them.

Saburo glanced around. The road was empty. He detected the scent of burning coal. Gray-black smoke rose from a vent in the high roof the building. An armory. Perfect. Nobody respectable—except warriors, of course—would want to soil their souls by coming around here.

Time to act!

The doorway stood empty. Where had they gone? Inside? Off to one of the other buildings? It didn't matter. He would kill her now and drag her body into the ravine. Nobody would know what happened to her.

He dashed toward the building.

But when he was but ten steps from the entrance, but two young men appeared.

Saburo darted to the side and hid around the corner.

The two men, hardly more than boys, dumped a large bucket of yellow-green liquid into a pile of rocks to the side. No indication they had seen him.

Saburo sighed. No witnesses. But to kill mere boys? He would avoid it if possible, but he would do what was necessary.

He edged around the armory to the field behind, where he saw a stable and a few small structures, fresh tracks in the snow leading to each of them.

No matter. She was here somewhere. Now was the time to strike.

FIFTY-TWO

BOOK OF LOVE

Hour of the Horse

IN THE GUESTHOUSE, the battle culminated with Yamabuki's surrender to Yoshinaka, and yet she did not in the slightest feel defeated. In fact she had achieved her aims. Now he lay next to her, sound asleep, his face innocent.

A distant tsurigane began its slow tolling. She rolled over and took some paper out of the saddlebag by the bed. For all the joy of intimacy with a man, afterward it was the woman who had to clean herself. Still, his wetness was strangely satisfying, she thought as she wiped along her legs.

Her mind wandered unbidden to one day when she was thirteen springs and a large boat rode out a storm in the Great Bay of Ō-Utsumi. There was much excitement, for the boat was filled with traders from Sòng Cháo. Nakagawa considered the occasion propitious for Yamabuki's education, and so he encouraged her to converse with the strangers and practice speaking their language. But the Taka princess began a different education that day, for among the strangers was one trader who spoke an indecipherable language but could make himself understood somewhat in the Common Language. He said he was from a place called Shā Xī, a great trading city in the far west beyond Sòng, and he had with him a text appropriate for young men and women who were nearing adulthood. But he would not show it to Yamabuki, only to Nakagawa, who, upon seeing it, became quite delighted—more than Yamabuki had seen him—and offered in trade his finest brocade kimono, one he always said was too fine to despoil on his mortal frame.

Soon after, the winds changed, and the traders departed. When Yamabuki asked Nakagawa about the text, he explained the language was of Tenjiku, the Center of Heaven, the land where the Buddha was born, a land as far from Sòng as Sòng was from Akitsushima. He explained that this language was not based on brush stroke but on musical symbols. The notes matched the sounds the human mouth made to form a word.

"You mean like women's writing and katakana?" Yamabuki asked.

"Even more complicated. A string of many shapes, one after the other, all connected like a long thread."

What a strange way to write. A langauge of musical notes on a thread.

"Perhaps one day we shall explore this language," he said, placing the scroll in the room where important manuscripts were stored.

The very next day, she retrieved it and took it to her shinden, where she and her handmaids could examine this strange language. Indeed, it looked like a row of jagged teeth. But far more interesting than indecipherable script were the drawings the manuscript contained—drawing that left nothing to the imagination as to their subject: handsome unclothed men and voluptuous unclothed women coupling with one another. No wonder a language based on musical notes needed drawings—drawings that needed no translation.

Now, as she watched Yoshinaka sleep, heat built up in her heart, and she recalled the resolution she had made that day: that long before she mastered the musical language, she would achieve all the pleasures pictured in the book of love.

She stood up and felt a chill. *Even colder than earlier this morning.* She tossed the paper with Yoshinaka's wetness onto the coals. Flames burst forth. She placed another piece of wood on the fire as a ninth bell strike rang out into silence.

"Burning the evidence?" Yoshinaka said, sitting up.

"Did I wake you? Or was it the bell?"

He shook his head. "I always sleep with an eye open." He tapped the tachi next to him.

"It's getting colder in here," she said, rubbing her arms.

"On this cold day, may I suggest we employ other means to keep warm and to purify ourselves?"

She smirked and said teasingly, "I already put another log in the fire."

"I mean warm up by taking a dip in the *onsen*."

"Hot springs?"

"Hai, hai. Where do you think all that steam comes from over by the cliffs? Maybe you don't have onsen on the Isle of Unknown Fires."

"We have steaming *kakkazan* from which living fire rock flows. Onsen in our prefecture could boil a rabbit."

"Ha!" Yoshinaka's eyes sparkled. "No doubt. We also have springs like that in Shinano. But I will take you to hot springs that I promise don't scald."

"Perhaps one day we will."

"No, no. I mean let's go now. Kōno's onsen."

"You've seen them?"

"Yes behind this guesthouse."

"Show me." She put on her shitagi and kimono, surreptitiously taking the three scrolls along.

Yoshinaka quickly donned his own kimono, leaving his undergarments where they lay.

Yamabuki thought about the shinobi and picked up Tiger Cub. "Bring your sword."

"Always. I would be naked without it."

They slipped on their boots and, before long, were making their way into the bluffs behind the armory and up a snow-filled narrow trail that twisted between narrow rock outcroppings, switching back and forth, and finally emerged on a small plateau.

Using his scabbarded tachi, Yoshinaka knocked through a drift of snow piled up between two high boulders and led her into a totally contained rocky ravine.

Above the surrounding high snowcapped cliffs, blue sky blazed bright, but the sun's warmth reached only partway down. Steam filled the air. Straight across from them, at about eye height, a small pool bubbled. Steaming water trickling down into a slightly larger pool below no wider than the reach of her arms. From there, a sheet of water flowed down through a channel into the largest of the pools.

She gazed all around, feeling like she had stepped into the mouth of a mountain. Except there was no musty odor. He laughed. "The onsen here are not so hot as Amaterasu, but warmer than the blood. This one carries the sweetness of life. And it's quite private. No one will find us here."

Yamabuki raised her brows and smiled.

A clump of ice fell from a steam-shrouded outcropping, and some pebbles tumbled down from above, splashing into the pool.

Yoshinaka grinned. "Shall we join those rocks?"

FIFTY-THREE

GODS OR MORTALS?

Third Quarter of Hour of the Horse

A S THE SUN PUSHED PAST MID-HEAVEN, two warriors approached Minezaki along the snow-covered road. At first all anyone knew was the clank and jingles of tack and weapons, the sounds of mounts—sounds familiar to a town used to the comings and goings of sakimori.

Where the road rose from the east, the tips of long blades appeared, aimed at the sky, moving up and down in easy rhythm, rising ever higher, until two riders came into view, side by side—each so exceptional that it was hard to decide which of them was the more stunning. Some townspeople just gawked; blood drained from their faces, and any sense of propriety drained from their bodies. Several commoners fell to their knees and bowed in awe. Two Gods had descended to the Autumn Creek Land to stir mere mortals.

One rider wore an open brocade kimono of the finest *nishiki*, its woven dye pattern blood red intermixed with rich indigo. Only someone from the highest echelon of the kuge class would dare to wear something so courtly; yet the yoroi underneath—crimson-lacquered platelets gleaming in the rays of the sun—suggested buke. And not just the armor, but the array of weapons that stood battle ready and menacing: a naginata with shaft well-worn from handling, a tightly strung bow with an ebira overflowing with black-and-white hawk-feathered war arrows, and a long tachi that hung in its fur-covered saya.

But what was so unearthly was the stranger's alabaster aspect: a young face of rare beauty covered in rice-white oshiroi appropriate for the Imperial Court, framed with long hair white as the snow. Even the horse, a magnificent half-tamed stallion, was argent like the clouds and had as much spirit as a tempest wind. As the green bridle flounce undulated, the horse almost pranced, its muscles rippling with every stride, its mane and tail combed by the gentle breeze.

"Ha!" the rider suddenly shouted—a female voice—and the stallion broke into a gallop.

The other rider likewise let out a womanly shout and galloped by, black hair streaming back. Her brilliant blue riding kimono fluttered open, revealing splendid white yoroi trimmed with indigo silk. The discerning eye could see she bore the distinctive Ine mon. She too was armed: naginata strapped to the saddle boot, its long tapered blade reaching up to slice the air; tightly strung yumi with ebira, replete with arrows; and tachi in a fur-covered saya fastened by braided blue-and-white sageo. With her kabuto strapped to the back of her saddle, a wreath of hollyhock adorned her head. How she came to wear these blossoms so early in the season, no one knew. Some suspected she was a master of magic who could conjure anything at will.

When the riders disappeared from sight, the commoners blinked, glancing at each other. Who or what had they just seen?

Without faltering, the riders galloped toward town. Now at a stately trot, they rode up the main street, sitting majestically in their saddles, glancing at the onlookers, although the gazes lingered only on those wearing armor or bearing weapons. The riders' expressions betrayed neither fear nor malice, just implacable disinterest. The townspeople withdrew far enough to feel safe, yet not so far as not to miss what might transpire.

As they approached the Saké House, the two samurai slowed their horses to a walk. At the entrance, a young Ōe guard leaned his hoko yari against the building's outer wall and ducked inside, immediately returning with Sadamasa. Several other sakimori followed.

Reining their mounts, the clinks and jangles of tack fell silent. The horses snorted, their breath steaming as, with casual dignity and the agility that comes from years spent on horseback, the woman warrior in blue slipped her leg from the stirrup, swung it over her mount's neck, and dropped down to the ground.

The other rider stayed in the saddle.

For the span of two breaths, the woman warrior and Sadamasa regarded each another. The more astute of observers might have noticed that

Sadamasa's breathing became shallow and his sword hand flexed by his side. As if in response to the pose Sadamasa struck, the tail of the woman's horse lifted and green excrement fell into the snow.

Sadamasa glanced around, glaring at anyone who dared meet his gaze, and stormed back into Saké House. The other sakimori glared at the two women before following Sadamasa—all but the two youngest, who resumed their posts, now with a renewed interest in projecting fierce strength.

The woman samurai led her horse down the alley.

The white warrior, still in her saddle, guided her white steed to follow.

They stopped in front of the House of Red Banners.

Before they could clap or call out, the front door slid open. "Welcome! Welcome, Aoi Shōgun!" cried a gaunt man as he ambled forward, bald head bobbing as he bowed repeatedly, his red-striped kimono dragging in the snow.

The dismounted warrior, Aoi Shōgun, gave him a perfunctory nod. "Hari-kun, grain for the horses. Food for us."

Hari bellowed a command toward the house and waited awkwardly since no one responded, grinning in the meantime at the general. He bowed to make it look like matters were in hand. All at once, there was the sound of scurrying feet on wooden flooring, and boy and a girl dashed out, bowing toward the newcomers.

Hari put on a severe expression, wagging his finger. "Take the horses to the stable!" The youngsters cried out in one voice, "Hai!"

The boy took the reins from Aoi, who said, "Comb down my horse. Put a blanket over him."

The girl, tall and just beyond her mogi year, rushed to the other horse. But the white rider withheld her reins and said, "Is Yoshinaka inside?"

Embarrassed, the girl shook her head.

Aoi addressed the girl in a rough voice made soft. "What about Ashita?"

The girl scrunched her face. "Ashita?"

"My brother."

Hari stepped up, bowing. "Nobody else has arrived, samurai-sama."

Aoi grunted and ducked in through the door.

Hari muttered something to the girl. She blanched and rushed inside after Aoi.

Hari bowed to the alabaster warrior. "May I be of help, samurai-sama?"

"Where's Yoshinaka?"

He bowed. "He leaves and he comes back. He never says where."

The white warrior tugged her reins and her argent stallion turned about, stomping and snorting. "No doubt he's on the prowl," she said with a smirk. "I'll find him." She left back up the alley at a trot.

Fifty-Four
Exposed

SABURO SWEPT ASIDE THE SNOW, revealing icy handholds in the cliff's outcroppings where he could plant his feet. He had to move fast now. He needed to catch the Taka warrior in a vulnerable moment—more difficult now that she was accompanied by Kiso. Saburo had just missed a clear chance when she was preoccupied in the guesthouse. He had foolishly assumed he had time for caution, avoiding even a chance of being seen by the people inside the armory. But before he could get close, she and the young lord had emerged and walked toward the bluffs, and now they were up in the crags somewhere.

To follow them, the shinobi scrambled up the rough rock face where nooks and crevasses meandered unpredictably but provided a quick way over the first rise. Let the terrain work to her disadvantage, where he would choose the moment of her death.

Accumulations of snow and ice made the way treacherous, but before long he cleared the crest. There he discovered a hidden canyon just beyond. He dropped to his hands and knees and slid across the snow-covered surface toward the far edge.

Cautiously he peered over the side.

The view, partially obscured by rising steam, revealed Yamabuki standing completely naked near a hot springs pool, her long hair tied into a coiled knot at the back of her neck. Ankle deep in the water, Minamoto faced her. The warriors below spoke, but wind gusted across the bluff, whistling in the ragged rocks, drowning out what little of the voices might have carried up this high.

Saburo edged even closer, but the packed ice under his body was slick and he found himself sliding down toward the drop-off.

Desperately, he reached out to grasp a rock outcropping, arresting his motion. But now he was too exposed.

However, he now had a clear view of the young man's beautiful body—lean, muscular, with the flush of youth—possibly more attractive than any man Saburo had ever seen. Two parallel scars, long since healed, crossed his shoulder. Only a truly adept fighter could have survived wounds like that. Probably the warrior at the other end of that sword had not been so fortunate.

Kiso took Yamabuki's hand and led her deeper into the hot waters. The water rose to his daikon. Momentarily Saburo felt his own twitch.

He cursed himself for becoming distracted and focused on Yamabuki. It was obvious she was about to give her skin. She stepped into the spring pool, and the emptiness in Saburo's heart began to fill with loathing animosity.

Kiso said something to her. Saburo could not make out, but they both swept their gazes around the canyon.

Certainly he'd been spotted.

But no. The two below remained totally intent on each other. This was perfect. She was distracted. Guard down. Completely focused on the man. Their swords leaned several steps away from the pool. Finally. Time to move in for the kill.

Saburo pushed away from the ledge and, crawling on hands and feet, found a route to descend the steep rock face. Saburo wrapped his finger around the tsuka of Shima's tachi.

We'll see who's holding the better tsuka at the end of this!

FIFTY-FIVE

THE WARMTH OF THE ONSEN

WAIST DEEP IN THE SPRING POOL, Yamabuki felt the heat seep into her legs. It felt wonderful, even as it continued to burn her skin. Steam rose all around.

Across from her, Yoshinaka, who was in the water up to his neck, grinned. "Better now, yes?"

"I'm not sure I can do this," she said. She crouched, and the hot water rose to just below her breasts. Her nipples grew firm, as much from anticipation as from the chill air.

"Don't worry. The toes have the most difficult adjustment."

"My toes are not the parts I'm thinking about."

He laughed. She lowered herself all the way in, water up to her neck. She gasped as the warmth embraced her. Yoshinaka's eyes twinkled. How unlike Ryuma he was! She found herself comparing them. She could not help herself. Both men were similar. Both men were different. Both men were tall, though she remembered that Ryuma seemed wider at the shoulder and wider at the *hara*—the belly, the seat of resolve.

But did Ryuma have resolve? The morning after their night together, as he led Mochizuki to the front of the Wakatake Inn, she and Ryuma exchanged a long moment, staring into each other's eyes. Who else knew what had happened? Maybe the entire inn. After all, it wasn't a Taka fortress. Still, propriety demanded formality. She knew many years might pass before the two saw each other again. Was it not already so? Six years had passed since their prior encounter. Maybe it would be six years again—maybe more. Most of the Good People died by their thirtieth year. By that reckoning, half of her own fleeting life was already gone. Maybe they would never meet again.

When she considered yesterday's duels, she realized how terribly close she had come to that being true.

And suppose after years yet to be recorded, she rode her steed into Kita, returning to the Inn of Young Bamboo? Might Ryuma have taken a wife? Perhaps one of the pretty servant-dancers. Maybe Ishi-tsuki, or perhaps Chi-ye. Both were lovely. Maybe he took both as his wives. They would have his babies. Yet she herself could not afford to let her attraction lead her in that direction—could not let herself feel what she in fact felt. She had to put Ryuma out of mind—the faithless Ryuma who would marry two women who would bear his babies.

Yoshinaka sat in the water, back against rock wall at the end of the pool. He looked at her intently. "Are you troubled?"

"No." She lied, of course. She would not say she was thinking about another man. Staying beneath the warm water she sloshed over to where he sat, his legs stretched out in front of him. She rose up and straddled him. As she lowered herself downward, her breasts moved passed his delighted face. He immediately became aroused.

"Lift your knees," she said.

"Oh, I'm lifting everything," he whispered back.

"Cradle me. Let me sit."

He adjusted himself so she could come down against him. She settled her weight on his thighs and rocked her hips gently, and the sun peeked over the south-facing cliff above and washed down upon them, illuminating the entire area in warmth.

Yoshinaka said, "Amaterasu is especially bright shining upon snow." He squinted up into the blindingly blue sky. "It is beautiful." He smiled. Such a beautiful smile.

"When I saw you come to the armory with the sun rising, I decided I would call you Asahi. All that she shines on is made beautiful by her rays."

"Asahi is it?"

"You are Asahi Shōgun."

He grinned, eyes wrinkling with pleasure. "Then I shall call you Yamabuki Shōgun. I have plans already drawn up to build a great fortress castle in the mountains. I shall name it Yamabuki-jō."

She raised an eyebrow, even as she continued rolling her hips. "Yamabuki Chéng? Am I that formidable?"

"You are that beautiful. It's the perfect name. Mountain Rose Castle. In the fortress mountains of Shinano."

She imagined herself in the mountains with the two of them looking across the domain. She had never been to Shinano, but that did not matter. She imagined a magnificent green land with brooks, lakes, and rivers. She imagined every day might be like this. He would lead her into their canopied sleeping area.

"Put your arms around me," she said, thinking back on the drawings in the picture book.

As he slid his arms around her back, she wrapped hers around his neck. Now he began to lift while she began to slide. Her saya moved toward him, but his tsuka was not where she wanted it. She reached down and held it steady, lowering her body until she could just feel him touch, and then she let go and allowed her weight to move her down, which pushed him inside her. Exquisite! Maybe because they had coupled earlier or because they were in the water, it went more smoothly. She lowered herself further and Yoshinaka slipped ever deeper into her. Her hara went numb and completely sensitive at the same time. And now she fully sat, and he was fully within her.

"Shall we have another battle?" She grinned wickedly and began to move up and down, and he did too in rhythm with her. She moaned with delight, and they continued with abandon. And her body experienced every sensation, every touch, every shiver that ran up her back.

Love.

Yamabuki moaned as another pulse of pleasure coursed through her. The embrace of the hot water trapped the heat building up within her. She felt Yoshinaka within, moving slowly but steadily. Her arms around his neck, she gasped, wanting him deeper. His strong hands, fists clenched at the small of her back, supported her. She directed the pace, rocking her hips. He moved in time in yet another dance they shared.

Stones skittered off the cliffs to her left. *Melting snow, no doubt.* She cast a sideways glance. Tiger Cub remained in easy reach. She let her mind slip back to the pleasure of Yoshinaka. A whistling breeze carried cold air across the water, sweeping aside the steam. She inhaled the coolness as the heat between her legs intensified. The guesthouse had been merely a preliminary compared to what she experienced now.

He thrust deeper. It ached yet it didn't. She wanted to ache. To hurt. But not in the way of injury. In the way of throbbing. Of entering ever further. The tightness of him inside thrilled her. Delighted her. And then Yoshinaka pressed his hips up, and his tsuka pulsed as his seed exploded inside her. Her entire body dissolved from the top of her head, through her neck, down her back, through her hips and legs to her curled toes. She moaned and almost screamed.

She touched his shoulder. He had to stop. She let him hold her as her body pulsed and throbbed, and the intensity began to die away.

His seed was in her yet again. She liked it. She liked the feeling. The seed had charm and power. Power over her—part of the bargain of surrender.

In the wind, a woman's voice sang out, "Somehow I knew this was what you were up to, Yoshi-chan."

FIFTY-SIX
THE ALABASTER WOMAN

YAMABUKI TRIED TO TURN toward the source, but Yoshinaka's arms slid up her back and pulled her close. She yielded. His chest vibrated against her. "Some people respect the intimacy between others. Leave us be."

"Some warlords respect their commitment to their warriors," the woman's voice said with a tone of scolding familiarity. "The general is awaiting your instructions. Get into your armor. I'll pay off your yahochi. Two coppers is the going rate, girl. No?"

Yamabuki's ire erupted like lava flowing from an angry mountain. She pushed away from Yoshinaka—groaning slightly at the loss of his presence within her, the full sensation of his tsuka sliding from her saya—and stood upright to face this intruder.

A woman warrior had positioned herself at the edge of the pool—and for a flash, Yamabuki was taken aback.

In full makeup, face oshiroi white, lips painted red in the fashion of a rosebud, with snowy white hair, obviously left untied for dramatic effect, draped across her shoulders and down her back, she stood as white as the vapor that filled the air. If not for her crimson red yoroi and two swords hanging at her side, she might have been an illusion from the roiling steam. However, it was the color of her eyes gave her an unearthly appearance—blue as pale as the heavens. Never had Yamabuki seen this eye color in a human. Only in cats: *neko. Yes, a pretentious cat, this one. Even the tachi she carried was of extra length.*

Yamabuki felt that her own eyes turn to flame. She pitched her voice in the high and haughty royal court accent that the Dowager had insisted she perfect. "Retract your insult!"

A startled expression crossed the other woman's face, which then transformed into a smirk. She purred musically, "Two copper's an insult?" She looked Yamabuki up and down. It was meant to be dismissive, but there was curiosity mixed in as her eyes lingered a bit longer than was polite. "Three then. I suppose he's obligated to pay extra for your supercilious pronunciation."

"At least I don't articulate like some backcountry bumpkin who's just crawled out of the Oku underbrush."

The pale blue eyes burned at Yamabuki. "Aren't you a caution!"

Yamabuki glared back. "Who is this *shirabyōshi* wearing armor and pompous makeup?" *A pretender who no doubt prefers the comforts of the inner shinden chambers to life in the world. One of Yoshinaka's lovers? His concubine?*

"Please stop this war of words, Yamabuki-san," Yoshinaka said, wading out of the onsen, unabashedly naked.

He stands naked in front of her. So, one of his lovers after all.

He raised his palms, looking plaintively at Yamabuki. "*Gomen nasai.* You have to excuse my sister."

Sister?

"Yamabuki-sama, may I present Imai Tomoe. Tomoe Shōgun, please respect our guest, Taka-gimi."

"Princess?" The woman named Tomoe both scowled and smirked.

"Princess and Taka Shōgun," he said. "Daughter of Taka Daimyō."

Tomoe smiled thinly, not showing her teeth. "You certainly have caught quite the man in my brother, Taka-*gimi.*"

"I don't *catch* men like someone who thinks she's a catcher of mice. And I'm not accustomed to being disrespected."

Tomoe flicked dismissively a hand as white as alabaster. "Welcome to the big rude world."

"Insults," Yamabuki said with restraint, "beget steel."

"Yours?" Tomoe laughed.

Yoshinaka shook his head. "Be careful, Tomoe. She fought in the Heiji Ran."

"Not possible." Tomoe sniffed.

"I saw it with my own eyes," he said with complete earnestness.

Tomoe huffed. "Now I know you are drunk."

"It is true. Last night she fought over saké bottles and sent several sakimori flying." Yoshinaka laughed, and Yamabuki recognized the homonym: Heiji Taira clan and wine bottles.

Tomoe did not answer.

Small rocks tumbled again from the cliff above. Tomoe looked up. "Someone's up there," she whispered.

Yamabuki scanned the cliffs but saw nothing.

Yoshinaka picked up his tachi. "Tomoe is right. Those rocks did not fall by themselves."

Tomoe's hand went to her sword hilt. "Animal? Maybe someone wanting to watch?"

The three listened intently in silence, but now only heard the wind whistling high above answered her ears.

Yamabuki retrieved Tiger Cub. *Is the assassin about to kill me? Is this how I am to die? Naked in a hot springs?*

Tomoe said, "Kiso-sama, you must get to a safe place. If someone is up there armed with yumi and arrows, we're easy targets."

"Perhaps we should take ourselves to our kimono and armor, Taka-gimi."

Frustrated and annoyed, Yamabuki met Yoshinaka's gaze and said, "Our business here is concluded anyway."

Tomoe glanced at her, pointedly taking in all of Yamabuki's nakedness, and her lips curled slightly. "Don't worry. I'll stand guard while you get into your shitagi, Hadaka-gimi."

Naked Princess!

Before Yamabuki could respond, Yoshinaka hissed, "Stop it!" and Tomoe turned away like a scolded child—a child wearing a ko-dachi and long tachi. Yoshinaka showed Tomoe a great deal of deference and nothing that smacked of indulgence. There was more to this woman than what she seemed. Quite possibly Tomoe knew how to use those weapons. Good. Yamabuki didn't like the idea of threatening a defenseless woman.

But Yoshinaka was right. This wasn't the place. Certainly not if Gankyū was lurking about.

Yamabuki retrieved her shitagi. At the edge of her vision, she caught Tomoe once again eying her before returning her attention to the rocks above.

FIFTY-SEVEN
ARMOR DONNED

WRAPPED IN HER SHITAGI AND KOSODE, the back of her head tingling—and not just from the cold—Yamabuki followed Yoshinaka down the rocky trail and out through the short rock-walled passageway, listening to the quiet steps of Tomoe behind her. They all walked in silence. When they emerged from the cliffs, Yoshinaka and Yamabuki headed directly toward the guesthouse.

"Where are you going?" Tomoe asked.

Yoshinaka grinned at her. "Kimono would be proper, ne?"

Tomoe's eyes scanned the cliffs. "I will stand post out here and protect you, brother."

The white warrior's concern about potential danger reminded Yamabuki that Yoshinaka, too, had enemies. The chill she had felt, barely acknowledged even to herself, when Tomoe had said someone was up on the rocks returned. How reckless she had been! Yamabuki had put the one-eyed assassin out of her mind. Now she felt foolish.

"Shall we?" Yoshinaka asked with a smile as he slid open the guesthouse door.

Just as foolish as giving my skin to Yoshinaka. Charming as he was, she scarcely knew him.

Inside the guesthouse, as Yoshinaka donned his kimono, Yamabuki immediately slipped into her own kimono and fastened her hakama.

Then she stood still while Yoshinaka dropped to a knee and expertly fitted her suneate. Neither of them spoke. She liked the touch of his hands, the firm but gentle touch of his fingers fastening the ties. A shiver ran down her back. Her skin still held memories. But as he fastened other armor pieces to her, one by one, a sense of relief came over her.

Something Shima had said now settled upon her awareness—that the assassin Gankyū worked only for clan traitors, that a Taka traitor was trying to have her killed. She had dismissed Shima's claims at the time as attempts to shake her before drawing steel on her. But was he right? Was there a traitor within the Taka clan?

Shima had claimed she was just a *chibi* being used as bait, and the scrolls likely were blank or even intended to fall into the wrong hands. But only her mother, her father, Tomoko, Hana-ye, and Lord Nakagawa had known she was leaving on musha shugyō. None of them would have sent a killer after her. Impossible.

But someone did. What purpose would her death serve? The mere question was almost too distasteful to consider. But there were hints. The two false monks had known of only two of the three scrolls. The traitor's information was incomplete. She had killed the false monks. As for Gankyū, the man Shima had said was named Saburo—*or was that a dream?*—he was still out there. *I've been fooled by three shinobi so far. I'm alive only because of my sword and luck. Anyone I meet could be an assassin.* Another shiver ran down her spine, this time cold and with foreboding.

Once her corselet was securely fastened, Yoshinaka stepped behind her and began to fasten a sode to her left shoulder.

"Yoshi-chan?" she asked softly.

"Hmm?"

"Who is Tomoe?"

"Ah. She's my brother's sister."

"Is she your sister?"

"Yes, but not by blood."

"Not by blood?"

"No. She is the sister of my milk brother, Shiro, so that makes her my sister."

She nodded. *Milk brothers, infants suckled by the same nursemaid.*

He began to attach the other sode to her right shoulder and said, "I told you about my uncle killing my father and taking our lands. I was to be executed as well. They could not bring themselves to kill a child, or so they say. We escaped from Musashi Prefecture and I was raised in Shinano."

The subject of family betrayals brought Yamabuki discomfort. "Your sister called you Kiso."

"Ah." He finished the last tie on the sode and stepped around in front of her. "I no longer go by Minamoto. Kiso is better—the mountains of Shinano."

"Kiso." She smiled, understanding exactly the significance: not Minamoto, not anymore, not in his loyalties. "Kiso Asahi Shōgun," she said. "And you've returned to power."

"Power of what? My cousin now rules Minamoto."

She saw pain in his eyes, and she felt a sadness for him. If she had been betrayed by her uncle, her father killed, her birthright taken, she would have been shattered. Could she have gone on with honor? Could she have rallied others to her side, in effect forging a new clan, or at least family of sorts, as Kiso obviously had?

Kiso Yoshinaka handed Yamabuki her short sword, and then tied his own tachi saya to his sash. "I also need my armor," he said, and he raised his brows mischievously, showing his self-confidence. "Especially with assassins lurking."

When they stepped outside, Tomoe stood waiting. She looked Yamabuki's armor up and down. Yamabuki stood ready for more insults, but Tomoe said simply, "It's an uncommon mon." She almost sounded impressed.

Moments later, they entered the armory. Yo-ichi rushed up to them and bowed to Tomoe. "Your horse is unsaddled, curried, blanketed, and fed in the stable, samurai-sama."

Tomoe grunted. "Take me stables. I want to see how Raski is curried. I've ridden him hard." Yo-ichi bowed lower this time, and the two of them headed for the stables.

Yamabuki muttered, "It's not just her horse she rides hard."

Yoshinaka smiled wickedly. "You know all about riding hard."

She blushed. He laughed. She laughed softly, casting a shy glance away.

Taro called out, "Samurai-sama!" Taro cradled Yamabuki's tachi in its scabbard, his palms up high. "I finished polishing your sword."

Yoshinaka whispered, "I'm glad my sword also got polished."

"What notches there were in fact were barely more than scratches. It was an honor to work on the blade of great master Yukiyasu," Taro said, and he bowed, presenting the sword to her.

Yamabuki bowed in return and accepted it.

She drew the blade out, tip only just still in the scabbard, and looked the blade up and down. "*Yoshi!*" she said in praise. She snugged the sword back in its scabbard, fastened the sageo to her waist sash, and let Tiger Claw hang free. Its weight comforted her.

She reached into her sleeve and retrieved the pouch with the agreed-upon fifty silver coins. She held it out.

Taro received the pouch and bowed low.

She said, "I expect to be leaving tomorrow, depending upon weather."

"You are most welcome here, samurai-sama."

Yoshinaka said, "Taro-san."

Taro grinned and bowed. "Your armor, samurai-sama. Hai!" He turned and shouted, "Eiji! Fuyuki!" The young men ran up from the back of the building. "Yoshinaka-sama is ready for his yoroi."

Taro's sons repeated for Yoshinaka the efficient process they had only an hour before done for Yamabuki—what Yoshinaka had done more tenderly, but with no less thoroughness, for her just moments before. She watched as they placed each piece on his body.

By the time they fastened his dō, he took on a splendid and formidable aspect, yet without any change in his demeanor. The deep-blue lacquer of the kozane platelets glinted in the daylight washing in from the open doors. The green and white silk only made the yoroi more impressive. When the azure-blue helmet was finally placed on his head, he seemed every bit the shōgun ready to lead battle.

He stepped around, swinging his arms this way and that—sword and archery motions. "Yes, yes."

Taro bowed low.

Yoshinaka glanced at the armorer. "I believe I paid you in advance."

Without hesitation, Taro bowed even more deeply. "I am most honored, Tennō."

Tennō? Yamabuki thought. If Kiso Yoshinaka drew this kind of support from people of all classes, perhaps his cause was not as hopeless as she had thought.

Mari's soft voice came from behind her. "Samurai-sama?"

Yamabuki turned, and the girl presented the kabuto that Yamabuki had declined to wear earlier. "May I assist you with this?"

Still not wanting to deal with her hair, especially now that it was still damp from the hot spring, yet not wanting to leave it behind again, she said, "Help me fasten it to my shoulder." It could hang on her back.

A boy's shouting voice shattered the respectful mood in the room.

"Samurai-sama! Samurai-sama!" A boy dashed inside—the same boy who had directed Yamabuki to this place the day before. Yoshinaka's spy. She tried to meet his gaze, but the boy had eyes only for Yoshinaka, who said, "Speak, Kani-kun"—and he chuckled—"when you can breathe."

Gasping, the boy said, "Dead men!"

FIFTY-EIGHT
DEAD MEN

M ORE DEAD MEN. Yamabuki was quite certain this had nothing to do with her. She wanted no part of it. She had enough troubles already. But Yoshinaka seemed quite concerned, so when he and Tomoe followed the boy out of the armory, Yamabuki came along—and almost immediately regretted it, for on Ledge Road, the three warriors walked into a brisk wind that blew loose snow from the trees and cut bitterly through Yamabuki's armor.

There's a snare to indulging in the comforts of onsen. She contained a smile. The fallen snow which had softened earlier now resisted their steps, giving in with a crunch. The swing of her tachi made her feel whole.

Next to her, Tomoe had put on a strange wooden mask that covered her face from brow to cheeks. It was far from a *mempō*. Not only was it wood, but it bore no fierce visage to frighten enemies. It was just plain wood with narrow slits cut into it, presumably so she could see where she was going. Was the mask to hide the blue color of her eyes?

Meanwhile, Yoshinaka questioned the boy, who chattered on, obviously excited about the spectacle.

"Kani-kun, tell me what happened."

"Bandits! They killed an Ōuchi warrior and monks yesterday."

"We already know this," Yoshinaka said, impatient.

"Someone killed the bandits. The sakimori are bringing the bodies into town."

"How many dead? Did you see?" Yoshinaka asked.

The boy touched his fingers, counting. "Six."

"All dead." It wasn't a question.

Kani said, barely ahead of his breath, "The bandits were killed in the woods, but a beast dragged one of the bodies to the road, and the guards saw it and found the others."

Tomoe said, "The guards are angry over dead bandits?"

"One of them says the Ōuchi did it. Revenge for killing their warrior."

This made sense to Yamabuki. Back home, the Ōuchi were known for revenge killings.

But Tomoe muttered, "Ōuchi? Is that even possible?"

Yoshinaka said, "Not likely."

Again, Yamabuki sensed she was missing something important.

Down in front of Saké House, on either side of the door stood two Ōe guards with spears. What were they doing there? Was a dignitary inside? The guards watched the three approaching warriors for a moment, but then turned their attention the opposite direction down Ledge Road.

When the intersection at North Road came into view, Yamabuki, Yoshinaka, and Tomoe stopped as one.

Down at North Road, a large group of Ōe warriors dragged boards bearing dead men—from their appearance, warrior-monks. Yamabuki recognized Sadamasa among the sakimori.

The procession stopped. Sadamasa shouted a command, and the guards unceremoniously let go of the planks. The monks fell to the muddy snowpacked road, their bodies sprawled in undignified death. Blood soaked their sōhei robes. Wild hair and thick beards covered the heads of all—except for one dead man whose head was missing. These were no warrior-monks. Yamabuki looked for clues as to their true identities, but she saw no weapons or banners. Either confiscated or already looted by others.

The Ōe guards spread out, glaring at the curious townspeople who had gathered to gawk.

"Who knows these men!" Sadamasa bellowed. Who recognizes any of them! Someone must!"

No one spoke up.

Tomoe and Yoshinaka shot long glances at each other.

"Kani-kun," Yoshinaka said. "Tell me if you learn anything else. You know where to find me." He held out a hand and the boy retrieved something from it. A coin?

"Hai!" the boy said, still pumped full of excitement, and ran back down the road.

Tomoe glanced at Yamabuki and said in dismissal, "Kiso and I have matters we must attend to. Leave us, Hadaka-gimi."

Anger flared in Yamabuki. She thought to draw Tiger Claw, but that would only attract the attention of the sakimori. *Perhaps it would be best to stay away from her, lest I get provoked into killing again.* She glared at the half-masked white woman.

Yoshinaka said, "Come with us, Yamabuki-sama."

"What?" Tomoe cried, whipping off her wooden mask to glare at him.

Ignoring her, he nodded at Yamabuki. His face no longer held the kindness of a lover. His eyes glistened and his jaw was set hard. "We all have matters to attend to."

Tomoe scowled at Yamabuki but said nothing.

"Come," Yoshinaka said, and he led them into the alley and to the House of Red Banners.

FIFTY-NINE
THE IMPORTANCE OF BLUE RICE

THE NIGHT BEFORE, Yamabuki had taken the House of Red Banners to be a room barely larger than the genkan where she and Yoshinaka removed their boots. But now heavy shōji were slid aside, revealing old but solidly built *yama* house. An irori burned in the center. Two braziers cast warm light on walls that bore no tapestries or banners. Nor did any mats or pillows decorate the plank floor, though its black lacquer's uneven color and lack of shine revealed years of use—a natural course of events given that this might have been the most well-made structure in this small town. Yamabuki briefly wondered if, years ago, an Imperial minister or governor might have lived here.

After they had removed their boots and stepped into the large room, Yoshinaka retrieved some items from a small box against a wall. A bowl, *sumi*, a small flask, and paper. He knelt on the floor and under brazier light prepared ink in the same way Yamabuki prepared her own for her pillow book.

The smell of pungent spice greeted her, and she realized Tomoe had lit some incense in a porcelain *kōro*. Now they both watched in silence as Yoshinaka laid out on the worn floor six square sheets of rice paper. He dipped his brush in the bowl and drew on one square, with elegant strokes, a name for one of the fallen warriors. A funerary remembrance. He dipped the brush again and marked the next square with another name. He marked each paper with a name.

He finished the last stroke on the last sheet, set down the brush, and sat back. Tomoe nodded in approval.

All attention turned to the front door as a warrior in brilliant white yoroi entered.

A woman. She slid the door firmly shut behind her and removed her boots. Moving as if her armor were part of her, the samurai stepped up from the genkan. For a moment, she stared at Yamabuki.

Yoshinaka said to Yamabuki, "This is Aoi Shōgun, my top commander."

Yamabuki stared back at Aoi. She was older, though not as old as Lady Taka. Like Yamabuki, and unlike Tomoe, she wore no oshiroi, and her cheeks held the color of a life led in the sun. Woven leather, stained dark from hand sweat, covered her tachi tsuka. Her kimono sleeves bore the rice-ear mon identical to those on Blue Rice's cotton trousers and saké flasks.

A knot tightened in Yamabuki's stomach. She had imagined Blue Rice's sister to be some helpless whisp of a woman, nothing like this formidable warrior; yet this had to be her. *"You have to tell her what happened,"* he had said. But that had been a dream.

Aoi shifted her attention to Yoshinaka and bowed. "Tennō! I was looking for you. I discovered bad news."

In answer, Yoshinaka gestured at the squares of paper. Aoi sighed. He rose to his feet and glanced at each of the warriors in turn—Tomoe, Aoi, and Yamabuki—and said, "Join me."

He walked solemnly to the far side of the irori and sat, facing the sandy pit. Tomoe seated herself to his left. Aoi, his right. Yamabuki sat across from him, her back to the entry. The glowing embers warmed her face.

Yoshinaka added two logs. Then he lifted the top off a taru resting next to him. One by one, he dipped bowls into the saké within, passing one to Tomoe, another to Aoi, who in turn passed it to Yamabuki—giving her a lingering questioning look in the process—and a last one again to Aoi before dipping one for himself.

He raised his bowl and said, "Namu Amida Butsu!" *I take refuge in the Amida Buddha.*

Tomoe smiled and repeated, "Namu Amida Butsu!"

The three others drank down their bowls, but Yamabuki hesitated, unsure. The Buddhist monks sanctioned by the Emperor had announced the accepted ways to honor the dead. The *nembutsu* was not one of them. Yamabuki had of course heard of Pure Land Buddhism, but it was not something the Taka practiced in Ō-Utsumi—and certainly not in the Imperial City. Still, she had read that the nembutsu was to be recited five hundred times for rebirth to be realized. Then again, every clan had their own practices handed down through the generations, each similar to others, yet unique.

She put her bowl to her lips and emptied it.

Tomoe lifted the funerary papers and touched them to her forehead, then held them in front of her mouth. She chanted words Yamabuki didn't understand while she dropped one of the sheets into the irori. The square seemed to float over the low fire, smoldering before flashing into flame. Ashes danced over the coals as sparks rose up toward the roof vent. Still chanting, the white-haired warrior released another marked paper into the coals. And then another, each one by one.

Tomoe's ritual seemed eclectic, resembling Shintō if not Jingi. Yamabuki wondered what Tomoe and Yoshinaka would think about the rituals the priests of the Taka clan performed in honoring the dead. *We are all as much strangers to each other as we are to the dead.*

As the ash from the last of the papers settled in the sand, Yoshinaka sighed. "Takaitori will be missed keenly by his Satake brothers."

"And by Otomo," said Tomoe.

"We need to find out who did this."

"I want to know *how*," Aoi said, and she opened her mouth to say more, but stopped herself and turned to Yamabuki. "Who are you? Why are you here? Tennō, why is she here?"

Yamabuki answered directly. "I am Taka Yamabuki, daughter of General Moroto."

"Taka-*gimi*," Yoshinaka added.

Aoi did not appear impressed, but she did bow her head slightly. "Why are you here, Taka-gimi?"

Yoshinaka said, "Taka-gimi might have some useful information about events that happened on the North Road."

"Among other useful aspects," his sister muttered.

Yamabuki bit off a retort and took a breath to calm herself. A coal sizzled and cracked. Several sparks floated up into the rafters.

"Takaitori's men were seasoned warriors," Yoshinaka said. "Not just anybody could kill them. Who? Who has the capability?"

"Who would dare?" Aoi asked.

Tomoe snorted. "Anyone with enough swords. Ōe. Ōuchi."

Yoshinaka turned his eyes to Yamabuki. "Taka-gimi, you were on the North Road yesterday. Who else did you see?"

"Nobody but those of whom I already told you," she replied. "Just a farmer family carrying dyed fabrics to the Strait. I encountered nobody else until I arrived in Minezaki."

He continued to gaze at her. "What about at the Strait? Who else crossed with you?"

"The Barrier Strait? You were there?" Aoi asked. "What did you see?"

Yamabuki shifted uncomfortably. She was being drawn into an intrigue she wanted no part of. When she had invited intimacy with Yoshinaka, this was not part of her plan. She took in a breath, considering her words, and decided to state the facts simply, without interpretation. Then they would realize there was nothing out of the ordinary—aside from the shinobi who attempted to kill her and the sword master who nearly did, but she was not about to get into *that*.

"In the morning, Hour of the Dragon, two jun low-level Ōuchi warriors arrived by kobune from Akamagaseki. Then I boarded with my colt. The other passengers were two Tendai monks, a sword master, a wanderer, and some silk merchants with a cart."

"Silk merchants?" Yoshinaka's face darkened. "You did not tell me."

"Why? Is it important to report of the travels of silk merchants?"

"Gomen." He took a calming breath and said, "This might be important Yamabuki-gimi."

"The cart was cumbersome. Heavy. The merchants appeared strong enough, but they were inept handling it. Why they didn't have an ox I have no idea."

"How many merchants?" asked Aoi.

Yamabuki checked her memory to make sure. "Six."

The others nodded almost as one.

Were the fabric merchants in fact Yoshinaka's men? That meant every passenger on that kobune—except for Blue Rice, and who knew what he might have been capable of?—was a killer of one sort or another. And she had not realized it, not even of herself.

"Did you kill them?" Tomoe declared, more an accusation than a question.

"Tomoe!" Yoshinaka snapped.

The alabaster woman snorted. "No, it's obvious she's incapable."

Yamabuki frowned. *Does she fear me? Is that why she's so hostile?* Yamabuki resolved to ignore Tomoe as much as possible. *Or she'll force me to kill her.*

"Gomen nasai." Yoshinaka bowed his head to Yamabuki. "Where did you see these silk merchants last?"

At this point, Yamabuki wanted to get this over with. Her temper was growing short. It was one thing to be interrogated by Nakagawa or challenged with bokken by other Taka warriors in training. It was quite something else to be questioned by armed warriors with revenge on their minds.

"I last saw them approaching Akamagaseki. They had struggled with their cart on beach. I was up North Road, a quarter hour ahead of them."

Aoi said, "The Tendai monks. Maybe they did it."

"Two against six?" said Tomoe "Monks?"

"They were no monks," said Yoshinaka.

Aoi and Tomoe looked at him, waiting for him to explain, but he said nothing, gazing at Yamabuki. He wanted her to tell them.

She sighed. "They were not monks, and they were dead by the Hour of the Horse."

"If not monks, who were they?" Aoi asked.

"They attacked me with blades tipped with fugu. I killed them."

"You killed them, Taka-gimi?" Tomoe narrowed her eyes. "How?"

Yamabuki touched her hand to Tiger Claw's hilt and said nothing.

Tomoe leaned forward. "And they were after you?"

"Apparently," Yamabuki said.

"Why?"

Yamabuki had no intention of elaborating. "A Taka matter."

Tomoe raised her eyebrows, skeptical.

Aoi struck a more polite tone. "Yamabuki-sama, you mentioned a sword master?"

Yamabuki nodded. "A large man with a nodachi. Wearing Ōuchi armor."

"Are you sure?"

Aoi turned to Yoshinaka. "It's possible a sword master could kill even six seasoned warriors."

Yamabuki said, "Not possible."

"Why not possible?"

"He also was dead by the Hour of the Horse."

"Dead? By you?" Tomoe asked.

Yamabuki met Tomoe's gaze. "He challenged. He insisted."

Tomoe's eyes crinkled, and a half-smile of half-admiration and half-menace appeared on her face. "You seem to attract trouble. You could have killed our men."

Now it was Yamabuki's turn to ask questions. "So they were your men?"

Tomoe spread her hands out and swept them over the irori, where the ashes from the rites still danced in the air currents.

Yoshinaka said, "I told you last night of my plan."

The eyes of the other two women flashed. "You told her?" Tomoe nearly shouted.

Yoshinaka growled, "We speak now with Taka Shōgun! Wasn't that the purpose of sending the envoys? To forge alliances with clans of the Isle of Unknown Fires?"

"Taka!" Tomoe said dismissively. "How many troops under your command, Taka Shōgun?"

Yamabuki narrowed her eyes. "My personal command?"

Tomoe nodded hard.

"All of them." Of course her father, the daimyō, was the ultimate commander, but she was still shōgun. Any Taka samurai she encountered would obey her command without question. She smiled thinly at Tomoe and said, "I do not see *you* with a retinue. Tomoe Shōgun, how many do *you* command? Or do you have so few that you need our numbers to swell your ranks?"

"This is pointless!" Yoshinaka roared. They fell silent. He took a deep breath. "We have lost six men and we bicker with someone who could be an ally."

Aoi looked very serious. "You mentioned an eleventh person on the kobune. A wanderer, you said. I am expecting my brother. He might have crossed with our envoys."

Yamabuki nodded slightly, steeling herself.

"Could you describe him?"

Time to fulfill her promise. "A loquacious and friendly man. Seemed to know a lot about the clans. He knew I was Taka. He did not approve of the Ōuchi. It was he who called them 'low-ranking' samurai." She decided it was best not to mention his particular affection for saké. "He said he had been of daimyō lineage, but he wore a commoner's tunic. Simple cotton trousers bearing the symbol of the rice plant."

Aoi smirked. "He offered you drink."

Yamabuki grinned sheepishly. "I declined."

"What happened? He's not with you?"

Yamabuki braced for another accusation from Tomoe, but the white warrior stared at the burning coals, saying nothing.

Yamabuki took a breath. "The seas were choppy. He did not bear it well. When we reached the shore, there was a checkpoint. Sakimori of the Ōe clan."

"And?" Aoi prompted, her face hardening.

Yamabuki realized she was drawing this out too long. Why torture her any more? "Ashore, he ran to the brush to lose his stomach. And—" She hesitated. *Tell her!*

"And?" Aoi prompted again.

"A sakimori warrior shot him with an arrow. He died instantly." Aoi did not seem to react. Yamabuki didn't want to say the next part, but she could not in good conscience hold it back, not from a respected general. "It was pointless," she said, letting her bitterness show. "A skill-test murder by one of the guards who claimed this unarmed man was making a run for it."

Aoi clenched her eyes tight. She whispered, "Risu-chan."

The dream name further tightened Yamabuki's stomach.

General Aoi opened her eyes. In an eerily calm voice, she asked, "Where is his body?"

Yamabuki shook her head. "I do not know. Last I saw, the sakimori left him there." She stifled a building rage. "They were too busy laughing."

"Where are these sakimori now?"

The question cooled Yamabuki's temper. *Yes, they met their just fates.* "I found out this morning, the kashira of the detachment, the man responsible, died last night along with several other Ōe as they tried to cross the pass through the snowstorm. The Yuki-onna took them."

The general lowered her head. In a strained voice, she asked, "Who held the yumi? What is his name? Whose arrows killed my brother?"

"A man named Misaki. He too was caught on the pass."

Aoi gazed with intensity at Yamabuki, and after some moments, bowed her head. "Yamabuki-sama, dōmo arigatō gozaimashita."

Yamabuki bowed in return.

Aoi's gaze moved to Yoshinaka. Tears welled in her eyes. "Tennō—" She choked on her words and turned her face away.

A distant bell began tolling the hour.

Yoshinaka said in a quiet voice, "When we return home, we will offer proper remembrance for our fallen."

Aoi said, "We need locks of hair from our men. For their families. I will get them."

She stood and stormed out to the genkan and put on her boots. A moment later, the outer door slid open and slammed shut just as the seventh toll rang out into silence. Hour of the Monkey.

Yoshinaka said, "Let Aoi-sama find herself. We need to decide what we're going to do."

Sixty
Not Just for the Moon Lords

Yoshinaka dipped a saké bowl into the taru and held it out toward where Aoi Shōgun had been sitting, while looking expectantly across the irori at Yamabuki. She met his gaze.

He wants me to discuss his plans? This is how he draws me into his endeavors. Am I to be his warrior-lover? That prospect made her both excited and uneasy. Still, this was just a conversation. Just talk. To refuse to sit next to him would be impolite.

In one smooth motion—not easily executed while wearing armor—Yamabuki rose to her feet, stepped to his right, and lowered herself back down. Eyes shining, he handed her the full cup, then dipped a bowl for Tomoe and one for himself.

Without a word, they all drank.

He collected Yamabuki's bowl and refilled it, and as he filled Tomoe's, he said, "We now walk in darkness. We don't know what news Takaitori was bringing. I may need to go there myself."

Tomoe said, "Too dangerous."

"Perhaps. But I must try."

"I don't know what you'd find," Yamabuki said. "If your men were the ones who visited my father days before I left—"

"He told you?" Yoshinaka's face lit up. "Is he interested? Or perhaps open to discussions of a pact?"

"What would be the benefit of such a pact? I do not know what it is you are trying to do, aside from reclaiming your birthright. Until yesterday, I did not even know you existed."

He collected and refilled everyone's saké bowls one by one. Then he began in his gentle voice to speak about what he called a better way to live, but which proved to be, at first, more of a litany of problems and injustices suffered across the land. "For example, the tax."

"We pay this every autumn," she said.

"Did you know that the tax rates were set hundreds of years ago? And no matter how land has changed, no matter the weather, droughts, floods, pestilence, famines, the amount never changes." He went into detail about lawless areas of the country, the ineffective and corrupt actions by Imperial officials, their failures to maintain roads and stations. And he spoke with some frustration about the self-absorption of the nobles in the Imperial City, their inward focus to the point of obsession. "Bandits are terrorizing the farmers while the Imperial ministers enjoy entertainments of monkey music. People starve in Shimotsuke while the ministers spend all day debating the fine points of what the acceptable brilliance of kimono colors should be for a middle-ranking lord."

Yamabuki found it not at all difficult to imagine ministers of petty concerns spending hours on trivial matters.

"Intrigue always shadows the Chrysanthemum Throne," said Yamabuki.

He slapped his knee for effect. "They do it for power. Not to change things, just to put themselves on top of the same stinking kuso pile!"

Yamabuki raised an eyebrow at his impolite language.

But he seemed not to notice as, eyes gleaming, he continued, "We are going to make it better for everyone. Not just for the moon lords!"

Yamabuki drank down her saké. Yoshinaka's enthusiastic interest surprised her. She could not betray her father's trust. "General Moroto's concern is always first with the Taka and the security of our borders. He did not tell me what message your men brought. He was interested in the news your envoys reported about the Kikuchi."

"You don't like them." Yoshinaka took the saké bowl from her hand. "I hear it in your voice."

"Relations with our neighbors is a Taka matter."

"A Taka matter!" Tomoe snorted.

Refusing to be provoked by her, Yamabuki waited as Yoshinaka handed her a brimming refill. "Takanao is the new daimyō. It is said he is young and ambitious. It is said he is not likely to remain sequestered. It is said he has disaffection for the Emperor."

Yoshinaka lit up. "Perhaps he could be made an ally?"

She shook her head slowly.

"What about the other clans? The Ōuchi?"

She grimaced. "The Taka have not had beneficial relations with the Ōuchi. Mostly we avoid one another."

"Do you know who of the western clans we might entreat?"

Yamabuki drank her saké while collecting her thoughts. "My father says that every daimyō must be acquainted with the game of Igo. It's about encirclement. Black and white stones are placed on a board that's scribed in squares."

"I know the game," Yoshinaka sounded interested.

"My father says it is more than a game. He says it is a teaching."

Yoshinaka nodded.

"It's a game the highborn in the Imperial City play very well. They build solid lines of stones and adroitly connect them at the critical moment." Yamabuki looked at Tomoe, who listened closely.

"True," Yoshinaka said, "but stones that linger on the edge have restricted liberty and can easily be captured, even if they take no great part."

"You mean like Ō-Utsumi? With water on two sides of our province, you think we risk being trapped in *atari*?"

"I mean like any piece whose freedom of movement is restricted."

Yamabuki nodded. "True, but every beginner also knows not to rush to the center to engage the opponent. For one, it is rude. For another, it rarely achieves anything lasting."

"What do you recommend, Taka-gimi?" Tomoe asked.

"Build a good foundation and to anticipate the enemy's structures and exploit weaknesses. As Nakagawa says, 'Every strength is also its weakness.'"

"Oh?" Yoshinaka leaned forward.

"Strong and fixed is good, but it cannot become supple and lithe."

He smiled. "A good player can turn one into the other by dropping the right stone in the right place at the right time."

"True, so long as the stone is not moved into atari or squandered. If it is your intent to win a game—"

"You mean, take the Imperial City?"

"—I mean any game, you can't let yourself walk into atari."

Yoshinaka said, "No one will deliberately go into atari."

"Sometimes even the brilliant attacker can miscalculate and end up sur-rounded. Sometimes it is better to lose a stone than to push a long line in hopes of saving one piece and end up losing a whole column."

"How do you mean that, Taka-gimi?"

"Tomoe Shōgun has advised that you not go to the Isle of Unknown Fires. I concur, not because you are in any real physical danger, but more that you are far from the center of the board."

"Didn't you just say it is rude to move to the center of the board?"

Tomoe said to her brother, "And didn't *you* just say that staying on the edge minimizes a stone's liberty?" Her deep blue eyes twinkled. "Taka Shōgun is saying we must first surround near the main area of play and not focus on the edges of the board."

Yoshinaka laughed. "How gracefully, Taka Shōgun, you tell someone that they need to rethink their strategy!" He laughed some more.

Yamabuki couldn't help but smile. "The Ōuchi and the Kikuchi will use you as a sacrificial stone, for they believe they have a chance of win-ning against Kiyomori. In the Hōgen Ran and the Heiji Ran, the enemy walked into the Imperial Capital. Walked into atari. Yet if you start at the edge, you yourself will be encircled before you break out. You are al-ready on the Main Isle. They must come to you."

"*Sōdesu ka*. Start close, but not foolishly close."

"Yes."

"And my words about taxes and lawlessness? What of these?"

"That's is where you lay your first stone."

"But everyone is affected."

"Start with those who are prospering without Imperial help, and thus pay the most for the least. These daimyō will understand your message immediately."

Yoshinaka nodded and began to brood. He appeared about to say some-thing but cut himself off.

He collected and refilled everyone's bowls.

At least there's good saké, Yamabuki thought.

He drank his down quickly and rose to his feet.

"I am going to find Aoi-sama. Make sure she doesn't kill anybody."

He said no more as he put his boots on and stepped outside. The door slid shut.

Yamabuki and Tomoe were alone in the House of Red Banners. Tomoe appeared to be amused, but for her own part, Yamabuki was both charmed and alarmed by Yoshinaka's headstrong nature—character that could be formidable in battle but also lead to blunders.

Tomoe broke the silence. "Shall we walk? My stomach tells me I would benefit from nabe."

After all the saké, the thought of food, even a steaming hot pot, did not hold appeal. However, a walk sounded quite the thing after such anxious conversation. But glancing at the alabaster woman, she hesitated.

Tomoe's eyes narrowed. "Tell me."

How could Yamabuki say this? "Last night, I sought out saké and because of this"—she touched the healing cut on her cheek—"I too thought it best to wear full makeup."

"Such are the decisions kuge women must make."

"I learned this morning, women in oshiroi are taken for yahochi."

Tomoe burst into laughter, a tittering musical laugh that was both courtly and almost bawdy. "You have a reputation, Taka-san!"

Yamabuki bristled. "That reputation is for *all* women in makeup."

If anything, Tomoe laughed harder. "They can try calling me yahochi, and my sword will reply."

"It's getting late. I'm going to see if the summit pass is in view. Maybe the weather is clearing."

"And if it isn't?"

"Well," she sighed, "I may have to go around on the East-West Highway."

"Then you can travel with us," said Tomoe and she smiled warmly. "I know my brother would like that."

Sixty-One
My Brother is Still Dead

Seven Bell Strikes, Hour of the Monkey

THE LAST NOTE of the distant tsurigane faded to silence under the thick gray sky as Aoi stepped into the crusted snow outside of the House of Red Banners. Her brother was dead, and there she stood, feeling nothing, looking at nothing, hearing nothing.

By standing around she achieved nothing, so she marched up the alley. The packed, refrozen snow made walking difficult, her steps sometimes sliding on hard-packed ice, other times breaking through crust and sinking to her ankles. She was thankful for her fur boots. Even rabbit hide was better than straw. Or nothing.

She found herself near the green banners of Saké House. Saké. That sounded good.

Two Ōe warriors, barely more than children, probably farmers, judging by their rough hands and shabby kimono, flanked either side of the entrance. They stiffened at her approach, trying to look fierce with their overly long hoko yari.

Aoi sniffed at them. "What were are going to do with those? Spear birds in the sky?"

The guards, suddenly uncertain, glanced up at the blades atop their polearms.

Aoi threw aside the door and stepped through.

Inside she found the place empty apart from five more Ōe sitting around several saké bottles. One of them the kashira she had stared down when she and Tomoe had first arrived in town.

Aoi snorted. *Real warriors.* She slammed the door shut. The warriors casually glanced at her, then looked again with appraising looks. She sniffed. *Let them look.* She picked a table close to the door, sat with her back to the wall, and said, "Hey!"

A bent old man emerged from a curtained-off back room.

"Saké," she said.

A moment later, he set a simple bottle down on the table. "A copper." She looked from the bottle to the old man's face. "Bowl?"

The saké man looked her up and down, then went into the back room, grumbling all the way, and returned with a drinking bowl.

She put a coin down and it disappeared into his hand. She poured and drank. Awful saké. Perfect for her mood. The world was awful. The Gods had abandoned the entire Autumn Creek Land. They had abandoned her. They had let her brother be killed. Little Risu, who had never hurt anybody. Who disliked fighting so much he refused to train with a bokken. Now he was dead. Killed by stupid warriors who thought killing an unarmed man was a test of skills. She glowered at the sakimori across the room. *Warriors like them.*

She drank the last of the sour liquid and she was about to call out for another bottle, when the front door slid open and two commoners, a man and a woman, entered. The woman carried a covered nabe. The man closed the door for her and they walked toward the back room. The woman said in a sweet, quiet voice, "Samurai-sama, I have some food." An indistinct voice came from the back room, and the two commoners ducked into the other room.

One of the Ōe warriors said, "We have to eat salted fish and he gets nabe. Lucky man."

"Lucky to lose only your fingers?" one of his fellows asked.

"Lucky to survive the Yuki-onna."

This caught Aoi's attention. She stared at her empty saké bottle, listening, watching the warriors at the side of her vision.

The senior guard—the kashira, she guessed from the extra colors woven into his armor—said, "You just want a woman to bring you hot broth."

All five warriors laughed quietly.

"Ōe Shōgun won't be pleased, though. Fingerless retainers are of no use to him."

"Maybe in the training hall?"

"Could you see that? An instructor? Misaki-san?"

A roaring thunder filling Aoi's ears drowned out the laughter of the men. Quietly, she rose to her feet and walked to where the five men sat. They looked at her. She said in a flat voice, "You said a name."

The kashira stood, facing her. "Who asks?" He seemed tense.

Aoi gazed at him calmly. "I know that name."

The Ōe warrior—kashira rank, from the look of him—squinted. "You know Misaki-san?"

Aoi ignored the question and glanced at the back room. "He's back there, isn't he?" she said, not expecting an answer.

She headed toward the curtained doorway.

Behind her, the guard growled, "Stop!"

She slowly turned.

The other four guards rose, and they all now glared at her. The kashira shouted, "You are not permitted to go in there!"

Aoi sniffed. "Who are you to tell me?"

He took a step toward her. "I am Sadamasa Kashira! I speak in the name of the Emperor!"

At that, Aoi laughed—but it was a bitter laugh, a mirthless laugh that vented her anger. "You? In the name of the Emperor? Does He know this?"

"Impudence!" He glanced at his men. "Apprehend her!"

The four warriors, hands on their sword hilts, spread out and approached her like silk moths to brazier fire. She stood still, her mind empty but for the pain of the her brother's death. But when they came within three strides of her, she let go of what held her and released her rage within.

She stepped once. Her tachi flashed out from its scabbard and cut across through one warrior's neck. The others froze as the man's head landed with a wet thump. The torso impossibly remained standing, blood gurgling out of its neck, before toppling over.

The warriors' eyes bulged, and they might have stood there like trees were it not for the roar of Sadamasa.

"Kill her!"

Aoi stepped again and cut another man through the chest, sending blood spraying. Sadamasa charged up from the back. Aoi stepped aside and shoved another guard into him, then whipped the sword through the leg of the third. Screams and blood filled the air as Aoi mercilessly moved through them, seeing where they would move, striking them where they were exposed. Before she had taken ten steps, the battle was over.

Five Ōe warriors dead.

The door guards clambered from outside, no doubt having heard the commotion, and saw the dead men and the woman holding the bloody sword.

"Ahh!" they cried and they began trembling. One aimed his polearm at Aoi. "You—!"

Aoi stepped toward them. The brave guard swung his yari back and slashed at her. Aoi parried the blade easily, but the polearm's reach still kept her at a distance, too far to strike back with her sword. Emboldened, the young guard grinned and swung back again, harder—but blade embedded in a wooden beam. He tugged on the shaft to free it, but in two quick strides Aoi was upon him. Her tachi cut through his neck. Blood sprayed. His eyes glazed. He collapsed.

His companion moaned, took a step back, dropped his spear, and sprinted out the front door.

So far, the battle was a rout. But Aoi felt no satisfaction. She felt nothing but black rage. She marched into the back room, where she startled everyone.

"Leave," Aoi said.

Grimacing with terror, the man and woman commoners slid along the wall, trying to stay away from the fearsome warrior, and dashed out of the room. The saké man followed. In the dim brazier light, a lone warrior lay on a mat next to an irori where coals burned red.

She said, "You are Misaki."

The man appeared to be unwell, but he answered in a surprisingly strong voice. "I am Misaki."

Aoi looked at him. He was nothing more than an insect. He peered at her with insect-like eyes. She said, "I am Ine Aoi, sister of Ine Ashita, and I avenge his death."

Misaki threw off his blankets and rolled to the side. With some difficulty, he pushed to his feet, grimacing, and stood—tottering, but with face hard, trying to maintain his dignity. "Your brother? He was the man at the Barrier Strait?"

Aoi shifted her position and raised her sword high.

Misaki just nodded. "I suppose it's better this way."

Aoi struck. Misaki was dead before his body hit the floor. His hand, missing all but two fingers, fell on the edge of the irori. Aoi gazed at that hand, the instrument of her brother's death, as it now lay lifeless in the flickering glow of the coals.

She heard a quiet step behind her, a familiar step. She turned around and gazed at Yoshinaka, whose eyes offered nothing but compassion. She felt tears run down her cheeks. But now that her rage was gone, she felt nothing but emptiness. Words came unbidden. "My brother is still dead."

Yoshinaka's mouth parted as if he was about to reply when a tsurigane began tolling in rapid rhythm.

Alarm!

Shouts outside, in the distance.

Yoshinaka stepped close and put his hands on her arms. "Aoi-sama," he said. For her, it was as though he spoke from the other side of the world. "Aoi-sama!" he shouted, but he was so far away. Yoshinaka too was all the way across on the other side of a veil. But right in front of her, she saw her brother, just six summers old, climbing high in a mulberry tree, laughing and squealing as he tried to chase a squirrel.

"Ine Shōgun!"

Aoi's eyes focused. "Tennō!" she whispered.

"We must leave town now! Take the East Highway. If we don't see each other, we will meet at the Inn of Dancing Butterflies in Aki Prefecture."

"Aki Prefecture," she repeated.

"Hai!"

"Aki Prefecture," she said again.

"Aoi-sama," Yoshinaka said. "There is still much to do. We must survive this day!"

Aoi took in a deep breath, and the cloud over her began to dissipate. The tolling alarm continued, and in her mind she pictured where the guards would be, blocking where roads intersected, watching at strategic points with clear sightlines. "We'll be safer together."

"If we can," Yoshinaka said. "My horse is at the armory, as is Tomoe-san's and Taka-gimi's. We will meet where North Road intersects East-West Highway."

Aoi nodded. "If the enemy is there, we should meet further beyond. A quarter hour at full gallop. They all will not sustain chase that long."

Yoshinaka grinned. "Shōgun!"

Aoi grinned. "Tennō!"

Together they strode through the main room of the Saké House and stepped outside. With a nod to each other, they parted. Yoshinaka dashed up Ledge Road. Aoi marched back into the alley to the House of Red Banners.

SIXTY-TWO
SNOWFALL

Second Quarter of Hour of the Monkey

WHEN YAMABUKI AND TOMOE stepped outside, they were met with fresh snowfall. They immediately headed toward the dead end of the alley. Tomoe had no interest in wandering around blindly searching for places where the Taka woman could see the pass, so she had rousted innkeeper Hari from his afternoon nap—late nights and early mornings were busy times for innkeepers—to get his advice. His answer was unexpected: simply venture up the alley to where it ended at the cliffs. "Look up the sheer wall, and you will see. This is why the town is called Peninsula Ridge."

They walked in silence. Rundown buildings lined both sides of the alley all the way to the end.

The cliff's rock face was indeed sheer. Dark gray and smooth as if a God had sliced off a piece of the mountain. The two warriors gazed skyward, but the summit remained cloaked in mists.

"The Imperial City lies ten days beyond the pass," Yamabuki said. "That is if the weather cooperates. Who can guess how long this freak storm will last?"

The snow conditions did not particularly interest Tomoe. She wanted to get to know better the future Taka warlord who had possibly stolen her brother's heart. Tomoe breathed hard. "With the loss of our men, it's too dangerous to stay here. We'll take the road eastward."

Yamabuki shook her head. "Going east adds five extra days to Heian-kyō."

Tomoe grunted. "We can't sit around and wait for the whatever pass to thaw."

"It's called the Pass of the Setting Sun." Yamabuki flashed a crooked smile. "It's in the northeast, where the sun rises—hardly a setting sun."

"Taka-gimi, you don't have the right viewpoint. From Kyōraku"—and certainly this Taka princess had to know that nobody called it Heian-kyō anymore, not in generations—"it's in the southwest. Everything is named in relation to the Imperial City. Besides, northeast is a badly as-pected direction."

Yamabuki gazed at the summit, frustration on her face. "We make our own luck. At least that's what my mother says."

Tomoe said, "You're not trapped here. You can wait for the pass to open, or"—she flashed her a smile—"you can accompany us and not let the el-ements waste your time. It'll be safer if we travel in numbers."

"No," Yamabuki said. "I will not leave Minezaki now. I have no rea-son to. I'll wait out the weather." She gave Tomoe a sideways glance. "Appealing though your invitation sounds."

A distant tsurigane began furious tolling in alarm.

Cries erupted down the alley, near the Saké House. Visible in the swirl-ing snow, black-clad sakimori dashed in all directions.

Tomoe's heart thumped hard. "What's this commotion?" She loos-ened her sword.

In a dry voice, Yamabuki said, "I knew Unagi's saké was wretched. Perhaps the soldiers are finally finding out." She started to laugh, then stopped.

Spear-carrying soldiers hurried in their direction. The men pointed at the two women and ran ever faster.

"I don't like the look of this?" Yamabuki loosened her own tachi.

"Spearmen." Tomoe stiffened. Even mediocre warriors could be dan-gers wielding hoko yari. "Dead-end. No getting away unless we smash through one of these hovels."

Yamabuki said, "If we run, we look weak—and guilty. Besides, it won't buy us anything if we head into the side streets. They don't lead anywhere."

Both women dropped their hands to their sides. Neither made any ag-gressive move. Their swords remained where they were, but they were at the ready.

The soldiers numbered a full jun, ten sakimori, counting their leader—one of those hotheads with more wildness in his eyes than brains in his head. They ran up as a bunch and spread out into a semicircular formation and lowered their spears, cornering the two women against the cliff. None of the soldiers, apart from the leader, wore any significant armor—only leather chest protectors and shin guards.

For a long moment no one said anything. It was Yamabuki who broke the silence. "What's this about?"

"You are under arrest," the leader growled.

"Arrest?" Yamabuki's eyes narrowed. "For what?"

"A woman warrior killed some of our men. It had to be one of you."

"We haven't killed anyone," Tomoe snapped. "You're out of your depth."

"Ha!" The leader sneered. "Put down your swords and come along. You don't want to challenge the Ōe!"

From a distance, anyone would have concluded this was no contest. The sakimori had the distinct advantage. Battle was futile.

But the two women examined closely the cohort, taking their measure. Warriors were not interchangeable, even though their tunics and weapons seemed to be. Tomoe and Yamabuki studied the men's eyes, looking for any sign of fear, any hesitation, any lapse in concentration, twitches . . . anything that would give them an advantage.

The men edged forward.

There was nowhere the women could go.

One of the sakimori shook his spear with menace. "Come with us."

"It has to be Aoi-sama they want," Tomoe whispered. She shook her head and raised her voice to proclaim to all within earshot, "We have nothing to do with this matter!"

The leader frowned petulantly, then nodded—some unspoken command—and the guard nearest to Tomoe started to poke his spear in her direction. "Move! You're coming with us."

Tomoe glared back with an expression that said, *Don't do this!*

Of course the sakimori guard ignored the warning, letting his spear dart back and forth like a prod. She stood her ground until the sharp edge almost touched her, so that she finally had to dance out of its way.

The man guffawed—but then he let out a ghastly scream.

The next anyone knew, Tomoe stood with her naked tachi held horizontally at shoulder height, gleaming blade dripping red. The falling snowflakes melted as they touched the blood's warmth.

The man's spear lay in the snow, an arm severed below the elbow, complete with hand, the fingers still clutching the spear. Now on his knees and shrieking horridly, with his good arm the man tried to staunch the bleeding, but the stump gushed blood with each heartbeat. He looked into the heavens, letting out another long shriek.

Tomoe's sword flashed a second time and the man's head rolled through the snow, leaving a bloody trail, stopping when it bumped against the side of one of the houses. Tomoe stood ready for battle in forward stance, her sword pointed downward along her front leg.

"He wouldn't have survived. Fatal cut. It was merciful," Tomoe whispered grimly. Her eyes remained locked on her targets. Yet she must have seen Yamabuki with eyes in the back of her head, for she muttered, "Classic stance, Denka?"

Yamabuki held her naked tachi extended high above her head, blade pointing toward the heavens. "Leave now," she growled low in the tone of a warlord, "and you leave with your lives."

The leader's hand moved to his tachi. "Kill them!"

At this point the fighting broke into two battles—three spearmen and the leader setting themselves on Tomoe, and four going at Yamabuki, while the last one held back, likely hoping the situation would resolve itself without his involvement.

Tomoe moved into a blur, using her speed and long sword to deadly advantage. One man saw his spearpoint sail off on its own before he saw nothing else. The other warrior was more cautious, trying to jab her from a distance. Tomoe leapt forward, tachi sweeping the polearm aside, and landed close, blade over her left shoulder. She spun. The man felt only an instant of pain before all went dark. One of the men thought this was his chance. With a fierce yell, he closed his eyes and thrust hard as he could, trying to drive the hooked blade of his polearm into her back. But his weapon met nothing. He opened his eyes to see her downward strike at his head. In an instant, his world turned red, then black.

For Yamabuki, time slowed. Four sakimori came at her at once, bellowing fearsomely. The one closest thrust his spear directly toward her corselet. In a single looping motion from up-to-down-to-up, her sword knocked the spear aside, into the legs of the man to his left. She brought Tiger Claw down against the top of the man's skull, splitting it wide as blood and brains plumed in every direction. The full-power blow continued down and through his jaw. He fell to his right.

She turned her attention to the next attacker, striking horizontally into his torso, blade passing through his lung. His eyes went blank.

The third guard had to deal with the first man, who fell in his path. Yamabuki reversed along the same horizontal line, cutting into the attacker's ribcage. Blood spurted into the air. The snow turned red.

The fourth sakimori leapt over the bodies of the first three men. However, to reach Yamabuki he bent at the waist. Yamabuki stepped on top of the first body and deflected the spear and delivered a full-power strike that cleaved his head.

The four guards had fallen in less than five heartbeats.

The last sakimori stood five strides away, spear directed at her chest. He shouted and charged.

Yamabuki leapt to the side, delivering a quick cut. Belly split, spilling innards, he screamed with his last breath before falling.

All the guards were dead. Yamabuki straightened, breathing deeply.

Tomoe, standing over her five kills, gasping through clenched teeth, muttered. "What took you so long?"

Yamabuki looked at Tomoe's handiwork and met her gaze.

"Next time don't make me wait," Tomoe said. "It gets boring watching you struggle so."

SIXTY-THREE
THE FISSURE YAWNS

FROM THE MOMENT THEY LEFT the House of Red Banners, Saburo shadowed Yamabuki and the alabaster woman. It was impossible to miss them, two women clad in beautiful yoroi. They carried their weapons casually as they strolled down the main street. Who was this woman with the Taka warrior? Ever since the onsen, he had tried to figure how she fit in. She had displayed extraordinary senses detecting his presence at the rim of the canyon. Was she a hired sword? A *yojimbō*? The bodyguard, if that's what she was, wore exquisite armor and was as haughty as she was beautiful, and she surely knew she was, for she brazenly flaunted an extra-long tachi.

And yet for all the military gear, Saburo could not help but have a growing impression that he followed a pair of young girls. They chatted in an animated and feminine way, gesturing with their hands and at times even laughing. As he paralleled them he saw Yamabuki had on a cheerful expression and open face. Almost innocent. Saburo wondered how she was even allowed to carry something so dangerous as a tachi.

His assessment of her started to shift when a squad of spearmen tried to arrest them. For a brief moment, Saburo thought they were after him. Maybe Ase's body had been discovered. He cursed himself. He had never killed indiscriminately. He prepared to take one of the escape routes he always noticed wherever he went.

The guards did not so much as glance in his direction. Just to be safe, though, he burst into one of the hovels, where a withered woman stooped peering through the window slats.

"Out!" he shouted and she almost fell over herself, leaving by the back. Saburo settled into her place at the window.

It appeared to him that the women had no choice but to surrender.

All that changed in an instant. Yamabuki's demeanor transformed, as though another being took over her body. Her smile dissolved. Her expression hardened. Her eyes turned to granite. Her mouth drew into a line. Her body erect, she grew half a head taller—not so much that anything physically changed, more that she called up something that she otherwise kept hidden.

Words were exchanged and spears were brandished.

Then in one glorious strike, the alabaster yojimbō decapitated one of the guards. She was as physically talented as she was beautiful. Like the snake of her mon, she struck fast. Blindingly fast. Fast and accurate— her sword a blur. Another spear carrier and then their leader fell in quick succession to her. For a brief moment Saburo wondered if it was the yojimbō who had killed Shima.

Meanwhile, the Taka Princess stood alone against the other men. Bad odds. The sakimori attacked as a unit. True, they were mere spearmen, but fighting close in with so many determined opponents took a coolness few possessed. A warrior was either born with this kind of ice or died young. This kind of nerve was something some men managed to feign. Fewer swordsmen actually possessed it. Most did not, but still had the presence of mind to bluff. Yamabuki's sword cut through men like a whirlwind. There was no bluffing. Saburo could barely keep up with the speed at which her sword dispatched them. Before one man even started to fall, her sword already found its mark on the next man. Saburo held his breath until the final sakimori fell.

"Magnificent," he whispered to himself.

And though Saburo favored men, if indeed he favored anyone, when Yamabuki flicked the blood from her sword and wiped the blade with rice paper, he found himself stirred. The Taka warrior excited him as no woman had, at least not since Sairyū at the market nineteen years before. Such a contrast: the sweet daughter of a weaver of straw baskets and a grim princess in dark green armor, a weaver of death. He did not know if he wanted to ravish the Taka warrior or if he even still wanted to kill her. *What kind of wife might she make? What offspring would we have? What would she be like if she gave her skin?*

But ever pragmatic, Saburo realized a warrior of this strength would never let any man possess her any more than Saburo would let any man possess him. Poor young Kiso would never possess her.

And there was more. Saburo saw the look in the alabaster yojimbō's eyes: lust. The alabaster woman's mouth might have twisted in disdain when she said something flippant to Yamabuki—something Saburo could not quite hear—but her eyes. Yes those eyes. What the yojimbō saw in Yamabuki was what he had seen. The look in the yojimbō's eyes was an admiration at least as great as Saburo's. No. He would never have any chance in Yamabuki's bedchamber. The only way he would conquer her was for her to fall beneath his sword.

His hand moved to the hilt of Shima's tachi. He took a deep breath, ready to act. No one would blame him—after all, Yamabuki now had killed sakimori, so her death would be deserved. The alabaster woman would be no easy target, but if he killed Yamabuki outright, the yojimbō would either choose to fight or make her getaway. The death of all the sakimori could be blamed on the Taka samurai. He stepped out the doorway.

Shouts drew his attention as a contingent of archers scurried up the street. Whereas spearmen were often raw recruits whose chief qualifications were youth, an ability to follow orders, and willingness to lift a polearm, archers were another matter.

Six of them and their commander halted some thirty long paces from the two women. The bodies of the dead, snow falling on them, lay in heaps in the street. The archers lifted their yumi, nocked their arrows, prepared to shoot.

One defensive tactic for Yamabuki and her yojimbō might have been to lift the dead bodies, using the corpses as a shield, but neither woman availed herself. Swords drawn, they eyed the archers. Saburo tensed. If they killed her, he would not have the pleasure of killing Yamabuki.

The leader gave the command. Six arrows sped toward the two women. The women's swords swept them from the air. Cut into pieces.

The commander ordered another volley. Again the arrows were intercepted. The commander called for his men to move in closer.

A small girl ran out, emerging from a break in the rock wall. Judging from her size, she was not even five springs, but the girl spoke animatedly and pointed toward the fissure. The archers leapt over their dead as Yamabuki and her yojimbō followed the child along the face cliff and one by one disappeared.

The archers reached the fissure. Three sat on the snow, extending their feet to hold their yumi and drew back the bowstrings, arrows directed into the fissure. The remaining three stood above them, ready to shoot at the same time. Clearly it would be impossible for anyone to dodge a volley within the narrow tunnel. The commander shouted.

The first volley was away, and they listened to hear the arrows hit, but there was no sound whatever.

Moments later, death was atop them. Saburo cut the archers down as they fumbled for their swords.

Another group of warriors, at least two jun, raced down the street, swords drawn. These odds were becoming impossible. Veiled partially by the snowfall, Saburo slipped into the cave.

Shouts erupted from the guards and they guards raced faster, leaping over the snow-covered bodies. The man in the kimono had killed saki-mori. No quarter would be given.

Yet when they arrived at the cliff face, they found only more dead bodies. The killer, along with the opening in the rock, had vanished, leaving only footprints in the snow.

Sixty-Four
Puppet Theater

THE BLOOD-SPATTERED SNOW of the street gave way to the welcome warmth and dryness of the cave. In single file, Yamabuki and Tomoe followed the small girl through a quiet, narrow, airless tunnel. The underground passage was lined improbably with braziers and torches. Sounds echoed musically, reverberating in harmony—a chorus endlessly repeating every footfall, utterance, and rasp.

Even after a hundred steps, the passage remained constricted with a low ceiling, though not so low that Yamabuki could not stand to full height. Still, the narrowness prevented her from seeing very far ahead. Within the confinement, conversations proved difficult, but she could see Kouma straight ahead. And Tomoe right behind. As far as she could tell, theirs were the only reflected sounds.

"You think anyone's followed us?"

Tomoe looked back over her shoulder. "The torches have gone out."

Kouma giggled gleefully. "No one's behind us. I closed it. The bad man is lost. He doesn't know the way, but I do."

"The bad man?" Yamabuki asked.

"The strange-eyed one who followed you across the water."

Yamabuki turned to Tomoe. "Can you keep watch if anyone's behind us. I don't want to have to fight in these confines. Even our short swords would be unwieldy. I'll have to fight with a tantō if it comes to it."

"You? If it comes to it?" Tomoe hissed as they turned sideways to move forward, squeezing by the encroaching walls. "There's no switching positions in here. If it comes to it, Denka, I'll be the one doing the fighting. Take down two or three, and the corpses will stop a brigade."

"Don't call me 'Denka.'"

"Don't look back. Bad luck," Kouma commanded. "Keep looking ahead."

They came to a series of chiseled rock steps that led steeply upward.

"Where does this lead?" Yamabuki asked.

"To your horses. You have to get away from the fox snows. They'll linger here just as long as you do." Kouma climbed quickly with a spring in her short stride.

"We may get out of here," Yamabuki said, "but it's far from over."

Tomoe grunted in affirmation. "Blood has been spilled. Lots of it. Once we get to the stables, we have to be ready to ride hard."

Every once in a while the corridor split and another set of steps led off in some other direction, sometimes glowing with warm light, sometimes fading into blackness. Yamabuki gazed into these other passages more out of curiosity than anything, but Kouma would always caution, "No. Not that way. That is not a good way. This way." She pointed to tunnels she favored.

Tomoe asked, "All of your spearmen? Kills?"

Yamabuki muttered, "All dead."

"No witnesses." She chuckled. "Maybe I should call you Shōgun."

Yamabuki shook her head. "The Ōe will question everyone."

"No." Tomoe laughed darkly. "They'll be riding full gallop after General Aoi, who, if I don't miss my guess, will outrun them. Head to Aki Prefecture where the Ōe won't be welcome. Neither you nor I can stay here. Not now. It's the East-West Highway for both of us. Soon as we get our horses, we head west. Let them chase Aoi-sama east. Draw them away."

Yamabuki breathed hard. This was not to her liking.

"Shhh," Kouma whispered. "This way." And the three disappeared into the shadows.

Saburo had followed right behind Yamabuki and the others into the cave—or so he thought—but total darkness greeted him.

He quickly lost his bearings. He stretched his hands out, seeking anything solid—rock, dirt, roots—but his fingertips encountered only emptiness. No matter where he reached, there was only wide-open, unseen vastness.

He bent, down feeling for the floor. Bits of broken rock and tiny boulders—all warm to the touch. Dry and dusty. Was he possibly teetering at a drop-off?

He stood back up and with one foot pushed some stones. They gave way. The sound of rock against rock, stones sliding downward, clunking one against the other echoed up and all around him. He sensed that he stood within an enormous chamber atop a massive mound of rubble that sloped away in every direction.

How did I get up here? How far to the bottom?

Murmuring voices drifted behind him, far away. He looked over his shoulder. More darkness. He stayed perfectly still. Listening. The murmuring died.

Tiny slivers of light bobbed up and down high above. Torchlight? It waned. *Follow it.* Or he might lose his way entirely. In fact, already he was lost. He vowed he would not let fear into his heart.

His eyes adjusted. Shapes ahead, dark within dark. He could just make out the ceiling of a cavern vault. More sounds. Dripping water. Murmuring voices. Torchlight above him—high and far up. Was that them?

He slid his foot forward so as not to stumble. Each step had to be planned. He moved within blackness over more rubble. Blinded by the darkness, his only recourse was to follow the sounds. They intensified, growing distinct. Wailing. Almost human. Screeching. Bats?

More torchlight. He glimpsed Yamabuki and the yojimbō walking upside down on the cavern roof. Was he looking up at them on the ceiling, or was he upside down while they walked below along the rock floor? All at once their torches went dark. How did Yamabuki move with such ease?

He tried to reconstruct his route. Again he put out his hands—and his palms came to rest against cool, solid rock walls. Solid rock where only moments before he encountered vast openness. Impossible. He needed lights. Follow the lights and intercept them. His only recourse. He had to find the lights.

He felt around some more. All he felt were walls. At last he encountered a passage. He could touch both sides by stretching out his arms wide. He could even reach the ceiling. He used his fingertips to follow the tunnel further and his foot as a feeler to confirm solid ground ahead.

He sensed he traveled downward.

The cries of children came out of the darkness. Children? Inside this cave? Screaming. Crying. The sounds of rocks being piled.

Steadily the cave grew brighter as if some sort of underground dawn had started to break. The light came from waters. Strangely colored ponds. He made his way toward the source—a chamber with hot yellowish-red boiling pools that smelled of brimstone. Too hot to stay, he retreated deeper inside the cavern, glad that he now could make out the features of his surroundings.

He entered another cave, one with obsidian walls and ceiling. Tiny fragments of feldspar glittered, embedded in black lava rock that almost looked like a night sky.

Voices echoed again. Loud voices. Not the children? Was it the two women warriors?

No.

Men, gruff and angry. The Ōe guards followed him in?

Steps carved in rock led up a hillside. He neared a rim of boulders tall as a man—and a familiar torii gate.

Soft Breeze Shrine? Impossible. Not inside this cave. And yet as he looked around he found himself outside.

When did I leave?

It was a night sky, not a lava ceiling. The moon shone full. He looked back down the steps. Was the mouth of the cave below? No. For a moment he thought he saw Shima holding the bridles of Raiden and Gaki, but then the image blew away like smoke—or more like whirling snow.

Saburo's heart sank as he heard voices he had never forgotten. The eleven Zodiac. He came upon the door to the shrine, which greeted him with granite guardian dogs and a chōzubachi to rinse his mouth. The basin was filled with sand. He was certain this was the Soft Breeze Shrine, and this night absolutely identical to the night ten years before. The raucous laughter. The bawdy singing. Was all this just a dream? More nightmare than anything.

Something inexplicable drew him to the door. And as on that fateful night, he clapped his hands to announce his arrival, but the door remained closed. Saburo clapped again, hard enough that his palms hurt and for an accomplished swordsman, that meant exceedingly hard. The raucous voices and bawdy songs continued. Saburo grew annoyed. He shoved the door open.

Everything fell silent, even the cicadas.

Inside, the bodies of eleven naked men lay slain, exactly as on the fifth night of Shūbun, just as he remembered.

Aka-rui's sword, which he had taken to kill the Zodiac, stood buried in Dragon's chest.

Saburo found himself strangely comforted at coming upon the scene, perhaps because it was his work. In fact over the years he had allowed himself to think about this scene, and it never caused him even the slightest moment of dread. If anything it gave him dark satisfaction.

But then Saburo gasped. Though the bodies lay perfectly still, the irezumi body art crawled along underneath the dead men's skin. Saburo looked down at Viper who lay splayed open. Though Viper's eyes stared emptily into space, the snake's glazed eyes darting with reptilian menace, its tongue flickering. It hissed, "Ssssshinobi."

Wolf's irezumi bared his canines. The dead man's chinko began to twitch. It pointed accusingly at Saburo. "Coward," growled Wolf's irezumi as it crouched to leap from the body at Saburo. But it could not free itself and merely writhed beneath the skin.

With increasing vitriol, one by one, the irezumi of each dead man denounced Saburo. *Killer. Fraud. Fallen priest. Murderer of infants. Liar. Baka mono. Impostor. Sham. Oni.* One of the irezumi would hurl a slur and the other ones would growl in echo. Louder and louder—it was growing hard for Saburo to think amid the din.

"Silence!" Saburo shouted, and all the angry words ceased.

Blade still deep in Dragon's chest, Aka-rui's sword started to move without moving. A shape crawled within the steel, just like the irezumi under the dead men's skins.

A boy's voice arose from nowhere. "You betrayed me, Dankotaru."

"Aka-rui?" Saburo would know that voice anywhere. "Where are you?"

The blade floated a vaporous, undulating figure. Aka-rui. He seemed to struggle to pull away, but could not succeed. "I am here," the figure said.

"Here?"

"Imprisoned in this blade."

"Imprisoned?"

Saburo stepped closer, and it was true. Aka-rui's image writhed like flame emanating from the ko-dachi. He appeared as he did in life, in pristine snow-white priest's garb, except for the slice across his chest where

Dragon's naginata had split the young man open. The wound did not bleed, though it was heavily caked in Aka-rui's own blood.

"Why?

"Because of your arrogance."

"Arrogance? I avenged you!" Saburo cried, shocked at seeing Aka-rui in this amorphous form, shocked that Aka-rui's body still showed the wounds, but mostly shocked at Aka-rui's accusation.

"Did you, now?" Aka-rui's eyes were no longer the ones Saburo remembered—the flashing eyes of mirthful youth. Their fire had gone out, replaced by pain and dullness. His image moved closer and further from the blade's edge.

Saburo said, "I did not betray you. I came back. I killed them."

"Did I ask you to?"

"There was no need to ask. It was my duty."

"Your duty?" Aka-rui almost sneered. "Your duty as what? As a syncretic priest? When had either of us ever taken such vows? When were we ever even asked to consider such a thing? Look where I must live now."

"In this shrine?"

"Shrine? This shrine does not stand. It exists only because of your memories of it. You see merely puppets—a *bunraku*. You're spared the true shape of the Ne-no-Kuni."

"The Hollow Land?"

"If your eyes saw the Land of Roots for what it is, you'd go blind at the very horror of it. If your mind experienced this place as it truly is, you would descend into complete insanity." Aka-rui pulled away from the steel, grimacing. "Yet it is in this place that I must remain until the Hour of the Ox, only to be called back when that short hour ends."

"Why are you here? You did nothing wrong. You are the one who was harmed."

"That may be. But then you stole my soul and left it with the men you killed."

"A soul can't be stolen."

"It can. And you did. A samurai's soul resides in his sword. I knew that since I was a boy. I *cleansed* my father's spirit from the sword I took. I know Shima told you the sword owner's soul rests within the blade."

"Shima? How do you know of him?"

"I was there. I witnessed the night you showed him my sword. I watched you from the steel. I watched as you honed your skills and sought your vengeance and then left my sword—my soul—buried in Dragon's chest. You have trapped me here with them. To be killed at Iwakawa-jiin was horrifying, but it ended quickly. But to be imprisoned with these beasts for an interminable term!"

For a moment, Aka-rui struggled. His image grew almost entirely clear, until finally he relented and was drawn back down to the sword. Small. Dark.

"If you wanted my sword so much, very well. You should simply have stolen it—but then it would have offended your arrogant priestly vows. You told yourself theft was base, but you should have faced it instead of turning your emptiness into some holy quest. Then I would not be trapped. You never made the weapon yours. You revered it, reveled in it, yes, but you never cleansed my spirit from the steel to free me. Until the night you attacked the Zodiac, you carried the blade like a religious relic, some love object of a moonstruck groom, though you never actually loved me—not the way I loved you—and thus this steel has doomed me."

"I only sought to honor you."

"Honor me! Like the one hundred sixty-seven memorial tablets in your self-styled temple at the headwaters of the River of Forty Thousand Sands? Where in your vanity you try to replicate Iwakawa-jiin? Where you think your killing can be atoned for by mumbling to pieces of wood?"

Saburo wanted to protest, but no words came.

Aka-rui said, "You told Shima you felt my grave marker was but empty stone. And now look at me." Aka-rui inserted his fingers into the gash in his chest. "My heart is rent."

"Done by Dragon," Saburo insisted.

"No. Done by you."

"My doing?" Saburo snarled.

"That you protest so much is proof your heart is empty, though it goes on beating. Somewhere your heart became empty, or maybe it was never full in the first place."

Saburo gritted his teeth and hissed. "You—I should—"

"What? What do you plan to do, Dankotaru? Kill me?" Aka-rui laughed manically. "If only you would!"

"I did it for Nin-tai!" Saburo's eyes flashed. "I always loved him. More than I ever loved you or anyone else!"

"Good that you speak the truth, for Nin-tai would be anguished if he saw what you had become."

"What do you expect of me?" Saburo cried. "I have done everything demanded of me by a warrior's obligation."

"Obligation? You have done what suited you."

"Well, it suits me to leave."

"Oh," Aka-rui laughed and said through laughter. "You couldn't stay even if you wanted to. Your time here will soon be up. You will leave the stage of this puppet show and return to the Veil of Tears, where other dark masters who hide behind black hoods will manipulate you. Fortunately for you, you will remember little of this place." And then his laughing stopped, followed by convulsive sobs. "If you ever loved me. If you every really loved me, you will take this accursed sword with you. Take it to Iwakawa-jiin."

"The monastery."

"Take the sword to where my body rests. There is a new abbot. He will expect you. Go to my grave. He will be there. Speak with him. Deliver this blade and set me to rest."

Saburo put his palms over his ears. He could not bear to hear Aka-rui's sobs, but the sobbing was not outside. It was inside. It was Saburo who sobbed. "I will take the sword! I will deliver it to the new abbot at Iwakawa-jiin."

"Arigatō gosaimas!" Aka-rui's voice boomed in relief, filling the cavern.

Saburo reached for the hilt, but the moment he touched it, a flash of blackness, if such a thing were possible, swept over the scene and everything—temple, bodies, sword—disappeared.

Saburo found himself standing totally alone in the dimness once again. Only the feldspar twinkled in the obsidian ceiling. Yet he held Aka-rui's sword in his grip.

He slipped the blade into his sash.

A young girl's voice pierced the silence. "You are a bad priest."

"What!"

"A bad priest." A girl stood further up the passage—the same girl who had led Yamabuki into the caves.

There was no time to argue with foolish children about priestliness. "You know where the two women warriors went?"

"Hai."

"Where are they?"

"I showed them the way out."

"Show me the way out."

"Ie." She shook her head. "Stay away from her!"

"You will show me the way out." He tapped the sheathed sword's hilt. The child shook her head. "Obstinate, are you?" He stepped toward her, ready to twist her wrist to force her into obedience.

But drawing closer, he saw her more clearly.

"Tōsō!" he gasped.

The pox—same as his mother. But this was much worse. Many times worse. The girl's face showed signs of advanced rot.

Corpse-like. Corruption.

When she smiled gently, it only made it look worse. "Come. Take my hand." She stretched out a skeletal appendage. "Let me lead you to where I dwell when it's daylight."

Saburo moaned with revulsion mixed with fear.

"I'll show you things you could never imagine." When she broke into a small smile, he could see through the sides of her cheeks where the flesh had fallen away.

She moved toward him. He stepped back.

"And those markers you burn incense for and pray over in your household temple? All those souls? Why look at pieces of wood when you can meet them as they are now? You can reacquaint yourself with them. Many are here—waiting for you!"

She pointed into the tunnel behind her.

"The tears of joy they will have at having you close to them again!" Without dropping her gaze, she stepped back into the shadows. "Come," she called from the darkness. "Come. Follow me"

Saburo turned, almost at a run, heading into the opposite passage.

Who is that ahead?

A shadowy figure beckoned Saburo to follow. Would it attack? No. It moved away from him as if it were afraid he would catch up, and this called on something within him that compelled him to follow.

The shadow was always just at the edge of his sight. Aka-rui? It beckoned again and vanished.

Alone, he plunged further into the corridor. At least he was not standing in total darkness on top of a pile of scree.

Saburo started to run. "Aka-rui!" he shouted. "Aka-rui." But the figure did not stop. It kept moving. Moments later he saw. Not Aka-rui, but Nin-tai!

Saburo called, but the figure kept moving, though he noticed they traveled steadily upward. Saburo's breathing grew labored. He thought to turn around and look back down from where he came, but he heard Nin-tai's voice whisper, his words perfectly clear, "Don't!" He sensed Nin-tai next to him. The bettō's voice entered Saburo's mind as if it were his own thoughts: "Seek out the mountain goat. Otherwise you risk taking his place."

Once again, Nin-tai stood further down the tunnel. Saburo dashed after him over the rough and rocky floor, but Nin-tai kept moving away until finally . . . daylight!

Despite what he had been told, Saburo started to turn to take a last look at where he had been—when a mighty shove hurled him out the passageway. He stumbled and fell.

The next thing he sensed was cold. He lay in a snow drift. Merciful daylight, though heavily gray with overcast, but daylight! He was in Minezaki. He looked for the passageway from which he came. There was none. He found himself at the waterfall, which had largely frozen. Judging by the snow accumulation, the road had not been traveled in some time.

"It was all a dream," he told himself. And then he gazed at Aka-rui's sword clutched in his hand.

Sixty-Five

The Hour of the Bird

Y AMABUKI CLIMBED THE STAIRS. The brazier had given out some time back, but daylight now led the way out into a drafty plank structure. She pushed out through the door onto the grounds behind the armory. What she had thought was a house near the stables merely covered the entrance to the network of caves.

Yamabuki breathed in the mountain air—cold but fresh—free of the cave's staleness. Tomoe emerged right behind her. Yamabuki grinned at her, then looked around. "Snow's falling hard."

Tomoe nodded. "The kind that piles up."

The girl was nowhere to be seen, not even tracks. "Where's Kouma?" She looked about. "Did Kouma not come out with us?"

Tomoe gave her a puzzled look. "Who?"

"Kouma, the little girl." Yamabuki headed back to the cave exit. "Ko-chan!" she called back into the cavern."

"Who's Kouma?" Tomoe asked.

"Kouma. The girl who led us through the tunnels."

"*You* led us through the tunnels."

"No. There was a girl ahead of us."

"I didn't see anyone."

"I must have blocked your view." Yamabuki again called, " Ko-chan!"

After a moment, a soft voice answered from the darkness, "Did you get out?"

"Yes. Yes. Gomen nasai. Come join us."

Her call was met only by silence.

"Ko-chan, come out."

Silence.

Yamabuki stood pondering the blackness of the cave when Yoshinaka's emerged from the stables. "We need to saddle up. The Ōe are looking for us. All of us."

"This has something to do with General Aoi, ne?" Tomoe said.

Face grim but confident, Yoshinaka nodded. "She found the man whose arrow killed her brother."

Yamabuki let out a long breath. "Misaki."

"She couldn't let her brother's death stand as long as the killer lived."

"I couldn't either," said Tomoe.

"She cut her way through at least eight guards to get to him."

Yamabuki sighed. "We had to kill ten more."

The simple gaze of understanding from Yoshinaka gave her some comfort.

"We're implicated. We ride out now." Tomoe's statement was more command than anything.

Something within Yoshinaka seemed to shift. Yamabuki could see it in his face. The charismatic noble was replaced by a general. He said, "I saddled up Uma. He's ready to ride. I'll stand guard until you can get your mounts ready. We'll go together and catch up to Aoi."

"No! Let her go east," said Tomoe. "We'll have to go where they won't follow. The closer we are to her, the more we'll be implicated."

"You will abandon her?" Yamabuki muttered.

"Ah!" Tomoe scoffed. "I pity anyone who takes it upon themselves to attack her."

"I mean at brigade strength."

"*Anyone*," said Yoshinaka and Tomoe in unison.

"I need to gather my things," said Yamabuki.

"We mount up first, ne?" Tomoe said and without waiting for agreement entered the stables.

Yamabuki started across the snow toward the guesthouse.

"What is so important?" Yoshinaka cried out. "You can get whatever it is once we're ready to ride."

"My ink and brushes. My pillow book and poems," she said, calling out. "Things I need!"

Out of breath, she burst into the room, kicking off her boots as decorum dictated. They fell against the straw boots no one claimed. *We're these*

Misaki's after all? Did Blue Rice take them? She caught herself. *I can't think about such foolishness now.*

She knelt down, gathered her saddlebag, making sure all her belongings were there—including the surreptitious weapons all Taka royals carried. Everything seemed complete."

"Yama-chan?"

Only Yoshinaka dared call her that. She met his eyes.

"You must ride out with us."

"You and Tomoe go ahead. Go west. If I decide that it makes sense, I may join you. Go without me."

He walked toward her. She did not like the deliberateness of his approach and so she rose. He looked deeply into her eyes. His own eyes half-closed, he said, "I have Tomoe-san saddling Raski and Full Moon."

She was ready to quip that Mochizuki would be a handful for such an inexperienced warrior, but from the look he gave her, she stopped her tongue before she said something she regretted. This was not a moment to make light. She could see it in his eyes. All she managed was to softly say, "What?"

"You must come with me, *anata.*" *My dearest one.*

"I am on a mission, a matter of giri."

"And what of ninjo? Is your heart so empty?"

Yamabuki suppressed the lump that formed in her throat. "You know what we are, you and I. I would feel nothing for you if we were not of the same cloth. The same steel. Surely you understand this."

"Then is there no place in your heart for me?"

"It is filled only with you, anata." She choked briefly "But duty comes first. How would it look if the next Taka daimyō simply rode away when it suited her?"

"And where are you riding?"

She smiled, a tears forming in her eyes. "To Heian-kyō. Rakuchū. To the Palace of Black Plums."

"Then I shall meet you there."

"I will be there but for a brief time. Then I must start my musha shugyō in earnest or risk all."

Yoshinaka put his arms, bulky with armor, around her armored shoulders and pulled her tight—armor to armor, face to face, breath to breath—looking deeply at her. "Then let's ride out quickly so we can see each other all the sooner again."

She smiled and felt herself blush. She gave a little push against him, armor to armor. He laughed.

They were most of the way back to the stables when Tomoe emerged. "The horses are ready." She threw Yamabuki a look. "Big horse."

"One of the breed that fell from the skies. Glad you managed to saddle him up. He's still half wild."

"I'm used to half-wild things." With a half-twisted smile, she looked Yamabuki up and down.

"Gomen," Yamabuki said, looking skyward at darkening skies.

"If we get separated, we'll rendezvous on the coastal road," Tomoe pronounced.

"I will not be going west."

Tomoe looked askance at her.

"It will add ten days to my journey."

"You are worried about *that*?" Tomoe scoffed.

"It's Taka Shōgun's decision." Yoshinaka swung into the saddle. "I'll ride a bit down Ledge Road to see if anyone's about."

"Doubtful in this weather," Yamabuki called after him as he rode off. She checked Mochizuki's tack. "I have to go to Heian-kyō," she said with a breath.

"Who's in the Imperial City that you need to get there so soon? Your betrothed?"

"Never that."

"Never? Have you told my brother that?"

"What happens between us is private."

"As private as the onsen?"

"As private as omeko." Yamabuki faced Tomoe. "If I did not care for him, you and I would not be speaking to each other." *Nor would I be involved in this embroilment.*

"What happened to Kiso-sama?"

Tomoe's question so simply stated gave Yamabuki a sense of dread. She squinted in the light. The firs were so laden with snow there was hardly any green. Even the leafing trees had accumulations that blocked much of the view up Ledge Road.

They moved over a few steps for a better line of sight.

In the distance, out where the road dropped down, was some kind of commotion. Yamabuki could see spears and helmets swarming around a man on horseback turning, charging, rearing, sword flying.

Yoshinaka!

Tomoe shouted, "He's in trouble!" and started for her horse.

Yamabuki called, "Hold!"

Tomoe spun, glaring at her. But Yamabuki focused on a mass of soldiers in black Ōe tunics charging toward them. "We have trouble of our own. I count fourteen." Her eyes scanned again.

Tomoe looked. "Twenty-five at least. At least and half of them archers."

"We can't go back through the cave. It will take us back to where we started. Besides the horses won't fit."

"I'm not going to surrender to them."

"Who said anything about surrendering? The question is how many arrows we have between us. You any good with a bow?"

Tomoe flashed Yamabuki a look. "Probably better than you."

"Well then, we should do quite well."

The sakimori approached in a loose formation.

Yamabuki and Tomoe led their horses to the other side of the stable, where they had some cover and a clear view of the road between the armory and the trees.

"Stop!" One of them, likely the leader, raised his *gumbai* over his head. A war fan—his symbol of authority all were to heed. He and is men were at least sixty paces from the half-walled stables.

"We can shoot from here," Yamabuki muttered. "We can't risk the horses by riding out. At least not yet. We stay here for the moment. Agreed?"

"Agreed."

Each grabbed an ebira and bow. Tomoe counted her arrows. "I have fifteen."

Yamabuki joined in a quick count. "Eighteen."

"Thirty-three." Tomoe breathed hard. "So every shot counts."

"You must come with us!" the man with the gumbai barked.

Yamabuki broke into a laugh. "No," she shouted back without the slightest sign of concern. "We are not under your jurisdiction. Only the Mikado Himself has the authority to arrest me, and I can assure you, He has no such intent, and I also guarantee He will be very cross if He discovers your effrontery."

The commander sputtered, shouting, "We have witnesses!"

"Silence, you fool!" Tomoe snapped. "Show your obedience! Bow before the Princess! All of you! Bow!"

The sakimori looked in confusion toward one another.

"She's no Princess!" a voice cried out from the back. "She's a yahochi! She gave me her skin last night."

The men more or less laughed and hooted as a group." Bow before a yahochi!" one cried, and the others joined in with rude noises. "Bow before this!" roared one of them, pointing at his privates, feigning ecstasy.

His laugh turned into a gurgle as an arrow pierced his neck, a plume of blood spurting into the air. The man fell back into the snow and did not move.

"Seventeen arrows left," Yamabuki muttered as she pulled a fresh arrow.

Tomoe put a hand to her mouth. "You dare mock us? Bow!"

Several men indeed bowed as they were told. The Ōe commander screamed, "Attack!"

The sakimori at the front broke into a run, drawing swords, charging through thickening snowdrifts that slowed them to at half speed.

"Start with the men at the edges," Tome said.

Yamabuki grinned at her. "Atari."

Tomoe nodded hard.

"Sixteen left," Yamabuki muttered as another fell.

Three more swordsmen fell in rapid succession, and Tomoe laughed. "You only shoot one arrow at a time? How boring."

"Very well." Yamabuki took three arrows in hand and shot them as quickly as she ever had. Accurately. Three men went down. "How many left?" Yamabuki asked.

"I have twelve arrows."

"No. How many men do you see?"

"I count sixteen."

"And we have twenty-five arrows between, still."

The remaining swordsmen, now within twenty strides of the stables, suddenly fell flat.

"What now?" Tomoe asked.

"You know. The archers next."

And sure enough, the sakimori archers took up positions. With the swordsmen so close and lying in the snow, their field of fire would be unobstructed.

"How many archers?" Tomoe shouted.

"Eight!"

Moments later, firing as a group, a volley of arrows sped toward the stables. Yamabuki and Tomoe ducked down, letting the half-walls shield them, and hoped the horses would survive. The arrows whizzed overhead. Timbers popped with impacts.

"The horses?" Tomoe yelled.

"No hits!" Yamabuki called out.

The archers ran forward, closing the distance. They were halfway across the armory grounds. In the meantime, the swordsmen were on their feet and running the final distance to the stables.

Tomoe and Yamabuki drew arrows and shot. Four men went down.

"Missed one!" Tomoe barked.

"So did I!"

"Swords!" Yamabuki barked. Disencumbering themselves from their ebira and bows, they leapt away from the building, cutting the remaining attackers down, though the Ōe swordsmanship was better than expected.

No sooner had the last of the swordsmen fallen than the eight archers grabbed arrows and moved into shooting position, thirty strides from the stable.

"Back inside!" Tomoe commanded, but Yamabuki was already inside with her bow and arrows.

The archers volleyed again in bursts of eight, three times in succession. The women lay low as the arrows struck all around them.

The archers broke into two groups. Half shot another volley while the other half dashed forward and took new positions—from which *they* volleyed as the first group charged forward. The archers repeated this tactic, gaining ground. But this worked only until they got so close to the stable that their own number got in the way of the shots.

Seizing this moment, Yamabuki and Tomoe moved back into position and released quick bursts, bringing down three of the closest archers. Yamabuki picked off another one of the furthest group.

Tomoe stepped outside and cut down the closest archer with her tachi.

"Three left!" Yamabuki cried.

"Mount up and get them!"

In moments the riders burst from the stables.

With only three of their original number, the archers broke into confusion. Though shooting from horseback was always more difficult, and the horses labored through the snow, Tomoe and Yamabuki got one archer each. They both aimed for the last archer. It was Yamabuki's arrow that felled him.

The two Ōe commanders turned and ran away down Ledge Road.

At the best gallop Raski could manage in the drifts, Tomoe, sword drawn, rode down the fleeing man, decapitating him with one magnificent strike.

My, she has that strike perfected, Yamabuki thought to herself, but she did not dwell on it, for the other Ōe commander fled into the woods where the horses could not follow.

In one leap, Yamabuki was out of the saddle, running in pursuit. She reached into her sleeve and drew out a *shuriken*. She threw it hard.

The throwing star struck him between the shoulder blades. He twitched and fell forward.

"Very precise," said Tomoe as she reigned her mount.

Yamabuki scowled as she got into the stirrups. "I was aiming for his neck."

Tomoe cast a sideways glance toward Yamabuki. "You Southerners seem to know how to fight," she said. She put out her hand, her palm upward. "It's snowing harder."

"And night is falling," Yamabuki added grimly.

The two rode to the intersection with North Road. Looking toward the heart of Minezaki, they saw a trail of bodies. Tomoe said, "That's Yoshinaka's work."

"He made it, you think?"

Tomoe laughed. "Why wouldn't he?"

Yamabuki gazed at the dead men strewn all over. How many were there? Twenty? Temporarily inured to seeing death, she started counting.

Shouts.

She glanced at Tomoe, who peered in every direction.

Right in front of them, not a hundred strides away, a black mass of Ōe samurai swarmed into view, blades drawn, filling the road. At least three jun warriors roared as one and charged through the snow at the two women.

"How many arrows?"

"Six," said Tomoe. "You?"

"Eight." Yamabuki sighed. "How long will they keep this up?"

"Don't worry about them. They're all on foot." Tomoe pointed at the mountains behind them—the way of the pass, though they couldn't see it through the white mist. "That's where we go."

"Into the storm?" Yamabuki cried in disbelief.

"We ride through it. The clouds are low."

"How do you surmise that?"

Tomoe laughed. "Where I'm from, any girl could tell you when the clouds are low. An hour's walk or ride and we'll see clear skies."

"And you know this for a fact?"

"No."

The approaching Ōe swordsmen had closed half the distance. Yamabuki squinted at the whiteness shrouding the mountains, trying to see through. She and Tomoe were had to make a decision. To attempt the pass at night? She saw nothing but clouds.

Tomoe said, "Ne, what's the alternative? Fight these Ōe? And who knows how many more?" She gave a crooked smile. "Besides, when we break through the clouds, it will be colder, and so more adventures lie ahead."

Her enthusiasm made Yamabuki smile. "Tomoe-san, I find it strange you think we can climb above the clouds."

Tomoe was unable to suppress a loud laugh. "Southern lowlander! I will teach you to climb above the clouds. Trust me, Yamabuki-san. I promise that you won't be disappointed."

The Ōe swordsmen were now only twenty strides away.

Tomoe spurred Raski and galloped through the virgin snow toward the pass. Following, Yamabuki could sense Mochizuki did not like the cold, and yet since she encouraged him, he did not protest.

They left the buildings behind. The North Road steepened, though it proved difficult to see where the trail actually went. And in the manner of spirited horses, the faster Raski strode, the more Mochizuki kept apace. Yamabuki held the colt back, which was not easy, but if Tomoe made a misstep, driving her horse as fast as she did, Yamabuki did not want to end up on top of the hapless horse and rider.

She seems to know where she's going. Maybe I'm the only one to not have any sense?

The wind picked up and the snow began to blow horizontally. Tomoe turned herself half-around in the saddle and cried, "Stay close. We're headed into a whiteout." Tomoe said something more, but the wind howled so that Yamabuki could not make out the words. Yet Tomoe was laughing about something. Something about the snow covering the dead as well as their tracks. Something about fools not following.

Yamabuki pulled her field coat tighter. *To what cold fate am I being led? Does this woman even know where she's going or what she's doing? Perhaps we should turn back from the fox elements?*

But there was no turning back, for when Yamabuki looked behind, she saw only a wall of swirling white.

EXCERPT FROM *COLD TRAIL*
SKIN TO SKIN

YAMABUKI EMBRACED A GODDESS. A naked Goddess. Within the ice-covered mountain temple, under the blue cast of the blue moon, the Taka princess held in her powerful arms the warrior named Tomoe. The dim light played across her slender body, alabaster white. Her amply muscled arms and legs and abundant breasts—extraordinary with the palest of nipples like silvery moons, large and round. Long ivory tresses past her shoulders, down her back. White brows. White lashes. Even snowy hair at the special place. All white. Except for her irises, intensely blue like the silk that bound Yamabuki's lacquered armor platelets. And Tomoe's plump lips—one of the few things the same hue as Yamabuki's. Her own lips started to ache. What would happen if she let her own lips join Tomoe's? An unthinkable act for someone of her class, an act frowned upon, and yet it had to be done. It had to be with her.

Yamabuki gazed without exactly staring at the other warrior, and pondered their two bodies—the samenesses and the differences. The sameness in that they were both women. Both warriors. Both survivors of the overwhelming onslaught of sakimori guards. Having vanished into the whiteout of the strange summer snowstorm—the fox snows is what Kouma had called them—blindly taking a dubious route, a road that vanished into drifts, likely leading them to their deaths, they had found their way to the summit of the Pass of the Setting Sun.

And they were alive.

At the Hour of the Dog, with heavy snow falling in almost full darkness, they had chanced upon the ramshackle temple. They pulled their horses inside and set alight some dry twigs in the irori.

"The fire won't last long," Tomoe said, her breath fogging in the ice air. "We might survive this night if we remove our clothes and bundle together under blankets."

"In our shitagi?"

"Skin to skin."

"Skin to skin?"

"Our shared body heat should be just enough to see us through." Tomoe tipped her head to the side. "You're a Southerner and know only palms and tropical breezes. You don't know the bitterness of winter."

"We know snow in Great Bay Prefecture and icy blasts off the ocean."

Tomoe smiled politely. "But not like in the mountain province of home."

"I know. Yoshinaka said you all live in Shinano Prefecture."

"We do now. But I'm from Watarishima, what you of the south call 'the Barbarian Isle.' Our cold's deeper and more intense than anything you know. I grew up with it and came to know it as both my friend and my enemy. If we are to survive, you must listen."

Mochizuki gave his head and neck a great shake. Raski stood quietly. Their clouding breath hung still in the faint light. Yamabuki said nothing. Thinking.

"The horses will do well enough," Tomoe said, and laid down every blanket they had between them near irori. "We'll stack our clothes, including the saddle blankets. And if the horses fall, it will be time to cut them open and crawl inside for warmth." Tomoe smiled darkly.

"Have you ever had to do that?"

Tomoe shook her head. "No, though there are many tales. There is a legend about two sworn enemies who were ready to duel at dawn. But then a terrible ice squall came. The two men found themselves snowed in. Facing a death by freezing, the enemies agreed to shed their clothing and encircle each other to survive the night . . . and then went out the next morning, drew swords, and fought to the death."

She pulled the blankets aside. The small irori embers sputtered but kept burning. The horses stood very still—likely already asleep. "Come. Come." Tomoe pulled the blankets over herself. "Slip under with me. I'll show you what to do."

"There's something to *do*?" Yamabuki tried not to smile.

"Oh yes." Tomoe laughed softly. "But nothing untoward."

Yamabuki, now also completely naked and shivering, joined her. They encircled their arms around each other, their breasts touching, nipples against nipples. Yamabuki was not sure they grew hard because of the cold or because she found Tomoe's body thrilling; and as if Tomoe could read Yamabuki's inner thoughts, Tomoe laughed wickedly and moved her legs down along Yamabuki's, her toes touching Yamabuki's shins. "You are tall," Tomoe purred. "So as we settle in, what we will do is each of us will put our heads at the other's toes."

Toes again, Yamabuki thought to herself.

"And," Tomoe continued, "we will massage and warm each other's feet during the night, staying close. We breathe inside the blankets so the heat of our breath does not escape, the blankets becoming our bed tent."

"Working each other's toes all night?"

"All night. We'll get some sleep in between, but we have to awaken once or twice every quarter hour and work the toes."

"I doubt we shall hear any temple bells this far up in the mountains."

"Ha-ha!" Tomoe grinned. "Our toes will tell us when they want to be warmed. Work them even if it hurts, especially if it hurts. Keep them moving, or we'll end up worse than the man whose toes you had to slice off."

Yamabuki was about to take her place at Tomoe's toes, but then an alabaster hand with strong fingers touched Yamabuki's shoulder tenderly. "But," Tomoe whispered in a low voice, "even with our best efforts in cold like this, we might not survive the night. Listen." And the two warriors listened to the wind wailing across the pass. "That kind of wind sucks away all heat. It's the Yuki-onna wind. It's said that when the crystalline woman of white opens her mouth, she blows the coldest air into your mouth and then sucks out your soul. They say it is hard to run for her, for her beauty is unmatched. One cannot help but gaze at her. Entirely white. Entirely ice."

Yamabuki sensed Tomoe's fingers sliding over her right breast. She drew slightly back and watched Tomoe trace a small circle around her areola Tomoe smiled warmly. "You afraid I'm the Yuki-onna?"

"You trace circles as you touch me, Tomoe, calligraphy for *she who circles*. Like the snake."

"A sacred animal, so you know that there's nothing to fear from me."

Mochizuki snorted.

Yamabuki hummed softly. "You are beautiful enough to be she, but there is nothing cold in your touch."

Tomoe burst out with a delighted laugh. "And you are the warmest warlord I have ever touched in my life in this particular way. Most warlords do not have such supple breasts. In fact, none that I can think of. You are the one warlord with lovely breasts." Tomoe slid down and put her mouth against Yamabuki's right nipple. Delight shot through her entire body.

Yamabuki, still beneath the covers, shifted onto her left knee and moved her right knee over Tomoe's leg, softly nudging Tomoe onto her back. "You see," said Yamabuki, "I am the taller of the two of us, and so you will need to let me cover you with my body. So you can feel my warmth. Skin to skin."

Tomoe giggled. "You are no isolated princess, I see."

"Oh, that would be a *terrible* outcome," Yamabuki said as she rose onto her elbow and, with Tomoe flat against the floor, rolled on top of her, encircling her in her arms, slowly lowered her body, making sure Tomoe could take the weight. It was easy for Tomoe, who sighed with delight and encouragement.

Yamabuki now shifted again and brought her knee up between Tomoe's legs, feeling the place of warm wetness—the soft sweetness—and lowered her own wetness against her thigh. Tomoe lifted her leg slightly in response, pressing between Yamabuki's. Slowly and gently, Yamabuki rocked back and forth, up and down, lifting, pushing, thrusting her knee, then backing away, and let her omeko slide over the top of Tomoe's leg.

Yamabuki gasped—the tactility so intense. Tomoe echoed. Their breathing grew heavier and ever more spasmodic, speaking that strange and singular language of moans uttered only by lovers and then only when in the throes.

The two communicated perfectly throughout the night and on until the dawn broke and the time came to journey further along the *kōri no michi*, the cold trail.

2018 Release. Order now.

AUTHOR'S NOTE

Some years back, a major publishing firm editor asked, "Yes, but how did Yamabuki become who she is?"

Yamabuki's back story moved up in priority to its chronological place in the series of Yamabuki projects and thus the books in the *Sword of the Taka Samurai* series were born.

Most series authors have at least some idea of the background of central characters be it Jack Aubrey or James Bond. On the other hand our culture almost demands to know upfront the details of any girl growing up who becomes a leader or person of action. It is usually unfamiliar and often exciting story in and of itself. The *Elizabeth R* series comes to mind.

How did Yamabuki become Yamabuki?

The book you see before you, *Cold Heart*, is the crux book. Yamabuki is truly on her own in a beautiful and brutal land. She and the reader experience this world largely for the first time and learn the rules as they go along which govern the realm outside of the palace.

Beta readers stumbled over how young all the characters are and how much they had to absorb and how early the lessons had to be learned, but the ages are based on actual historic records and are correct. Life expectancy was short and people got on with life early.

Does this book conclude the young Yamabuki series? No. There is far more to the story than delivering three scrolls to the Imperial capital. For me the journey is part of the pleasure, not just the destination. I hope you agree.

KML
Boulder, Colorado
First Quarter Moon, Seventh Day
of Last Month, Akihito 28

CHARACTERS

AKA-RUI: Saburo's friend at Iwakawa-jiin.

AKIBŌ: A monk.

AOI: Woman warrior of the Ine clan and general for Yoshinaka.

ATSUMICHI: Yamabuki's cousin, son of Tachibana.

BLUE RICE: A traveler and friend of Yamabuki.

BUNZŌ: An Ōe sakimori guard.

DAIMARU: A priest at Iwakawa-jiin.

DAYU-SUKE: A bettō of Iwakawa-jiin.

DRAGON: Leader of The Eleven, named for his tattoo.

EIJI: Taro's son.

THE ELEVEN: The remaining eleven members of the Zodiac.

ETSU: A personal bodyguard to General Moroto.

FUSA-ICHI: A musician to the Taka Court.

FUYUKI: Taro's son.

GANKYŪ: Nickname for Saburo; "eyeball" *(literal)*.

GIICHI: Senior personal bodyguard to General Moroto.

GUN-KUN: Shima's nickname for Saburo; "fellow soldier" *(literal)*.

HANA-YE: Youngest handmaid to Yamabuki.

HARI: Innkeeper of House of Red Banners.

HIMEYO: Saburo's father's new wife.

IEBŌ: A monk.

INU: Innkeeper of Wakatake.

JUN: A personal bodyguard to General Moroto.

KANI: A boy in Minezaki who's Yoshinaka's spy.

KIRI: Saburo's housemaid.

KISO: Yoshinaka.

KOUMA: Daughter of Kōno Taro. Also the childhood nickname of Yamabuki.

KUMA: Pseudonym of Yo-aki, given to Saburo; "bear" *(literal)*.

LONG SWORD: Yamabuki's nickname for Shima.

MARI: Taro's daughter.

MASAHITO: Former Emperor of Akitsushima *[reign 1155–1158 CE]*, Cloistered Emperor thereafter. *[Posthumous name Go-Shirakawa.]*

MIKA-GEISHI: Saburo's father.

MISAKI: An Ōe sakimori lieutenant.

MOROTO: Lord Taka, daimyō of Ō-Utsumi Prefecture and Yamabuki's titular father. Also known as General Moroto.

NAKAGAWA: Yamabuki's tutor.

NARIHITO: Former Emperor of Akitsushima [Emperor Konoe, reign 1142–1155 CE].

NIN-TAI: Bettō of Iwakawa-jiin.

REI: Youngest handmaid to Lady Taka.

RÈNXÌNG: Beautiful woman who appears in Saburo's dream.

RYUMA: Guard at the Wakatake Inn.

SADAMASA: An Ōe sakimori commander in Minezaki.

SAIRYŪ: A weaver's daughter.

SABURO: Expert assassin pursuing Yamabuki.

SHIMA: Shima Sa-me, a sword master.

TACHIBANA: General Moroto's younger brother and Yamabuki's uncle.

LADY TAKA: General Moroto's wife and Yamabuki's mother, née Itō Sumi.

TARO: Kōno Taro, armorer in Minezaki.

TETSU: A kobune captain.

TOMOE: Adoptive sister of Yoshinaka and formidable warrior.

TOMOKO: Personal handmaid to Yamabuki.

UNAGI: Saké house man in Minezaki.

YAMABUKI: Princess and heir to the Taka clan.

YO-AKI: Pseudonym of a Taka traitor.

YO-ICHI: Taro's son.

YOSHINAKA: Kiso no Yoshinaka, a dispossessed Minamoto prince; adoptive brother of Tomoe.

YUKIYASU: Master swordsmith to the Taka clan.

GLOSSARY

AJISAI: Blue hydrangea flower. Thought to mean apologies and gratitude.

AKAMAGASEKI: Port city in Nagato on the Main Isle at the Barrier Strait.

AKITSUSHIMA: Ancient name of Japan; "Autumn Creek Land" *(literal)*.

AKUTŌ: Rogues.

AMIGASA: Braided wide-brimmed straw hat.

ANATA: My dearest one.

ARIGATŌ: "Thanks."

ARIGATŌ GOSAIMAS: "Thank you for what you are doing."

ARIGATŌ GOZAIMASHITA: "Thank you for what you have done."

ASA: Bowstring.

ATARI: In the game of Go, having one's piece(s) surrounded on all sides but one, in danger of being captured.

AWABI: Abalone.

BAKA: "Stupid" *(literal)*.

BAKA MONO: Monster; "stupid thing" *(literal)*.

BARBARIAN ISLE: Isle to the north of Akitsushima *[Hokkaidō]*.

BARRIER STRAIT: Narrow water passage between Honshū and Kyūshū.

BENIBANA: Ruby-red dye used to color cheeks and lips.

BOKKEN: Wooden sword used for training.

BUKE: Warrior; military house.

BUNGO STRAIT: Narrow water passage between the Kyūshū and Shikoku; "back way" *(literal)*.

BUNRAKU: Puppet theater.

BURI: Yellowtail variety of jack fish.

-CHAN: Diminutive suffix used toward an endearing person or child.

CHÉNG: *[Chinese]* Castle.

CHIBI: Runt.

CHIGO: Male student or young priest who is a sexual partner to an older male.

CHIKUZEN PROVINCE: Northwestern-most district of the Isle of Unknown Fires.

CHINKO: Penis.

CHŌ: Thick eyebrows drawn high on the forehead, above the natural browline; "butterflies" *(literal)*.

CHŌSEN: Ancient empire on the Korean peninsula *[2333–108 BCE]*.

CHŌZUBACHI: Stone bowl at a temple's entrance to hold water for ablution prior to entering; "hand water bowl" *(literal)*.

COMMON TONGUE: Mandarin.

KŌSHI: Confucius.

DAIMYŌ: Ruler of hereditary landholdings. Often translated as warlord.

DENKA: Honorific for non-sovereign royalty. Similar to "Your Majesty."

DŌ: Armor corselet chest protector.

DOJO: Martial arts training studio.

DŌMO: Thanks. Sometimes combined with arigatō and its variations.

DAIKON: Japanese white radish. Slang for penis.

EBIRA: Quiver for holding arrows.

ENGAWA: Outer walkway of a building.

FUGU: Puffer fish. Can be poisonous to eat.

FUKAGETSU: Straw boots.

FUNDOSHI: Loincloth.

FUNE: Largest of boats.

FUJIWARA: One of most powerful clans.

GAGAKU: Chinese music preferred by Japanese royalty.

GENKAN: Entryway to home or building where footwear is removed.

GENPEI WAR: Civil war *[1180–1185 CE]* marking the end of the Heian era.

GENPUKU: Coming-of-age ceremony for twelve-year-old boys; "taking the crown" *(literal)*.

-GIMI: Honorific suffix meaning "princess."

GIRI: Duty.

GOKENIN: Imperial guards; banner men.

GORYEO: Kingdom on Korean peninsula *[est. 918 CE]*.

GOSHOGURUMA: Enclosed two-wheeled ox-drawn cart.

GREAT BAY PROVINCE: Name for Ō-Utsumi Prefecture.

-GŪ: Suffix meaning Shinto shrine.

GUMBAI: Military fan carried by high-ranking officers to claim authority.

HACHIMAKI: Cloth headband; "helmet scarf" *(literal)*.

HACHIMAN: The War God.

HAGURO: Teeth blackening, a tradition practiced by married women and some men.

HAI: Yes.

HAKAMA: Split trouser-skirt, with ankle cords.

HAMON: The temper line of a blade.

HANABISHI: Fire flower; the Ōuchi mon.

HAORI: Field coat.

HARA: Belly.

HASHI: Chopsticks.

HEIAN-KYŌ: Traditional name of the Imperial City of Akitsushima; Kyōto.

HEIJI RAN: Attempted coup against the Emperor *[January 19–February 5, 1160 CE]*; "the Heiji disturbance" *(literal).*

HININ: Outcast class at the bottom of the social order; "non-human" *(literal).*

HISASHI: Roofed, enclosed veranda surrounding a shinden.

HŌ: Old Japanese name for China.

HŌGEN RAN: Attempted coup against the Emperor *[July 28–August 16, 1156 CE]*; "the Hōgen disturbance" *(literal).*

HOKO YARI: Polearm with bladed tip.

ICHIBAN: Best.

IGO: Go, the game.

ĪE: "No" *(polite form).*

INE: Rice plant.

IRORI: Hearth; fire pit set in the middle of the floor, used for cooking.

IREZUMI: Tattoos; ink on skin.

IRRASHAI: "Welcome" *(informal).*

IRRASHIMASE: "Welcome" *(formal).*

ISLE OF TWO KINGDOMS: The isle to the south of the Main Isle *[Shikoku].*

ISLE OF UNKNOWN FIRES: The southwestern-most isle *[Kyūshū].*

-JIIN: Suffix meaning syncretic compound, temple, monastery, shrine.

JIGOKU: Buddhist hell.

JIMMU: The first Emperor of Japan.

JINGI: Ancient religion, precursor to Shintō.

JINGŪ: Ancient Empress, mother of Hachiman.

JŌ: Length or distance measurement of 10 shaku, approximately 3 meters.

JUN: Ten.

JŪNIHITOE: Elegant, highly complex kimono worn only by court ladies; "twelve layers" *(literal).*

KABUTO: Warrior helmet.

KAGE: General Moroto's horse; "shadow" *(literal).*

KAGO: Single-person palanquin-type transportation, usually lightweight, carried by two or four men.

KAIKI SHOHO: Gold coins.

KAIMYŌ: Death name.

KAKKAZAN: Active volcano.

KAMI: Spirits worshipped in Shintō.

KAMI-DANA: Household shrine.

KANI: Crabs.

KANJI: Calligraphy of Japan adapted from Chinese; "Han characters" *(literal)* .

KANZASHI: Hair-band crown.

KARAGINUMO: T'ang-style sheath and skirt composed of multiple kimono layers.

KARAHASHI: T'ang-style bridge.

KASHIRA: A military command rank.

KATAKANA: One component of Japanese written language, along with hiragana and kanji.

KATANA: Curved sword, shorter than a tachi, favored by lower-rank warriors.

KATCHŪ-SHI: Armor maker.

KANTŌ BUSHI: Warriors from the east.

KEBIISHI: Capitol police investigator.

KEBIISHI-CHŌ: Imperial City police.

KEHITO: Name used to refer to peoples of the Barbarian Isle; "hairy people" *(literal)*.

KIBI: Millet.

KICHŌ: Drapes.

KISSAKI: The curved tip of a sword blade.

KITA: City at the Barrier Strait, in Chikuzen, on the Isle of Unknown Fires.

KO-DACHI: Short tachi; a short sword commonly used as a secondary sword.

KOBUNE: Flat-bottomed water craft used to ferry passengers and property.

KŌJIN-BIWA: A stringed instrument.

KOKU: Volume of measurement. Basic unit for measuring rice stipends and taxes.

KŌRO: Incense burner.

KOSODE: Simple short-sleeved cotton kimono worn under clothing or armor.

KOZANE: Scales; platelets used in the construction of yoroi armor.

KUGE: Court nobility; aristocratic class defined by heredity.

KUGUTSU: Puppet.

KUGYŌ: Senior nobles in the Imperial government.

KUMA: Bear.

-KUN: Honorific suffix added when addressing someone of junior status.

KUSHI: Drink made from fermented barley; "mysterious thing" *(literal)*.

KUSO: Shit *(colloquial)*.

KYŌFŪ: Gale; "strong wind" *(literal)*.

KYOJIN: Giant.

KYŌRAKU: Commonly used name to refer to Heian-kyō. *See* Raku.

LEEWARD SEA: Sea between Akitsushima and the mainland *[Sea of Japan]*.

MAIN ISLE: The largest island of the archipelago *[Honshū]*.

MEMPŌ: Armor mask covering the face from nose down to chin.

MIFUNE: Seagoing boat.

MINAMOTO: Powerful clan ruled by Yoshinaka's uncle.

MINKA: Commoner's wooden home, typically with thatched roof; "private house" *(literal)*.

MINMINZEMI: Cicadas. Known for their pulsing musical mating call.

MISU: Screens.

MIYABI: A concept of appreciation of beauty and personal refinement.

MIYAGE: Souvenir.

MIZU: Water.

MIZUKI: Significant trading city on the Isle of Unknown Fires, on the road to the Barrier Strait.

MOCHIZUKI: Yamabuki's horse; "full moon" *(literal)*.

MOE KUSA: Burning herb to treat infection.

MOGI: Coming-of-age ceremony for girls; "adult clothes" *(literal)*.

MOON LORDS: Poetic reference to higher ranking nobles for their proximity to the Emperor as the sun.

MON: Crest or symbol representing a clan.

MOYA: An inner room of a shinden.

MUSHA SHUGYŌ: Samurai warrior's quest or pilgrimage of self-discovery and skill testing; "warrior training" *(literal)*.

MUSHI: Bedbugs.

NABE: Iron pot or kettle. Also can refer to a meal served in an iron pot.

NAGATO: Prefecture on west end of the Main Isle.

NAGINATA: Polearm with a sword blade.

NAKAHARA: Clan that raised Yoshinaka from infancy.

NAKAZASHI: War arrows used by only the highest ranking military.

NAMARI: Lead (the metal).

NAMU AMIDA BUTSU: The nembutsu; "I take refuge in Amida Buddha" *(literal)*.

NAMAZU: Giant catfish that causes earthquakes.

NANDŌ: Male homosexuality; "the way of men" *(literal)*.

NANIGASHI: Kuge name for common people; "certain person" *(literal)*.

NANSHOKU: Male homosexuality; "male colors" *(literal)*.

NE: Exclamation to get someone's attention or emphasize a point.

NEMBUTSU: A chanted repetition of the name of the Amida Buddha.

NE-NO-KUNI: Underworld of the dead; "Land of Roots" *(literal)*.

NINJA: Spy or covert agent; "to sneak" *(literal)*. Word is often used interchangeably with shinobi.

NINJO: Human feelings.

NISHIKI: Fine silk brocade.

NODACHI: Field sword; a very long, heavy battle sword.

NOSHI: Small origami worn at ceremonies.

NURIGOME: Private inner room, or moya, of a shinden-zukuri estate house.

NURUDE: Paste made of rust, stale saké vinegar, and ground nuts used for haguro, the blackening of teeth.

NYŌBŌ: Handmaid(s).

Ō-UTSUMI PREFECTURE: Yamabuki's home. Ruled by the Taka clan. Also referred to as Great Bay Province.

OBĀ-SAN: Term of affection toward an elder woman; "grandma" *(literal)*.

OBI: Cloth waist sash tied around kimono.

ODOSHI: Brightly colored leather or silk-braid lacing used in yoroi armor to tie platelets (kozane) together in overlapping patterns.

ŌE: Clan in Nagato.

ŌGANE: Largest and deepest temple bell.

OJI-SAN: Term of affection toward an elder man; "uncle" *(literal)*.

OMAMORI: Amulet.

OMEKO: Slang for vagina *(vulgar)*.

OMIKI: Saké that's offered to the Gods.

ONMYŌJI: Religious practitioners of cosmological divination and magic.

ONSEN: Hot springs.

OSHIROI: White rice-powder makeup.

Ōuchi: Clan on the Isle of Unknown Fires. Also controls territory on the Main Isle.

pillow book: A diary.

polearm: Handheld weapon of a long pole tipped with a blade or point, such as a lance, spear, or naginata.

Pure Land Buddhism: A branch of Buddhism teachings focused on the Amida Buddha.

Qin: Ancient imperial dynasty of the Yellow River Delta *[221–206 BCE]*.

Raijin: The Storm God.

Raku: Commonly used name for Heian-kyō. Specifically refers to an eastern district within the Imperial City.

Rakuchū: "Within Raku" *(literal)*.

Rakugai: Urban area of Heian-kyō outside of Raku; "outside Raku" *(literal)*.

reikoku: "Cold heart" *(literal)*.

reiu: "Cold rain" *(literal)*.

River of Forty-Thousand Sands: River on the Isle of Two Kingdoms. Where Saburo lives.

River of Wild Ducks: Kamo River. Runs along east side of Heian-kyō.

ryō: Gold coin currency unit.

ryokan: Inns along the main roads.

Sagami Prefecture: Home of the Hayakawa clan.

sageo: Braided cord to secure a saya to the warrior's waist sash. The sword in scabbard hangs loose to not interfere with riding.

Sairyū: Streamlet.

sakimori: Border guards.

-sama: Honorific suffix when addressing someone of higher rank or senior status, or to express admiration.

samisen: A Japanese guitar with three strings.

-san: Honorific suffix used between equals.

sanba: Midwife.

sangu: Components of yoroi armor that protect the extremities.

saya: Scabbard for sword or knife.

senchou: Boat chief.

shakuhachi: Japanese flute.

Shin-en: A monkey in Saburo's mind.

Shinano Prefecture: Province on the Main Isle. Home of Yoshinaka.

shinden: Private main house within a mansion estate.

SHINDEN-ZUKURI: Popular style walled mansion compound with several buildings and garden.

SHINMOE-DAKE: Volcanic mountain on the Isle of Unknown Fires.

SHINOBI: Secret assassin; "person who hides" *(literal)*. Word is often used interchangeably with ninja.

SHIRABYŌSHI: Female dancer known for wearing men's attire and white makeup.

SHITAGASANE: Kimono train.

SHITAGI: Under-sheath, underwear.

SHINTŌ: Traditional religion of Japan; "the way of the Gods" *(literal)*.

SHŌBEN: To piss, urinate.

SHŌGUN: Military leader. Akin to rank of general.

SHŌJI: Sliding doors made of solid wood, usually painted or lacquered.

SHURIKEN: Throwing star weapon.

SODE: Shoulder guards on yoroi armor.

SŌDESU KA: "Is that so" *(literal)*.

SŌHEI: Warrior-monks.

SÒNG: Imperial dynasty of the Yellow River Delta *[est. 960 CE]*.

SUGATA: The curvature of a sword, mark of a swordsmith's overall style.

SUMI: Inkstick, solid ink ground and dissolved in water to make ink.

TACHI: Long sword commonly worn by samurai.

TAI-SHŌGUN: Big military commander.

TAKA: Yamabuki's clan; "hawk" *(literal)*.

TAMAHAGANE: Steel used in Japanese swords and arrowheads.

TANTŌ: Slightly curved dagger.

TARU: Barrel.

TASUKI: A narrow sash used by samurai to tie back loose kimono sleeves.

TENDAI SECT: A Buddhist sect.

TENNŌ: Majesty *(honorific)*.

TESSEN: War fan made out of metal.

TIGER CLAW: Name Yamabuki has given her tachi.

TIGER CUB: Name Yamabuki has given her medium-length personal sword.

TOI: Name given for invaders from Goryeo.

TOMOE: Circular pin-wheel symbol.

TORII: Traditional gate commonly found at the entrance of Shintō shrines.

TŌSHŌ: Frostbite.

TŌSŌ: The pox.

TSUCHI: Soil.

TSUKA: Sword hilt.

TSUKIMONO: Evil spirit intent on possession.

TSUKUSHI: Ancient name for the Isle of Unknown Fires.

TSURIGANE: Medium-sized bell.

USHIGATANA: Sword shorter than the tachi, with more curvature, designed for wearing in a waist sash.

URŪ: "Leap" *(literal)*. Used to designate leap month.

WA: *[Chinese]* Ancient name for Japan.

WAKATAKE INN: An inn in Kita; "young bamboo" *(literal)*.

WAKIZASHI: Short sword.

WATARISHIMA: Isle north of the Main Isle *[Hokkaidō]*.

WÉIQÍ: *[Chinese]* The game of Go.

WINDWARD SEA: Pacific Ocean.

YAHOCHI: Prostitute.

YAMA HOUSE: Style of house built by commoners, with a steep shingled roof and plank walls built to withstand snow and wind; "mountain house" *(literal)*.

YAMABUSHI: Reclusive Buddhist monks known to wander the mountains. Considered mystics.

YAMAZARU: Monkey.

YELLOW RIVER DELTA: The mainland to the west and its series of ruling dynasties.

YOJIMBŌ: Bodyguard; hired sword.

YOROI: Full armor made of lacquered platelets, usually metal, woven together with leather and/or silk.

YOSHI: Good.

YUKI-ONNA: Winter woman of myth who steals people's vitality; "snow woman" *(literal)*.

YUMI: Japanese bow, typically over two meters long.

Japanese Years, Seasons, and Time

Solar Stems

Solar stems are based on the position of the sun. Risshun begins at the exact midpoint between Winter Solstice and Spring Equinox.

	Romanji	Kanji	Start Date	Name
1	Risshun	立春	February 4	*Beginning of spring*
2	Usui	雨水	February 18	*Rain water*
3	Keichitsu	啓蟄	March 5	*Awakening of Insects*
4	Shunbun	春分	March 20	*Vernal equinox*
5	Seimei	清明	April 4	*Clear and bright*
6	Kokuu	穀雨	April 20	*Grain rain*
7	Rikka	立夏	May 5	*Beginning of summer*
8	Shōman	小満	May 21	*Grain Fills*
9	Bōshu	芒種	June 5	*Grain in Ear*
10	Geshi	夏至	June 21	*Summer Solstice*
11	Shōsho	小暑	July 7	*Little Heat*
12	Taisho	大暑	July 23	*Great Heat*
13	Risshū	立秋	August 7	*Beginning of Autumn*
14	Shosho	処暑	August 23	*End of Heat*
15	Hakuro	白露	September 7	*Descent of White Dew*
16	Shūbun	秋分	September 23	*Autumnal Equinox*
17	Kanro	寒露	October 8	*Cold Dew*
18	Sōkō	霜降	October 23	*Descent of Frost*
19	Rittō	立冬	November 7	*Beginning of Winter*
20	Shōsetsu	小雪	November 22	*Little Snow*
21	Taisetsu	大雪	December 7	*Great Snow*
22	Tōji	冬至	December 22	*Winter Solstice*
23	Shōkan	小寒	January 5	*Little Cold*
24	Daikan	大寒	January 20	*Great Cold*

Months

Each month begins with the Dark Moon (New Moon). Sprouting Month, the First Day of Spring, begins on the first Dark Moon to fall on or after the first day of the solar stem of Risshun (February 4).

Because the lunar cycle does not coincide perfectly with the solar year, intercalary months, or urū months, are added every few years. *For example*, in the year 1172, the Dark Moon on 16 January 1172 marks the beginning of Urū Twelfth Month, and the year 1173 officially starts on the next Dark Moon on 14 February 1173; in 1156, Urū Ninth Month begins on 16 October 1156. *(See "Years" section.)*

Month 1: **Sprouting Month** — First day of Spring

Month 2: **Clothes-Lining Month**

Month 3: **Flowery Month**

Month 4: **Unohana Month** — First day of Summer

Month 5: **Rice-Sprouting Month**

Month 6: **Watery Month**

Month 7: **Poem-composing Month** — First day of Autumn

Month 8: **Leaf Month**

Month 9: **Long Month**

Month 10: **Gods Month** — First day of Winter

Month 11: **Frost Month**

Month 12: **Last Month**

YEARS

Years are marked by twelve or thirteen months and designated by era names, often named after the ruling Emperor.

Because the lunar cycle does not coincide perfectly with the solar year, intercalary months, or urū months, are added every few years. All western dates refer to the Julian calendar.

KIŪAN 1–6 25 January 1145 – 19 January 1151
Kiūan 1 has an urū month starting 16 November 1148
Kiūan 5 has an urū month starting 18 July 1148

NIMBIŌ 1–3 20 January 1151 – 13 February 1154
Nimbiō 1 has an urū month starting 18 May 1151
Nimbiō 3 has an urū month starting 16 January 1154

KYŪJU 1–2 14 February 1154 – 20 January 1156

HŌGEN 1–3 21 January 1156 – 20 January 1159
Hōgen 1 has an urū month starting 16 October 1156

HEIJI 1 21 January 1159 – 8 February 1160
Heiji 1 has an urū month starting 18 June 1159

EIRIAKU 1 9 February 1160 – 27 January 1161

ŌHŌ 1–2 28 January 1161 – 4 February 1163
Ōhō 2 has an urū month starting 17 April 1162

CHŌKWAN 1–2 5 February 1163 – 12 February 1165
Chōkwan 2 has an urū month starting 16 December 1164

EIMAN 1 13 February 1165 – 2 February 1166

NIN-AN 1–3 3 February 1166 – 29 January 1169
Nin-an 2 has an urū month starting 17 August 1167

KAŌ 1–2 30 January 1169 – 6 February 1171
Kaō 2 has an urū month starting 18 May 1170

SHŌAN 1–4 7 February 1171 – 23 January 1175
Shōan 2 has an urū month starting 16 January 1173

ANGEN 1–2 24 January 1175 – 31 January 1177
Angen 1 has an urū month starting 17 October 1175

Japanese Hours

The hours of the day are defined as divisions of time between sunrise and sunset, and back to sunrise again. Sunrise marks the middle of the Hour of the Rabbit; sunset marks the middle of the Hour of the Bird. There are only twelve hours in each day—six hours of daytime and six hours of night—therefore each hour is *approximately* two hours in modern reckoning. The new day always starts at sunrise.

Naturally, as the seasons change—days longer and nights shorter during summer, and vice versa during winter—the actual duration of daytime and nighttime hours will vary throughout the year.

HOUR	BELL STRIKES	SOLAR TIME
RABBIT	6	5 – 7 AM
DRAGON	5	7 – 9 AM
SNAKE	4	9 – 11 AM
HORSE	9	11 AM – 1 PM *(Noon)*
SHEEP	8	1 – 3 PM
MONKEY	7	3 – 5 PM
BIRD	6	5 – 7 PM
DOG – *Shokō, First Watch*	5	7 – 9 PM
PIG – *Nikō, Second Watch*	4	9 – 11 PM
MOUSE – *Saukō, Third Watch*	9	11 PM – 1 AM *(Midnight)*
OX – *Shikō, Fourth Watch*	8	1 – 3 AM *("witching hour")*
TIGER – *Gokō, Fifth Watch*	7	3 – 5 AM

ACKNOWLEDGMENTS

This book and series exist because of Laura Lis Scott, my indefatigable editor and publisher extraordinaire. She is an editor in the truest and deepest sense of the word, whose suggestions and insights are major league. Her understanding of structure, organization, and storytelling show themselves on every page. She threw herself into this project with fact-checking, research, and scholarship in which she ended up channeling Heian Japan. Her Zen-like knowledge of the *Chicago Manual of Style* once again pulled all my scribbling together into a unified whole. And as always, her years of experience in book layout, art direction, even cartography and abilities in software were vital in the professional look of the entire project.

I would be remiss if I did not acknowledge my deep appreciation for the encouragement and insight offered by Tonia Hurst, who embraced every draft and gave insightful feedback. Some of her touches include the *onsen* as part of the backdrop.

I also want to thank Jane Campbell of the Bonsai Cit Group, as well as the Rocky Mountain Fiction Writers Crit Group members Lesley Smith, Paige Danes, and Janet Bigelow for their critical readings of the early texts and their unflagging encouragement.

I want to thank Carolyn Burke for her helpful insights into wordsmithing.

I thank Dana Densmore, the Kwan Jang Nim of the martial art of Ja Shin Do, whose training was invaluable and whose additional teachings as an MIT Outing Club ARC Leader and winter mountaineering guide came out in this book.

And also, as always, for any errors, omissions, or problems with the text, I take all responsibility for such shortcomings.

EDITORIAL NOTE

Katherine M. Lawrence's Yamabuki novels are works of fantasy fiction. Nevertheless, your series editor and the author have collectively endeavored to present the stories in a historically accurate context. Scores of scholarly books and hundreds of academic and historically minded websites have proven invaluable in our efforts to incorporate ecological, geological, geographical, linguistic, cultural, economic, political, interpersonal, and religious details of life in 12th-century Japan. However, as many historians note, the available historical documentation and records of Japan over eight centuries ago have been, to date, inconsistently translated and indexed. For historians professional and amateur, this is part of the delight in learning about ancient times. Every day we learn new things and gain what we hope is a deeper understanding.

Unfortunately, one inevitable consequence of this continual research into an ancient era—especially when working in translation—is that, now and then, we discover that a detail in a book we have already published is in fact incorrect. These errors are our own. For this, we deeply apologize.

Moving forward, we have opted to prioritize accuracy over continuity with prior publications. Therefore, the attentive reader of the earlier books in this series, *Cold Blood* and *Cold Rain*, may in *Cold Heart* note some changes in certain details—the name of a year, the spelling of a word. We ask the reader's indulgence.

Laura Lis Scott
Series Editor

ABOUT THE AUTHOR

For several years, Katherine M. Lawrence has been researching and writing the adventures of Yamabuki, an actual historic female samurai who lived in the Heian Era of Japan. Inspired by several decades in the martial arts halls led by women—Ja Shin Do, the San Jose State University Kendo Club, and Pai Lum White Lotus Fist: Crane style—Katherine set out to write about the experiences of women who train in warriors' skills . . . and Yamabuki in particular. The first books to be published from that effort are *Cold Saké*, *Cold Blood*, *Cold Rain*, and this book, *Cold Heart*.

Katherine graduated from the University of Washington with an undergraduate degree in both History and Chemistry, and continued with work on a Masters in History at the Far Eastern and Slavic Institute. She also received an MBA from Harvard University.

She is currently developing further books about the adventures of Yamabuki. She lives in Boulder, Colorado.

Kate blogs at KateLore.com

Follow her on Twitter: @pingkate

To get advance notifications on Kate's upcoming releases, sign up for her newsletter at http://eepurl.com/K8IIf

BOOKS BY
KATHERINE M. LAWRENCE

COLD SAKÉ

SWORD OF THE TAKA SAMURAI series
COLD BLOOD

COLD RAIN

COLD HEART

COLD TRAIL*

COLD FIRE*

COLD STEEL*

COLD FATE*

Swords of the Immortals series
THE BROKEN LAND*

* Coming Soon

ABOUT TOOT SWEET INK

Toot Sweet Ink is an imprint of Toot Sweet Inc., an independent publisher based in Boulder, Colorado.

Watch for our upcoming releases in science fiction, non-fiction, women's contemporary fiction, humor, and historical fiction, including more Yamabuki stories by Katherine M. Lawrence.

Follow us on Twitter: @TootSweetInk

Facebook: www.facebook.com/tootsweetink

Website: TootSweet.ink

Sign up for our Inkvine newsletter to get updates and learn about new releases and discount opportunities on our upcoming titles, at https://eepurl.com/K8XVn

73380699R00192

Made in the USA
San Bernardino, CA
04 April 2018